The Athena Syndicate

Charles Mossop

Print ISBNs
BWL Print 9780228614364
Amazon Print 9780228614371
B&N Print 9780228614388

BWL Publishing Inc.

Books we love to write ...
Authors around the world.

http://bwlpublishing.ca

Dedication

For my wife, Louise, on the occasion of our fiftieth wedding anniversary

Acknowledgements

I am indebted to Mr. Pranav Lal and Ms. Adeline Pasichnyk for their generous assistance in the preparation of the final manuscript. Also, to Mr. John Rafferty and Ms. Shampa Bose for help with research. Their valuable comments and suggestions are gratefully acknowledged.

Prologue

London, England 2014

If young Terry Preston had known taking a photograph would cost him his life, he would never have touched his mobile phone. But he didn't know, and he died.

The last night of his life was a very pleasant occasion spent with long-time friend Michael Barrow, thirty-one and strongly built with dark hair and blue eyes, at Barrow's flat in Knightsbridge. Preston, six years Barrow's junior, was his opposite in build, with a full head of unruly, fair hair. He wore thick glasses, which Barrow said made him look like an owl. They drank wine and ate a superb dinner of beef wellington prepared by Barrow, who was, in Preston's words, *a damn fine cook.* Following the after-dinner coffee and liqueurs they played a game of chess which Preston won handily as he almost always did, thanks to Barrow's utter lack of patience and consequent ill-considered decisions.

After a flourishing declaration of checkmate, Preston chuckled and shook his head. "You never learn, Mike. You need to take the time to set a strategy, not just charge forward with everything on the board as if you were storming the Bastille."

"I know," said Barrow, with a rueful grin, "but the blitzkrieg gambit does work sometimes, even on you."

"Only when I'm tired," said Preston, "and in case you didn't know, blitzkrieg was very carefully planned and highly organized."

"More brandy?" asked Barrow. "There's another bottle of the best sitting there in the kitchen feeling alone and neglected."

Without waiting for an answer, he made for the kitchen, but muttered, "Damn," as his mobile phone chirped its electronic summons. Glancing at the screen, he smiled apologetically and said, "It's the boss," and disappeared into his bedroom, shutting the door behind him.

Preston, left alone, looked around the spacious, expensively furnished sitting room. He knew it well. Leather sofa and deep armchairs, a sizeable flat screen television on one wall with all the auxiliary sound and video accoutrements anyone could wish for. Old maps and documents, all elegantly matted and framed, hung on the other walls. To his left, floor-to-ceiling bookshelves stood on either side of a glass door providing access to a small balcony which overlooked the building's landscaped central courtyard.

Preston often wondered where Barrow got all his money. He said he worked for a firm of consultants headquartered in Germany but evaded any further questions.

"Can't tell you much more," he would say. "Security and all that, you know."

Occasionally, Preston conjectured that Barrow might work for MI 5 or 6, or some other such agency, and lived a James Bond-like existence. It was an entertaining thought, but somehow, he couldn't see his friend suavely insinuating himself into the inner sanctums of foreign governments, much less into the beds of glamorous female spies from the Balkans, or anywhere else, for that matter. He was not a bad-looking fellow, Preston reflected, but no one would have said he was handsome. His parents had not been particularly well off — he made no secret of that — his father having gone from one dead-end job to another all his life. However, they now lived in a posh retirement development in Bristol, the colossal rent covered by Barrow faithfully each month. Preston also knew Barrow travelled a good deal, although he never revealed his destinations, saying only it was *all part of the job*. Preston concluded, therefore, whatever his consulting work was, it paid bloody well, and that was certain.

Barrow's muffled voice drifted out to Preston as he let his eye wander over the bookshelves. He was on the point of deciding he would go and get the brandy himself, when his attention was unexpectedly arrested by something he had never seen before. The bookshelves were devoted to almost everything except books, but Preston knew his friend was not a great reader. When he did read — salacious novels usually — it was almost always in electronic form, so in the general absence of books, the shelves were home to porcelain vases and Toby jugs, crystal glassware, and other pieces of costly ornamentation. What brought Preston to his feet and hurrying across the room, however, was none of those things. What he had seen, resting on a carved wooden stand, was a flat, roughly oblong piece of bone, divided into squares by fine grooves, and about the size of a dinner plate. The bone, which was, in fact, the plastron or underside shell of a freshwater turtle, was partly covered by columns of small symbols which had been incised into its surface, and the surface itself displayed a network of cracks radiating like the root tendrils of grass from a point at the top where the bone was slightly blackened. Preston stared at the object for a moment, hardly able to believe what he saw, before whipping his phone from its belt holster, nearly dropping it in his haste, and taking a picture. Quickly entering a series of commands, he watched as the image was emailed away.

Willard needs to see this, he thought. The old boy's going to go apoplectic with excitement.

"Sorry about that," came Barrow's voice from behind him. "I'll just get that bottle of rotgut."

"Mike," said Preston, pointing to the bone as Barrow returned with the brandy, "where on earth did you get that?"

Barrow's eyes narrowed, giving him a momentary look akin to wariness, or even guilt, but when he spoke, his voice was casual, off-hand.

"That? Oh, I picked it up in an antique shop a few days ago. Why?"

"Do you know what it is?"

"Haven't a clue," said Barrow, decanting the brandy into their glasses, his voice still neutral. "Just thought it looked intriguing, that's all."

"It's a *jiagu*."

"A what?"

"A Chinese oracle bone," said Preston, grinning. "You can find loads of fakes, but this one's real. Dates from the bronze age, you see. Around thirty-six hundred years ago, give or take a century or two."

"Hardly," said Barrow, coming to stand next to Preston and handing him his drink. "It only cost me fifteen quid."

"No, it's genuine," said Preston, studying it again. "I've seen others, and I can read most of the characters on this one. In fact, I've seen it before, or a photo of it, at any rate."

"Oh yes," said Barrow, "I keep forgetting you're into Chinese epi-something-or-other."

"Epigraphy," Preston said. "The study of inscriptions."

"Right."

"Oracle bones," Preston went on as they reseated themselves, "were used for divination, just as the name suggests. That one's especially interesting, because the inscription — "

"Oh, no, Terry," Barrow held up his hands, laughing, "I surrender. Please...not another Chinese history lecture."

"All right," said Preston, chuckling, "no lecture. But suffice it to say the inscription on that bone solves a couple of significant problems in Chinese history."

"Okay," said Barrow, after a sip of brandy, "I'll take your word for it, but it's a little hard to believe."

"Well, it's true," said Preston, "and I took a photo of it and emailed it to Dr. Willard, my tutor at Oxford." He paused for a moment before adding, somewhat diffidently, "I...I hope that was okay, Mike. I didn't think to ask, I'm afraid."

"No worries," answered Barrow, with a wave of his hand, his blue eyes shining. "What did you tell him?"

"Nothing at all," said Preston, with a grin. "I just sent the image. He'll be beside himself with curiosity by the time I see him."

"That's a dirty trick," said Barrow, laughing.

"Old Willard can read bronze age inscriptions as easily as he can a newspaper," said Preston, "and if I'm right about what it says on that bone, we may have to re-write some history."

"Really?"

"Yes, really, and I know something else as well. When word gets out, every sinologist from here to Mongolia will be clamoring to hear more about it."

"Sounds all very dramatic," Barrow observed.

"So, what's the name of the shop where you found it?" Preston asked, after another mouthful of brandy. "Did they have any more of them?"

"You know," said Barrow, frowning slightly, "I can't recall the name just now, but I think that was the only one I saw. I told you it was cheap. Are you *certain* it's not a fake?"

"Yes," said Preston, "it's authentic, and it really belongs in a museum."

"No kidding?" said Barrow, with a grin. "Then maybe I can make some money off it."

"Maybe," said Preston, thinking it a little odd Barrow should so soon have forgotten where he bought the bone, but he mentally shrugged it off for the time being. The first priority was to translate the inscription, and then he'd try to persuade Barrow to donate the bone to the Ashmolean, Oxford University's ancient and venerable museum of art and archeology. He hoped Willard would be able to see enough from the photo to translate what was there. For a moment, he toyed with the idea of asking Barrow if he could take it with him to Oxford but decided against it. He did not want to be responsible for it, and it was probably perfectly safe where it was.

By eleven o'clock, the tide had gone completely out in the bottle of brandy, and Preston got to his feet.

"I must get me gone, as Shakespeare would say. I'm off back to Oxford tomorrow, and I want to get an early start."

"Well," said Barrow, walking over to the glass door and peering out into the darkness, "I think it's raining, and I know it's damn cold, so let me give you a lift."

"Heaven forefend," said Preston, rolling his eyes to the ceiling. "You're much too full of alcohol. I can easily walk. It's not that far."

"It is in this weather," countered Barrow. "You could catch a bus."

"Not worth the wait," said Preston. "I'll be fine on foot."

"You sure?" asked Barrow, as Preston retrieved his hat and coat from their peg in the hall.

"Perfectly, thanks anyway, Mike. I'll be home in a quarter of an hour. Twenty minutes, tops."

Preston shrugged on a heavy raincoat and planted a wool cap firmly on his head before bidding Barrow a cheery farewell, and a promise to be in touch again soon.

"I'm sure you'll be interested in what old Willard says about that *jiagu*," he finished, as he walked out into the corridor. "'Night Mike."

Once outside, Preston turned right and set off at a brisk pace through the chilly February night. The road and sidewalk glistened in the incandescence of the streetlamps, and vehicles passed in a hiss of flying spray, their headlights speckled by the drizzling rain. Oblivious to the weather, however, he strode on, preoccupied with thoughts of the oracle bone. He was dwelling on its potential significance as he rounded the corner and started down the street on which he lived and was so absorbed he failed to notice the dark-clad figure stepping out of a shadowed alley as he passed. Preston hit the pavement a moment later, having never so much as heard the muffled cough of the silenced pistol shot that killed him.

9

Part One
The Valley of the Huang He, China
The Late Xia Period, c. 1605 to 1600 BCE

Chapter One

Chang the Hunter tightened his grip on the spear he held, hardly daring to breathe. The muntjac was close, but had neither smelled nor heard him, thanks to Chang's stealth and the still air in the forest. These tiny, red and brown deer were seldom seen in the valley of the Yellow River, and Chang offered a brief silent prayer of gratitude to his ancestors and the spirits of the forest for their generosity. He had hunted all day, moving cautiously through the thickly tangled undergrowth bordering the mighty river, but without reward — not so much as a mangy squirrel — until now. His family had eaten no meat for many days, but here, at last, was a chance. The forest surrounding him was dim; the sunlight barely penetrating the interwoven, green canopy overhead, and bushes and vines grew in tight profusion between the gnarled trunks of ancient trees. The small deer, standing in a patch of dappled sunshine slanting into a narrow, natural clearing by a shallow pool of spring water, browsed contentedly on the abundant leaves and berries.

It was by no means an easy throw, but Chang dared not move from where he stood, lest he give himself away. With infinite care, he drew back his arm, aimed, then, summoning all his strength, he sent the bronze-headed lance streaking between the trees. The well-honed point sank deep into the animal's side, and it collapsed, its legs flailing as it died in a final paroxysmal attempt to flee. Jubilant, Chang ran towards the clearing, leaping over bushes and tearing vines out of his way, and dropped to his knees beside the deer. At last he could take meat home to his wife and eight-year-old son. He spared a moment to thank the spirits for giving up this living thing to him for his sustenance, stopping just short of reminding them their largesse had been rather long delayed. Removing his spear from the carcass, he wiped the blade and examined it for possible damage.

He was proud of his bronze spear, and it had enabled him to become the finest hunter in his village. Other men used spear points of carefully flaked flint, or sometimes black obsidian traded from the mysterious hairy peoples of the cold northern regions, and Chang had made such points for himself for years. Many a patient hour had he spent chipping a lump of stone, striking off large pieces for rough shaping, before using a piece of bone or antler to detach smaller flakes, thinner and more precise, until he had a strong and sharp point or blade of the size he wanted. He then attached them to carefully made wooden handles or shafts with gum and wet leather thongs that shrank and hardened as they dried. In that way, he made arrows and spears, as well as reaping knives and other domestic tools. It was an arduous and time-consuming craft, at which he was an acknowledged master, and he still made many such weapons and implements for his fellow villagers, but he no longer made spear points for himself.

Two years before, the spirits had smiled upon Chang.

On his way home from market, he came upon a wealthy man, his wife, and children, whose cartwheel had broken. They were stranded on the open road, the six men-at-arms escorting them powerless to help for lack of skill. Chang, a gifted worker in wood as well as stone, roughly shaped new spokes from the branches of a tree and repaired the shattered wheel. The grateful man — Chang never learned his name — offered him a heavy gold pin with a garnet at its head, but such a bauble, valuable as it undoubtedly was, meant nothing to Chang; he could not bring down an animal with a gold pin, garnet or no garnet. He asked instead for one of the spears being carried by the guards, and the nobleman, happy, if a little bewildered, to have purchased his salvation so cheaply, agreed at once. So great was the value of that spear, both to Chang and his whole village, he slept with it by his side each night for fear of its being stolen.

Bronze, the alloy of copper and tin, was prized for its ability to take and retain a keen edge. Only royalty and the nobility could afford the daily use of bronze implements and utensils, but it was the priests who made greatest use of the valuable metal. They commissioned the casting of highly decorated three and four-legged vessels of all sizes, some too heavy for a man to lift unaided, which were used to hold ritual wine or boil herbs and grain for ceremonial feasts and sacrifices.

Now, having satisfied himself the point was undamaged, Chang tied the deer's legs together and slung the carcass across his back. Picking up his weapon, he walked out of the forest towards Liushu Village where he and his family lived in the summer. The declining sun warmed him as he trudged along the narrow forest path. To his right and left the trees grew thick, casting long shadows across the ground. Chang, tall and muscular, did not find the deer particularly heavy — he wished it had been larger — but the meat would be welcome, however much or little there was. He would try to save something to share with his neighbors, as was the custom, but he knew all too soon it would be gone. The rains had been sparse in recent months, the millet and vegetable crops had suffered, so after payment of tribute to the king and rent to the landlord, there was precious little left. Although Chang and his fellow villagers were inured to an uncertain existence that was never bountiful, this year was uncommonly lean.

As it always did, this thought set his heart smoldering with anger. The nobleman who owned the land on which the village stood did so simply because of who he was. The land was his birthright, and Chang often wondered how that had come to be. At least he was known to the peasants, for he came each year to collect his rent and survey his property, but the king was a different matter. Neither Chang, nor anyone he knew, had ever set eyes on Jie, seventeenth king of Xia, ensconced as he was in his fortified city far away, yet tribute was paid to him. Worse still, his soldiers marauded throughout the countryside pillaging and enslaving at will as they collected the bags of grain the king demanded.

Can that be right and just, Chang asked himself. The gods and spirits had placed the king on his throne, and he was a divine being, that was understood by all, and yet should a divine being act with such ruthless barbarity? Did he not have a duty towards his people, his subjects? The priests declared the king had obligations to no one, and counselled fortitude and forbearance, but Chang could not suppress the questions in his heart. Were the gods so malignant as to visit hardship and fear on simple folk who were powerless to resist? Had the divine ones no compassion? Or, he wondered as he walked, were the scarcity of game and the summer's drought signals that the gods were no longer content to see Jie on his throne? Could it be that heaven itself was turning against this tyrannous monster? It was said by some that the gods sometimes manifested their displeasure through the manipulation of natural disasters; so was this such a time, then? How were mere mortal men to know?

As he neared home, Chang began to smell smoke, but thought little of it. It was late afternoon by now, and the cooking fires would be burning. His anger cooled somewhat as he pictured the rejoicing that would ensue as he entered the village with his prize. The people of his village kept pigs and chickens, but all that could be killed and eaten had long ago been consumed. Those that remained had to be kept alive to replenish the stock for next year.

Rounding a bend, the broadening pathway emerged from the forest at the extreme edge of a wide expense of fields surrounding Liushu, and forgetting the ache growing in his shoulder, he quickened his pace. Once amongst the fields he was able to see the village clearly, and he stopped, paralyzed, staring in horror at what he beheld.

His village was ablaze. The houses, built afresh each summer of bamboo and thatch, burned fiercely, and far to his right he saw horsemen, perhaps as many as a hundred, galloping into the distance, leaving a churning cloud of yellow dust behind them. He saw no other living souls.

Dropping his burden, Chang ran towards the burning houses, his heart hammering in his chest as though to crack his very ribs. As he drew closer to the fires, he heard the crackle of the devouring flames and glowing embers drifted on the light breeze. Gasping for breath, he reached the devastated village, seeing bodies strewn on the ground, some decapitated, others bearing the fearful wounds inflicted by swords and clubs. Approaching the smoldering ruins of his own hut, Chang shrieked in anguish and sank to his knees as he recognized the bodies of his wife and son, their skulls split like melons. Raising his arms skyward and throwing back his head, he cried out to heaven, pleading with the gods that he, himself, might die, for he had no further wish to live.

* * *

Seven women and three men had managed to escape the carnage, but all the rest had either been killed or carried off as slaves. As night fell, the survivors crept out of the forest's protective depths, and Chang, numb with shock and despair, somehow contrived to organize the men to help him build a crude shelter of bamboo and rough thatch. A man was sent to retrieve the dead deer, but he returned empty-handed, the carcass evidently dragged off and eaten by forest scavengers. The remnant of the village huddled together all that interminable night. No one slept, and the silence was disturbed only by muffled weeping and the occasional crackling of the dying fires. Trying to extinguish them would have been a pointless waste of effort and water; nothing remained to save.

Chang himself, seeking solitude, sat outside under a sky emblazoned with an infinitude of glittering stars. The air he breathed remained heavy with the stench of smoke and burnt flesh. He stared at the bodies of his wife and son where they lay next to him and vowed before all the gods and the spirits of his ancestors, he would one day avenge their deaths. His indescribable grief, a pain deeper than any he had ever known, slowly transformed into an anger so bitter and monumental as to consume his very soul.

* * *

At daybreak, one of the women was sent to Hongshan, the neighboring village, to tell the news. She returned in the late afternoon with a shaman, a woman of about fifty with black hair hanging past her waist and dressed in a gray robe, who began at once to prepare for the funeral rites. She had brought herbs and leaves to be burned and two chickens for sacrifice, and she busied herself laying the fire in the prescribed manner and trussing the chickens so their throats could later be cut. Chang and the three surviving men of Liushu spent the day digging graves, twenty-three in all, and as they worked, Chang heard the story of the previous day's horror.

"They rode in just after midday," said one, as he wielded his wooden spade, "and after collecting the tribute grain for the king they asked for food and water. We gave them what we had, but they demanded meat. When we told them there was none, they slaughtered all the pigs and chickens, and then threatened to kill us as well. We begged for mercy. Their leader, I think his name was Fu, said they had come to collect the king's tribute, and when Bau Ling told them we had just paid it, he demanded we pay it again.

15

When Bau Ling said we could not, Fu seized his daughter and, before us all, he raped and killed her."

"And you did *nothing*!" Chang snapped, flinging aside a spade-full of earth, too overwrought to realize the stupidity and injustice of the accusation. Anguish and fury robbed him of reason.

"What would you expect us to do, in the name of heaven?" the men retorted, heaving a large stone up and out of the grave he was digging. "We are not soldiers. They wore armor and carried swords and lances of bronze. We were powerless."

"So, you did not even try to resist? You just waited for the slaughter like a flock of frightened ducks."

"I told you," said the man, indignantly, "there was nothing we could do."

"There must have been something," Chang muttered, his grief still mastering his common sense, and the man turned on him in outright rage.

"You were not here, Chang. If you had seen what we saw, seen what they did... It is easy for you to blame us for not trying to save ourselves, but they were many and we were few. We are farmers; they were warriors. And mark this," the man went on, his finger raised, "We shall bury my wife and my two daughters this day, as we shall bury your wife and son. Do not tell me what I should or should not have done, for there is no need. I will ask myself those questions from now until the day I die."

Chang thrust his spade savagely into the ground, saying nothing, as he tried to smother his shame.

I will avenge them all, he told himself. Hear this, my revered ancestors, and remember well what I say. Every soul that cries out from the earth of this place shall be redeemed. King Jie will fall. The scales of heaven shall be balanced, I swear it.

Chang worked on in grim silence, anger still showing in his dark eyes and compressed lips.

"They raped many of the women and girls, young and old," said another of the men, "then set fire to the houses. My family and I ran for the forest, but a soldier rode after

16

us and cut down my wife and children. I reached the trees, where he could not follow. I know not how the others escaped. I watched as they bound the women's hands and put them on the horses behind the soldiers. The children they put across their saddles. They rode away, leaving the dead and dying where they lay."

Chang listened, his fury surpassing any he had ever known. If nothing was done yesterday, he thought, then something will be done tomorrow. King Jie and his henchmen will pay for this.

When the woman returned with the shaman, she was accompanied as well by a small group of men and women. The men helped dig the last few graves, while the women set out the food they had brought. The two villages shared many kinsfolk through intermarriage, but today there were no happy greetings, no cheerful talk and chatter, as there would normally have been. There were only murmured words of sorrow, while people's faces wore somber expressions of bleak resignation. As the sun set, the burial ceremonies were completed under the direction of the shaman who delivered the souls of the dead to the afterlife amongst their ancestors through prayers, ritual burning, and sacrifices to the spirits of the trees, the mountains, the sky, the sun, moon, and stars, promising them as she did so the everlasting reverence and obedience of those left behind.

Chang wept openly as the savaged bodies of his wife and son were covered in cold, dry earth. He was the last of his family now. He had no living relatives. Without a son, his name would disappear and there would be no grandchildren to revere his spirit when he joined his ancestors.

"You must marry again," said the shaman, her efforts at consolation being somewhat misplaced, "and have another son. Such a thing would be pleasing to the gods and spirits."

"And what about the demons?" Chang asked. "What pleases the demons? The deaths of innocent children such as took place here?"

17

"We fight the demons through the power of good," answered the shaman, placing a hand on Chang's shoulder. "Heaven must prevail in the end if we do the best we can and do all that is right."

"Heaven did not prevail against the demons who did this," snapped Chang, gesturing towards the earth heaped up over the new graves, "and the demons responsible were made of flesh and blood. The demon soldiers of King Jie, the foulest demon of them all."

"You mourn, and you are angry, young sir," said the shaman, in a gentle voice. "That is easily understood. But in time, anger and sorrow fade, and the world is made anew for the sufferer. The sovereign lords of heaven who created all things make this possible."

Chang stared at the old woman, finding nothing to say. He had heard such mystical words for as long as he could remember, but their familiarity held no solace for him today.

"There are only a few weeks of summer remaining," the shaman said to Chang and the small group of survivors an hour later, "We shall send men here to harvest what they can when the time comes. Your grain and vegetables will not be wasted. After that you can move to your winter village, if you wish, although I fear now there is nothing for you there, either. It is my honor, therefore, to invite you to stay with us and join our people."

Following the harvest, all the farmers in the river valley left their summer fields and villages — taking food supplies and livestock with them — and moved to their winter settlements close outside the walled cities. There, the houses were built of mud brick, rather than flimsy bamboo, affording protection from howling storms and deadly cold during the months when no farming could be done.

"You are generous," answered Chang, taking it upon himself to speak for the group of survivors of Liushu. "We shall come, and we shall revere you and your kinsmen for your kindness."

"Not so," said one of the three other surviving men. "I, and these other two, do not choose to go with you. We ask only that the women be taken into your families and cared for."

"I swear it shall be done," said the shaman, bowing, "but what of you?"

"We shall go our own way," the man said, "and find new lives for ourselves elsewhere."

All attempts at persuasion proved fruitless. Taking up the small bundles of food made ready for them, they bowed in thanks once again before walking down the track into the distance and eventually out of sight.

"They will die," said Chang, soberly, as he watched them go. "They were my friends and neighbors, but they will die."

"Perhaps that is what they want," answered the shaman, waving a frond of sacred bamboo after them in a final blessing. "Great sorrow can sometimes cause men to lose sight even of their own lives. It is as though they exist, but do not live."

"The king has taken our lives from us, although we still live," Chang said, as he turned away, "but it shall not be forgotten."

And so it was, that Chang and the seven women turned their backs on the still-smoldering remnants of Liushu, and in grief, departed. Chang, carrying his only possession, his bronze-bladed spear, went with them. Casting a final backward glance at the grave-mounds of his wife and son close by the blackened shards of the hut he had built for them to live in, he trudged out of the devastated village. In his tumultuous thoughts, the tiny seed of a plan was germinating and beginning to grow. Sorrow and rage clamored within his very soul, and he vowed yet again he would kill King Jie with his own hand. If the gods and spirits of heaven and earth were moved to help him, so much the better. If not, however, he would do it without them or die in the attempt. At that moment, he had never felt so utterly and monstrously alone.

Chapter Two

The merciless heat of late summer slowly relinquished its hold on the desiccated countryside as autumn drew on. The days shortened as Chang helped the men and women of Hongshan gather in the vegetable and millet harvests in preparation for the return to their winter settlement. They had been compassionate and generous to him, helping him build a small hut for himself, and giving him a full share of the harvest, meager though it was, thanks to the persistent drought. In return, he spent many hours hunting, providing Hongshan with venison and the meat of wild buffalo and boar. And the hours were numerous indeed, for the chase was arduous. The game had retreated from the crucible-like heat of the valley to more comfortable feeding grounds in the cool hills, but he pursued his quarries relentlessly, all the while nurturing the plan he had made, nourishing it, and watching it grow.

He became popular amongst the villagers, but he kept to himself as much as politeness would allow.

"Sharpening your spear again?" the villagers would ask, with a cheerful wave, seeing him sitting on a four-legged stool outside his hut, patiently honing the blade with a flat piece of black basalt he had found one day as he stalked a deer. It was the perfect hardness, and after that he polished the metal to a gleaming finish with a thick piece of boar's hide he had cured for the very purpose. He nodded and waved in return, but as he stroked the blade with the stone, his thoughts dwelt not on the hunt, but on plunging the weapon into the heart of King Jie of Xia.

At summer's end, the villagers urged him to accompany them to their winter settlement.

"Make your home with us," they said, and eventually he agreed. He had first thought to return to his own winter village, but as he pictured it, he could not face living in the house he had once shared with his wife and son. He saw himself alone throughout the bitter days and black nights which were to come, with wind-driven snow scouring the land, and the ground as hard as stone. For all that he desired solitude, it was more than he could bear. He had no fear of loneliness itself, but what he did fear were his own thoughts and memories. Sweet memories of living in that house in winters past with his small family around him. Far from sustaining him in his sorrow, he feared those memories would drive him mad.

* * *

In the middle of the ninth month, the residents of Hongshan departed, leaving their bamboo summer houses to collapse under the inevitable burden of winter snow. Preparations for the trek had been underway all the previous week. Carts were loaded with wooden boxes of grain, large earthenware jars of dried fruit and pickled vegetables. Bamboo cages were fashioned for raucously protesting chickens, quacking ducks, and squealing pigs. There were boxes of clothing, and two carts reserved for spades, hoes, obsidian-bladed reaping knives and saw-edged sickles, hammers, chisels, and a multitude of other tools and accoutrements which made life possible. One cart had been piled high with stools and small pieces of furniture, while each family carefully packed its own cooking pots and wooden utensils. It was an immemorial ritual, performed every autumn, and again in the spring for the return. Everyone knew what had to be done.

On the day appointed by the men of the village for departure, a day selected in consultation with shamans who themselves consulted the spirits of the land and forests, oxen were yoked to the heaviest carts, while men assembled to push or pull the lighter ones. Women and older children walked with bundles on their backs, while youngsters rode in carts. Elderly villagers sat on the loaded ox carts, many of them holding a bundle on their knees or in their arms. Everyone helped who was able to, and the procession moved off down the dusty track at mid-morning amid much talk and laughter, the cacophonous cackle of poultry and livestock mingling with the squeaking of wooden wheels on inadequately greased axles.

Ten men, Chang amongst them, acted as guards, carrying nothing apart from spears and wooden clubs. Two walked at the head of the column, two at the rear, and three ranged on either side. Many villages were on the move at this time of year, and bandits abounded, but the greater menace by far was the marauding squads of soldiers, eager for easy plunder, very little of which, if any at all, was ever presented to the king as it should have been.

Casting his gaze about him constantly as he walked, Chang was reminded of why this summer village was named Hongshan — Red Mountain. Behind the expanse of level ground enclosing the houses and fields, there rose a low hill covered in thick stands of deciduous trees, their autumn leaves turning the slopes into a patchwork of vivid reds and golds. The day was cool, but it made the walking easier. Although the drought had finally broken, albeit too late to help the crops, there had been several days without rain prior to departure allowing the track to dry out, for which small mercy everyone gave grateful thanks. A single day's rain could turn the road into a morass of viscous, yellow mud which sucked and grasped at everything that walked through it, bringing even the oxen to an exhausted standstill.

Notwithstanding the absence of mud, progress was still slow. Frequent rests were necessary, and while the lumbering brown oxen plodded along steadily enough, they certainly did not do so speedily. An entire day was lost when a woman went into labor, and in the afternoon was delivered of a healthy son. There was much jubilant rejoicing, but the wailing of the new-born infant tore at

Chang's heart. He, his wife and son, along with the rest of Liushu village, had made the journey to their winter settlement many times, but this year he was alone, bereft, in spite of the kindness shown him by those he now walked beside and guarded.

As the journey progressed, however, the birth brought him an unexpected solace, slight though it was. The cries of the new, tiny being heralded the perpetual renewal of life, and Chang, sitting one day under the spreading branches of a gnarled old oak tree, found himself reflecting upon the unquenchable strength of life. Despite whatever disaster might befall mortals, life itself endured, eternal and tenacious. Was this the will of heaven, he asked himself, or was it simply the *Dao*, the irresistible way of nature? As he raised his eyes to the massive branches of the mighty tree above him, he blessed the woman's child as he had blessed his own son on the day of his birth. He did not know how to explain the world, but for better or worse, the world was where mortals found themselves, so they must live in it as best they could. But that small glimpse into the unfathomable did nothing to palliate his inflexible determination to avenge the horror of what had been done at his village. He thought again of the words spoken by the elders and shamans he had heard so often before, but which had now become his creed.

"Kings rule at the behest of heaven, but heaven's mandate may be withdrawn if a king is prideful, unjust, or disobedient to the dictates of heaven."

"How do men know the will of the gods?" he had once asked. "To whom does heaven speak?"

"Heaven speaks to no man," was the quick reply, "but heaven shows its abandonment of an evil ruler by bringing upon his kingdom great misfortunes and catastrophes. Storms, floods, droughts, even earthquakes. Heaven's anger is unleashed upon all."

Then surely, he said to himself, listening again to the crying child, men must have the right to act as the instruments of heaven and overthrow an evil ruler. There have been months of drought, and they say there have been terrible storms of wind and dust in the western regions that have buried fields and killed the crops. Is not this the time? If Jie has displeased the gods, as surely he must have, then I shall bring about his downfall. This child shall grow up in a better world than the one into which he has been born. I pledge it to him.

* * *

The people of Hongshan called the collection of meager mud-brick houses huddled close by the walled city of Li, *Dongtian de zhusuo*, the Winter Dwelling Place, or Dongzhu for short. After seven toilsome days, during which Chang and the other guards repelled two attacks by brigands on the open road, a child was born, and a chicken and two ducks died, the tired and footsore villagers reached their home. Chang had no possessions apart from his treasured spear when he arrived in Hongshan, but now he owned a stool, two cooking pots of different sizes, and a reaping knife of his own manufacture. These items were carried for him to the winter settlement on a small handcart pushed by a ten-year-old lad for whom he had fashioned a bow and five arrows in a deerskin quiver. Now they had arrived he stood alone by the cart, for he had nowhere to take it. He had thought about this from time to time during the journey and decided he would try to find a vacant hut somewhere nearby and take work in the city as a carpenter or maker of tools. As he scanned the scene before him, however, his eyes ranging along the line of houses to his right and left, he saw no unoccupied dwellings. Families were dispersing to their homes. People moved in and out of the houses unloading carts and unpacking boxes, young children played outside, and wisps of blue smoke were already beginning to curl up through chimney holes. He would have to build a shelter of some kind for himself, he decided, but where was he to obtain the materials?

"Do not worry, my friend," said a hearty voice from behind him, as though someone had divined his thoughts. Turning in astonishment, he saw Zhou Ma, an elder of the village, approaching with a broad, gap-toothed smile on his thin, wrinkled face.

"Did you think we would leave you to the rats, Master Hunter?" said he, clapping Chang on the shoulder with a strength belying his age. "Come."

Pushing the small cart, Chang followed the old man to a small house with a tiled roof, into whose single interior room he was ushered with a flourish of Zhou's boney hand. The floor was bare earth, pressed as hard and smooth as polished stone by generations of feet. Zhou left the door open for light, there being no window openings. The room was unfurnished save for a clay stove in one corner, but it was by no means unoccupied. There were other living things already in residence. Chang could smell them, even if he could not yet see them; the acrid, sickening stench was unmistakable. He could hear them as well. A rustling susurration filled the dim space. His eyes growing used to the half-light, he looked around, certain of what he would see, and sure enough, it was as if the very walls were moving. They undulated, almost writhed. He saw exactly what he expected to see. An uncountable multitude of black cockroaches swarming thickly everywhere, disturbed, no doubt, by the unheralded appearance of human intruders in the domain they had hitherto called their own.

It did not concern him unduly, however. Such pestilential invasions were commonplace, an inescapable part of life, and he knew what would have to be done. A torch of blazing pitch would drive out the hordes of sharp-jawed insects, leaving thousands of them dead. He had done it many times in his own house every autumn, but no sooner had that recollection come to mind than it was supplanted by the realization that this was not his house. Then what of its real owners, he wondered.

"This is where you shall live," announced Zhou, answering his thoughts for a second time. "The owner of this house died a year ago, and it has been unoccupied ever since. We have decided to give it to you." Zhou gestured expansively towards the open door, and said, "See what now comes."

As Chang watched in mute astonishment, a group of men carried in a wooden table and four stools, while women brought boxes and pots of preserved food; dried fruit, grain, meat, both dried and pickled. More than enough to last him through the hardest winter. He would have no need to work.

"All for you," said Zhou, as the men grinned, and the women giggled at his bewilderment. "We wish you to stay here and be one of us, good Master Chang, and later," he went on, more diffidently, "later you may find a wife from amongst our daughters…"

Chang could no more think of marrying again than he could of flying to heaven to converse with the gods. He was only twenty-seven, and a wife and children would normally have been an urgent goal, but his bereavement was still too recent, too raw a wound, and in any case, there was something he had to do before ever he thought of resuming the life of a simple village hunter and farmer. Nevertheless, he recognized the generosity of his new friends, and was touched by their abundant kindness.

"I give you all my deepest thanks," he said to Zhou and the others who had assembled in the dim interior of the small, mud-brick house. "I am moved by your invitation and your goodness. I would be honored to dwell here." And he bowed.

They received his words with smiles, nods, and happy laughter.

"You shall be my brother," said Zhou. "It is we who are honored. You shall venerate our ancestors, and we shall venerate yours."

"You are all very kind," he said, and then, looking at the floor and seeing the army of cockroaches approaching his feet, he went on hastily, "but before anything else, I should be most grateful if someone would bring me fire with which to purge my new home of its present tenants before all is lost."

Zhou laughed and said, "It seems you have many tenants, but I fear they pay no rent."

He gave an order to a couple of young men who scurried away, returning a few minutes later with blazing torches, and the house was soon filled with black smoke and the vile, stomach-turning stink of the burned insects. Chang and his two helpers coughed and gagged as they scoured the walls and the inside of the clay stove. After twenty long minutes they were finished, and the three of them staggered outside to draw grateful gulps of fresh air into their congested lungs. Finally, Chang, finding a broom made of rice straw amongst the household utensils he had so recently been given, ventured back inside to sweep the dead and dying cockroaches, each one looking like a shard of charcoal, into heaps which the two men shoveled outside and buried. They had won this battle, but Chang knew the war was never-ending; the black insects were as tenacious as they were numerous, and they were as numerous as the stars. There were a thousand replacements for each one killed, and they would invade again almost immediately. Once he was in residence himself, however, their legions could never overwhelm the house as they had when it was empty. He stood in the middle of the floor and surveyed his house in the light of a tallow lamp on the table and was content.

Thus, Chang the Hunter became a man of the Hongshan people. Zhou and his kinsfolk, both men and women, treated him as a true relation, and, in his turn, he assumed the roles of brother, nephew, brother-in-law, cousin, and uncle. Throughout that winter he learned to be a part of his new extended family. Using his skill as a maker of wooden furniture, boxes, and other necessities as a means of contributing to the village, he did his best to settle into the community. As an adopted member of Zhou's family, he took part in the many ceremonies of ancestor worship and the winter festivals honoring both the spiritual and natural worlds. But, in spite of it all, he felt himself an outsider, an observer rather than a true participant. He lived in a house but could not feel he had a home. He kept his spear by the door, reminding him of what he had promised himself to do. And so, during the long, cold nights of winter, as bitter winds from the north and west raked the countryside and heaped the snow into mountains, he sat alone, his house warmed by the clay stove and lit by the yellow glow of tallow lamps, planning, encompassing in his mind the death of King Jie, and the extirpation of the House of Xia.

* * *

Protected by the walls of the city of Li beside which Dongzhu was built, the nobility and other wealthy landowning families dwelt in lavish houses. They lived their lives in easeful contentment, surrounded by legions of slaves and servants, and guarded by men armed with bronze weapons. To venture inside the walls without a legitimate reason was to risk a fearful flogging, or worse, but Chang had neither wish, nor reason, to explore the city. His interests lay not within the walls, but outside them. Outside, their year-round houses built right against the high walls, lived the common folk. These people were not hunters or farmers but workers who derived their sustenance from serving the urban gentry. They were shopkeepers, metalworkers, carpenters, potters, jade and ivory carvers, sellers of silk, stone cutters, gem merchants, and other artisans and tradesmen. Chang spent many hours cultivating friendships amongst them, for the information he gleaned held the key to his plans. He wanted to hear the rumors and stories these people told, those laborers whose daily toils and moils made possible the excesses of the arrogant, heedless few living in their walled fastness.

Although the world of the wealthy was a foreign place to him, Chang did not question its right to exist, nor did he believe that wealth itself was intrinsically illegitimate or evil. He shared the general understanding that a few men were favored by the gods in the circumstances of their

29

birth, and the rest were not. It was a simple enough proposition. Such was the way of heaven, and such was the consequent way of the world beneath heaven, capricious though heaven might sometimes seem.

What he did question, however, was the wanton and abhorrent cruelty of those favored few. Was there not a moral and honorable way to live amongst one's fellow beings, he asked himself, without regard to a man's rank or the size of his house? Should wealth and privilege be granted to men for no better purpose than the oppression of others less fortunate? Did gold, lapis, and jade give men the right to kill? Most people, rich and poor alike, seemed to think they did; the rich believing in their innate and indisputable superiority, while the poor believed they could do nothing, save endure in silence.

As winter swooped down like a predatory bird, sinking its frozen talons into the shivering ground, Chang spent as much time as he could talking to his new friends living against the city walls. He found a kindred spirit in the person of Lai, the jade carver, a wizened, gray-bearded old man of nearly sixty years — a prodigious age — who was much celebrated for his technique and artistry. When the summer weather was kindly, neither too wet nor too hot, Lai walked from city to city, hawking his wares or delivering pieces to those from whom he had received commissions.

"It is all that walking which keeps my legs strong and my heart young," he told Chang, with a cheerful laugh.

Lai, a man of keen perception, invariably returned from these expeditions with his head full of information, and Chang rapidly discovered how valuable it was. One cold, snowy evening, just after the mid-winter festival, Lai and Chang sat talking together in Lai's small workshop house, sipping steaming cups of herb tea and warming themselves over a clay stove. To one side of the single room stood a stout workbench Chang had made for his friend out of durable blackwood, after seeing him working cross-legged on the earthen floor. Several lumps of raw jade, some emerald green, others white or variegated, lay on the bench along with an array of chisels and grindstones which were the tools of Lai's trade. Around the bench, shards of jade, many of them as sharp as a fine bronze sword, littered the floor.

"Now look, my friend," said Chang, gesturing towards the workbench, "you carve a fine piece of jade and sell it to some rich man or other, and what does he pay you for it? He pays you barely enough to buy food for a week. Am I not right? It is an unjust and dishonorable thing that is done to you."

"At least I eat that week," said Lai, with a rueful smile. "But that is the way of things. He is what he is, and I am what I am. What can be done? Nothing at all. Is that not so?"

"He feeds you for that week, yes," said Chang, nodding, "but what of the week after, and the one after that?"

"The next week," Lai said, with a shrug, "I sell something else. I told you, it is the way of the world, and who can change it? I cannot hunt as you do, my friend, nor do I know anything of crops and livestock. Heaven, therefore, has graciously provided me another way by which to live." Lai paused, then added, "I am a jade carver, and few men have my skill. The gods have been generous to me in their own way."

Chang sipped his tea, contemplating what Lai had said. He, Chang, could track an animal and bring it down with a sure throw of his spear, but if he were to try to carve jade, he would not know even how to begin. The gods had not deserted their people, but why, then, did heaven allow the rape and pillage of peaceful villages, and the murder of innocents? Why were the rich allowed to enslave defenseless folk, or pay a pittance for a fine carving? It made no sense to him, but he left the subject for the time being, resolving to dwell further upon it at a later time.

"Have you heard anything recently?" he asked Lai. "What is being whispered elsewhere?"

"Well now," said Lai, finishing his tea and casting Chang a conspiratorial glance, "I do have news which may be of interest."

"Go on," said Chang, his eyes wide with anticipation. "What is it?"

"I have not been able to travel much since the end of the summer, but I hear the Shang village of Bo, twelve day's walk to the west of here, has been savaged by the soldiers of King Jie of Xia. Many died, and many more were taken as slaves."

"That evil man is the worst of tyrants," Chang growled. "My heart overflows with hatred for him and his people. I would have them consumed by a plague, had I the power to command it."

"It is said the destruction of Bo was an act of revenge," continued Lai, pouring himself more tea from a copper jug steaming on the stove.

"Revenge?" Chang held out his own cup.

"Just so," said Lai, nodding. "Revenge for Jie's defeat in battle."

"He has been defeated in battle?" Chang was exultant. *At last.* King Jie is not invincible after all. He is not mightier than heaven "Are you sure?" he asked, half afraid Lai would say it was all rumor or mere wishful thinking.

"Yes," said Lai. "There has been a battle. I have a friend who journeyed back from the river which yields up her jade to us, and he found a wounded soldier who told him of it before he died. It was not a great battle, mind you, really a minor skirmish, I gather, but the soldiers of Jie were routed by warriors of the Shang. Bo was attacked in reprisal."

Chang's eyes glittered in fierce delight. Was heaven finally turning against him?

"And who led the men of Shang?" he asked.

"Well," said Lai, stretching out his calloused hands to the warm stove, "it seems a powerful Shang king has risen far to the west, whose name is Tang, although many now call him Da Yi. He is the leader of the clan of Zi, the hereditary rulers of all the Shang, but until now, no Shang

32

king has ever been strong enough to unite the Shang peoples and challenge the House of Xia."

"I have never heard of this king," said Chang, "but if he is the enemy of Xia, then perhaps he is a man to watch."

"I cannot say," answered Lai. "The man I spoke to could tell me very little of the battle itself. He said he believes many smaller clans and lineages are coming under Da Yi's sway, either willingly or by conquest. It is said Da Yi is a mighty man, just and honorable, who declares he has the mandate of heaven to rule all people."

"So also says King Jie," replied Chang, angrily. "But think now…if what you were told is true, perhaps we shall see which of them is right."

Chapter Three

With an imperious beckoning wave, King Da Yi summoned Chang to come before him. Chang, feeling decidedly ill at ease in this royal place, stepped forward and bowed deeply.

"Lord King."

"Who are you?" demanded Da Yi, transfixing Chang with an appraising gaze from his dark, penetrating eyes. "Why have you come here?"

"To serve you, Lord King," said Chang, raising himself a little to avoid the appearance of addressing the floor.

"To judge by your speech," said Da Yi, frowning slightly, "you are not of Shang. You are not even of this region."

Straightening himself fully, Chang looked at the king of the Shang people. His clothing was of white silk, a wide-sleeved cross-collar tunic with decorative stitching at its borders and secured around his waist by a wide, black sash. A calf-length kilt stamped with circular designs in red completed his attire, but it was the king's physical appearance which at once arrested Chang's attention. The stories he had heard of military prowess had led him to imagine Da Yi would be a tall, powerfully built fighting man with a fierce expression of warlike determination fixed upon his face and wearing bronze-studded armor, but seeing him now, he could scarcely credit the evidence of his eyes. The king was thirty or thereabouts, short and slight of physique, not looking to Chang as if he could lift a sword, let alone wield one in battle. Chang was a head taller than the king, and his many years of hunting, farming, and carpentry had given him broad shoulders and muscular arms. No, Da Yi did not look like a warrior king, but Chang soon came to know he behaved like one.

"I have come from the east, Lord King," said Chang, "from the lands conquered by King Jie of Xia, and I offer myself to you as a soldier and vassal."

"A single man alone?" asked Da Yi, his eyebrows raised. "That is not so mighty an army, I think."

A rustle of dutiful laughter emanated from the assembled courtiers and ministers in the hall, while Chang stood in some perplexity and disappointment. He had expected at least a few words of welcome from this king, this ruler who had by now brought nearly forty other kingdoms and clans under his suzerainty.

"Indeed, I am but one man, Lord King," he said, striving for a humble tone, "yet I am pledged to die in your cause, if that is the will of heaven."

"And why are you thus pledged?" Da Yi sat back in his chair, regarding Chang with an intense, unwavering stare. "And what is my cause, as you call it?"

Here, at last, was the question Chang had anticipated. His answer came swiftly and with conviction as he spoke the words he had so often rehearsed in his mind.

"My lord, I have been touched by the blood-stained fingers of the king of Xia. I have seen his cruelty. My wife and son died at the hands of his lawless soldiers when they raided my village, killing, raping, and enslaving. Surely such a man is not fit to rule. Can heaven countenance so evil a king?"

"And who are *you* to decide who is fit to rule and who is not?" demanded Da Yi, in a voice as cold as a high mountain stream.

Chang hesitated, sensing he might be venturing onto dangerous ground. Speaking of fitness to rule in the presence of one who does rule is not always prudent.

"I...I am no one, Lord King," he said. "The spirits of the sun, the rivers, the winds, and the souls of our ancestors govern us all, even those who reign on earth, but how long will the spirits allow an unrighteous man to rule? There have been droughts and floods, Lord King, storms, and landslides. A hideous sickness came upon several hill villages last year which caused the limbs of children to swell until they burst, and there has been sore famine in many lands. Could that not be the gods of heaven and earth declaring to us they no longer grant the king of Xia the right to rule?"

He had shot his last arrow; there was nothing more he could say.

Da Yi said nothing, and Chang, fearing he had been injudicious yet again in the plainness of his speech, waited. The thunderous silence lengthened as the assembled courtiers watched the king's impassive face. Chang heard the crowing of a rooster somewhere a great way off, incongruous, yet reassuringly familiar, and he realized he was barely breathing. Finally, after an eon of suspenseful expectation, Da Yi nodded slowly, and said, "Perhaps it is as you say, but if so, to whom has the mandate been transferred, I wonder? If calamities portend the withdrawal of the mandate, by what means are we then to know upon whom the mandate now rests?"

Chang was dumbstruck. In all his mental deliberations and planning he had never considered that particular saliency, and he had no answer.

Unexpectedly, Da Yi threw back his head with a loud laugh, and all those present obediently did the same, albeit with some bewilderment. Chang was equally confused. What on earth was coming now? The best he could manage was a sheepish grin.

"You see," Da Yi said, "you are neither a mighty army, nor a mighty philosopher."

Chang felt embarrassed and humiliated, but Da Yi appeared not to notice. His tone became severe once again as he said, addressing the entire assembly, "Listen to me, all of you, and mark well what I say. Heaven shares no secrets with men, no matter they be high-born or base-born, king or slave. Each of us is what heaven has made us. If the mandate has been taken from one and given to another, we shall know it in heaven's good time. All a man can hope to do is believe in his own destiny and strive to follow it."

Believe in his own destiny, Chang repeated to himself, and strive to follow it. Was that not what he was trying to do? Was that not the very thing which had brought him here?

Standing there before the king of Shang, surrounded by his royal courtiers, advisors, generals, and servants, Chang was unexpectedly overcome with memories. He relived the mental turmoil he had experienced as he wrestled with the conflicting desires and emotions surging within him all those months ago. He had found a new life with the good people of Hongshan Village, a life offering him familial contentment and peace, were he to embrace it, but there still remained within him the conviction that life held more for him than the daily labor of a peasant farmer, continually at the mercy of weather and pestilence. He had journeyed for weeks in order to stand where now he stood. Why had he done it, if not to follow the destiny he believed in, if not to wreak the revenge he had promised his slain wife and child?

It had been in the warm weather of early spring that Chang bade farewell to Lai the jade carver and the other friends he had made while at the winter settlement and returned to Hongshan Village with his new kinsfolk. The procession wound its ponderous way from the city and back to the countryside along the same dusty track it had followed the previous autumn. As he journeyed, Chang became ever more resolute in his determination to find the king of Shang, this Da Yi, and become his liegeman.

At the village site, the men cut new bamboo, and Chang helped build huts to replace the ones destroyed by winter. The fields were made ready, crops planted, and the immemorial cycle of farming life resumed. Although he knew the ways of farming, Chang preferred the solitude of the hunt, and so most days he took up his spear and went into the forest in search of game, sometimes staying away for two or three days. He was a canny hunter who knew the habits of his quarry, so he usually returned with venison to supplement the chicken and pork which formed the basic diet, along with eggs, vegetables, grain gruel, and powerfully strong millet beer. The people of the village had so taken him to their hearts they fully expected him to stay forever, yet he knew he did not truly belong there with them. He had become convinced his destiny lay elsewhere, and his lust for revenge was undiminished.

"You are restless, Younger Brother," said Zhou, one warm evening towards midsummer as the two sat with pots of beer outside Zhou's hut. "What is it that so troubles your soul? Are you not happy here?"

"This village has become my home, Older Brother," he answered, "but I cannot stay."

Old Zhou smiled knowingly and nodded.

"I thought as much. You have other work to do."

"The king of the Shang people is leading a rebellion of some kind against King Jie. I am called to that cause."

"Then you must surely go," said Zhou, with firm conviction. "Perchance you are to be the instrument by which heaven will destroy the king of Xia."

"I have heard the king of Shang is called Da Yi, and his kingdom lies in the direction of the western mountains. He has defeated Jie in battle, and I am told he believes he possesses the mandate of heaven to rule."

"And what if Da Yi's belief in the mandate is mere vanity, Younger Brother?" asked Zhou, in a gentle voice, entirely without sarcasm or mockery.

"Then I may lose my life as recompense for my inability to discern evil from good, but surely heaven sees the horrors wrought by Jie. They cannot be so perfidious as to ignore them and condemn so many people to such suffering."

Zhou nodded slowly, and with a grave smile said again, "You must go, Younger Brother, and we shall pray and make sacrifice for you. These are mighty matters, and you are but a mortal man."

"The stories of Da Yi may be nothing but rumor," Chang said, "but I must find out. If, indeed, he is so great a king, then I wish to serve him."

Two weeks thereafter, Chang gathered together a few necessities along with a little food, and, slinging them over his shoulder in a deerskin pouch made for him by Zhou's youngest daughter, he took up his spear and bade farewell to his friends and putative kinsfolk of Hongshan Village. They saw him off down the dusty summer road with tears and waves, as a shaman chanted a solemn prayer for his safety. He stepped resolutely forward, but his thoughts were in turmoil.

Am I a complete fool, he asked himself, as he rounded a bend and the village was lost to sight, an idiot? One family has been torn from me, and now I am deliberately abandoning another. Is it sheer arrogance to think I can aid heaven in the accomplishment of its purpose? And do I really know that purpose, or am I an addle-headed dreamer of dreams?

He stopped where he was and looked around at the mighty forest which lined each side of the track, and then, unable to settle his whirling thoughts and mounting doubts, he prayed aloud.

"Be with me, revered ancestors. Watch over me, you great ones who have gone before. I shall honor you always, wherever I may be. Guide me now. I will accept my destiny. If I am to die, then I shall ride the dragon to bow before you in paradise, but if I am to live, then help me be worthy of the life I am to lead. Is it your wish that I go on into the unknown?"

He waited, unsure how, or if, an answer would come. He believed in the spirits of his ancestors and was conscious of their presence, but had they heard him now?

The answer was not long in coming.

As he stood in silence, his pack over his shoulder and his spear in hand, the sun emerged from behind a cloud, flooding him and all that was around him in radiant warmth. Murmuring words of thanks, he bowed in each of the four cardinal directions and then knelt to touch his forehead to the ground. That done, he took firm hold of his spear, hitched up his pack, squared his shoulders, and walked on, feeling the spirits of his ancestors at his side.

The journey was arduous. He walked westward for many *li* until he finally stood on a high hill and saw before him a broad plain with a wide river beyond, its sinuous curves resembling the undulations of a gigantic snake lying across the expanse of green fields and dense forests. Here and there across the cultivated land, villages showed themselves as clusters of thatched huts, but nowhere could he see anything which might be the royal city of Shang. He thrust the shaft of his spear into the ground and surveyed the landscape, shading his eyes against the harsh glare of the declining sun.

I will ask at one of the villages. Perhaps they will know where I can find the city.

Realizing he could not reach even the nearest settlement before dark, he decided to go no further that night. The sound of a stream reminded him he had not tasted water for hours, and he drank deeply at the bubbling spring providence had placed nearby before finding a suitable place to camp. Sitting with his back against a convenient boulder, Chang ate some of the venison he had dried in yesterday's sunshine, and after watching the sun slide below the western horizon in a shimmering blaze of red and gold, he lay down on the leaf-strewn forest floor and slept soundly. Rising at first light, he ate a little more venison with a small millet cake, replenished his water jar at the spring, and set off for the nearest village where he arrived as the sun was approaching its zenith.

Halting outside the small group of dilapidated bamboo huts, Chang shouted a greeting, declaring he came in peace, but the only response was absolute silence.

Is there no one here, he wondered.

He shouted again, and this time a woman appeared — he could not guess her age. She was not tall, but thin and bony almost to the point of emaciation. She stood at the doorway of the nearest hut, fear on her pinched, angular face, but with defiance in her voice.

"Be off. Go. You have taken everything already."

"Do not be afraid, good woman," said Chang, laying down his spear. "I mean you no harm. I seek nothing from you but information."

A spindly-legged old man with a wispy gray beard appeared behind the woman, leaning heavily on a rough-hewn stick. He wore only a tattered loincloth and looked to Chang like a living corpse, so skull-like was his ancient face.

"What is your business here?" the old man demanded, in a high, querulous voice.

"I travel to the royal city of Shang, venerable sir," Chang answered, bowing. "I have come to beg your generosity in giving me directions."

"You are not a soldier of King Jie?" squeaked the skeletal old man, putting a protective hand on the woman's boney shoulder.

"No, indeed I am not," protested Chang. "Heaven forfend. I am the sworn enemy of the king of Xia."

The old man stared at Chang, now somewhat ragged and dirty after his long march and many nights spent in the open, and evidently decided he could be trusted in spite of his bedraggled appearance. In any event, no matter who or what he was, if giving him simple directions would get rid of him, the old man apparently decided it was worth the attempt.

"Royal Shang is four days' journey west and a little south of here," he said, pointing. "I wish you good fortune. We have no love for King Jie."

At the old man's command, the woman hurried out with some fresh fruit and an earthenware pot of water, but Chang bowed, saying, "Do not trouble yourself, good woman. I have all I need, and you have so little."

"You are kind to us," she said, her narrow features softening a little.

"What did you mean," Chang inquired, "when you said everything has already been taken?"

"The king of Xia taxes our food and takes it for himself and his nobles," wheezed the old man, bitterly. "We are alone here now. The rest of our people were taken.

Men, women, and children, to labor for King Jie in the enlarging and fortifying of his capital city many *li* away. I was considered too old to be of use, and they allowed my daughter to stay with me. They said she was of no use to anyone save perhaps as a whore, but she was too old and ugly even for that. We have done what we could to survive, but there is almost no food left."

"Heaven's curse be upon this king of Xia," Chang muttered. "Would that I could see him lying dead before me this very moment."

Chang spent the rest of that day with the old man and his daughter. He gathered as much firewood for them as he could, speared a deer which he could barely manage to drag out of the forest, and then skinned and butchered it so the strips of meat could be dried. He camped that night in the desolate village, and the following morning departed, carrying with him the gratitude and blessings of its two lone inhabitants. He looked back to see them standing, waving, outside their tumbledown hovel, then, with a wave of his own, he walked on.

The valley of the Yellow River offered flat ground, a welcome relief from the hills he had struggled over previously, and he made good progress. He found well-trodden paths through the forest, the broad canopies and sturdy branches of the ancient trees almost meeting high above his head, so that at times he felt as though he walked through a fragrant, green tunnel, into which the hot sun penetrated only in bright, dappled patches. As he travelled, the forest gradually thinned, yielding place to well-tended fields of millet, rice, and vegetables. He passed villages where men and women went purposefully about their business, while children played in front of well-built houses.

After three days, he fell in with a man driving a rough-hewn ox cart laden with vegetables. Chang noticed he was carrying only a flint knife, virtually useless as a weapon. The man obviously had no fear of being attacked and robbed.

"Are these the lands of Shang?" Chang asked, cautious, notwithstanding.

"They are," replied the farmer, with a cheerful smile.

"I have come to fight for the king of Shang," Chang declared, emboldened by the man's openness.

"You are welcome," said the farmer, "but take heed. You are close to the city and you are a stranger. If you see soldiers, lay down your spear and fall to your knees. King Da Yi fears spies, and if you are suspected, he will have you flayed alive."

Early the next morning, Chang had cause to be grateful for the advice. Rounding a bend in the track he was following through a small patch of forest he saw a troop of some twenty well-armed and armored soldiers coming towards him.

"Stand fast or die," roared one of them.

Chang did not need to be told twice. He at once dropped his spear and knelt down on the dusty path.

"Who are you?" snapped the commander, "and why are you armed? Speak the truth, lest you die."

"I am not of this land," said Chang, remaining on his knees. "I have come from a distant place to offer my weapon in the service of the most noble and mighty King Da Yi of Shang."

The commander, his bronze sword poised at the ready, regarded Chang narrowly, appraisingly.

"How do I know you are not come to spy?"

Chang looked up at the commander, a youngish man but strongly built, who handled his weapon with a familiarity born of training and experience in battle. Chang decided he was a man to be reckoned with in spite of his comparative youth.

"Had I come to spy, Lord," he said, "would I have walked boldly through this forest in broad daylight and bearing a spear? I would be a poor spy indeed."

The commander gazed at him steadily for a few moments more, and then, evidently coming to a decision, shouted to his men, "Let him up. We shall take him to the king, and he shall decide what is to be done with him."

These memories crowded in upon Chang, and he stood, oblivious of his surroundings as he relived the arduous journey. Had it been his destiny, or his death?

"Well," roared King Da Yi, bringing Chang back from his reverie with a crashing jolt, "did you not hear me? Where is your tongue? Answer me."

Chang blinked and stammered, "Forgive me, Lord King. I —"

"Oh, never mind," snapped Da Yi, waving an impatient hand. Chang heard the irritation in his voice and strove to concentrate. "I said," the king went on, "now you are here, what do you want?"

In his waking and sleeping dreams, Chang had seen himself welcomed by the king of Shang, gathered gratefully into his army, and sent forth to crush the forces of Xia. He had foreseen nothing else. What else was there? He had not exactly imagined himself carousing at the king's table, but nor had he expected this mockery and incivility. He felt Da Yi's gaze boring into him like an ivory carver's drill. The assembled court was waiting to hear his answer, and, praise heaven, inspiration came.

"Lord King," he said, spreading his hands in a gesture of supplication, "grant me, I beg you, but a single opportunity to prove myself. An opportunity of your own devising, whatever it may be. That is all I ask."

Da Yi sat back in his chair, an unadorned piece of plain wooden furniture, continuing to stare at Chang, who hoped those dark eyes could see into his soul and discern his sincerity. The distant rooster crowed again, clear in the absolute stillness. Chang prayed the sound was an omen, for the rooster was a symbol of honesty, but the king remained silent.

Da Yi's expression betrayed nothing, until, at last, his face relaxed and he stood up.

"What did you say your name was?"

"Chang, Lord King."

"Very well, Chang. I shall prove you as you request. If you fail, if you betray me, if you take even the smallest false step, you will die, and I promise your death will be of a most unpleasant nature. Will you agree to do whatever I ask?"

Chang swallowed, his heart thundering in his chest as though to be heard by everyone in the hall.

"I will, Lord King."

"Then hear me well, Chang," said Da Yi, portentously. "You will journey to the court of Jie, King of Xia, in the company of my envoy, Minister Yi Yin. You will obey him in all things, and when he instructs you to do so, you will return here with messages for me. Do you understand?"

Chang was thunderstruck, but conscious of his tenuous situation, he mastered his emotions.

"I do, Lord King," he said, with a deep bow. His life had been spared, but for what? To stand before the monster whose soldiers murdered his wife and child, and destroyed his village? He had expected his trial to be some test of arms, some feat of soldiery, not service as a messenger boy.

What Chang did not understand, however, was that despite his conquests and enlargements to the lands of Shang, Da Yi was not an independent ruler. In the strictly hierarchical edifice of the feudal world, he was but a liegeman of the ruler of Xia. King Jie would normally have been highly delighted to have a vassal so successful in expanding the borders of Xia and the consequent enrichment of tax revenues, but the recent clashes between the armies of Xia and Shang, along with Da Yi's practice of absorbing conquered territories in his own kingdom rather than into the realm of Xia, had placed a marked strain on the feudatory relationship between the two kings. Da Yi envisioned independence, while Jie smelled treason and rebellion.

Chang listened as these intricacies were explained to him later by one of Yi Yin's clerks, an impatient young man who clearly regarded Chang's illiteracy and unworldliness as things of wonder.

"So, you see," the clerk concluded, "Minister Yi Yin must serve King Da Yi while appearing to serve King Jie. It is a dangerous task, for no king likes a spy."

45

"But will we not all be spies also?" asked Chang, but for answer the man merely smiled and inclined his head.

Chang was stunned by these revelations. He had always assumed Da Yi and Jie were mortal enemies. However, despite his unfamiliarity with high statecraft, Chang was sufficiently astute to realize the delicacy of the situation, and so made up his mind to remain alert, to watch, learn, and remember.

* * *

After Da Yi dismissed him with an imperious wave of his hand, Chang scarcely had time to gather up a few necessities for the journey before someone was shouting at him to make haste or be left behind. Seizing his pouch, he ran to join Yi Yin's entourage of soldiers, servants, slaves, clerks, and sundry other functionaries.

Now, as he sat in an ox cart lumbering and lurching slowly towards the capital city of Xia, Chang continued to contemplate the mysteries of politics. If the armies of Xia and Shang had fought each other, if Xia had sacked Shang villages, and Shang had retaliated in kind, why was there not open civil war by now? Why was the solution not a purely military one, without all this subterfuge and diplomatic maneuvering? It was utterly beyond him but he had been told of Yi Yin's celebrity as a scholar and man of unimpeachable honor, so he concluded this mission to the court of Xia must be of some importance, even if he, Chang, did not comprehend its nature.

And since it is so important, he said to himself, as his ox cart squeaked and rattled its tedious way along the track, there may come an opportunity for me to do some great thing for the king of Shang. I will not believe my destiny is to be nothing more than an errand boy at the beck and call of other men.

He gritted his teeth and hung on as his cart crashed into, and then out of, a large pothole in the uneven track.

At least I do not have to walk, he reminded himself, looking at those footsore members of the column who trudged along beside the heavy-wheeled wooden carts. He was designated a personal messenger and private servant to Yi Yin, and this lofty appellation spared him the walk, but as the cart bumped and jolted its ponderous way along, he sometimes thought walking might have been a lot easier on his back and backside.

At first, the sun was warm, rather than hot — heaven be thanked — as the small procession wended its way past fields and villages, but then, after nearly a week of good progress, heaven apparently lost interest as black clouds marshalled themselves on the horizon before overwhelming the blue sky and unleashing such a torrent of rain as Chang had seldom ever seen. The air was riven by lightning, thunder pealed and reverberated across the lowering, ragged sky, while the rain lashed the countryside, turning the track into a sea of viscous, yellow mud. Chang sat in his ox cart, the rain plastering his long, black hair onto his head and streaming into his eyes as he watched the minister's cart ahead, protected by a hooped wooden canopy beneath which Yi Yin undoubtedly sat in dry, cushioned comfort.

One day, he promised himself, I shall be the one in the covered cart. I shall be the one who is dry and comfortable. Heaven favors other men, why should it not favor me, as well?

The sun reappeared the next morning, but its effect was anemic at best. It was mid-afternoon before its feeble warmth finally managed to dry Chang's sodden clothes, and he was able to take a little more interest in his surroundings. By then, they were far to the east and north of the Shang capital, and the landscape was hilly, the forests less dense. On the tenth day of their journey there appeared before them at last a large city girded by massively thick mud brick walls. As with all such cities, small houses were built against the outside of the walls, and as they approached, the procession passed through villages whose inhabitants' lot in life was to raise crops and livestock for consumption by those fortunate enough to live within the city walls rather than outside them. They also passed by the workshops and smelters of metalsmiths whose shimmering furnaces filled the air with acrid fumes of burning charcoal and molten metals — copper, tin, bronze, silver, and gold.

"Is this the city of Xia?" Chang asked the driver of his cart. The man nodded.

"Yes, and it is as evil a place as ever could be found. I wish you good fortune during your time here, sir, but I am bound to say I feel glad I will not be with you."

Chang had no desire to be there either and he reflected sourly on it as the ox cart passed through the gates into the city of King Jie, the tyrant whom he had vowed to slay. He had always envisioned striking Jie down with a sword or spear on the battlefield, but on the other hand, he now reflected, my stay here might provide me an opportunity to put a knife into his belly and he would then be just as dead.

Chapter Four

Nearly two years have passed since Chang's arrival at the court of Xia, and he had become inured to its excesses, although he kept himself aloof from them as much as his position allowed. Jie and his courtiers lived a life of debauchery, lasciviousness, and gluttony beyond all imagination. Mountains of food were prepared, served, and often wasted. Wine and millet beer flowed like the Yellow River itself, while women, both young and old, were abused as carnal playthings.

But, finally, an opportunity had come for him to act and begin to fulfill his destiny.

"Who are you?" Jie had roared as Chang and Yi Yin stood before him after their arrival, Jie was a strongly built man of about forty years, carrying an intricately carved green jade scepter as long as his arm. He wore a tunic and kilt of black silk; the Xia people believing black to be the most dignified of all colors. His eyes were small, and Chang thought them menacing and cruel. He had a prodigious moustache, heavily waxed, which extended on either side of his nose by more than the length of a man's hand, and his sallow skin evidenced the general dissipation of his daily life.

"I am Minister Yi Yin, Lord King," answered Yi, bowing deeply. "I and my servants and slaves are come hither from the king of Shang, your vassal in the eastern regions, in the valley of the great river."

"Ah…yes," said Jie, with a sarcastic sneer, "the *great* king of the Shang clans. I know of him. He conquers all the kingdoms around him. He covets power and wealth. He attacks my soldiers, and yet he calls himself my vassal."

"He conquers on your behalf and in your name, Lord King," said Yi, his tone humble, "and as to the incidents between his soldiers and yours, we can only say they were most regrettable misunderstandings which we beg you in your graciousness to overlook. Lord Da Yi is your obedient liegeman, Lord King, and we are here to serve you in token of his fealty."

So, thought Chang, as he listened, this is how the truth is bent, twisted, re-shaped, and re-spoken. I would rather fight with a sword than with words like these. We grovel and debase ourselves before this monster and it is called diplomacy.

"Ha," Jie guffawed. "Vassal he may be, but *obedient*, I think not. I should have you all executed for the liars you are. What say you to that, Minister of Shang?"

Cold fear clutched Chang's vitals. I should have stayed in Hongshan, he thought, as he waited for Yi's response. I have stood in the presence of two kings, and each has threatened to kill me.

"Our lives are yours to take, Lord King," said Yi, and Jie stared at him, narrow-eyed.

"You speak with a slippery tongue," he said, at length, "but you shall live, and when I give you leave to go, you shall return to the king of Shang and speak my words to him."

Yi bowed and began to speak, but Jie forestalled him.

"But hear me, Minister. If your intention is to spy, I shall roast you alive, you and all your followers."

"As you command, Lord," said Yi, bowing again, and Chang remembered Da Yi's instructions that he carry messages from Yi Yin back to the Shang court, and fear gripped him tighter.

Why am I here? Is this what heaven has ordained?

A slave conducted Chang to a small room, sparsely furnished with a table and two stools. By the meager yellow light of a tallow lamp standing on the table, he saw a bed of rice straw on the floor in one corner; the floor itself being of beaten earth like that in his house in the winter settlement, but at least there were no cockroaches here. There were no shuttered windows or even bare openings to the outside air, and the atmosphere was heavy with the smoke curling upwards in a thin, black thread from the tip of the lamp's small flame.

The slave, an emaciated lad of about twelve, said nothing, merely bowing before he departed. Chang closed the wooden door behind him and was about to bar it with a stout piece of wood he retrieved from the corner, when he heard a knock. Re-opening the door, he saw before him in the dark passageway not the slave boy he had expected, but a girl of perhaps sixteen.

"Who are you?" he asked.

"I am your gift from King Jie," she answered, slipping nimbly into the room. "And now you may bar the door."

Chang stood looking at the new arrival. She was very pretty, with dark eyes and hair which covered her back in a sweep of lustrous ebony. She wore a plain robe, devoid of ornamentation or embroidery, dyed a pale blue.

"What do you want?" he asked, acutely aware of how foolish the question sounded, but unable to find other words.

For answer, the girl let the robe fall from her shoulders and stood completely naked in the pale lamplight.

"I am called Sai," she said, "and I am sent here by King Jie for your pleasure. Please bar the door. I do not like it when others watch."

Chang had been alone since the death of his wife. He had paid no heed to the flirting of the girls in Hongshan, but now he stared at the comely girl's body with a sudden, reawakened desire. He stepped closer to her, reaching out to caress the smooth skin of her shoulder and down to the exquisite softness of her breast. She tilted her head to one side, smiling at him with a sweetness of expression that touched his heart.

"I was afraid to come here," she said, almost in a whisper, "but you are gentler than the others I visit."

Chang withdrew his hand as new thoughts raced through his mind. This young slave girl had been sent to him by the king, but to accept the gift would be to render himself beholden to Jie, and worse, make himself like him — lustful and cruel. And might she not be a spy, commanded to report all he said back to the king?

Stooping, he picked up the robe and draped it over her shoulders.

"You do not desire me?" she asked, a puzzled look on her oval face.

"I am almost old enough to be your father," he said.

"That is no matter," she answered, apparently genuinely confused by his lack of carnal appetite. It occurred to him it was not at all what she was used to.

"Go now," he said, but she did not move.

"If you do not lie with me," she said, a tear running down her soft cheek, "I will be beaten with a bamboo cane. It has happened to other girls, and I have heard them scream. I beg you not to let it happen to me."

What a place is this, Chang asked himself.

"Here is what you shall do," he said, leading her to the door. "Tell everyone I lay with you and my happiness was complete. Make up a fine story, and I will thank the king for his lovely gift."

Sai smiled up at him; a shy look of gratitude.

"Ask for me again, Lord. Perhaps another day you will feel better."

"Perhaps," he said, closing the door behind her.

* * *

As the weeks went by, Chang saw little of Yi Yin, and knew nothing of what the minister might be doing as a member of Jie's court. Unlike his initial cordiality, Yi now barely spoke to him, hardly deigning to recognize his existence, and it seemed Chang was to be relegated to his small, airless chamber, presumably to pass his time in obscurity. It suited him well.

The months since his arrival had been little more than day after empty day of boring inactivity — or so he intended everyone to believe.

"I have nothing to do," he would complain to anyone who would listen. "There is nowhere to go. I am at my wits end. Surely I shall lose my mind."

The fact of the matter was that he had long since determined to return to the court of Shang with as much valuable information as he could carry, and to that end he was continuously at work. Ostensibly merely looking for something to fill his time, he talked to servants, slaves, and soldiers. He insinuated himself into their confidence, learning the workings of the court and striving to understand the factions vying for the king's ear and favor. From the servants and slaves, he learned how Jie's taxes were collected, how money was apportioned, and how Jie's kingdom was administered, but his prime sources were the soldiers. They provided the information he wanted above all. From them he learned how the army of Xia was structured, its size, disposition, and weaponry, but that was not enough.

The men he talked to were not rank-holders but simple foot-soldiers who did what they were ordered to do and lived or died as fate would have it. He needed to know more. Eventually, therefore, after befriending one of the king's captains who possessed a strong belief in his own military prowess and an equally strong affinity for millet beer, he became a student of the battle tactics of the army of Xia, if tactics they could be called, which was doubtful. From what he could gather, the customary plan amounted to little more than a wild, headlong charge straight at the enemy.

Chang knew of the thing called writing, of course, but had no skill in it himself, so he memorized everything he heard, repeating it over and over to himself as he sat in the dim light of the tallow lamp in his tiny room. He had become convinced there would be open civil war one day, and the forces of Xia and Shang would collide in one grand struggle which would destroy the Xia and establish Da Yi

53

of Shang as ruler. When that day came, he, Chang, would be at Da Yi's side. He would see the Xia defeated. It was his destiny, and if heaven and his ancestors were generous, he would kill King Jie with his own hand.

Sai, the gentle young slave girl, was of inestimable value to him in his new vocation of spy. Choosing one of the not infrequent moments when Jie was all but totally intoxicated, he had told the king of the great pleasure she bestowed upon him, expressing humble gratitude for so generous a gift. Jie responded exactly as he hoped.

"She is yours," he grunted after a loud belch, haphazardly waving a cup of wine in the air. "Keep her and do with her as you will. I had once thought to take her as a wife, but her father is only a weaver of cloth. She is far from noble, but for you, a nonentity, she is well suited. If you tire of her, send her to the barracks, and we shall find you another furrow to hoe."

Chang was content to bow and say nothing further as three slaves hurried forward. Two to save the king from sliding off his chair, and one to hold a bowl for him to vomit into.

"The man of Shang is speechless with joy, Lord King," mocked a nobleman hardly less inebriated when order had been restored, and the king guffawed loudly, belched again, and then choked and spluttered on his wine.

Since she now belonged to Chang by royal decree, Sai was no longer required to go to other men, and came almost every evening to his small room where she told him of all the gossip she had heard that day. His long months of cold celibacy had finally become too much for him, and he surrendered himself to the girl's ineffable sweetness and her gentle caresses. He satiated himself night after night, and she responded with all the ardor and warmth of her youthful sensuality. She became the light which illumined the otherwise drab world he lived in at the court of Xia. At first, his desire for the girl made him feel guilty, unfaithful to the memory of his dead wife, but the closeness of her, her happy smile each evening she visited him, began gradually to possess his soul. He had not wanted to find pleasure with her, but his body betrayed him as he kissed her and made love to her.

One evening, twenty-two months after his arrival, Sai, now nearly eighteen, brought him something wholly unexpected. She came to his room an hour after his invariable evening meal of chicken dumplings, rice, and millet bread, her eyes sparkling with excitement.

"Such news, Master," she bubbled, in high glee, after their customary kiss and embrace.

"Quietly, quietly," he hissed. "There may be someone outside the door."

"I am sorry, Master," she whispered, giggling.

He had at first objected to being called *Master* — the ownership of a slave being beyond his expectations and experience — but she eventually convinced him it was right and reflected the proper order of things. As a guest of the king, after all, he had become used to being attended by many slaves. There were those who brought him fresh straw for his bed, cooked his food, and emptied his honey bucket; there was even a scruffy little boy of ten who came twice a week to bathe him and pick the lice from his long hair. He owned none of those, and they served many others as well as himself, but Sai was his, and his alone. He found that fact pleasantly satisfying and came to enjoy dwelling on it from time to time. Many people owned slaves, so why not him?

"What is this amazing news?" he asked, keeping his voice low. "I have been out hunting all day with some of the soldiers, and I have heard nothing."

They lay on his straw bed, and she snuggled against him.

"The court is in an uproar," she whispered, her lips close to his ear so that he felt her warm breath on his cheek. "The king's rage burns like the sun."

"What happened?"

"The royal historian, the great Zhong Gu himself, has displeased the king, and has gone into hiding to preserve his life. It is said he refused an order from the king."

"Most unwise," observed Chang, thinking a man like Zhong should have known better than to tweak the tiger's tail. "What was the order?"

"Zhong Gu was with the king and some noblemen in the king's private chamber. Zhong Gu read to him from the annals of the kingdom, as is his duty. Zhong read of the small battle between the soldiers of Xia and Shang, in which the men of Xia were defeated."

"That is a true account," said Chang, stroking the inside of Sai's silken thigh. "It was widely spoken of at the time and cannot have been unknown to King Jie."

"Yes, Master, but it seems the king ordered Zhong to change the writing to say the victory belonged to Xia. Zhong Gu fell to his knees at once, begging the king to understand that honor required he write the truth. King Jie flew into a great rage and Zhong fled from his presence and disappeared. He was truly fortunate. Had guards been present, Zhong would be dead already."

"Indeed, he would," murmured Chang, almost to himself, his hand wandering to the girl's soft breast. "What happened after that?"

"How can I tell you while you make my heart flutter so," she giggled. "Come into me quickly, and then I shall tell you the rest."

"Now," he asked, a little short of breath when they had finished, "what else is there?"

"King Jie has ordered Zhong Gu found and brought back to the palace," she said, after collecting herself for a few moments. "He says he is to be flayed alive before all the people."

Chang found difficulty believing such a thing could happen. Could Zhong Gu have been so foolish? True, he occupied a lofty position at court, one commanding power and respect, but no man could refuse the king his wish. Zhong was the keeper of all records and the chronicler of the reign. He was known as a mighty man of learning and philosophy, a maker of writing, and a seer. Jie had scant respect for any man as far as Chang had ever seen, yet when Zhong Gu spoke, the king listened. This time, however, he had clearly not liked what he heard. Zhong Gu's honor had proved stronger than his obedience to the king, and he would not record a lie.

A plan leapt fully formed into Chang's mind. A plan whereby he could leave this place and at the same time prove his allegiance to the king of Shang. It was perfection itself, but it was perilous.

"Does anyone know where Zhong Gu has gone, do you think?" he asked Sai, and she shook her head, her long hair rippling across her shoulders. "Are there any rumors?" he asked. "Are there any speculations, no matter how vague?"

"Some say he has left the city, others that he must be hiding here in the palace. No one really knows."

"I do not believe he could hide within the palace," said Chang, rolling onto his back in the straw. "He is either somewhere in the city or has escaped altogether."

"Perhaps," she answered, shrugging. "He hides now from the wrath of the king, but he may come back if the king's anger cools. If not, they say he will never be seen again."

Rising from the straw pallet, Chang seated himself on a stool, and Sai came to sit on his lap, her arm around his shoulders.

"What is in your heart, Master? I know there is something."

"Might the shamans and priests know where Zhong hides?" he asked, after a few moments' thought, but Sai shook her head again.

"They are dead. The lord king ordered they be buried alive this afternoon when they could not divine for him where the great Zhong had gone."

How can the court exist without priests and shamans? Chang asked himself. Who will propitiate the gods and spirits? Who will seek for intercession? Can Jie be so arrogant as to believe himself greater than all heaven and earth?

"And where is King Jie now?" he asked.

57

"He sits alone, drinking beer. The soldiers are searching the city, house by house, and the palace room by room."

As if in answer to her words, there came a thunderous pounding on the door, accompanied by demands the door be opened. Scrambling to her feet, Sai threw her robe around herself while Chang seized his loincloth before unbarring the door. Four soldiers, one carrying a blazing torch, pushed their way in, and looked around the room. After plunging his spear several times into the straw bed, the captain snapped, "He is not here. Come on."

As the man with the torch reached the door, he turned, casting a hungry glance at Sai.

"We are sorry to have disturbed you," he said, grinning lasciviously. "We shall leave you to your work, unless, of course, you would like some help."

He raised his eyebrows, and Sai stepped back, clutching her robe more tightly around her shoulders.

"Get out," Chang barked, and the soldier laughed.

"Pigs, all of them," Sai whispered, shuddering, as Chang re-barred the door.

"I must find Zhong Gu," said Chang, almost to himself, as the sound of the soldier's laughter faded.

"I am afraid for you, Master," said Sai. "If you should displease the king you will forfeit your life. I could not bear to lose you." He barely heard her, so deep was his preoccupation.

"Sai," he said, looking into her fathomless dark eyes, "help me find Zhong Gu. Listen to what others say. Hear what they guess, what they imagine. Bring me anything you can find out. Anything at all."

"Master," she said, staring at Chang, her eyes now filled with terror, "if the king hears of it, he will have me killed."

"No, no," he said, hastily. "You must say nothing, ask nothing. Only listen and watch, as you do already. Be my eyes and ears in places I cannot go. If I can find Zhong Gu, I shall have the means to fulfill my destiny."

58

"And what is to become of me?" she asked, still wide-eyed, but he did not answer.

Chapter Five

It seemed Zhong Gu had vanished into the void. King Jie's wrath did not abate but intensified to a pitch unseen before. Everyone at court sought to avoid him. When one of his most trusted generals was forced to admit Zhong had not been found, the wretched man was lucky to escape with his life, hurrying from the room as Jie flung pots and stools after him, shrieking that he was an ill-begotten imbecile.

Throughout this incendiary turmoil, Sai faithfully brought Chang news of every rumor, every whisper, she heard. But she grew more fearful each day Zhong remained unfound as the king's fury blossomed like a fire in the forest. Finally, after five harrowing days, she came late one night, a hood over her head, and slipped soundlessly into his room.

"Bar the door, Master," she whispered, as though afraid the very walls would betray her.

Placing the wooden beam across the door, Chang led her to the table, and they sat close together on four-legged stools. Her fear was palpable, but although he was consumed by curiosity, he waited for her to collect herself.

"You are safe here," he said. "Do not be afraid."

Drawing a deep, shuddering breath, she paused for a long moment more before beginning her story.

"I heard two of Zhong's servants talking," she said, her voice barely audible. "The one said to the other, *he will never be found, even though he is so close. In time he will be able to escape.*"

"What did he mean?"

"I know nothing more, Master."

"Why have those servants not fled?" he asked.

60

"Where could they go?" she answered. "How far could they get? It is safer for them to stay in the palace and pretend to aid in the search. That is what they are doing."

"This is intriguing news," he said, "but little more. Yet you are fearful and come here hooded."

"They saw me as they spoke, Master," she said, "and knew I had overheard. They said if I told anyone of it, they would find me and kill me. They remain loyal to Zhong."

"They cannot hurt you," he said, putting an arm around her shoulders. "You are my property, and you cannot be taken away. You belong to me as a possession. I have the right to kill anyone who touches you, and those men know it. Do not be afraid."

So, Zhong has not escaped, he thought, his mind running in a separate direction as he spoke to Sai. They have not found him in the palace, yet he is close. He must be somewhere in the city. If he leaves the city, I shall never find him.

The king's soldiers had turned the city first upon its head and then upon its heels, in their desperate efforts to find Zhong Gu, but it seemed he was cleverer than they supposed.

"You have done well," he said to Sai, wrapping his arms around her and squeezing her tightly. "Go now and see if there is more to be learned. I cannot go myself. I am a man of Shang, and I would arouse suspicion. I must rely on you."

Reluctant to leave, she held him in her arms, and as she did so, a new thought came to him.

"Say to everyone I have grown tired of you," he told her, "and you are seeking pleasure elsewhere. Find the servants you overheard, and perhaps, in the arms of one of them, you will learn what he knows."

She recoiled from him with a cry of revulsion.

"Only for now," he said, seeing the horror in her eyes. "Until I have found Zhong Gu. Do this for me."

"You make me a whore again," she said. "Do I mean nothing to you, after all?"

61

"You were a whore before I came here," he answered, wondering why she could not see the value of his idea. "Why is it so terrible now?"

She stared at him, backing away as he took a step towards her. What in the name of great heaven was wrong with the girl? A few nights with other men; was it so much to ask if it led him to Zhong Gu? Why could she not understand?

She left him without a further word, and he did not see her again for four days. When she at last knocked on his door, he flung it open in towering impatience.

"Well?"

"Zhong Gu hides in the house of Wu, the king's cousin," she told him, her voice flat and cold. "That is all I could find out."

She had done as he asked, and now he had his answer. He began to thank her, opening his arms, but she turned and left him where he stood, her eyes empty. He stared at the door she closed behind her, shaking his head in utter incomprehension.

* * *

Banishing all thoughts of Sai, Chang sat at the wooden table in the dim light of the tallow lamp, dwelling on his plans. He knew where Zhong Gu was — assuming Sai had been given reliable information — so now it was a question of finding a way to speak to him. But even if I do, he mused, will Zhong Gu accept my proposal? He is a great man, and I am but an insect by comparison. Why should he trust me? He stared at the small flame of the clay lamp with its thread of black smoke undulating upwards from its tip. "He will trust me," he said, under his breath, "because he will have no choice. If he is found, he is a dead man, and how long can he remain where he is undetected? I will show him a way to escape. I will place it before his very eyes."

It now occurred to him he may not have much time in which to act. If Jie took it into his head to turn Zhong's servants over to his torturers, he would soon learn their secret. Loyal they may be, but how long could they endure the streams of molten metal that would be poured on them? It was surprising it had not happened already. They must be men of a sturdy constitution and steady nerves to risk such a fate.

He wondered if he should contrive a means of talking to Yi Yin, but dismissed the idea almost at once. He had not even seen the minister for at least a month, and when they had met by chance in a narrow passageway in the palace, he bowed, wishing Yi long life and good health, but the minister, appearing much preoccupied, pushed by without so much as a word. He could obviously not be relied upon.

"No," he said, aloud. "I must do this alone. Involving others is too dangerous."

The following night, therefore, Chang cautiously traversed the dark streets and alleyways to the house of Wu, a wealthy, arrogant man, known in the city of Xia for his gluttony and lasciviousness. Men such as he, attract rumors as dung attracts flies, and the whisper ran abroad that he coveted the throne. He lived in a large house, little smaller than Jie's own palace. Constructed of the same mud brick as the city walls, the dwelling had two floors, a great many rooms, a host of servants, a veritable army of slaves, and a strong contingent of well-armed guards. Chang stood in the long purple shadows of a moonlit stand of acacia trees twenty paces from the house and pictured Zhong Gu hiding somewhere within. As he did so, it occurred to him that Wu might well be planning to use Zhong in some manner in an attempt to seize the throne from his cousin. Why else would Wu risk hiding him? If such were the case, time might be even shorter than he had thought. However, he could think of no ruse or pretext by which to gain entry to the house, much less be afforded an opportunity to talk to Zhong Gu. Even to reveal that he knew, or suspected, Zhong was in the house would mean immediate arrest and execution by Wu's soldiers. If Zhong Gu truly was in the house, and he had no proof of that beyond the word of a man who might simply have been eager to impress the girl lying in his arms, then someone else would have to get him out before an escape could be accomplished. But who was to do that, he wondered, and how was the escape to be made? If Wu did indeed plan to usurp the throne, perhaps Zhong had already agreed to support him, seeing his own salvation in King Jie's overthrow, but how was this to be ascertained?

These questions and many others revolved in his mind for hours after he returned to his tiny chamber, but at last an idea emerged slowly from the mists of these perplexities. An idea he refined and polished like a metalsmith shaping, sharpening, and annealing a fine bronze sword. If it worked, he would be a hero; if not, he would certainly die a hideous death. Gathering his courage, he went to work.

* * *

"Well," barked the king, as Chang knelt before him five days later, "where is Zhong Gu? If you can tell me that, you will be well rewarded, but if you lie, I shall have you cut into little pieces very slowly."

Chang had seen men executed by this means, and the very thought of it made him shudder, but he had asked for an audience with the king and there was no turning back. He told his story as carefully as he could, remaining on his knees, his head bowed.

"But, Lord King," said the captain of the palace guard as soon as Chang had finished, "Lord Wu allowed us to search his house. I was there myself, and we found nothing."

Now, Chang thought, do I live, or do I die? He knew Wu's house had been searched, and if Jie believed his soldiers had been thorough, all was lost. He would die for attempting to deceive the king and for complicity in Zhong Gu's disappearance. On the other hand, it was widely known that Jie distrusted his cousin and suspected him of plotting against the throne.

"Of course," Jie snapped at the officer, "what else would you expect, you imbecile? My *beloved* Cousin Wu is as crafty as a weasel and just as trustworthy. If you searched his house, then perhaps I should have you cut in pieces for not finding Zhong Gu there in the first place."

Chang breathed an almost audible sigh of relief.

The captain went pale and stepped back hastily, probably wishing he had never spoken, but Jie had turned his full fury on Wu.

The king clenched his fists, raising his arms and eyes towards heaven.

"In the house of First Cousin Wu," he roared. "I might have known. There is treason here, and I will root it out."

Chang saw his opportunity and dared to speak.

"Lord King," he said, as humbly as he was able, "I ask but one thing if Zhong and Wu are found and taken."

Jie, now on his feet, stared at Chang for a long moment, his eyes narrowed in sudden suspicion.

"And what might that be?" he demanded in a voice as cold as a winter's frost.

"I ask that they be given to me, that I, your subject, may deliver them to you here in person. Such a service would be a high honor for me, and for my family forever."

"Very well," said the king, after a moment's reflection, "that shall be your reward. But betray me, and you die. Remember that."

"You should have asked for a chest of gold," whispered Yi Yin, as Chang backed away from the king and came to stand beside him.

"Would he have given it to me?"

"Of course not."

Jie summoned one of his generals and gave him his orders. The soldier bowed and hurried off, taking Chang with him. A troop of two hundred men was speedily assembled, and an hour after midnight Wu's house was surrounded and attacked in a fury of blood-lust. Those inside were taken entirely by surprise. Jie had ordered that if Zhong were found, he and Wu were to be taken alive, while the remaining occupants of the house were to be slaughtered where they stood. Watching from a safe distance, Chang saw two figures dragged out bound with leather thongs, and he was exultant. It had been a great risk, but Sai had not let him down.

The pillage continued for an hour. The men of the household and the guards were put to the sword or clubbed to death, while the women, regardless of age or rank, were raped and beaten before being slaughtered in their turn. Chang had never heard such screaming, seen so much blood, such terrible savagery, and he wondered if this was how it had been when these same soldiers of King Jie destroyed his village so long ago. He thought of his wife and son lying dead and renewed his vow to see an end to the rule of Xia.

The carnage having at last ended, Chang joined the soldiers as they marched the two prisoners through the city to the palace and flung them into small, barred dungeons. As they went, the flickering light of their blazing pitch torches made shadows leap over the ground and across the walls of shops and houses. Occasionally, citizens appeared, no doubt disturbed by the noise, only to retreat in haste as soon as they saw the procession. At one point, Wu, who walked with a pronounced limp, stumbled, falling to his knees, and was hauled to his feet with blows, kicks, and fearful curses.

"I shudder to think of the death awaiting them," muttered a soldier, as the march resumed.

"Guard them well, Master Chang," snapped the commander, his leather armor bespattered with gore and brains. "We will return at daybreak to escort you and the prisoners to the lord king."

The soldiers departed, laughing and retelling stories of the night's exploits. No one appeared to spare any further thought for Chang, which was precisely as he had hoped.

Chapter Six

"You are many times most warmly welcome here, Lord Zhong," said King Da Yi of Shang, raising his hands in greeting, "and I give thanks to my trusty subject, General Chang, for his courage in conveying you safely to this city."

Zhong Gu, on his knees before Da Yi, had sworn fealty to the clan of Zi, to the king of the Shang peoples, and declared his vow to serve his new master. Chang, wearing new leather armor, his hand on the hilt of his bronze sword, stood behind him, reveling in the glory of his new rank and basking in the radiance of Da Yi's gratitude.

Disguised as peasant farmers, he and Zhong Gu had walked for weeks in their escape from the city of Xia. As soon as the soldiers left him alone outside the cell in which Zhong was imprisoned, Chang removed the bar from the door and entered, carrying a tallow lamp.

"Lord Zhong," he whispered, "I come to take you to safety. I beg you to make no sound in case Wu should hear us."

"Who are you?" Zhong Gu hissed, "and why do you offer me help? You must know you risk your life."

The feeble flame of the lamp revealed Zhong to be a thin man of about fifty with a long, wispy gray beard and moustache. He wore a blue silk robe, now torn in several places, and there was a cut on his cheek outlined in dried blood.

"I am not a man of Xia," said Chang. "I came here with Lord Yi Yin from the city of the Shang. I can take you there. The Lord Da Yi will be gracious to you. He has declared King Jie no longer holds the mandate of heaven."

"How can we go to the city of the Shang?" whispered Zhong. "It is not possible."

"It is possible," said Chang. "I have made everything ready for us, but we must make great haste. We have but a few hours before sunrise. Trust me, Lord, I beg you."

"Very well," said Zhong Gu. "I have little to lose if you are false, for I am dead if I stay here."

The two men crept out of the cell, and, by the light of the small lamp, Chang led the way outside. To his vast relief, there was no sound from Wu's cell. Extinguishing the lamp, Chang conducted Zhong by the route he had planned, down narrow streets and alleys towards the city walls. The moon was a mere feather, drifting in and out of the clouds, silvering their edges in pale radiance, but there was enough light for them as they hastened past the dark, high-walled houses of rich noblemen and landowners.

"We will be caught by the night patrols," whispered Zhong, but Chang shook his head.

"They are fools. They carry torches which proclaim their coming. If we are careful, we shall be safe from them."

Twice they saw a warning orange glow approaching and retreated into the shadows where they lay hidden as the squads of soldiers passed by, their bronze weapons reflecting the light from their pitch torches. Once all was clear, they rose cautiously and continued on their way, at last reaching the wall at the place Chang had chosen.

"Follow me," whispered Chang, leading Zhong Gu along the base of the enormous structure to a point where repairs were being made. The work was almost complete, the wall near its full height and thickness, but there were still piles of brick everywhere, as well as hand carts and, best of all, ladders. He had at first decided against this place as a way of escape, deeming it far too dangerous, but following two nights' observation, he marveled to discover it was not being guarded at all. It appeared there must be a greater interest in keeping marauders out than in keeping citizens in.

Placing a ladder against the wall, they climbed to the top of a scaffold, and thence to the parapet at the summit of the wall itself where they crouched in the darkness.

"How are we to get down the other side?" whispered Zhong, very much out of breath from such unwonted exertions. Men of learning such as he did not run through city streets, much less climb ladders to the tops of high walls.

"You shall see," said Chang. "Follow me but be careful of the rubble they have left up here."

Crawling along the narrow parapet to avoid being silhouetted against the pale moonlight, they came to a place where a large house had been constructed against the outside of the wall, no doubt the home of a successful tradesman or artisan.

"We must jump down onto the roof," Chang whispered. "No one will hear. The owners are not here."

"I cannot," whispered Zhong, desperately. "The drop is too great."

"There is no other way," hissed Chang into Zhong's ear. "We have no choice. I will go first. Just do as I do."

As expected, there was no sound from within the house as Chang dropped onto the thatch, and he silently thanked his ancestors for their protection.

"Come," he called softly. "It is safe, and the thatch will break your fall."

He ground his teeth in exasperation as he watched Zhong Gu teetering hesitantly on the edge of the brick parapet above him. Was all to be lost because the man would not jump?

"Hurry, for the love of heaven."

After an eternity of indecision, Zhong dropped onto the thatch beside Chang in a heap of flailing arms and legs, uttering a cry of pain as he landed.

"What happened?" Chang asked in alarm, but Zhong only shook his head.

"It is nothing. Let us get out of sight."

Chang pulled away some of the thatch, and they scrambled into an upper room and then down to the ground floor and out of the house. No one was to be seen anywhere. Nothing stirred.

"Come, Lord," said Chang, "we have not far to go now."

"I cannot run much further," gasped Zhong, after a few minutes, and they slowed to a brisk walk which Zhong, now panting heavily, barely managed to maintain.

"I am sorry, Lord," said Chang, "but we dare not loiter."

"I know," Zhong gasped. "I am trying my best."

They passed fields of grain and vegetables dotted with occasional stands of trees, ghost-like in the soft radiance of the declining moon, before reaching a broad expanse of bare ground where Chang found the hiding place he had prepared for them.

"Here we are," he said, halting by a large pile of stones at the base of a rocky outcrop. Moving aside several stones, he revealed a narrow opening which appeared to be the entrance to a cave.

"I am to go in there?" Zhong wheezed, uncertainly, and Chang nodded. "But I will never fit," he protested.

Chang showed Zhong how to wriggle into the tunnel, and then followed him before pulling the stones back from inside to conceal the opening.

"We shall not be found here, Lord," he said, lighting his lamp again. "I found this place several days ago. It is an ancient copper mine, long disused. No one knows of it. We must wait until the hue and cry dies down which it will surely do, once they believe we are far away. I have brought food and water for us for as long as we need."

"You have done so much for me, young sir," said Zhong. "My gratitude is boundless."

They settled themselves on the rocky floor, their backs to the wall of the tunnel, and after pouring water from a large jug into two clay cups, Chang explained his plan for their final escape from the kingdom of the Xia.

"But shall we not be recognized?" asked Zhong, his breath returning after a long drink.

71

Chang smiled, and said, "Without doubt, Lord, were we to go in the clothes we wear now, but we shall go in the guise of ordinary farmers. I have clothing here for both of us."

Zhong Gu looked around in the dim lamplight, plainly unnerved by all that had happened that night — the terrifying raid on Wu's house, his capture and imprisonment, then his miraculous deliverance at the hands of a man completely unknown to him. Such high drama and perilous adventure were as foreign to him as anything in life could possibly be. He had faced certain death, and his life had been given back to him by the young man now sitting beside him in this subterranean sanctuary calmly pouring him another drink of water.

"I owe you my life, young sir," he said. "but may I ask you a question?"

"Of course, Lord."

"What is your name?"

* * *

As Chang had predicted, the frenzied hunt finally ended a week later, but not before he and Zhong had endured an agonizing two hours of breathless terror one day when a troop of soldiers camped at midday by their subterranean hiding place. Several of them sat eating and drinking on the pile of stones concealing the mine's entrance while the two fugitives crouched in the dark just below them, not daring to move. They listened as the soldiers laughed and talked.

"They are gone forever," said one. "The Lord King may shout all he likes, but it will not bring them back."

"His cousin, Lord Wu, was skinned alive," said another, "and the slave girl the king gave to the man of Shang was put to death as well, I hear."

"Yes, she was," said the first. "The king accused her of aiding the escape. She denied it on the bones of her ancestors, but he had her executed anyway."

"How?'

"I do not know, but I am sure it would not have been pleasant."

The soldier chuckled, and then belched loudly.

Chang felt a pang of regret as he listened. Sai had been a loving companion, and without her, Zhong Gu's rescue would never have been possible. But, he reflected, it seems her destiny was to enable me to achieve mine. The gods must have judged her life less important than mine. She was, after all, my property, and the lives of slaves can never be more valuable than the lives of their masters. If her destiny had been of greater importance than mine, I would have been her property, would I not? It is a proof of the righteousness of my cause.

However, righteous cause or not, he tried hard not to contemplate the numerous, hideous forms of execution he had been forced to witness while at King Jie's court.

Regardless of the search, the days in hiding proved necessary for an entirely different reason as well. Zhong Gu had damaged his left ankle in the jump from the city wall, and although he made no complaint, it swelled and discolored in a most alarming manner. Chang watched it with mounting anxiety. Such an injury, which he could never have foreseen, might ruin everything. Their food and water would not last forever, and he was considering the possibility of returning to the city to steal more supplies, but so risky a venture was unnecessary in the end. Within three or four days, to Chang's immeasurable relief, the joint returned to its normal shape and color, and Zhong pronounced it sound.

When Chang judged it safe to go, they emerged from their tunnel like cautious mice.

Wearing nothing but loincloths and homespun jackets with rice straw belts around their waists, they walked, day after weary day, begging for food and water until they reached the city of Shang. To his surprise, Chang

73

discovered Minister Yi Yin was already there, having fled on horseback from Jie's fury.

"You shall be one of my generals, Lord Chang," Da Yi proclaimed. "We shall wage war and vanquish the ignoble king of Xia."

"I am yours to command, Lord King," said Chang, bowing. "My sword and my life belong only to you."

And so, as Da Yi's strength flourished, Chang, who rapidly gained fame as his military prowess grew, led soldiers of Shang on raids deep into the lands of the Xia, overrunning many smaller kingdoms which had come under Jie's suzerainty and securing their allegiance to Da Yi. He watched with contempt as King Jie's soldiers fled the battlefields like frightened rabbits and took savage delight in killing prisoners and those who lay wounded. Da Yi soon made him a member of his high military council, so that thereafter he stood with the other, more senior, commanders as the king planned the campaigns which were taking him ever closer to the final defeat of Xia.

"We must entice the Xia into a single great engagement," said one of the commanders, a battle-scarred old warrior who had lost his left eye to one of Da Yi's enemies many years before. "There is no other way, Lord King."

"Yes," said Da Yi, nodding, "but the time is not yet propitious. The clans of Gu and Wei have made common cause with Jie, and together they are too many for us."

"The Wei alone field a mighty army," said another, "and their commanders are courageous men."

"I shall overcome the Wei," Chang declared. "Give me but two months, and I shall either destroy them or turn them into our allies."

"Bah," snorted the old general. "Two months? You are a dreamer, General Chang. I know you to be a fearless man in battle, but you are a dreamer, notwithstanding."

"On what grounds do you ask me to risk an entire army in such a venture?" asked Da Yi. "This sounds like sheer bravado."

"I have studied the battle tactics of the Wei," said Chang. "There is a means by which a relatively small force can defeat them."

"How small?"

"I would need a thousand good men."

"A thousand only?" guffawed the old general. "This is sheer folly, Lord King."

"Tell us," commanded the king, and Chang set forth his plan. Da Yi and the other commanders listened without interruption as Chang pointed out the necessary features on a drawing and described the disposition of his forces.

"And so, Lord King," he finished, "I ask leave to undertake this venture for your greater glory and power."

"It is far too risky, Lord King," protested the old general, shaking his hoary head. "It bases the entire battle on one strategy alone, without tactical options if things do not go as anticipated. Moreover, the plan requires one particular piece of ground, and what is to be done if it cannot be reached? The slightest miscalculation or unforeseen circumstance will result in disaster, and we would lose a thousand men for nothing."

"I have thought of everything, Lord King," said Chang. "I am sure of success. With the Wei subdued, your path to victory over the Xia is assured. The army of Gu is small and ill-equipped, and King Jie's forces are demoralized. This is the moment to strike down the Wei. The army of Xia will then be forced into a final battle and delivered by heaven into your hand."

Da Yi studied the drawing, rubbing his chin, and every eye rested upon him.

"Go," he said, after a long pause. "Take whatever men you need. But," and here he raised a warning forefinger, his eyes narrowed, "if you fail in this, do not trouble to return."

The king's final words rang in his ears like the tolling of portentous bells as Chang bowed and withdrew from the council chamber.

A mere six weeks later, Chang returned triumphant, and the king of the Wei peoples bent his knee to Da Yi and swore allegiance. Chang was a hero, and the king made him rich.

After leaving the council, he carefully chose a thousand seasoned fighting men and equipped them with new weapons and armor. For several weeks, they hounded and harassed the army of Wei in a series of raids in daylight and darkness, always avoiding a pitched battle. Eventually, just as Chang had anticipated, the king of Wei was infuriated to the point of gathering his troops into a single force and marching on Chang's small army which had, by design, disposed itself in what appeared to be a temptingly vulnerable position. Chang and his army fled in mock disarray, and the men of Wei, in high hopes of routing their enemy permanently, pursued them into the place Chang had chosen. After more games of cat-and-mouse, the king of Wei, in a sad display of military ineptitude, allowed himself to be lured into the narrow defile where Chang had prepared the final, terrible slaughter. Too late, did the king of Wei see his fatal blunder and order his men to withdraw. Chang's troops at once blocked the paths both in and out, and rained spears, arrows, boulders, and blazing bundles of wood down upon their helpless enemies. Surrender came swiftly, and the king was found cowering under a thorn bush, from whence he was conveyed in chains to the court of Da Yi, eager to transfer his loyalty from Xia to Shang and thereby preserve his life.

In the entire campaign, Chang lost no more than a hundred warriors, and in gratitude, Da Yi gave him a carved jade baton of deep emerald green — an honor no other commander had ever received. He further bestowed on him a great weight of gold and bronze, a fortune in cowrie shell money, and a hundred slaves — prisoners from the defeated army of Wei — to serve him in the luxurious house he now occupied in the city of Shang. Five weeks later, Da Yi dispatched him to crush the Gu clan, which he speedily accomplished — they capitulated almost at once — and with that final minor impediment removed, the massed armies of Shang and its allies marched against the king of Xia.

Choosing his ground with utmost care, Da Yi ranged his forces across a broad, level plain at a place called Mingtiao. Two days after their arrival, as Da Yi and his four generals sat together in a large tent eating, drinking, and talking battle tactics, a messenger begged leave to enter, and, kneeling, made his report.

"Our scouts tell us the army of the Xia has been drawing up all day, Lord King. It is believed they number nearly six thousand men with foot soldiers, archers, horsemen, and charioteers. It is a mighty host."

"Mighty indeed," said Da Yi, "but with heaven's help, we shall prevail." He paused for a moment, then said to the messenger, "Go now. Fetch me the old seer."

A few minutes later, there appeared a willow-thin woman of about sixty, with a face as wrinkled as a dried plum. She wore a black, knee-length tunic, and a black silk scarf knotted around her head. Her smile revealed very few teeth as she entered the tent, bowing repeatedly as she came.

"Lord King?"

"Old and venerable one," said Da Yi, "I wish you to conjure the gods of heaven and tell me the outcome of the battle we shall fight in this place tomorrow."

"I shall burn the shell of a turtle," the priestess said, bowing yet again, "and by this we shall know the will of heaven, if the gods themselves wish it to be known."

"So be it," said Da Yi.

"But there is a question, Lord King," the priestess put in.

"Well?"

"Whom shall I say commands the army of Shang?"

"I command, of course," snapped Da Yi, with a flash of irritation, "and the Lord Chang is my deputy. Why should heaven care who commands?"

"Because, Lord King," the priestess said, with a knowing smile on her furrowed face, "heaven blesses men, not armies, and heaven will not reward or prosper unrighteous men, no matter the strength of their armies."

Da Yi grunted, and the woman nodded.

"If you will come with me, Lord King, all things will be revealed."

Da Yi, Chang and the three other generals followed the woman to where a fire burned in a three-legged bronze cauldron. Other priestesses stood nearby, bowing as the king approached, and the woman spoke a curt command. One of her assistants took up a bronze rod about the thickness of a man's thumb and thrust it into the glowing coals. While the rod heated, the high priestess reached into a deerskin bag, withdrawing a dozen or so plastrons of the fresh-water turtles which abounded in the rivers and lakes thereabouts. She examined each one with sedulous care, muttering to herself and occasionally shaking her head. After discarding several of them, she finally chose one somewhat larger than the span of her hand which looked to Chang exactly the same as all the others.

Get on with it, he thought, fingering the pommel of his sword impatiently.

"This is the one for today," she announced, holding it aloft. Delving into her bag once more, she produced a short bronze awl, and, sitting cross-legged on the ground, she proceeded to incise the question asked by Da Yi onto the flat shell using a special script reserved for such divinations. All eyes were fixed on her as she worked, and the only sound was the scratching of her awl and an occasional crackle from the fire. At length, she looked up and read back what she had inscribed.

The great and noble King, Da Yi of Shang, humbly asks if he and his great general, the Lord Chang, will prevail at Mingtiao against the hosts of King Jie of Xia.

Getting to her feet, she approached the hot cauldron, where, by that time, the end of the bronze rod glowed a bright red. Wrapping a cloth around the end, the old priestess held the hot metal rod in one hand, the plastron in the other, and extended her arms skyward.

"Witness this, great ones of heaven," she cried. "Show us mercy and answer the petition of the Lord King Da Yi."

No one stirred or spoke as she stood thus for almost a full minute. Inwardly, Chang fumed with impatience. Then,

78

after bowing in each of the four cardinal directions, she pressed the red-hot end of the rod to the turtle shell. For a few moments nothing happened, then with a soft crackle and a curl of black smoke, a lattice pattern of tiny, thread-like cracks appeared on the surface of the plastron, radiating from the point where the rod had touched it. Raising her arms again, she blessed and thanked heaven before dropping the rod. Approaching Da Yi, she bowed and presented him with the shell. He looked at it for a moment before handing it back.

"Heaven reveals nothing to me. Tell us the meaning of it, old one."

The priestess studied the shell for several minutes, all eyes still fixed on her in fascinated expectation. Chang watched the king for signs of impatience, but there were none. Da Yi now appeared content to await the verdict of heaven, rather than insist on haste. Perhaps, Chang reflected, he does not wish to risk angering the gods and spirits on so important a matter. Turning his attention to the priestess, he watched her as she puckered her lined face into a frown, pursed her thin mouth, and then chewed a little on her lower lip, before addressing Da Yi.

"Lord King, heaven tells you this. Tomorrow, many men will die. The unrighteous will be defeated at this place called Mingtiao, and an unworthy king shall be driven from the land."

Da Yi gave the priestess cowry shell money and then watched the completion of the ritual. Sitting on the ground, she incised the answer on the plastron as custom dictated, before giving it to the king's historian, who had the solemn charge of keeping it safe. When Da Yi was eventually gathered into the arms of his ancestors, the bone, along with the hundreds of others accumulated during his reign, would be placed in his tomb. There, they would form an indispensable record of his deeds as the gods and demons vied for possession of his soul.

* * *

Dawn the following day prophesied a storm. Towering flat-topped thunderheads massed themselves on the horizon, and the humid air lay motionless on the land like a hot blanket. Chang, helped by two slaves, donned his bronze-studded leather armor, and his heavy bronze battle helmet which all but obscured his face, leaving him only narrow slits through which to see. He had commissioned the finest metalsmith in the city of Shang to craft a new bronze sword to his own exacting specifications, and he hefted it in his hand with great satisfaction before sheathing it in the leather scabbard at his side. Today, heaven willing, he would kill Jie with that very sword and so fulfill the vow he had made so long ago. It had taken five years, but the time had finally come. He laughed in fierce anticipation. Although many said the answer from heaven told them nothing, was mere equivocation, Chang believed it foretold the end of Xia and the demise of its king. In his mind, it could not be otherwise, for was it not his destiny to see the destruction of Xia?

After a short prayer and the sacrifice of a chicken, Da Yi issued his orders to Chang and the other commanders. The strategy was bold, not without risk, but Chang was confident it would succeed, simply because it would be wholly unexpected. On his return to Shang he reported all he had learned about the battle tactics of Xia, and his information had been confirmed by Zhong Gu, now elevated in the Shang court to a position of high esteem and dignity. Da Yi had planned accordingly.

"We shall not attack," he said. "They must come to us before the trap can be sprung."

Hours passed, and the sky darkened menacingly until just before noon the blare of trumpets was heard from the camp of Xia.

"At last," said Chang aloud, and then shouted, "Come, Jie of Xia. Come and die."

As if in answer to the call to arms, lightning leapt across the sky, and the damp, oppressive air was riven by a mighty peal of thunder. The black clouds opened as though they were vessels full of water, and the downpour all but blinded man and beast alike. The storm's climactic eruption also released a wind which howled across the plain, driving the rain before it, turning the drops into a hail of needles.

Heedless of the rampaging storm, the Xia army hurled itself forward across the open ground in a wild, shrieking stampede, expecting, no doubt, to overwhelm the forces of Shang in a single charge.

Exactly as expected, you fools, thought Chang smugly, remembering what he had told Da Yi about Xia's lack of discipline.

The warriors of Shang stood resolute, waiting for the onslaught. Then, at the last conceivable moment, when the Xia were all but upon them, Da Yi's heralds sounded three blasts on their bronze trumpets. Immediately, the Shang army divided to allow the attacking hoard to blunder headlong into the space between the two halves. Jie's over-confident indiscipline now proved his undoing. The two flanking sides of the Shang army fell on his bewildered troops and wrought a bloody slaughter. The air rang and reverberated with the clash of weapons, the thundering of hooves, blood-chilling war cries, and the screams of the wounded and dying. Jie's forces collapsed in complete disarray, and by mid-afternoon, the carnage was over. Chang found Da Yi, his sword arm blood-covered to the elbow, standing, his breath labored, amongst the dead and wounded of both sides.

"It is done, Lord King," he said, sheathing his sword. "The Xia are no more. Theirs was the army whose defeat the seer foretold yesterday, and Jie was the unrighteous king."

"Where is King Jie now?" asked Da Yi," and Chang, removing his heavy battle helmet, shook his head.

"He has fled like the coward he is."

"Find him," ordered Da Yi, vehemently. "We must know where he is."

Chang bowed before hurrying away. Three of Jie's commanders had been captured, and for the next two hours they swore they knew nothing of his hiding place, but Chang looked into their defiant eyes and knew they were lying. In spite of himself, he was impressed by their unyielding loyalty to their defeated king, but impressed or not, he eventually lost patience. Choosing one of them and stripping him naked, he heated a large kettle of water until it boiled and bubbled in clouds of steam. Without a word, he poured the scalding water over the man, and nothing further was needed.

"Jie has gone to Nanchao, Lord King," he reported to Da Yi. "He has only a handful of men with him."

"Take two hundred horsemen," Da Yi commanded, "and follow him. Tell him if ever he so much as sets one of his feet outside the city of Nanchao, he will die. Tell him I swear it on the bones of my fathers and bring me word of his answer."

"You exile him?" asked Chang, surprised and disappointed. "May I not execute him, Lord King? I would rather bring you his head than his words."

"No," said Da Yi. "The mandate of heaven has passed to me, and that is enough. Jie's death is not necessary, nor was it foretold by the seer."

It is necessary to me, Chang thought, as he led his mounted troops towards Nanchao. He felt a bitter frustration at being unable to kill the man whose soldiers murdered his family and destroyed his village, yet angry as he was, his heart told him Da Yi was right. Jie had lost the mandate, and once lost, it could never be recovered. Jie would never rule again; heaven would destroy him if he tried, and in letting him live, Da Yi was condemning him to exilic obscurity and poverty. Chang contented himself with that thought. He pictured Jie many years hence, gaunt and thin, gray-bearded and toothless, in a threadbare tunic, telling anyone who would listen that he used to be a powerful king. Adults would nod and smile indulgently, and grimy street urchins would mock him and call him a silly old man, bowing before him and laughing. Surely that was a fittingly ignominious end for a man once so arrogant and cruel.

Chang eased himself in his wooden saddle. For years he had nourished the belief that his destiny was to kill King Jie, but that was not to be. What is my destiny, then, he asked himself?

Perhaps I am to become a king myself. Perhaps the mandate will pass to me. Is kingship my destiny?

He found the thought intriguing.

Part Two
London, England 2014

Chapter Seven

"Your job is to tell me if something goes wrong," Sylvia Becker shouted at Michael Barrow, "not to go around shooting people. You've put the entire syndicate at risk, you moron. My family worked damned hard to build up this organization, and I will not have it jeopardized by clowns like you who don't stop to consider what they're doing."

"I thought —" Barrow began, but she cut him short, her voice harsh and abrasive.

"No, Mike, you *didn't* think. That's the trouble. And how the hell did he get a look at that bone in the first place?" She paused for a moment before snapping, "For God's sake don't tell me you actually *showed* it to him."

"Of course, I didn't, Sylvia. I left it on a shelf, that's all. It wasn't stuck out in the middle of the room. I suppose I forgot it was there, but I didn't think he'd notice it."

Sylvia's anger became luminous as she shouted, "You didn't think he'd notice it? Are you serious? That bone is a Chinese artifact, and you told me Preston's an archeologist and sinologist. And you didn't think he'd *notice*?" She ground out her black Turkish cigarette. "I'm surrounded by imbeciles."

"It wasn't a routine acquisition," Barrow pointed out in an attempt at self-defense. "The bone wasn't stolen. It's your personal property and you're selling it. There was no reason to hide it like we hide the other stuff. This operation's perfectly legit."

"My property?" Sylvia retorted. "I have no idea where it came from or who it might once have belonged to. All I know about it is that it came into my family's possession at the end of the war. It might well have been stolen, and in which case someone may want it back. My great-grandfather was mixed up with Nazi treasure thieves, so God knows what the bone might really be, weird though it is."

"I'm sorry," Barrow said, withering under Sylvia's onslaught. "I should have realized..." His voice trailed off.

"You're damn right you should," she muttered, almost growling.

"I'm sorry," he repeated quietly, but the apology seemed only to enflame her further.

"Well," she said, her slight German accent laden with vitriolic sarcasm, "being sorry doesn't help us much, does it? As usual with all you people, if you make a mess, I'm the one who has to clean it up."

Jesus, thought Barrow, and Terry sent a picture of it to his professor at Oxford. Maybe I'll have to take him out as well, except I have no idea what his name was. I should have made a note of it before I smashed Terry's phone. If I tell her about that, she'll have a seizure.

"And there's another thing," Sylvia was continuing. "What possessed you to move the body? Why didn't you just leave it where it was instead of loading it into your car, of all things?"

"I wanted to hide it," said Barrow. "I didn't want it discovered until I got clear. As far as I know, it hasn't been found yet."

Sylvia turned in the direction of a short, thick-set man in a nondescript, gray overcoat who sat inconspicuously by the door, and he stood up, anticipating her question.

"Carl?"

"I'm here, *Fraulein* Becker." His German accent gave his deep voice a guttural timbre.

"Find a way to get rid of Mike's car," she told him. "It's probably got blood stains and God knows what all over it."

"*Ja*, of course," and turning to Barrow he snapped his fingers and held out his hand. "Keys."

"And dump his gun somewhere as well," Sylvia added, before bursting out, "My God, I don't believe this. How could you have been so bloody, bloody stupid? We could lose everything. How many times have I told all of you that I'm the only one who approves maximum responses? If we have to eliminate someone, I set it up. No one else. It's happened enough times for you to know it by now. It's a security issue. It's meant to prevent exactly the sort of mess we're in now."

Barrow, feeling humiliated and angry, handed over his car keys without a word, and retrieved the gun from his coat pocket. He loved his sporty little car and his gun gave him a sense of importance, but he knew he would never see either of them again. The man in the raincoat left the room, saying no more than, "Leave it all to me."

Watching Carl go, Barrow realized he had left the gun's silencer at home. Too late now, he thought, fighting off a momentary panic as he resumed his seat. I'll have to remember to get rid of it myself somehow.

As the door closed, Sylvia sat back in her chair, breathing a long sigh as an eloquent expression of sheer exasperation. Reaching to her left, she found the polished mahogany table beside her chair, and patted her way across the top until she located a pack of cigarettes wrapped in gold foil. Lighting a black cigarette, she drew in a lung-full of smoke. Her mother had begun smoking Turkish tobacco when Sylvia was a child. Directly she left school, she tried it herself, and came to enjoy it. She indulged frequently, despite the fact that her mother was now confined almost permanently to her house in Berlin as emphysema slowly robbed her of breath and life.

She settled herself more comfortably, assuming the position she habitually adopted when smoking, holding the cigarette in her left hand while resting her left elbow in the

86

palm of her right hand. As she smoked, the anger making her hands tremble slightly gradually subsided. Barrow, and the two others left with her in the room, stayed silent. They knew if Sylvia's volatile temper had anything remotely resembling a redeeming feature, it was that it was almost always short-lived, and so they waited for the storm to abate. Sylvia often said the best way to die quickly is to make decisions when you're angry, so although her outbursts of rage were fierce and frequent, she knew herself well enough to exercise control when she needed it. Her pungent — some said dreadful — black cigarettes were her faithful helpers.

After about two minutes, each of which stretched like eons to Mike Barrow, she sat forward again, apparently composed, and there was a palpable relaxation everywhere around the room.

"All right," she said, stubbing out the cigarette, "we have some business to attend to. Are the twins still here?"

The two men left in the room with Barrow had said nothing thus far. They sat somewhat rigidly on a sofa, as though feeling out of place in the spacious sitting room of the flat in London's fashionable Russell Square. The furnishings were opulent. Oil paintings, some of them dark with age, adorned the walls, while crystal and porcelain pieces stood on tables and shelves. Barrow was impressed by the room and had tried to emulate it in his Knightsbridge flat.

Sylvia's mother, Gabriella, had purchased the flat shortly after her own mother, Ellen's, death in 2001, and eventually it had become the head office of the syndicate. Sylvia, now in virtual control of the organization, much preferred London to Berlin, and did not often see her ailing mother except when she needed advice. Gabriella's lungs were occluded by the tar and grime of a lifetime of smoking, but her mind was still as sharp as a snake's fang, and Sylvia knew it.

She sat in a large leather armchair; her slim, elegant legs crossed. She wore a dark blue dress, perfectly cut and tailored for her five-foot-six-inch stature. Her nails were manicured to perfection, and her long, blonde hair covered her shoulders, framing an oval face with wide-set green eyes. Her complexion was flawless. Mike Barrow had always regarded her as an incandescently beautiful woman, in spite of the black, wrap-around glasses she habitually wore. Beside her chair, stretched languidly on the thick carpet, sprawled a golden retriever wearing a harness and handle.

"Mike," she said, "I want you out of London quickly. Can you be trusted to carry that oracle bone to the client in Caen without shooting anybody?" Her tone was sarcastic, but without its former causticity.

"I'll be fine, Sylvia," he answered, trying not to sound as annoyed as he felt. He was convinced leaving Terry Preston to go blabbing to his old professor — what the hell was his name, anyway — would have been a fatal mistake, bringing more trouble down on everyone than killing him ever would. Yes, he knew *maximum response*, Sylvia's quaint euphemism for killing, was her call, but there hadn't been time for the niceties in this case. He also knew Sylvia's first and most important principle was *obey the rules*, but he was sure he had done the right thing, in spite of what she said. He had taken the initiative and killed his best friend for the good of the syndicate, and he felt ill-used by Sylvia Becker and deeply resentful.

"You better be fine," Sylvia snapped. "If you screw up like that again, it'll be you they find stuffed in an alley somewhere with a stiletto in your eye. Do I make myself abundantly clear?"

Her tone was almost conversational by now, which made her words all the more menacing, and the hair on the back of Barrow's neck rose. The syndicate was at the very core of Sylvia Becker's being, and she would defend it with all the ferocity of a lioness her cubs. She had killed to safeguard it before, and by God she would certainly do it again if required.

"Yes, Sylvia," he said, "but I really think I —"

"Leave it, Mike," she said, anger beginning to creep back into her voice, and Barrow backed off.

"All right," she said, "you should be out of London no later than this evening, preferably sooner. You know the delivery arrangements in Caen?"

"Yes, I've memorized the address, and we use the doorstep drop system."

"Correct," said Sylvia. "The client has a secretary and he'll receive the merchandise from you. He'll be expecting Paul Ellis, so use the right ID. As you know, this is not a top tier security delivery because the bone hasn't been stolen, or at least not recently."

In a top tier security delivery, Barrow would pass the merchandise to a known syndicate agent but the delivery might actually involve a further chain of several other people, none of them knowing the names of anyone else in the string, but all of them aware of the syndicate's second principle, *obey your own orders and don't ask unnecessary questions*. Occasionally, Barrow knew who the client was, but not as a rule.

"Got it," said Barrow. "It's certainly not the same as when I delivered that old manuscript last year to our man in Bordeaux. The Paul Ellis ID is good for another couple of years at least."

"Ah, yes, Bordeaux," said Sylvia, with a smile, her tone now quite mellow. "The tenth century Qur'an we acquired from the Topkapi Palace Museum in Istanbul. That was a complicated operation. The museum security was a real challenge."

"That's right," said one of the rigid men on the sofa, speaking for the first time. "Had to shoot a guard, though. Too bad, that. Otherwise it was pretty cleanly done."

"Sylvia," Barrow ventured, diffidently, "I know that Chinese bone thing has been in your family a long time. Are you sure you really want to get rid of it? Pardon my asking, but..." his voice trailed off, as Sylvia snorted. It was a derisive, contemptuous sound.

"It's worth money," she said. "My mother got someone to decipher it, and it's very significant in Chinese history, although I have no idea why. Mother's too sick to care very much anymore, and obviously I can't see the damn thing. Apparently, my grandmother used to say it reminded her of the war and the tough times, although I never knew what the connection was. Anyway, our client is paying a quarter-of-a-million dollars for it, which is all I care about."

"A very easy acquisition," commented the second rigid man on the sofa.

"Yes, but we have a much more difficult one facing us now, Graham," Sylvia said, leaning back in her deep leather chair again. "This is a new project and I want to get the general planning done for this one before I go back to Berlin tomorrow to pay my goodwill visit to my mother."

"Sylvia," said Graham, "if you want to, you can leave the planning work to us. Just give us the target details and we'll look after the rest. You can go off to Germany and not have to worry."

Sylvia answered the question by remaining completely silent, and Barrow simply waited to see what would come next. Graham's remark was ill-advised, and he should have known better. The awkward silence was finally broken by the man sitting next to Graham.

"What's the operation, Sylvia?"

"There's a new client," Sylvia began. "He's in China. Shanghai, to be precise. He's been vetted and given number one-five-two-nine. He collects sculpture, mainly Chinese, of course, but he has interests in all styles. Seems to think it's very prestigious, or something. Anyway, he's in the market for something Greek. Specifically, bronze, not too large, and preferably of considerable rarity. I put Research to work on it, and they suggested something by Polykleitos should work."

"Who's she?" asked the second man, grinning, but Sylvia only sighed. The pun was not particularly funny, but Graham guffawed while Sylvia made an exasperated clicking sound with her tongue.

"Richard, you constantly remind me of why I employ you for your skills as a thief, and not as an advisor on fine art and antiquities."

"Well, I just never heard of that person before," said Richard, a man of about forty with close-set dark eyes, and a think mop of unruly brown hair.

"*She* is a *he*, actually," said Sylvia, in an elaborately patient voice. "A Greek sculptor of the fifth century BC. He's known as one of the greatest masters, but the works of his that have survived are too large for the most part. They're too difficult for us to deal with in logistical terms. It wouldn't be impossible, but even this client isn't willing to take the risk, let alone cover the cost. Not that he's short of a pound, I'll tell you. But we're in luck. Research found a small statue which may, in fact, be the working model or study for one of his most famous pieces, the *Doryphoros*, or *Spear-carrier*. It's only about a meter in height, and the client agreed with our recommendation to go with it."

"Sounds like another museum job," said Graham, a man of Richard's age, but of lighter complexion and hair color. He also had a rather large nose which tended to dominate his facial appearance. He and Richard were not twins, not even brothers, but Sylvia always called them *the twins*, and so did everyone else. They certainly were not gay, although gossip said they certainly were.

Sylvia shook her head, her long, honey-blonde hair swaying gently in a manner Barrow found deliciously alluring.

"We did think we'd have to go to Greece for this one, but I spoke to our agent in Athens, and he told me about this particular piece. Fortunately for us, it's here in England, in a private house in Norfolk belonging to the Robertson-Hyde family. It seems one of their ancestors picked it up on a grand tour in the eighteenth century sometime and brought it home. Well-off country gentlemen did that sort of thing in those days, you know. Our agent tells me the statue is something of a *cause célèbre* in Greece because of its uniqueness. The National Historical Museum in Athens asked for it back, then demanded it back, and finally offered to buy it back, but the Robertson-Hyde family won't give it up. They say it was legitimately purchased, even if it was two-hundred-and-fifty years ago.

The Shanghai client is willing to pay up to three million dollars for it, so we made the usual agreement."

Barrow knew that did not mean a signed contract. Rather, it meant Sylvia, who was the only person ever to communicate directly with syndicate clients over matters of price and payment, had made a verbal agreement to supply the piece in question. The entire syndicate operated on the basis of what Sylvia — always ready to display her classical education — said was *ultimo bonum fidei*, which she translated as *ultimate good faith*, and Barrow and the others knew very well what happened to clients who did not possess that special virtue. The police in Bogota were still trying to discover how multibillionaire and celebrated drug lord, Juan Espino, ended up tied to a tree in the garden of his palatial mansion with his femoral artery cut. Known only as Client 1719, Espino had ordered a Sumerian alabaster vase, specifying it must be at least five thousand years old, and in pristine condition. Such a vase was duly acquired from an archeological museum in Jordan — the curator being short of money at the time — and smuggled to Cairo in the hold of an Arab fishing dhow. Then, following the transfer of some funds to an Egyptian shipping agent, the piece travelled to Colombia aboard a ship sailing from Porsa'īd in a container marked *Agricultural Machinery*. The vase, carefully padded and packed, was concealed in the discharge chute of a combine harvester, and after offloading and being conveniently overlooked by a Customs and Excise inspector who then went out and bought himself a new car, Barrow had the implement transported to a location pre-arranged by Sylvia where Espino collected it a day later. Barrow had no idea who the client actually was; he simply had the machine parked where he was told to leave it. Sylvia arranged everything.

However, the bank draft used to transfer the hefty cost of the ancient vase to one of the syndicate's many Swiss bank accounts proved worthless, and Espino refused to make good what he owed in spite of numerous negotiations and a personal visit from a frustrated and furious Sylvia

Becker. He laughed at her and made crude and supercilious jokes about a woman trying to run a criminal organization — and a blind woman at that.

"Go back to England, Missy," he sneered, "and leave such things to men who know what they're doing and can see where they're going."

It had not proved a good career move for him, and it did not take long for the secret, dark world of illicit trading in antiquities to spawn the rumor that his death was a reward for trying to double-cross the implacable Athena, whoever she was. Barrow smiled to himself as he thought of the police trying to decide why there was a combine harvester in Espino's driveway.

Thanks to the assistance of a local team of very professional housebreakers contracted by the syndicate's agent in Bogota, the vase was retrieved, shipped north, and now resided in a secret vault in the home of a reclusive American financier with highly questionable ties to the Middle East and Russia who lived in a fortified mansion in the Rocky Mountains of Colorado. He had done business with Sylvia before, and he always paid his bills.

Barrow was not a decision-maker; he was one of Sylvia's delivery boys, and nothing more. However, she gave him the riskiest and most difficult jobs, and paid him very well for what he did. As he listened, he wondered if getting the Greek statue to China might present some technical challenges. It could be tricky, he reflected, but Sylvia, seeming to read his thoughts, said, "You shouldn't have any trouble with the delivery, Mike. Our Polish friends are available to us again, and the client has what he calls *influence* at the port of Shanghai. You can fly there, meet the ship, and oversee the delivery in person. You'll get full details nearer the time."

"Sounds good to me," said Barrow, smiling. "Nothing like a bit of official corruption to smooth things along."

"Just don't take a gun with you," said Graham, smirking, and Barrow darted him an angry glance.

"That's enough," Sylvia snapped, and Richard subsided, a little crestfallen.

She provided Graham and Richard with the details of the sculpture's location, and everything was quickly settled. She gave them instructions on how to effect the acquisition and all was agreed. She trusted them, and they had never let her down.

"So, I think we're finished here," she said, standing up, and the dog beside her chair, galvanized into action, scrambled to its feet and shook itself vigorously, its harness rattling and clattering. Putting her hand down, she found the handle on the dog's back.

"Lombardi," she said, firmly, but not at all roughly, "find the door, we're going for a walk."

Familiar with the routine, Barrow crossed the room, the dog threading its way around the chairs and tables with Sylvia at its side. Barrow opened the door, then closed it behind them.

"Why's her dog called Lombardi?" asked Graham, as Barrow seated himself again. "I've often wondered about it."

"I asked once," said Barrow. "I thought maybe he'd been born in Italy or something like that, but it's not that complicated. Lombardi was the dog's name when she got him from the training school, and apparently it can't be changed, which makes sense. She told me it's all a matter of what the dog's trained to recognize."

"Weird," said Graham. "Dogs are supposed to be called Prince, or Fido, or Rover, or something. I don't much like dogs, anyway."

"Was your mother frightened by a chihuahua?" Barrow asked, happy to return Graham's recent barb, and Richard laughed before saying, "We had a dog when I was a kid. Lovely collie, she was. We called her Lady, because that's what she was."

"Lady," said Graham, affecting an exaggeratedly snooty accent. "Sounds a bit toffee-nosed to me."

"Shut up, you two," said Barrow, grinning. "If it's all the same to you, I'd like to go over the plan for this statue. It's your job to pinch it, but it's mine to take it off you and send it to bloody Shanghai."

Chapter Eight

Detective Superintendent Harry Stuart, fifty-seven years of age, and a thirty-two-year veteran of the London Metropolitan Police, felt deathly ill. His nose felt as if it had been crammed full of that stuff they insulate houses with, his eyes hurt, he had a sore throat, and a headache that could have been measured with a seismograph. Sitting at his desk in his small office at Scotland Yard, he ran his fingers through his graying hair, put his face in his hands, and wondered how soon he could expect to die.

"Don't go to work, Harry, for heaven's sake," his wife, Emily, admonished him at breakfast. "You're just being stupid and stubborn, as usual."

"Get off with your bother," he answered, in the rich accent of his native Glasgow. "I'll be perfectly all right."

"Well, think of everyone else," Emily said, "if you won't think of yourself. D'you really imagine they want you there, sneezing and blowing like a grampus, spreading microbes far and wide? Have at least a little consideration for them."

Stuart was not widely known for thinking of others, so he ignored her. He shrugged into a heavy overcoat, planted a flat cap firmly on his head, and went out into the cold rain of the morning.

She's nothing but a fuss-pot, he said to himself, as he rounded the corner, walked face-first into the full blast of an icy wind, and picked up his pace as he headed for the Tube station ten minutes' walk away.

But now, at three o'clock that afternoon, after spending the morning interviewing a foul-mouthed young suspect banged up on a charge of grievous bodily harm and then gulping down a remarkably leathery toasted cheese sandwich in the canteen, he stared morosely at the pile of paperwork on his desk feeling it was mocking him. He pictured himself at home in his own warm sitting room nursing a hot toddy, and sincerely wished he had listened to Emily.

"It doesn't matter, anyway," he muttered, "I'm going to die any moment now." He washed down another two Aspirins with the cold remains of a cup of tea and sighed.

He looked around his office, as if to be sure no one had heard him. There was not much to see. There was his desk, a little knocked about now after so many years, two vinyl-covered wooden chairs in front of it, a coat rack in one corner, a small window in the wall opposite him offering a less than inspiring view of a plain brick wall across an alley, a whiteboard on the left-hand wall, and that was it. All very institutional and utilitarian, devoid of character. He sometimes thought it was not much to show for his years of service, but, on the whole, he was happy with his career and content with where it had taken him from his first days as a beat constable in uniform in Glasgow to his present rank on the plainclothes side of the house here at Scotland Yard.

He debated the idea of simply saying he was ill and going home early, but that would be to admit Emily had been right, which she had been, of course. However, he imagined the *I told you so* expression with which she would greet him as he walked in the door and he steeled himself to stay the course. He told himself he could last out the day, provided nothing came along to make a mess of it.

Which, naturally, it did.

About ten minutes later, as he was making a desultory attempt at composing a report on the morning's GBH interview, the phone on his desk trilled its electronic summons.

"Oh God," he groaned under his breath, sniffing, as he reached for the receiver.

"Stuart."

"Fielding here, sir. We've a dead bloke in an alley near Canary Wharf."

"That's all I bloody need," Stuart croaked, his sore throat and blocked nasal passages making it sound like, *dat's all I bloody deed.*

"Are you all right, sir?" asked Detective Sergeant David Fielding, Stuart's right-hand man for the past three years.

"No, I'm not all right, but never mind that. Get the car, will you?"

With Fielding at the wheel, they drove towards what used to be the rather dilapidated dock and warehouse district in London's east end. A casualty of London's gradual post-war decline as a seaport, the area fell into disuse until its transformation into a major international financial center in the 1990s. Not for the first time, Stuart noticed Fielding's peculiar habit of addressing the drivers of other vehicles around him on the road, telling them under his breath to get going, stay where they were, or, more usually, to get out of his way.

The relentless rain hammered on the roof of the car, and Stuart gloomily realized that if the temperature dropped a couple of degrees, it would all turn to freezing slush and snow. Other cars, slowed by the deluge crawled along the streets, making progress grindingly tedious. Stuart sat next to Fielding, his raincoat pulled around him and his hat well down on his head, feeling worse by the minute. He finally admitted to himself his condition was not a simple chill after all, but a full-on case of galloping influenza.

Emily's going to give me hell when I get home.

"You should have stayed at home this morning, sir," said Fielding, edging the car towards a right-hand turn.

"Don't you start," Stuart coughed, then sneezed explosively. "I'll take it easy over the weekend. I'll be fine by Monday."

"Don't count on it," said Fielding. "There's some nasty stuff going about this winter. My sister's been off work for the last ten days."

"Thanks very much for that welcome bit of encouragement," said Stuart, sniffing. "How far is this place, anyway?"

"We'd have been there ten minutes ago if it weren't for the traffic and this damn rain. It's been like this all day. I often think the only difference between this weather and Noah's flood is that today we have better drains."

"I don't suppose you brought an umbrella, did you?" asked Stuart, fearing the worst.

"Afraid not, sir."

"Wonderful."

After another ten minutes of stop-and-go driving and concurrent running commentary, Fielding guided the car into a side street surrounded by towering office buildings and pulled up by the entrance to a narrow alley between two shiny blocks of flats. As Fielding parked behind an ambulance and another squad car, Stuart collected his mental resources for the task ahead. He had investigated innumerable murders in his time, and seen innumerable dead bodies, but not usually when he was feeling near death himself. Yellow crime scene tape was festooned everywhere, and they ducked under it after showing their identification to an unhappy-looking uniformed constable wearing a plastic rain cape. Stuart found himself at the entrance to an alley barely wide enough to allow them to walk abreast. About twenty paces from the road they came upon a knot of people gathered under a tent-like rain shelter. The group parted for them, and Stuart studied the scene before him. The body of a young man in his mid-to-late twenties lay curled as if asleep on the granite paving squares where it had been pushed behind a couple of metal rubbish bins. The clothing was saturated, and through the open raincoat and jacket, he saw a copious bloodstain on his white shirt.

"Who is it?" he asked.

"Don't know yet, sir," said one of the paramedics. "Dr. Crane's still busy with him."

"Shot?" asked Fielding.

A woman of about forty looked up from where she knelt by the corpse.

"Yes. Very close range, I'd say, and small caliber."

Dr. Alison Crane got to her feet and removed her latex gloves.

"How long's he been dead?" asked Stuart.

"I'll know better once I get him on the slab," she said, "but off-hand I'd say he's been here at least a couple of days."

"So probably dumped on Tuesday or Wednesday night," said Stuart.

"Quite likely, yes."

"Look there, sir," said Fielding, pointing. "His left shoe is half off his foot. That could mean he was dragged down here after getting himself shot somewhere else."

"Could well be," said Stuart, nodding. "Anyway, get Uniform to canvas the area. See if anyone heard or saw anything the last couple of nights. Oh, and interview whoever it was that found him. Forensics should be here any minute, so we can clear off. Are you finished, Dr. Crane?"

"Pretty much," she answered, taking up her bag. "I should be able to tell you more after I do the PM. And, by the way, Superintendent, you sound awful. You should be at home, not prancing about back alleys in this sort of weather. Next thing is I'll be doing a PM on you if you're not careful."

"I know, I know," said Stuart, sounding as miserable as he looked and trying not to remind himself how much of an idiot he was. The damp cold had seeped into every bone and joint in his body, and his sinuses ached abominably.

Leaving the group, Stuart and Fielding returned to their car, both more than happy to be out of the rain which showed no signs of abating. As Fielding edged the car back onto the main road, Stuart glanced over at him hearing him mutter something to the driver of a white Toyota. Fielding

100

was thirty-two, a full six feet three inches tall, with well-cared-for fair hair, hazel eyes, and a strong, square jaw. His promotion to detective inspector would come soon, and Stuart would be happy to see it. Fielding was an asset to the Force, and the sooner he rose in rank, the better.

* * *

Stuart spent the weekend in bed, and was then ordered by his physician, a rotund and disgustingly cheerful little man in a tweed suit, to spend the following week there as well. He opened his mouth to protest, but on catching sight of the expression on Emily's face he thought better of it immediately. The sentence had been handed down and it was clear any appeal would be denied. Thus, it was nine days before he returned to Scotland Yard, but thanks to the rest, a solid course of antibiotics, and Emily's tender, loving, and rigidly strict ministrations, he felt a great deal better. Walking to the Tube station that Monday morning, therefore, he decided with relief he was not going to die after all. Sitting down behind his desk, he booted up his computer, and stared at the list of accumulated unread emails. He derived a perverse sense of satisfaction from seeing how many departmental and other meetings he had missed, but after prioritizing the emails into his customary three action categories. *Now*, *Later*, and *Never*, he set about getting up to speed on his caseload.

What about the bloke in the alley? he asked himself, scrolling down to find the folder.

There was a preliminary report from Fielding revealing the victim's identity as a certain Terence Preston, aged twenty-five, London address, and a graduate student at Oxford in archeology and sinology. Fielding had begun the process of interviewing Preston's known friends and acquaintances, but thus far had found nothing whatever to explain why anyone would want to kill him. Stuart called Fielding in.

Fielding settled himself onto one of the vinyl chairs before Stuarts desk saying, "You look a lot better, Guv."

"What's happening with this Preston chap?" he asked, ignoring the sergeant's solicitudes.

"Interesting thing about him," said Fielding. "He turns out to have been the nephew of Detective Inspector William Foy, now retired."

"Bill Foy?" asked Stuart, in some surprise. "Good God."

"Yes," said Fielding. "I've had him on the phone several times last week trying to find out what we're doing and how we're doing it."

"I'll just bet you have," Stuart grunted, with evident feeling. "He always did have the idea that most of us didn't know what we were doing or how to do it. Wasn't afraid to say so, either. Used to get him into trouble sometimes."

The mere mention of Foy's name called up bad memories for Stuart. He disliked the man, and he could foresee potential trouble. Why the hell did Terence Preston have to be his nephew?

What a lousy coincidence.

"So, I've heard," said Fielding, grinning, "but he's very polite when he talks to me."

"Glad to hear it," said Stuart. "We don't want him breathing down our necks the whole time." He paused a moment, then resumed. "Anyway, what about Preston? Where are we now?"

"Dead end at the moment," said Fielding. "Excuse the pun. I'm still doing the rounds of people who knew him, but there's nothing about him, his life, or his background, to suggest he might wind up dead in an east end alley."

"Robbery?"

"No, indeed. He had his wallet on him with fifty-three quid in it. He had his watch on as well, and a small gold signet ring. All untouched. Whoever topped him wasn't after money."

"Post-mortem results?"

"Nothing much more than we heard at the time. Shot at close range with a nine-millimeter handgun. Dr. Crane

102

retrieved the bullet and judging from the location of the wound and angle of entry, Preston wasn't facing his killer. Most likely standing, or perhaps sitting, on his or her right. Ballistics couldn't find a match to anything on file but did say the gun almost certainly had a silencer on it."

"A silencer?" echoed Stuart, his eyebrows arched. "Well, that tells us something about the killer, doesn't it? Perhaps it was a professional hit."

"Possibly, sir," said Fielding, looking dubious, "but what on earth for? I mean, why would a pro have anything to do with a young Oxford egghead?"

"We don't know yet, do we, but stranger things have happened. It's worth following up."

"I doubt a professional would use a nine-mill peashooter, sir, nor go with a single shot."

"Well, check the data banks anyway. See if there's anything there." Stuart sighed before adding, "You know the drill, Fielding. *No stone unturned*, and all that sort of thing."

"Will do, Guv," said Fielding, making a note.

"Time of death?"

"Some time on Wednesday evening."

"Forensics?"

"He'd been killed, then dumped where he was found on Friday afternoon just as we originally speculated."

"How'd they know that?"

"Well, there was the shoe I noticed, but also a tear in one of Preston's trouser legs as well as a stain matching oil on the pavement in the alley. The main point, though, was that there was no blood residue. He'd done his bleeding elsewhere. They reckon he was dragged in from the street."

"Brought there by car."

"Presumably, yes."

"Anything to suggest where he was actually killed?" asked Stuart, thinking the leads here were thin, at best.

"Nothing, I'm afraid."

Stuart thought that was hardly surprising, and asked, "Did Uniform come up with anything? Strange noises? Cars stopped at odd hours? That sort of thing?"

103

Fielding shook his head, saying, "No one heard or saw anything on the Wednesday night, and there's no surveillance camera coverage in that particular area, which, I suppose, may be why the killer chose it."

"If that's true," mused Stuart, "it makes it sound all the more like a professional effort."

"Yes, it does," said Fielding, "but, to reiterate, there's nothing to connect Preston with anything that might warrant his being killed at all, let alone in a professional, targeted hit."

"Terrific," snorted Stuart. "And who found him?"

"Two blokes who came to empty the rubbish bins. I talked to both of them." Here, Fielding shrugged expressively before saying, "Routine. They came, they saw, they called nine-nine-nine. They did have the sense not to touch anything."

"So, we're nowhere," said Stuart, after a short pause.

"Pretty well nowhere, yes."

And Bill Foy circling around out there like a vulture, Stuart reflected sourly, before another thought struck him, and he asked if the victim had a mobile phone.

"There was no phone on him," said Fielding. "Forgot to mention that, but I'm—"

"Did you check that out?" Stuart interrupted.

It was a stupid question, but Stuart was totally oblivious. Fielding, expressionless, simply said, "Yes, and he did use one. I'm—"

"But no sign of it?"

Another daft question, but once again Fielding did not react. "I'm getting the phone records," he said.

"Good," said Stuart, "but it's odd, don't you think? The killer leaves Preston's wallet and his watch but pinches his mobile...if he had it on him, that is."

"Well," said Fielding, "it wasn't in his flat."

"Then we have to assume he had it with him, and it was taken," said Stuart, grasping the obvious. "What does that tell us?"

Fielding paused, perhaps waiting for Stuart to answer his own question, then said, "I'd suggest there was something about the phone, and the killer knew what it was."

"Right," said Stuart. "But what was it, I wonder? Did anything turn up when you searched his flat?"

"Nothing at all. Just mountains of papers, articles, notes, books, and that sort of thing. All stuff on Chinese history and archeology, just as you might expect, and a good deal of it actually in Chinese, to boot. There's a small team still going through it, so perhaps something might show up. I rather doubt it, though."

"Let's hope something does," Stuart said, "but the place was clean otherwise, was it?"

It seemed to be Stuart's morning for repetitious questions, but by this time he was suffering from a depressing feeling that the case had got away from him and there was no way to retrieve it. Without leads to follow, he was like the proverbial drowning man thrashing about in search of a straw, and he hated that feeling. Not only might there not be an arrest, but also, he felt that he had no control over the situation, and that was the worst of all.

"Clean as a whistle," answered Fielding.

"Not even a wee bit of the wacky backy?" There was a note of desperation in his voice.

Fielding shook his head.

"So, we've an unblemished, unremarkable, perfectly ordinary young student who gets himself shot and dumped in an alleyway. He's not robbed, but perhaps the killer swipes his mobile phone for a souvenir, or something."

"We might be able to find out who he last spoke to when we get the records," said Fielding.

"Okay, let me know."

"Will do."

Another thought struck Stuart, and he asked, "What about his parents, other family members?"

"Both parents are dead, no brothers or sisters."

"Of course." Stuart grunted. "Why aren't I surprised?" He sat silent for a moment, ruminating. The landscape looked very bleak to him. "Well," he said, "just tell me there's one, tiny thing we have to go on here, can you do that much, Sergeant?"

"Well, actually, I think I can, sir," said Fielding. "The techies had a go at Preston's computer. There's a load of stuff on it related to his work at Oxford with a Professor Sir Donald Willard. I talked to his office, but he's away at some conference or other in Chicago. Left two weeks ago and won't be back for another five days because he's going on to Harvard. I'll talk to him when he's back because Preston sent him a message the night he died. It—"

"What did it say?" Stuart's impatience showed clearly in his tone.

"It didn't say anything," said Fielding. "There was no message, not even a subject. There was an attachment, but it hadn't downloaded to the computer for some reason. Hopefully, Willard can retrieve it."

"I hope so," said Stuart, not wanting to contemplate losing hold of a possible straw. "Anything else?"

"Could be," said Fielding, checking his notes. "There's quite a string of messages with someone named Mike Barrow setting up a dinner at Barrow's flat on the night Preston was killed. I've spent the last two days combing through it all. I found the Barrow messages late last night."

Relief swept over Stuart like a tsunami.

"Well," he said, getting to his feet, "thank God there's something we can actually do. Let's have a word with this Mr. Barrow, shall we? Where's he live?"

"Knightsbridge."

Chapter Nine

Michael Barrow ushered the two detectives into the spacious sitting room of his flat and invited them to sit.

"I assume this is about my car," he said, settling himself on the sofa opposite them.

"Your car, sir?" asked Fielding.

"Well...yes, my car," said Barrow, a bewildered expression on his face. "Don't you know it was stolen?"

"We...er..." Stuart fumbled for words, feeling a complete fool.

"I'd been abroad, you see," Barrow went on, "and I reported the car missing as soon as I got home last Thursday. They called me yesterday afternoon with the news they'd found it in a field near Peterborough, burnt to a crisp."

"I'm sorry, sir," said Stuart, nonplussed to say the least. "Robbery isn't actually my department, but I'm sure the theft is being competently investigated."

"Then what's going on?" asked Barrow, still looking confused. "Don't you people read your emails anymore?"

I'll murder Fielding, Stuart fumed. Why the hell hadn't he run Barrow's name through the current case files and got this background, instead of making us look like clowns on their day off from the circus?

"We're here on another matter entirely, sir," Fielding put in, no doubt seeing Stuart's face red with embarrassment and fury.

"What other matter?" asked Barrow. "I was hoping you'd come to tell me you'd arrested whoever stole the car. My insurance company isn't being overly cooperative, you know."

"I'm sure the theft is being competently investigated, sir," Stuart repeated, and it sounded just as lame to him as it had the first time. "I trust there'll be a result very soon. But, in fact, we're here about your friend, Mr. Terence Preston."

"Terry?" asked Barrow, eyebrows raised. "What about him? Has something happened?"

Fielding cleared his throat in preparation for taking over the conversation. He knew Stuart found it difficult to frame the words to break this sort of bad news, and tended either to sound too emotional, or, more usually, simply uncaring. He seemed never to be able to find an appropriate approach to what was, after all, a difficult situation.

"We're very sorry to have to tell you Mr. Preston was found shot to death twelve days ago."

"*What*?" Barrow stared at Fielding, looking stunned. "You're saying Terry was *murdered*?"

"We're treating it as a homicide, yes, sir," said Fielding, "and we're here because we've reason to believe you might well be the last person to have seen Mr. Preston alive."

"Me?" Barrow sat up straight on the sofa, wide-eyed.

"Yes, sir," said Stuart, now on firmer ground. "Was Mr. Preston not here for dinner with you on the evening of the eighteenth of this month? A week ago, Wednesday?"

"Yes, he was," said Barrow, nodding. "But...look...I'm having a lot of trouble with this. Are you sure it was Terry? He was one of my best friends."

"There's no mistake, sir," said Fielding. "I'm sorry."

"What time did he leave here that night?" asked Stuart.

"Oh...about seven, I think," said Barrow. "It was a lousy night, so I said I'd drive him home, but he wouldn't hear of it. Said he'd get a bus. There's a stop just around the corner from here, and he often goes...or went...home that way. I just saw him out of the flat, and that was it."

"Do you know of anyone Mr. Preston was having any sort of disagreement or dispute with?" asked Fielding, taking notes. "Did he ever mention any sort of problems like that?"

"Not to me," answered Barrow. "He was a very easy-going chap, and a bit of a loner, I'd have to say. Didn't have a lot of friends, kept himself busy with work on his doctorate at Oxford. I'd almost say he was obsessed with it, in fact."

"I don't suppose you own a gun, sir, do you?" Stuart asked, and Barrow's head jerked up.

"No, Superintendent, I bloody well don't. I don't know the first thing about guns."

"Then I think that's all for now, sir," said Stuart, rising. Pausing at the door, however, he asked, "When, exactly, did you go abroad, sir?"

"A week last Thursday morning. The day after Terry was here."

"The nineteenth?"

"Yes."

"Thank you, Mr. Barrow," said Stuart. "If there's anything further we need, we'll be in touch."

"Please don't hesitate," said Barrow. "Poor old Terry. He'd never have hurt a living soul. I hope you get the bastard who killed him."

* * *

Upon hearing Professor Willard had returned to Oxford, Fielding telephoned him, but the professor, although appalled at Preston's death, could offer no assistance.

"I've not heard from him for some time," he said, "but Terry was due back to continue his research on certain events which took place during the Bronze Age in China. In fact, I was beginning to wonder why he hadn't yet come to see me. He knew when I was returning from America."

"I see," said Fielding, who knew slightly less about the Chinese Bronze Age than he did about nuclear fission and sub-particle physics, "but we saw a good deal of

109

correspondence between yourself and Preston in Preston's email."

"Oh, indeed," said Willard, "we were in touch often, but I've been away, as I say."

"Yes, sir."

"And, come to think about it, I hadn't received anything from him recently."

"But Professor Willard," Fielding put in, "the phone records show Preston sent you a message on the eighteenth of this month, the night he died. It also showed up on his home computer. There was an attachment with it."

"My goodness," said Willard, "I'm sure I don't remember anything like that. Just a moment, please."

Fielding heard Willard keyboarding, and muttering, "Preston…Preston…" before saying, "No, I'm afraid not. I always save all the emails I receive from my students. There's nothing from Terry Preston on the night you specify."

Damn and blast, Fielding thought. We're screwed because of an email glitch.

"You're quite certain, sir?"

"Absolutely. I assure you I keep most meticulous records."

Dead end again, at least for now, Fielding told himself.

"Well, thank you, sir," he said. "If we require anything further, we'll be in touch. Thanks again."

* * *

Three days after Fielding's call to Professor Willard, the twins, Richard and Graham, travelled to Norfolk on separate trains. Then, soberly dressed in suits and ties, and declaring themselves to be disciples of the Christian Congregation of the Resurrected Lord, they called at the sprawling country house owned by the Robertson-Hyde family.

Ignoring the sign at the front door addressing the kinds of people who should use the back one, they rang the doorbell, and waited. Somewhere in the depths of the old house they heard a faint, sonorous chime. It was a raw day, and they stood with their hands in their overcoat pockets, their shoulders hunched against the wind, until a tall woman of about fifty, presumably Mrs. Robertson-Hyde, opened the heavy wooden door. She was a little on the corpulent side with iron-gray hair and wore a plain white skirt with a red woolen sweater.

"Are you selling something?" she demanded peremptorily, her expression hostile and her tone supercilious.

"We are selling nothing, madam," answered Graham, with a warm smile. "What we have to offer is available free of any charge, yet it is precious beyond any price. We offer the kingdom of hea—"

"Go away," said the woman, in a manner suggesting she was not used to being disobeyed. "I'm not in the least bit interested."

She started to close the door, but Richard spoke up, his voice full of self-deprecation.

"Madam, we won't trouble you further, if that's how you truly feel, but would you be kind enough to allow us to make use of your bathroom, please? We've been out all morning, you see. We'd be ever so grateful."

The woman hesitated. Richard and Graham did their best to look cold and in desperate need. The woman glared at them before sighing loudly.

"Oh, all right then, come in. There's a bathroom just through here."

She preceded them across the large, tiled foyer where a wide staircase curved upwards in a great sweep of polished oak and thick, red carpet, before leading the way down a short corridor whose walls were decorated with framed prints of eighteenth-century foxhunting scenes.

"First on the left. Please don't be long. And just so you're aware, my husband is upstairs."

111

The two men went into the bathroom in turn, came back to the foyer, thanked the woman who did not acknowledge their existence any further, and left the house.

"What a charming old boot she was," muttered Richard, as the door closed behind them with a dismissive thump. "She probably wishes slavery was still legal."

Walking back to where they had hidden their hired car behind a high yew hedge at the edge of a field, they compared notes.

"Simple front door," said Richard, with satisfaction, as he pulled off the dark wig he had been wearing. "Lock's a breeze. Five minutes work at the most. Windows are even easier if we want to try one of them instead."

"The alarm system's as old as the hills," added Graham, wincing a little as he tore off his false moustache. "No surveillance cameras. Candy from a baby, this one. People like them never learn, thank Christ. They're too busy counting their money to know anything about the rest of the world. They look down their noses at it, but they don't see it."

"Yes. We can tell Sylvia this one's pure routine," said Richard, grinning, while he stuffed his disguise into a plastic bag.

"God, it's freezing," said Graham, as he moved the car out onto the narrow lane and accelerated away. "Let's find a pub."

Richard sent a coded text message to Sylvia that evening and she cleared the operation to proceed. Forty-eight hours later, therefore, Mr. and Mrs. Robertson-Hyde were found in their bedroom by their astonished housekeeper, bound, gagged, terrified, but otherwise unharmed, with nothing whatever disturbed in the house apart from the removal of a small, bronze statue from its stand in Mr. Robertson-Hyde's oak-paneled study. Investigations by the Norfolk constabulary revealed not a single fingerprint or fragment of evidence, and Mrs. Robertson-Hyde made no mention of the two itinerant evangelists who had needed to use the bathroom, because she had forgotten them entirely.

112

The twins, using new identities as employees of a non-existent firm of auctioneers in Chichester and with false license plates on their vehicles handed the crated statue over to Mike Barrow, the ostensible purchaser, complete with papers and receipt in case anyone ever asked. The transfer took place at a pre-arranged drop-off in the rear parking lot of a warehouse just outside the city of Norwich owned by a man well paid to look the other way. The exchange was made in broad daylight on the theory that skulking about doing it in the dark could easily look suspicious.

"No need to tempt fate," said Richard.

Two days after the *acquisition*, as such thefts were called by the syndicate, Barrow stood on a narrow metal catwalk above the bilges of a Polish container ship at anchor off Felixstowe, the largest container port in the United Kingdom, on the North Sea coast of Suffolk. The stale air reeked of bilge water and rusty steel, and, situated as it was below the waterline, the space was clammy and cold. On the bulkhead to his right was a maze of pipes and conduit carrying the fluids and electrical cables which gave life to the ship, and as he looked at it in the harsh yellow glare of the overhead lights, Barrow wondered how the hell anyone could keep track of it all. The cold steel around him hummed and reverberated with the distant throb of the ship's diesel generators, and the sound increased the claustrophobia that was beginning to oppress him. He wanted to get out. The steel walls encased him like a coffin, and the vibrating air itself seemed to press in on him, making it difficult to breathe.

With an effort, he forced his attention back to the thing which had brought him there in the first place, and he stood with his hands in his pockets watching three sailors unscrew a panel on the front of a large metal cabinet into which many of the conduits disappeared. As the panel was removed, Barrow saw the interior of the cabinet was filled with smaller junction boxes and intertwined electrical cable.

"There's room at the bottom," said the officer in heavily accented English.

"Okay," said Barrow, nodding. "Just tell them to make sure it isn't able to bang around in there with the motion of the ship. It's bronze, but it's not indestructible. It has to be delivered to its new owner in Shanghai in good condition."

The officer spoke to the men in rapid Polish as they placed the sculpture, tightly wrapped and padded, into its hiding place. Barrow was glad to see it go. He had driven to Felixstowe with the sculpture in the back seat of his car, nervous every inch of the way that he would be stopped for some bizarre reason and his car searched. The rational portion of his mind told him there was no cause whatever for such a thing to happen, but that did nothing to lessen his apprehension. He had never driven so carefully in all his life.

"The inspectors don't usually come down here," the officer said, as the panel was being replaced, "and even if they do, they don't start taking things apart, especially electrical boxes with big red warnings signs on them. But when we get to Shanghai, you better be there to take this thing off our hands. If you're not, it goes over the side. We take no unnecessary risks."

"I'll be there," said Barrow, "but if something comes up and I can't meet you myself, someone else will take care of it, don't worry. Now can we get out of here, please? I feel as if I'm being buried alive."

Laughing, the officer led the way back along the catwalk, their shoes clanging and echoing on the steel floor, to a metal ladder which took them into the hold, and then to a lift which whisked them all up into that part of the ship used as living quarters. Barrow paid the officer ten thousand American dollars, promising the remaining ten thousand upon delivery in Shanghai, and was then conveyed back to Felixstowe by the same launch that brought him. Sitting in the stern sheets of the small motorboat feeling the wind in his hair and inhaling the salty smells of the sea, Barrow had never been so happy to be out in the fresh air.

Over the ensuing weeks, Stuart and Fielding followed up what few lines of inquiry they had. They spoke to Preston's Oxford landlady, interviewed his fellow graduate students, but all to no avail. There also seemed no connection between Preston's death and Michael Barrow's burned-out car, although the squad investigating the theft never actually identified a suspect, let alone made an arrest. Stuart ordered the re-canvas of the neighborhood, but the results were the same. No one saw or heard anything on the night of the eighteenth of February, apart from a very elderly gentleman who, on being questioned a second time, thought, he perhaps remembered hearing a car door slam late that night, or the night before...or perhaps the one after, although that was when his sister, Iris, was visiting from Bournemouth...but, no, she left on February the nineteenth, or was it the thirteenth? The gentleman admitted to being rather deaf, and his hearing aid was being repaired at the time...he thought, anyway.

"Oh, God," muttered Stuart, as he read the interview report, feeling the case going colder by the minute.

As time passed, the death of Terence Preston receded in importance as other cases took precedence. The investigation was not actually closed — murder investigations never were — but less and less attention was paid to it until it came eventually to reside on a list of unsolved murders that most people at Scotland Yard tried not to think about.

One day in October, Stuart received the latest in a series of telephone calls from Bill Foy.

"What the hell's going on, Harry?" Foy demanded. "It's been eight months."

"What can I tell you, Bill? The well's dry. You know what that's like. I wish there was something else we could do, but just now, there isn't."

"You could kick a few backsides for one thing," said Foy, his voice harsh. "Get them moving."

"That kind of talk doesn't help, Bill," said Stuart, striving for patience. "I know you're upset. I would be as well, but—"

"Just get the finger out," Foy interrupted, and hung up.

As Stuart replaced the receiver, he had an uncomfortable feeling Bill Foy was going to cause him a lot of trouble before too much longer.

Part Three
China and Germany 1933 - 1935

Chapter Ten

Dr. Aaron Weiskopf, Professor of Archeology and Oriental Antiquities, looked at the fragment of carved jade the young Chinese boy had brought him. Weiskopf had spent eighteen seasons excavating in the region of the Yellow River valley, and he knew a piece of Shang sculpture when he saw it. This one, the head and left shoulder of a figurine, had been very skillfully wrought, evidence of its having been made for someone of wealth and importance, perhaps even a king.

It was mid-April, and Weiskopf had just arrived in Zhengzhou, capital city of Henan Province in east-central China, for his nineteenth summer of work. He was well known in the busy city. This lad had come to the guesthouse on the city's outskirts where Weiskopf and his team habitually stayed and loitered outside until the *foreign devil who digs things up* appeared on the verandah to drink his morning coffee and smoke his ornately carved Meerschaum pipe.

Weiskopf, fifty-six years of age, with dark hair showing almost no gray, brown eyes, and a round face, had excavated dozens of tombs and village sites over the years. He had shipped vast quantities of material home to his university in Leipzig, but his greatest ambition had so far remained unfulfilled. His dream was to find and excavate the tomb of Da Yi, first king of the Shang, and his plan for this year was to continue the search. Chinese and European archeologists had excavated many Shang cities and tombs since the early years of the twentieth century, but the final resting place of Da Yi had eluded them all.

Since its founding by the Republican government of China, the *Guomindang*, in 1928, archeologists from the *Academia Sinica* had been excavating a site at Yinxu, near the city of Anyang, which appeared to be the site of the largest known Shang city. This urban center, called Yin, had become the probable Shang capital long after Da Yi's death, and Weiskopf doubted his tomb would be found anywhere near there. There were older Shang sites near Zhengzhou, including an entire city, and he believed he had a better chance of finding the tomb here, if it still existed.

One of Europe's most celebrated sinologists, Weiskopf was able to read the divinatory inscriptions on Shang oracle bones fluently, as well as the characters on cast bronze vessels and other artifacts. He was also considered an authority on the ancient texts of the Zhou and Qin Dynasties which followed the Shang. His numerous publications had added greatly to the general academic understanding of Shang society and governance, while his excavations had contributed to an enlarged appreciation of the power and wealth of Shang kings. Folk traditions declared these monarchs to be buried with all manner of grave goods designed to serve them in the hereafter.

117

Horses, chariots, a fortune in cowry shell currency, ceramics, bronze weapons and ritual vessels of every size and description, gold jewelry, ivory, jade, tiger skins, and the bodies of hundreds, if not thousands, of slaves. Excavations of royal tombs had shown many of these wondrous tales to be exaggerations — perhaps attempts by classical historians to distinguish themselves through the revelation of such glittering details — but, archeologists reasoned, there must be a grain of truth in it all somewhere. Of the eleven Shang royal tombs excavated since the turn of the twentieth century, only one had been found intact, and the treasures it contained, although not as prodigious as tradition predicted, suggested Da Yi's resting place, if undisturbed by thieves and vandals, might well yield an artifact assemblage of unparalleled worth and importance.

Now, studying the broken piece of carved jade, Weiskopf wondered what it might mean. Clearly it was a Shang sculpture, the style and method of manufacture confirmed that fact, but beyond that, nothing could be learned from the fragment itself. Its quality alone did not guarantee it came from the tomb of a king, much less that of Da Yi. It could easily be from the grave of a high official, a royal wife or concubine, a military leader, a nobleman or woman, or even a wealthy merchant, yet there existed the tantalizing possibility it could be from the tomb of a king, and if a king, why not Da Yi himself? Speaking perfect Chinese, he asked the young lad how he had obtained the jade.

"I found it," he answered, with an enigmatic smile. "They say you are a foreign devil who digs up old things, so I brought it here for you to buy."

Well, thought Weiskopf, at least he's clear about that, and I'll bet he's no more than ten or eleven years old.

Feeling in his pocket, Weiskopf withdrew a Yuan *Shikai* dollar, and the youngster's eyes shone at the sight of it. This was real money.

Introduced in 1914 during the short-lived presidency of General Yuan Shikai following the overthrow of the Empress Dowager, the coin Weiskopf offered was prized for its guaranteed weight and silver content; much sought after in comparison to the numerous base metal trade dollars, cheap copper coins, and the dubious paper currency which could all be found everywhere alongside the old, square-holed bronze coinage of the Manchu Qing Dynasty. The Yuan silver dollar bore an unusually large representation of the president's head on its obverse and was thus often called a *Yuan Da Tou*.

"A Yuan Big Head," exclaimed the lad in delight.

"It is indeed," said Weiskopf, handing over the coin.

"Thank you, thank you, thank you."

"One *thank you* is quite enough, young man," said Weiskopf, laughing. "but now you listen to me carefully. That dollar is for you in payment for the jade, but I will give you five more if you show me where you found it."

* * *

The following morning Weiskopf breakfasted with his assistant for the last two seasons, Dr. Eduard Schilling, and showed him the jade. Schilling, an energetic man of forty-five with blue eyes and a full, iron-gray beard, studied the fragment intently, turning it over in his large hand several times before nodding.

"It's Shang all right. Might have come from anywhere, but it's worth an exploration at any rate."

"Yes, I agree." Weiskopf finished a steamed savory bun, and then, downing the last of his coffee, he stood up. "Let's go, shall we? How's the truck?"

Schilling snorted and shrugged.

"We need a new one, but the budget won't rise to it."

Outside in the pleasant morning sunshine they managed to instill some life, albeit tenuous, into the engine of their antiquated Ford truck, and drove, pursued by a cloud of exhaust smoke and noxious fumes, through the crowded streets of Zhengzhou and into the countryside. Weiskopf had obtained directions to the village where they were to meet their young guide, and they passed many isolated huts and smallholdings as they left the city behind.

"What a place," said Schilling, as they approached the four small, brick-built huts, thatch-roofed and windowless, which comprised the village. Erected adjacent to each dwelling was a pigsty and a fenced yard containing a few bedraggled chickens clucking and pecking at the ground. Around this hamlet, which their guide-to-be had told Weiskopf went by the more than incongruous name of Imperial Forest Village, stretched vegetable fields and rice paddies, their plentiful early growth attesting to the fertility of the soil here in this valley of the Yellow River.

"No sign of a forest or an emperor," said Weiskopf, as he parked the truck at the side of the dirt road.

As they walked towards the nearest hut, a woman, whose age they could not judge, emerged carrying a wicker basket, the contents of which she flung into the sty, causing a cacophonous squealing and grunting from the dirt-covered pigs. She was thin and boney; her black hair, lank and greasy, straggled down past her angular shoulders. She wore a stained cotton garment which might once have been a blouse, and baggy gray trousers. After staring, hollow-eyed, at the two foreigners for a few moments, she turned her head towards the hut and shrieked in a harsh and piercing voice, "Lai."

Immediately the youngster, wearing the same ragged blue t-shirt and brown shorts as the day before when Weiskopf met him, bounded out and ran to meet them.

"I was not sure you would come."

"I promised I would," said Weiskopf, with a smile. He found Lai an engaging young scamp, but the young scamp's next words betrayed the reason for his delight in seeing the two visitors.

"Did you bring my five dollars?" He held out his hand.

"You will get them *after* you show us where you found the jade," said Weiskopf, "and not before."

"If the jade is so important," Lai said, his eyes fathomless pools of innocence, "perhaps seven dollars are better than five?"

"No," said Weiskopf firmly.

The youngster's eyes narrowed in obvious suspicion, but he said nothing more.

They coaxed the truck back into life, and with Lai sitting between them, they set off again down the road.

"It is not far," said Lai, and then, looking intently at Schilling's beard, he observed, "You are very hairy. A lot of foreigners are hairy. My father has a beard, but it is very thin. Why do you have a beard?"

"My beard means I don't have to shave, and it keeps the flies away," said Schilling, in a solemn voice, and after digesting this explanation for a moment or two, Lai nodded.

"I thought it meant you were very old and wise, but that is not so. You are just lazy, and you don't like flies."

Weiskopf laughed, glancing sideways at Schilling, who seemed irked by the boy's impudence.

"Tell me," he said to Lai, swerving to avoid a deep pothole, and then swerving back again to avoid five white ducks parading in an orderly line across the road, "your crops look very promising, yet your village appears poor. Can you not sell what you grow?"

"What is there to sell?" answered Lai. "We give almost everything to the landlord for rent. There is not much left over, but we are used to being hungry. We do not notice it any longer. My father says it has been that way since he was a boy, and his father before him."

"No wonder he wants the money," said Schilling in German, and Weiskopf nodded.

"*Ja*, it's as I expected. It's the same all over China."

At Lai's direction, Weiskopf steered the Ford off the road to follow a narrow dirt track running between small fields, some lying fallow, others in grains or vegetables. The truck bounced and jolted its way along until they came to a broad expanse of open, uncultivated ground.

"Here," said Lai.

"Are you sure?" asked Schilling, "this looks like useless earth."

"Of course, I am sure," said Lai. "Can I have my money now?"

"No," said Weiskopf, "not until you show us the exact place."

They left the truck and followed the young lad to a patch of stony, uneven ground covered with clumps of dry grass and scrubby, low-growing bushes.

"No one owns this land," Lai said, as they picked their way across the rough terrain.

"I'm not surprised," muttered Schilling. "Who would want it, for God's sake?"

"I came here with my father to see if it could be planted," Lai want on, "but my father said it could not. He also said there was something underneath." And pointing in front of him, he said, "See?"

"See what?" asked Schilling.

"Like this," said Lai, crouching, and putting his head on one side.

"My God, Eduard," said Weiskopf, sighting across the ground as Lai had demonstrated. "Do you see it?"

"Yes," said Schilling. "There's a very slight depression."

"I'd have missed it if it hadn't been pointed out," said Weiskopf.

Lai said, "My father told me that sometimes people have found old things here, so I came by myself one day and tried to dig. There is the hole where I found the jade. It was very easy."

After drawing a rough sketch outline of the area and the depression which Weiskopf paced out at about ten by six meters, they paid Lai his five Big Heads and drove him home.

"We'll do a test pit first," said Weiskopf, as they reached the main road and turned for Zhengzhou. "If there have been artifacts found there in the past, the site may well have been looted, but it's certainly worth investigating."

"It may not be a tomb at all," Schilling pointed out.

"Of course," said Weiskopf, negotiating a narrow space around a plodding bullock cart laden with what

122

looked like turnips driven by an old man sitting round-backed and oblivious to the world around him, "but there's only one way to find out. Tomorrow, you go to the local authorities and make sure Lai's father was right about the land's not being owned. It will cost a few dollars to bribe someone to look through the records, but just pay it and get written proof with a seal. We have to be absolutely sure about it, because if it is someone's property and we start an excavation the fines and bribes will be astronomical. Let alone that we might end up in jail hoping the university will pay to get us out."

Schilling snorted. "Bergdorf would probably pay to keep us in if we caused that much trouble."

Weiskopf grinned and went on, "Beijing decreed all deeds of land ownership were to be updated and corrected several years ago, so the information should be available. The whole exercise was basically for the benefit of the landlords, of course. Thousands of them simply bribed local officials to enlarge their holdings in the government records. The result was that millions of peasant families who knew nothing about the new laws suddenly found themselves living on someone else's land and owing rent after perhaps centuries of farming it for themselves."

"Outrageous," grunted Schilling.

"Yes," answered Weiskopf. "I often wonder, you know, if the Chinese people are really better off with their shiny new republic."

"Not so shiny, I think," said Schilling. "Pretty tarnished, actually. Such corruption would never be tolerated in Germany."

* * *

As it transpired, it cost forty silver dollars to persuade a minor bureaucrat in the land registry office in Zhengzhou to confirm the land was not private property, although it took him three days to rummage his way through the welter of files and papers filling his office to overflowing. Weiskopf used the time to assemble a crew of laborers and arrange for an old army truck to convey them — at prodigal expense — to the excavation site.

"Everything costs a fortune," Schilling grumbled, as he and Weiskopf, both in brown overalls and broad hats, led the way out of the city in the smoking Ford.

"Everyone has to get what he can, when he can," said Weiskopf, with a shrug, "because the future is highly uncertain. The *Guomindang* has only a tenuous hold on government, the Japanese have had a strong and well-equipped army in Manchuria for the last eighteen months, so God only knows what they intend to do. North China could muster very little resistance to a Japanese invasion because the region is still recovering from what they call the time of the warlords, Wu Peifu and all his cronies, which devastated much of the countryside.

"Many people do expect an invasion," Schilling said, and Weiskopf nodded, slowing the truck behind a group of men pushing flat-decked wooden handcarts and engaging loudly in animated conversation. Weiskopf pressed the horn repeatedly to move them aside.

"The Sino-Japanese War ended in eighteen-ninety-five," he went on, changing gears as the truck picked up speed again, "but China and Japan are still mortal enemies. And on top of it all, there's the communists down in the southeast."

"That rabble won't amount to anything," snorted Schilling. "They'll be like all communists everywhere. Thugs, that's all they are. Leaderless thugs, intent on troublemaking and destruction all in the name of what they call working people. They know nothing else. They're poison, that's what the Reds are."

Weiskopf had heard these outbursts before.

"Don't be too sure," he said, as the Ford crashed into, and then out of, a large pothole. "I hear there's increasing support for a couple of them who seem to be very shrewd. The foremost is a certain Mao Zedong. Calls himself a peasant, but his father was actually a small-time landowner and sort of gentleman-farmer. This Mao fellow has the support of an influential young intellectual by the name of Zhou Enlai. He's an historian, I understand, and studied in Paris, no less. He and Mao met when they worked together as teachers in Canton in the mid-twenties."

Schilling stared stone-faced at the road ahead as Weiskopf came to his point. "So…in the face of all that, what would you do if you were an ordinary citizen trying to stay alive and keep your family fed, hmm?"

"All right," said Schilling, a little morosely, "I see what you mean in the case of ordinary people but having to bribe government employees really galls me. After all, damn it, they're getting paid for what they do, aren't they?"

"Yes, they are," said Weiskopf, "but they're paid precious little. And when it comes to officials, there's a separate issue. The problem is that for the last two thousand years, men who held positions in the civil service were barely paid anything at all and were expected to make their actual living through what we would term corrupt practices." He grinned, adding, "So by asking for a little something extra, the officials today are simply honoring an age-old tradition and keeping it alive."

"Well," said Schilling, "that's as may be, but that sort of corruption should have been eradicated years ago when the old imperial system was turfed out."

Weiskopf, concentrating on his driving for the moment as the truck threaded its way through a huge flock of clamorous white ducks being chivvied across the road in a flurry of feathers by three bare-footed young girls, said nothing, and Schilling clenched his fist before declaring, "China has no strong leader, that's her real trouble, Aaron. She needs a man like Adolph Hitler who can get rid of the Reds, the racketeers, the profiteers, and the left-wing agitators. You know what I mean. The lawless elements and those who want to drag us all down to their own dead level."

Weiskopf felt as if he were in a beer hall in Munich or reading a Hitler speech in a pro-Nazi newspaper. It was not a pleasant sensation.

"China needs a leader who can damn well get things *done!*" Schilling finished.

"Such as getting the trains to run on time?" asked Weiskopf, with a sideways glance at Schilling.

"Well, they sure as hell don't run on time here now," Schilling snapped, in a tone suggesting there was nothing more to be said.

Weiskopf had long suspected Schilling's National Socialist proclivities. He noted Schilling had made no mention of Hitler's virulent anti-Semitism, but like many others, Weiskopf suspected Hitler would soon go too far for the moderates in Germany. Once that happened, they would throw him out; send him back into obscurity where he and other such lunatics belonged, and men like Schilling would then have to hitch their wagons to a more practical, less opportunistic and demagogic, star. Germany needed more substance and less sound than the Nazis were offering, although he could not deny their current popularity.

Weiskopf drew the truck to a stop at the side of the dirt track, glad of the chance to end that particular conversation.

"And here we are," he announced.

It was mid-morning by now and the sun was getting hot as it mounted towards its zenith. Tools and equipment were unloaded by the laborers, and then all eyes turned to Weiskopf. They watched him as he walked this way and that around the site carefully studying the terrain, all the while rubbing his chin as was his habit when deep in thought.

"All right, Eduard," he said at last, "I think our best chance is to situate the test pit where artifacts have been most recently recovered. I see nothing here to suggest any other course of action. There is no evidence of buildings, walls or foundations to be seen, so if there is anything here it's not showing itself on the surface, that's certain."

Schilling agreed, and four stakes were driven into the ground under Weiskopf's close supervision. Thin white cord was then strung between them to delineate an area of ground three meters square around the place Lai claimed to have found the carved jade. The workmen were shown how

126

to clear the ground of weeds and tufts of grass while disturbing the soil as little as possible, and then Schilling and two others who had worked with Weiskopf in previous seasons, began the systematic excavation.

It was painstaking work. Some of the laborers shook their heads, wondering why they were not allowed to use picks and spades to get the job done more quickly.

"These foreign devils with their round eyes and big noses will get nowhere like this," averred one of them, forgetting that both Weiskopf and Schilling spoke Chinese.

Small flat trowels of the sort used by bricklayers were the only digging tools used, and if anything appeared, the soil was brushed away from it with a small paintbrush while Weiskopf took photographs and kept meticulous notes on its location and depth in the slowly deepening pit. Nothing conclusive appeared, however. Objects which could have been artifacts turned out to be pieces of ordinary wood, naturally chipped stone, or broken bits of recent pottery. Short-lived excitement was caused by Schilling's discovery of a rust-encrusted arrowhead which might have been Shang in origin had it not proved to be made of steel. Its presence was interesting, but nothing more.

Several of the workmen laughed, asking why so much care was being taken over such odd things, but they dutifully carried away the buckets of soil the excavators filled, wondering, no doubt, if anything truly valuable would ever be uncovered.

"Even if it is," Weiskopf heard one of them say, "at the speed they dig we shall not live to see it."

Weiskopf and Schilling, absorbed in their work, spared no time to explain. Patience was paramount, but they had both dug too many unproductive pits to let their imaginations run away with them.

It had been necessary to promise the laborers lunch as well as money, so Weiskopf engaged the services of the cook he had employed on many previous occasions. This ancient and wrinkled little man, seventy-five if he was a day, and completely without teeth, set up a makeshift kitchen under a tarpaulin rigged between two stunted trees.

Chattering with irrepressible cheerfulness, regardless of whether anyone was listening, he produced an excellent meal of rice, chicken, and vegetables using nothing but an oil stove and a large wok. Schilling and his two assistants rested briefly, smoked a cigarette or two, and then returned to the pit, by then barely twenty centimeters deep. Hardly had they begun, however, when Schilling let out a whoop of excitement.

"What is it?" shouted Weiskopf, hurrying to where Schilling knelt in one corner of the excavation.

"Bricks," answered Schilling, wielding his brush to reveal two sunbaked bricks laid side by side. They were old, and obviously not there by natural occurrence.

"Are they a floor?" asked Weiskopf, thinking this may be nothing more than the remains of an ancient dwelling or temple, but Schilling shook his head.

"No, they are not level. They slope to the left, going deeper. And they extend beyond the pit wall as well. Right under where you're standing, as a matter of fact, but I can't yet tell how far they go."

"All right," said Weiskopf, trying to appear calm, but not wholly succeeding. Was it a ramp? he wondered. Bronze age tombs belonging to important people often exhibited entrance ramps. "We'll follow where they lead and see where we end up."

By sunset they had exposed half a meter of brick pathway nearly four meters wide and were following it half a meter deeper into the ground.

"It's an entrance ramp all right," said Schilling, and Weiskopf agreed.

"Yes, it certainly looks like it. It's a tomb in all probability, but whose is it and has it been disturbed?"

Weiskopf felt the familiar surge of excitement he always experienced when excavating a new site, but as he stood looking at the rows of carefully laid bricks exposed to view for the first time in millennia, he became conscious of something else as well. He did not know whether to call it a premonition or a mere feeling, but he was somehow sure this find would be of greater significance than any of his others. Pushing these thoughts aside with some difficulty, he concentrated on what was before him.

Assuming it is a tomb, there is no evidence so far to suggest it is a royal one. But no matter who might be buried here, if tomb robbers have been here already, there may be little, or nothing, left.

As he watched Schilling and the others at work, he studied the newly exposed path. There was no doubt the ramp was uncommonly wide, and the bricks of an uncommonly fine quality.

"Da Yi, Aaron?" asked Schilling with a smile, obviously knowing what was going through his mind, and Weiskopf shrugged.

"Who can tell?" His casual attitude and off-hand words belied the turmoil of his thoughts.

Could it be Da Yi after all these years?

Weiskopf and Schilling ate their evening meal sitting cross-legged on the ground, their kerosene lanterns creating luminous pools of pale-yellow radiance around them in the starlit darkness. The light inevitably attracted a teeming host of moths, gnats, and other flying insects, to the point they both lit their pipes in hopes the smoke would keep the swarm away, which it did not. They soon retreated to their tent where they discussed and edited Weiskopf's notes, and by nine o'clock they were rolled in blankets and sound asleep.

Rising with the sun, Weiskopf left Schilling to continue exposing the brick ramp, while he returned to Zhengzhou. As he maneuvered the clattering, smoking old Ford around and between the pedestrians, carts, and other vehicles on the narrow country road, he pondered the numerous problems associated with running the dig, which he was now convinced would be a full-scale excavation. How many new laborers should he hire? What additional tools and supplies would be needed? And the overarching question of what the budget would bear loomed before him. There was never enough money. His frustration grew as he drove. If this was a major tomb discovery, its excavation would be expensive, as would transporting the artifact assemblage back to Leipzig. Why did the university governors always expect him to make bricks without straw? Now fuming with exasperation, he rounded a bend in the road.

Damnation!

He swerved violently to avoid a bullock cart. Calm down, for heaven's sake, he instructed himself, severely. Watch where you're going, or you won't be excavating anything.

In Zhengzhou he enlisted the aid of Mr. Wu, the owner of the guesthouse, who had become a firm friend after so many years. Wu took his quiet way into the labyrinthine streets and alleys of the ancient city, where he located twenty reliable men Weiskopf could safely hire as ordinary laborers, as well as four strong-looking ex-soldiers for whose honesty he personally vouched, to serve as night watchmen. At the same time, Wu's wife, a stridulent harridan, took the list Weiskopf had brought from the cook and departed to do shrill battle with the street and market stall vendors she habitually referred to as cheats, liars, and crooks. Weiskopf sent telegrams to the departments of archeology at Beijing University, Qinghua University, and Nankai University asking for volunteers from amongst their graduate students. If this was a major tomb, and all indications were that it probably was, he would need as many trained hands and eyes as he could acquire. He then sent a telegram to Professor Irwin Bergdorf, head of the archeology department at the University of Leipzig.

April 20 1933 Zhengzhou China

Excavating large bronze-age tomb stop Perhaps royal stop Will advise soonest stop Weiskopf

That should keep the old boy happy, he thought, as he left the telegraph office having handed over two dollars to send the wires, and another five to ensure they actually would be sent.

Following that, he drove back to the guesthouse where Wu had assembled the new recruits for his inspection. Surveying the men standing in two ranks before him, he told them they would be picked up at dawn two days hence,

130

and anyone not on time would be left behind without question. They would be paid at the end of each week, and if any man proved lazy, he would be dismissed forthwith and be obliged to walk back to Zhengzhou.

"There is one final thing," and making his voice harsh and threatening, he said, "If any man attempts to steal anything we unearth in our work, no matter how small it may be, he will be turned over to the police immediately and severely punished. This, I solemnly promise you."

Some men bowed, others merely nodded, as he bent a meaningful stare on them to emphasize his words. He had had trouble with theft in the past and was not about to risk it now. He derived no satisfaction from the thought of men being flogged into insensibility with bamboo canes — on the contrary, he considered it a barbarous practice — but such was the punishment invariably prescribed for thieves. However, he was not prepared to lose precious artifacts to light-fingered casual laborers, and so he repeated, "Severely punished. Remember that, all of you."

He and Wu then ate a fine dinner together in the company of Wu's strident wife and their five children before retiring to bed, tired, but excited and happy.

Returning to the telegraph office the next morning at ten o'clock he was told by a sad-faced and apologetic little man in a creased and stained dark blue suit that there were no messages for him. However, upon his receiving three Big Heads, his mood at once brightened and he was miraculously able to find five telegrams which he had *forgotten about.*

"Forgive my failing memory, good sir." This with a self-deprecating smile and an obsequious bow.

Standing outside in the warm sunshine on the steps of the office with the tumult of pedestrians, cars, trucks, carts, and rickshaws all contending for room on the road before him, he read that ten graduate students would be on their way to Zhengzhou by train that evening, arriving at six o'clock tomorrow morning, and could he send someone to meet them and conduct them to the site?

131

Good, he thought, tearing open the final wire and reading.

Understood stop Stay within budget stop Bergdorf

What's he think I'm going to do, Weiskopf fumed, run up a huge debt and ask the department to pay it for me? Pausing for a moment, he was chagrined to recall that he had actually done that once several years ago, thereby incurring the ire of the university's governors expressed to him in a strongly worded letter of reprimand. Their anger, however, paled into insignificance when compared to the wrath of *Herr* Professor Dr. Irwin Bergdorf.

After procuring many more trowels, several small spades, two dozen brushes, and eight hundred paper bags of varying sizes, he collected the provisions Wu's wife had purchased and packed and drove back to the excavation site, arriving in the late afternoon.

He saw at once Schilling had made good progress. The upper extremity of the ramp was fully exposed, measuring a little under six meters in width. Schilling and his small team had also uncovered two meters of its length, at which point it was just over a meter below the datum line, a horizontal string set about three centimeters above the surface of the ground to serve as the uniform level from which all depths were measured. This method removed the inconsistencies inevitably resulting if measurements were taken from the uneven and undulating surface of the ground itself.

"It's been disturbed, I'm afraid, Aaron," Schilling reported, with a disappointed expression on his bearded face, as he took off his hat and wiped his forehead with his sleeve. "You can see it."

He pointed to the wall of the pit at the base of which the paved ramp disappeared underground, and Weiskopf saw immediately he was right. His heart sank. On the far right-hand end of the wall, the color of the soil changed from dark brown to pale gray. It contained much more sand than the original earth, and it was clear someone, hundreds of years ago perhaps, had burrowed his way down the ramp. There was a chance, albeit a slim one, that the

132

unknown vandal had given up before he reached the far end of the ramp and had not plundered the actual burial, but Weiskopf put very little faith in that idea. In any event, whether he reached the tomb or not, he had left his tunnel to be filled in by natural means. Weiskopf shook his head, bitter disappointment choking any words he may have wished to say.

Chapter Eleven

It was now late August of that same year. The season was rapidly coming to an end, and Dr. Weiskopf was a happy, happy man. He had at last found the tomb of King Da Yi of Shang, and although one small corner had been looted, the rest of the tomb was intact, pristine, and brilliant. A rich assemblage of artifacts had been recovered, and the world of Chinese archeology was all agog.

Surveying the excavation in the dripping heat of a summer afternoon, Weiskopf, borrowing freely from Dante Alighieri's *Divina Commedia*, observed to Schilling that they had at first been in the depths of the *Inferno* when they found the tomb had been disturbed, then in the *Purgatorio* of uncertainty until it was discovered all was not lost after all.

"Then, we were transported to *Paradiso*," he finished, with a flourish. "What a season it has been, Eduard. What a time we have had."

As the summer progressed, and the excavation with it, more laborers were hired, and more students arrived as word spread of the momentous discovery. The dig gained international fame, thanks to the appearance of a staff writer and photographer from *Life Magazine* in the United States and other members of the foreign press, all eager to tell the tale of China's ancient wonders.

An English newspaper trumpeted, *It is the greatest archeological discovery since the excavation of the tomb of King Tutankhamun in Egypt's Valley of the Kings by Howard Carter in 1922.*

Visitors came from near and far. Government luminaries, distinguished scholars from major Chinese and foreign universities, and even three officials from the illustrious *Academia Sinica* journeyed from Beijing to gaze enraptured at what had been found. The merely curious came in their thousands as well, compelling a worried Weiskopf to hire more guards. He was unused to the notoriety his work had attracted, and he did not like it at all. He feared for the safety of his crew and the artifacts.

The size of that crew had been increased in June by the University of Leipzig's sending of four of its most promising graduate students to China, apparently without regard to any budgetary concerns *Herr* Bergdorf might have had. The university basked in the reflected glory of Weiskopf's fame, and suddenly nothing was too expensive.

One of the four, a fresh-faced young fellow of only twenty named Gerhard Martins, so impressed Weiskopf with his skills and brilliance, he gave him responsibility for artifact photography, cataloging, and classification, thereby freeing Schilling for full-time duties as assistant director.

Even the puissant Professor Bergdorf himself travelled to the site, enduring hours of deafening discomfort aboard a propeller-driven aircraft, followed by an overnight ordeal on a dilapidated Chinese train with, in his words, *the hardest seats known to God or man*. Hands behind his back and wearing a broad straw hat to protect his balding pate, he walked about the site, carefully observing the work, asking numerous questions, and becoming progressively more impressed and excited. Notwithstanding his interest, however, he staunchly refused to sleep at the site in a tent. He insisted on staying at the Zhengzhou guesthouse and being driven to and fro each day. Weiskopf decided it would be less than prudent to point out the considerable additional cost in fuel this service represented, although he would dearly have loved to do so.

"You have crowned your career with this find, Aaron," Bergdorf said one evening as the Ford bounced along the road to the city. "The university is proud of you, and you will be remembered for this great accomplishment."

After a five-day stay, an hour of which was spent studying Weiskopf's account books followed by a perfunctory nod of approval, Bergdorf bade the team a hearty farewell, wished them continued success, and departed. One incident had marred his visit. Weiskopf told him he had made a bargain with the *Academia Sinica* that the artifacts would be returned to China after being studied and briefly displayed in Germany.

"What possessed you?" demanded Bergdorf. "We have not done that before. Why send these things back? They will all be better off in our museum. I doubt the Chinese will take proper care of them, anyway, and it will be expensive to return everything. Why should we be asked to pay for that?"

"I had no choice, *Herr* Professor," Weiskopf explained as humbly as he could. He wanted to avoid an outright confrontation. "The *Academia* was threatening to take over the excavation and that would have been a disaster for the university."

"Were they indeed?" asked Bergdorf, in a dry voice. "Well, we shall see. It is we who have paid for everything, not they. China is on the brink of civil war, while Germany has never been better led than she is now. Where will these treasures be safer, here or there? The answer is obvious."

"I think they are entrusting the collection to us until China, herself, achieves stability," Weiskopf suggested respectfully, and Bergdorf responded with a derisive snort.

"And when will that be? The oriental peoples are like the Slavs, Aaron. They have no concept of orderly government. They are anarchists at heart."

Weiskopf could tell Bergdorf was envisioning the entire glittering collection on prominent display in the university museum in perpetuity.

"I gave them my word," he said. "I promised that when we had studied the assemblage, photographed everything, and published our findings and conclusions, we would return everything to China. It is a matter of honor."

"*You* promised them," growled Bergdorf, "not I."

Bergdorf was adamant, and Weiskopf let the matter drop. In any case, it would take years to study fully the vast collection, and who knew what the situation would be by then? He decided he would cross that bridge when he came to it.

I wonder when Professor Bergdorf is due to retire.

"Well," he said, "let us finish the work and get the collection home to Leipzig. There will be plenty of time to decide what to do after that."

"Just so," said Bergdorf, stone-faced.

One afternoon, three weeks after Bergdorf's departure, Weiskopf, in the bottom of the excavation, got up off his knees, his joints cracking as he straightened his legs. The pit was now almost twelve meters long by six wide; its floor divided into squares by lengths of white cord. In each square, two or three men knelt carefully clearing away the dry earth with trowels and brushes. A constant parade of other men, each carrying a basket of earth, moved up a slope dug into the end of the pit opposite the brick ramp, while another line came down, their baskets empty. Weiskopf's brown overalls hung loosely on his lean frame, and he wore his customary broad-brimmed hat as protection from the merciless sun which beat down into the deep excavation, turning it into a shimmering crucible. He put his hands on his hips, surveying the scene around him with satisfaction. He had made many remarkable discoveries in his years of work in China, but here, in this excavation in the Yellow River valley, he had unearthed nothing short of a treasure trove. He and his team had recovered over a thousand oracle bones, along with the remains of chariots, carts, horses, bronze weapons by the score, and bronze vessels of every sort. There was a great deal of gold and many precious gemstones as well as jade, agate and lapis jewelry. It seemed every day brought the revelation of new wonders.

The site was also rich in artifacts from non-Shang traditions, confirming Weiskopf's contention that trade was widespread and well-established. The masterful jade carvings of the Liangzhu peoples were of special interest to him, as were the intricately decorated black ceramic vases and bowls from the Neolithic culture of the Longshan, which had survived well into Shang times in remote areas.

137

Ivory from the southern regions was abundant, along with ornaments and a vast fortune in cowry shell money. The bones of Da Yi himself had come to light in late July, resting amid the rotted remains of his red lacquered wooden sarcophagus, along with the skeletons of several concubines and the decapitated corpses of three-hundred-and-twenty-eight slaves.

But now, at the end of August, the excavation was virtually complete. The workers on the pit floor were beginning to encounter sterile soil, devoid of artifacts and showing no trace of human activity. There was almost nothing more to be done. Tons of soil had been carried by hand out of the pit, and every gram of it had been sieved and scrutinized. Not a bead or a chip of bone had been overlooked. The numerous artifacts, large and small, had all been recorded, classified, and catalogued by the endlessly energetic young Gerhard Martins, and before long, it would be time to think of closing down.

Calling to Schilling, Weiskopf pointed to where he had been kneeling.

"I think there's an oracle bone there, Eduard. Do you see the tip of it…just at the surface? Shall we have a look?"

The two men knelt and with Schilling wielding a small, flat trowel, and Weiskopf a soft paintbrush, they carefully cleared the loose, sandy soil away from the flat object which soon revealed itself as the plastron of a turtle, the surface of which was covered with a pattern of branching cracks like the fine tendrils of a plant.

"Aha, another one," said Schilling, beckoning Martins to come and photograph the object *in situ* before lifting it clear of the ground.

"Let's see what it says," said Weiskopf, as they got to their feet. Taking the plastron, he brushed away the last of the soil, muttering, "It'll probably be about the best place for the king to go hunting, and what he'll kill there if he does."

"Excuse me, *Herr* Professor," said Martins, "just look this way for a moment, please, and hold the bone where we can see it." The shutter clicked. "Excellent. Thank you."

Turning the bone into the sunlight, Weiskopf studied the incised characters for nearly a full minute, occasionally using his brush or blowing away grains of soil, before looking at Schilling, his eyes wide.

"Well, Eduard, we really have something here." Weiskopf's dark eyes positively sparkled. "This is definitely *not* just another ordinary oracle bone."

"What is it, Aaron? You look as if you've just inherited a million marks."

"Better than that, Eduard, he said. "It's direct confirmation of the battle of Mingtiao, and the existence of Lord Chang. So far as I'm aware, it's the only such confirmation in existence. It'll cause a sensation when we publish this."

"That's wonderful, *Herr* Professor," said Martins, who had stayed to listen. "My congratulations."

"But surely, we've known of them before, have we not?" queried Schilling.

"Ah, yes," said Weiskopf, nodding, "but only in apocryphal stories and legends that could never be verified."

"Sima Qian speaks of them both in the *Records of the Grand Historian*," Schilling pointed out.

"Yes, he does," Weiskopf agreed, "but he was writing during the Han Dynasty, more than fifteen hundred years after the event. There was no guarantee of reliability without contemporary evidence and verification. This bone was inscribed at the very time, and to think it was not with the others. It was lying just here, by itself. We might have missed it altogether. I wonder how it became separated from all the other."

"Impossible to say," said Schilling, with a shrug. "Dropped by someone during the funeral rites, or even by the tomb robbers. Who knows? But at least it isn't damaged, which is the main thing."

Martins held out his hand, saying, "I will photograph it, *Herr* Professor, and put it with the rest," but Weiskopf shook his head.

"Photograph it by all means, number, and record it as well, but then find a strong specimen bag for it, and bring it back to me. I want to make sure it comes to no harm. Whatever else we may have found here; this plastron is truly and lastingly significant."

* * *

Within a month of finding what Weiskopf began to call the *Mingtiao*, the excavation of the Da Yi tomb site was finished. By the first week of September, sterile earth was everywhere; there was nothing more to be found. After a careful evaluation, during which he walked or crawled over every square centimeter of the pit floor, Weiskopf declared the work to be at an end and ordered the pit refilled with the excavated soil, a small mountain of which, more than twice the height of a man, had steadily arisen about ten meters from the rectangular cut. This was tedious and exhausting work which had to be done by hand. A bulldozer would have accomplished the task within thirty minutes at most, but when Weiskopf inquired if one might be available, no one knew what he was talking about. Mr. Wu, therefore, recruited twenty-five additional men to help, and the work progressed with buckets and a brigade of wheelbarrows.

The artifacts were packed into wooden crates under Schilling's exacting eye. Every one, that is, except the Mingtiao, which Weiskopf kept in a leather bag securely tied around his waist.

"Nothing must happen to it," he said, when Schilling protested. "I know I'm probably being silly, Eduard, but I feel better knowing it's with me at all times."

Schilling grinned. He knew Weiskopf's little idiosyncrasies, and he was enough of an historian to appreciate the artifact's importance.

Special care was taken over the ceramics, most of which were wrapped in layers of cloth before being put into their own individual crates made especially for them by a master carpenter in Zhengzhou recommended by the apparently omniscient Mr. Wu. The man spent weeks at the site, measuring each piece with sedulous care before crafting boxes of a perfect fit.

The larger bronze ceremonial vessels, some weighing over a hundred kilos, were protected by wooden frames packed with rice straw before being loaded, along with hundreds of crates and boxes, onto the eight rickety trucks Weiskopf had managed to hire, albeit at prodigal expense.

"I doubt they'll make it ten kilometers," grumbled Schilling, staring disapprovingly at the rusty hulks.

"They were all I could find," said Weiskopf, shrugging. "Let us hope they will survive."

He and Schilling, grateful the pitiless heat of previous weeks was beginning to diminish, if only slightly, exhausted themselves supervising the work. The arid dust raised by dozens of pairs of feet filled their mouths and nostrils, caking on their lips and in their throats.

"God deliver us from this," Schilling croaked, one afternoon, as he wiped his mouth after a long drink brought to him by young Lai, employed as water carrier and endlessly energetic in the performance of his duties.

"We shall soon be ready," said Weiskopf, patting Schilling on the shoulder. "Have courage. I have heard from the shipping agents in Tianjin, and they will be waiting for us. We will take the train to Beijing, and then on to Tianjin. I have our tickets and permissions to travel, as well as the freight certificates from the local authorities. I've received the necessary export license for the artifacts from the *Academia Sinica*, so all is now prepared."

He spoke lightly of the bureaucratic tangle through which he had been obliged to navigate, but in reality, it had been a long and arduous journey. At each step of the way, payments were needed to guarantee the next door would be opened. The travel and freight papers had been the most complicated items and had taken the longest to finalize. Obtaining appointments to see the dignified and urbane scholars at the *Academia* had cost a minor fortune, all of which disappeared into the pockets of clerks, secretaries, and other underlings. With smiles and cordial bows, the governing officials reminded him of his promise to return everything he was being allowed to take away. He reaffirmed his agreement as the small, red seals with their special characters were stamped on the certificates.

"I trust we will be safe on route," said Schilling, a note of concern in his voice, after Weiskopf had explained these things to him. "Lawless behavior has increased this summer."

"There are bandits hereabouts, all right," said Weiskopf, "but the *Guomindang* army keeps them in their place."

"Well," Schilling grunted, wiping his forehead and replacing his hat, "that may be so, but I am not a great admirer of Chiang Kai-shek or his army. He has been in power since ...what...?"

"Nineteen-twenty-eight," Weiskopf supplied, and Schilling nodded.

"The last five years, yes, but he strikes me as little better than the warlords he replaced, and in our time here we have seen many a local thug come and go, haven't we?"

"The communists continue to establish themselves," said Weiskopf, accepting a drink from Lai. "Would you prefer them to the Nationalists?"

"I would prefer to go home," said Schilling, "before I have to deal with either of them. China is going to fall to pieces, and I have no desire to be here when it does."

"We shall be on our way very soon," chuckled Weiskopf, "but, tell me, what will you have to complain about once you get home?"

Schilling, ignoring the gentle jibe, continued. "My brother has written to me to say the National Socialists have come to power, led by Adolph Hitler. He is the man for Germany now, Aaron. He will restore us to our position of prominence and tear up the Versailles Treaty once and for all. I am looking forward to seeing what he can do."

"Ah yes, Corporal Hitler," said Weiskopf, in an almost musing tone. "He used to hang wallpaper, I believe.

Admirable preparation for national office, wouldn't you say?"

Schilling grunted again.

"My brother says he's doing things to give people jobs and restore social order."

"And I understand he and his SA Storm Troopers were responsible for much of the disorder in the first place," said Weiskopf. "Street riots, beatings, and God knows what besides. Is that the Germany you're looking forward to?"

Schilling ignored the question. In a dogmatic tone of voice, he repeated, "I believe Hitler is what Germany needs." To Weiskopf he sounded as if he were reading from a script.

"Someone has to take charge, Aaron. Surely you must see that. Someone has to *lead*. Hindenburg can't live much longer. The old ideas and the outmoded class structure no longer serve us."

This was rapidly becoming something of a tirade, and Weiskopf sought to calm the waters.

"Well, we shall see," he said. "All in good time, I think?"

"Excuse me, sir," said a young Chinese man who had appeared at Weiskopf's side, "all is finished."

"Excellent," said Weiskopf, with a smile. "Eduard, see that the men we no longer need are paid what we owe them, and then we shall be off."

The graduate students from Leipzig had been invited by the *Academia* to spend four weeks in Beijing participating in a series of colloquia and lectures on ancient Chinese history, and they came to say their goodbyes before driving off in a hired car.

"I shall miss them," said Weiskopf, waving. "Especially young Martins. He's a brilliant lad. At least we shall see them again once we are home."

After speeches of farewell and a long series of personal goodbyes to young Lai, Mr. Wu, and Mr. Wu's numerous family and associates, all of whom had travelled from Zhengzhou for this occasion, Weiskopf and Schilling, replete with parting gifts, climbed into the battered Ford to begin the long journey homeward. A journey Weiskopf would later describe as a tragedy and a nightmare.

Chapter Twelve

The procession of nine vehicles moved off in clouds of yellow dust and black diesel smoke to the accompaniment of cheers and waves from those gathered to see them go. Although it was late summer, the sun blazed down on the convoy of trucks, each bearing its cargo of crates, boxes, wooden frames, and packing cases, each numbered and listed with its contents.

Notwithstanding the many wonders discovered, the turtle shell which Weiskopf kept securely at his waist was to him, the season's greatest treasure. As he drove, he began to compose in his mind the paper he would write announcing his find. To begin, he thought, there will be a full description of the site, its geographical coordinates, and a map, as well as several photographs of the excavation at various stages of the work. Then would come details of the recovery of the bone, its depth and location in the excavation — with a diagram, of course — and a list of its precise dimensions followed by an analysis of the provenance to establish its age and absolute authenticity. Martins' *in situ* photograph, along with photographs of the bone both front and back, would have to be included, and, when all that was done, his translation — he thought of it now as his *triumphant* translation — of the inscription. And to conclude, he thought, a brief description of the historical placement of General Chang and the now-confirmed battle. He could envision the entire article in his mind already. It was simple, and, best of all, the evidence was indisputable. It was free of speculation. Other epigraphists would no doubt carefully scrutinize his translation, but he was entirely confident. The incised characters were clearly visible. There was neither illegibility nor gaps in the text. He had had, therefore, no need of interpretational guesswork of the kind scholars, including himself, love to poke holes in. He felt the pouch for the hundredth time and experienced the familiar surge of excitement.

The procession left the excavation site and turned towards Zhengzhou. To everyone's relief, Schilling's pessimistic prediction about the condition of the trucks, that they *would not get ten kilometers*, did not come to pass, and although their engines rasped and growled, coughing out dense billows of acrid smoke, they all kept grinding forward. Weiskopf had been told by a shipping agent in Tianjin that a German tramp steamer, the *Sonne*, was sailing for Bremerhaven in mid-September with a mixed cargo of hardwoods, furniture, silk, and silver. There would be room for the crates of artifacts, and after a little haggling and a lot of alcohol, cabins were also secured for himself and Schilling. A price was agreed, and all was done. He walked out of the office with the signed contracts in his hand, leaving the agent smiling, happy, and three parts intoxicated.

"I won't be sorry to board that ship," said Schilling, as they jolted and banged their way out onto the main road. "We haven't been home for six months, and a lot has been happening in Germany since we left."

"I'll be relieved to get all these boxes and crates safely back to Leipzig," said Weiskopf, "It won't be an easy journey to Tianjin, and the *Sonne* didn't sound like much of an ocean-going vessel to me."

"Why do we have to take the train at all?" asked Schilling. "Can't we drive to Tianjin?"

"We could," said Weiskopf, with a nod, "except for the fact no one would rent me the trucks to go there. Mr. Wu did his best, but everyone told him the same thing." He steered the truck around a farmer on the road carrying a long, flexible pole on his shoulder with a large basket of what looked like turnips suspended from each end. The man, barefoot and clad only in baggy brown trousers and a ragged shirt which might once have been white, matched

146

his steps to the rhythmic upward spring of the pole and thus saved himself from some of the weight of his burden as he walked. Schilling waited.

"The trucks would never be returned to their owners," Weiskopf resumed. "Once we got to Tianjin, the truck drivers would simply sell the vehicles and pocket the money. Wu said the only solution was for me to buy the trucks and sell them in Tianjin myself, but there's no money left for that sort of thing. The good *Herr* Professor Bergdorf would have a seizure. And besides," he added, with a sideways glance at Schilling, "the price quoted for the trucks was extortionate. I had enough trouble getting an agreement on hiring them even for this short time."

At the Zhengzhou railway station Weiskopf edged the Ford into a narrow space outside the main terminus, and then, by dint of a lot of waving and shouting, he and Schilling managed to get the other eight vehicles positioned close to the platforms. As they prepared to enter the station building, they were accosted by a man wearing a rumpled gray suit, a battered fedora, and an ingratiating, gap-toothed smile.

"Excuse me," he said in halting English, "but do you wish to sell your truck?"

In Weiskopf's estimation the ancient Ford was almost worthless, and he had simply planned to abandon it, but here was an unexpected opportunity.

"You see," the man was continuing, his smile now obsequious, "I can take it to pieces and sell the parts. I understand you are leaving China, so you will have no more use for it. I will give you sixty silver dollars."

Well, thought Weiskopf, the bush telegraph is working with its customary efficiency.

"One hundred," he countered in Chinese, to the man's evident surprise.

"Sixty-five," said the man, his equilibrium shaken.

"Ninety-five."

"Seventy," snapped the man, in exasperation. Weiskopf could see he had not been expecting this sort of difficulty in doing business with a foreign devil. Many

147

round-eyes were uncomfortable with the custom of haggling and tended to pay the asking price or accept the first offer.

"Ninety," answered Weiskopf. "Take it or leave it."

The man's good humor had quickly evaporated, but he paid the money, albeit with no good grace, caught the keys Weiskopf threw him, and disappeared into the noisy crowds thronging the station's forecourt. He reappeared in a moment or two accompanied by another man who looked equally disreputable, and they clambered into the truck, banging the doors shut with a tinny clank.

"There isn't anything on that truck worth selling," said Schilling, as he and Weiskopf watched the Ford's new owner fighting unsuccessfully to start the engine.

"It's a business opportunity," said Weiskopf, grinning. "If he didn't think he could make money off it somehow, he wouldn't have bought it."

"But you were just going to leave it here anyway," said Schilling. "He might have got the thing for nothing."

"True," said Weiskopf, with another grin, "but he didn't know that, did he? As I said, he saw a business opportunity, but so did I."

The truck still would not start. Schilling looked at Weiskopf and said, "Well, your opportunity was a lot better than his, I think."

Inside the station, they were confronted by a scene of bewildering pandemonium. On every side there were milling, shouting crowds, surging lines of people, demanding to buy tickets. The din was intensified by squealing herds of terrified pigs being pushed into holding pens, and dozens of crates of quacking ducks piled anywhere space could be found. The thick air reeked of dung, coal smoke, and the pungent aroma of unwashed human bodies.

"Is this a railway station or a farmyard?" grunted Schilling, shouldering aside a young woman shrieking in a voice to shatter glass that she had a ticket to Shanghai she was willing to sell.

"Follow me," Weiskopf shouted, squeezing through a narrow steel-barred gate into the main station's inner concourse.

"I'm trying to," gasped Schilling, somewhere behind him. "There are entirely too many people in this country, and they're all in this railway station."

"We have our tickets already," shouted Weiskopf, and he thought he heard Schilling answer, "Praise God," but he was not sure.

"What we need now, Eduard," said Weiskopf, once they reached a place of relative calm, "is some men to help us unload."

Weiskopf knew the station well. There were always men loitering about on the chance someone would want help with luggage or freight.

"Come on," he said, heading for the platforms.

Within a few minutes he had found a squad of men happy to unload the eight trucks and transfer the cargo to the special boxcar attached at the rear of the regular passenger train. The men, most of them wearing only baggy trousers, were organized by Schilling into a work party, and soon proved appearances to be deceiving. In spite of their thin arms and narrow chests, they showed themselves strong and energetic. As each item was transferred, Schilling checked it off against his master list while Weiskopf supervised the loading of the train. It was tedious, but the risk of theft was too omnipresent to leave the work to the railway officials who stood watching, anger and resentment etched clearly on their disapproving faces.

"They expected to be paid in return for allowing us to load," said Weiskopf, in German. "They were not at all pleased to see we had authorization from the provincial government. There was no way they could prevent us from loading, nor could they demand a bribe."

As Schilling checked off the last crate, a bronze cauldron which it took four men to move, a young soldier wearing the brown uniform of a *Guomindang* officer strode up to Weiskopf, his expression a good deal less than friendly.

149

"Who are you, and what is in all these packing cases? Where are your papers?"

Weiskopf was all too familiar with this sort of individual. Here in Zhengzhou, as in much of the rest of the country, the influence of the Beijing government was scarcely felt, leaving petty civic bureaucrats and junior officers from the local garrison to run the city and the surrounding countryside almost as a private fiefdom. Bureaucrats kept records — of a sort — while soldiers kept order — of a sort — and imperfect as it was, the system somehow managed to prevent China from disintegrating into anarchy, but only just. When he spoke to this belligerent young man, therefore, Weiskopf kept his voice level and respectful. A confrontation could be disastrous.

"I am Dr. Aaron Weiskopf, of the University of Leipzig, Germany, sir, and the cases you see here contain archeological material which I have permission to take out of China for study. Here is a copy of the certificate of authorization from your government through the *Academia Sinica* in Beijing."

"It is a forgery," snapped the officer, barely glancing at the sheet of paper Weiskopf held out. "This is all stolen property. You are thieves and criminals."

"No, sir, it is not a forgery," said Weiskopf, patiently, "and we are not thieves. I have worked in China for many years, and my writings on Chinese history are well known in your finest universities. This paper bears the seal of the Department of Antiquities, and, as you know, to forge it would be a capital offence."

Out of the corner of his eye, Weiskopf saw the men hauling shut the sliding door of the freight car, while Schilling stood by with a heavy padlock. Even though the trains seldom ran on time these days, Weiskopf knew it would not wait for him if he were detained arguing with this arrogant young martinet.

"With your permission, sir," he said, "I must go now. The train is leaving."

"You do not have my permission," said the officer. "I wish to question you further."

"I must go, sir," Weiskopf repeated, being careful not to sound peremptory or condescending.

The man hesitated, then, glancing at the train, its steam locomotive belching gray billows of coal smoke, he turned without a further word, and stalked off, leaving Weiskopf with a strong feeling the encounter did not bode well.

As whistles sounded and doors slammed up and down the length of the train, the locomotive discharged a great hissing cloud of steam from the cylinders whose glistening steel pistons delivered power to the three huge driving wheels on each side. Beginning to roll ponderously forward, it repeatedly chuffed tall columns of smoke into the evening air. Weiskopf, his heart pounding, sprinted for the door Schilling held open for him.

"Run, Aaron," Schilling shouted, quite unnecessarily. "Come on…you can do it."

The train faltered for a moment as the driving wheels lost their grip and spun on the rails, but it was all Weiskopf needed. In that short second or two he was able to fling himself into the compartment, gasping for breath. The train regained speed, and they were underway.

Dropping into their seats facing each other, Schilling withdrew a flask from an inside pocket, tapped it with his forefinger, and smiled.

"Here's what we need."

* * *

"What's going on?" Weiskopf mumbled, startled from a deep sleep by the shriek and squeal of steel on steel as the train braked hard. Their compartment shuddered as the train ground to a halt amid the banging and clanking of couplings.

"God knows," Schilling answered, lowering the window and looking out into the night. Weiskopf joined him, and as they peered towards the front of the train, glaring yellow floodlights leapt into life, revealing dozens, perhaps hundreds, of soldiers lining the tracks.

"What the hell's going on?" asked Schilling.

"They've stopped the train," said Weiskopf. "Something must be up. Bandits somewhere, perhaps, or a skirmish with some local tin-pot warlord who wants to be an emperor."

They heard the sound of heavy boots coming down the corridor, and someone shouted, "European professor, professor from Germany. Identify yourself immediately"

"There's no use in trying to hide," said Weiskopf. "They obviously know we're here. That officer in Zhengzhou must have called ahead."

Weiskopf slid the door open, and three *Guomindang* soldiers, one of them a senior officer judging from the red epaulettes and brass buttons on his well-tailored uniform, crowded into the compartment.

"We have information you are attempting to steal ancient treasures from China," snapped the officer, a thin-faced man of about fifty. "I order you to unlock the freight wagon at the rear of this train."

"We have permission from—" Weiskopf began, but the officer interrupted, shouting, "You have no such thing. You will open the door to the freight wagon, or we shall blow it open."

"They want the gold," said Schilling in German, and Weiskopf nodded.

"There's nothing we can do."

"Bribe?" suggested Schilling, but Weiskopf shook his head.

"What are you saying?" shouted the officer. "Speak Chinese. Unlock the wagon, *now!*"

Climbing down from the train, Weiskopf, fearing the loss of all they had worked so hard for, led the way to the rear of the train. He felt numb. It was as if he were watching, incredulous, from some external place, removed from the reality of what was happening. There were soldiers everywhere, the harsh glare of the floodlights illuminating the expressions of anger, hostility, and greed on their young faces.

Mere boys, thought Weiskopf, bleakly. Do they seriously think any of the treasure will be shared with them?

As though in some waking nightmare, he undid the padlock securing the heavy wooden door and it was flung open with a crash. Soldiers leapt into the freight car and began throwing out boxes and crates. Weiskopf saw the train had been diverted onto a siding in a small rural station and knew with certainty the entire ambush had been carefully planned. Here was the Chinese army itself, behaving like the very bandits from which it was supposed to protect both he and his precious cargo. Glancing at his pocket watch, he saw it had been but two hours since they had left Zhengzhou; more than enough time to arrange this reception. Appalled and sickened, he watched the boxes being split and broken open as they were flung out of the boxcar. Schilling, who had come up behind him, lost his temper entirely and began shouting in German.

"Stop it, you ignorant savages, you…you vandals, you uncouth barbarians."

A soldier raised his rifle, and Weiskopf hissed, "Shut up, Eduard, for God's sake. You'll get us killed."

Weiskopf, consumed by impotent rage and horror saw box after box torn open, its contents tipped onto the ground. A soldier picked up a large ceramic jar, and Weiskopf moved forward, his hands outstretched.

"*No*! Be careful. Please don't damage that."

Three more soldiers levelled their weapons at them, and he stopped where he was. The soldier threw the jar out of the train, and it shattered on the ground, as men began shouting and cursing.

"There's nothing here but old pottery and other useless junk. We're wasting our time."

"Keep looking," the thin-faced officer barked, and within a few more minutes they found what they were after. The gold and silver, the gemstones, and jade pieces had been packed in plain wooden boxes to avoid attracting undue attention, but they were soon pried open with whoops of triumph. The crates were delivered to the officer where he stood next to Weiskopf.

"So," he sneered, with a malicious smile, as the boxes were unpacked on the ground before him, the gold and gemstones gleaming in the yellow light, "it is as I thought. You are stealing this treasure. I could have you shot, here and now. China will no longer allow her riches to be pillaged by foreign racketeers. Those days are finished."

"Does he seriously think that little bit of high-sounding jingoism justifies what he is doing?" asked Schilling, bitterly. "And he calls *us* thieves."

"Speak Chinese," shouted the officer.

Weiskopf, all but overwhelmed by grief and crushing disappointment, could do nothing but stare in dumb horror at the scene before him.

A soldier standing at the open freight wagon door shouted, "There are many boxes of old bones in here. Do you want them?"

"No," the officer shouted, "but go through them to be sure nothing has been hidden there."

The soldiers tipped out the boxes of oracle bones while others stamped on them, shattering the fragile plastrons into countless fragments. Weiskopf, aghast at the wanton destruction of so much valuable historical material, became suddenly conscious of the pouch at his side containing the Mingtiao bone, and blessed his decision not to allow it to be packed with the others. He prayed no one would think to search him. The thought of losing the Mingtiao tormented him as he stood, trembling, in the brassy light.

At length, the ruinous rampage was finished. The soldiers were formed into a column and marched away, leaving Weiskopf and Schilling standing with the officer. The ground was littered with empty boxes, shredded packing paper, straw, and broken pieces of wood. Ceramics lay shattered, oracle bones scattered in disarray or smashed. Anger welled up in Weiskopf like hot lava within a volcano to a pitch almost beyond endurance. This had never before happened to him in all his years in China, and the sight of such mindless carnage sickened and disgusted him. Only the largest bronze vessels remained untouched; the soldiers declaring they were too ugly and heavy to bother with.

"This is outrageous," he shouted at the officer. "Look what your men have done here. Irreplaceable treasures, all gone. You are worse than a gang of bandits. You call yourselves soldiers? You are thieves, that's all you are."

"I am a soldier in the army of the Republic of China," retorted the officer, glaring at Weiskopf. "The valuables my men have found hidden by you amongst this old junk belong to China. How can you presume to accuse me of stealing what is already ours?"

"Bah," snorted Schilling, and the officer rounded on him aggressively.

"You should consider yourselves very lucky you are not under arrest. I advise you to board the train and leave here before I change my mind. The valuables you were attempting to steal will be displayed in a museum here in China where they belong."

And on the day that happens, thought Weiskopf bitterly, the dead will rise and dance the polka.

The taste of bitter disappointment corroded his throat like an acid.

"Does he think we're fools?" asked Schilling, as they watched the officer strutting away after his men.

"He will have it all sold and the money pocketed within the hour," said Weiskopf. He felt empty, drained, and defeated, but the train's whistle jarred him back to reality.

"Hurry Eduard, for God's sake."

They rushed to collect what they could, rapidly stuffing oracle bones and any small artifacts and ceramics they could find that remained unbroken into boxes, but within a few minutes the whistle sounded a second peremptory warning blast. Schilling took Weiskopf by the elbow and pulled him away.

"Come, Aaron, there's nothing more we can do. We must get back on the train."

Shaking Schilling's hand away, Weiskopf continued to search for undamaged articles until Schilling forcibly restrained him. He quickly loaded the boxes they had filled and told Weiskopf to find the lock.

Schilling slid the door shut, locked it, although there was very little remaining inside, and they pelted back to their compartment as the train began slowly to move off in clouds of smoke and steam. As it pulled out of the siding and rejoined the main line, some unseen hand somewhere turned off the floodlights leaving everywhere as dark as a stage at the end of a play.

Chapter Thirteen

"And the voyage to Bremerhaven was tedious beyond words," said Weiskopf to Professor Bergdorf, as he finished his narration of the journey from China. "The *Sonne* was a very old ship, and I swear it would have fallen apart if the rust hadn't held it together. After we left Tianjin, the captain announced we were stopping in Singapore and Bombay on the way back, which is why we were six weeks late. Furthermore, he made us pay for the original cargo even though we ended up with much less, thanks to the Chinese army."

"So," said Bergdorf, his face red and eyes narrowed in anger, "the entire debacle cost us a great deal of money, and what have we to show for it? A season of work wasted, and one of the greatest finds of modern times lost. The university will be a laughing stock. I will look a fool. How could you be so thoughtless as to risk train travel in such circumstances? You should have gone by road, traveling during daylight in ordinary vehicles so as not to attract attention, not pulling a wagon-load of priceless treasures behind a passenger train for all to see. And then to trust an unreliable ship and a dishonest captain...where was your judgement? Your conduct is reprehensible, *Herr* Professor."

Weiskopf, appalled and stung by the monstrous injustice of the accusation, rose to his defense in righteous indignation. He stared at Bergdorf. Was the money all he cared about? We could have lost our lives, and he calls me thoughtless?

"*Herr* Professor Berg—" he began, trying to moderate his tone, but Bergdorf forestalled him with an elaborate and exaggerated sigh.

"Well…what were you left with, then? What am I to tell the university governors to save my reputation?"

"*Your* reputation?" Weiskopf could not keep the incredulity out of his voice.

"Of course, mine. Whose do you think? I am the one who authorized the expenditures, not you. I am the one who will have to explain the loss to the governors, not you. So, I ask you again, what did you bring home when all is said and done?"

"All eight large bronze ritual vessels survived," Weiskopf answered, his anger unabated. "Each of them very fine specimens, tri-pedal, highly decorated, and bearing considerable amounts of text. Two of them are of a style hitherto unknown. Most of the smaller bronze pieces are also safe. The soldiers saw no value in them."

"Ceramics?" asked Bergdorf.

"Virtually all destroyed," said Weiskopf, in a tired voice, the enormity of the loss weighing him down once again. He felt sick with disappointment and frustration. "Irretrievably shattered, even if we'd had time to collect the fragments. There are only two large jars remaining and one small Longshan bowl."

"Anything else?" Bergdorf shook his head. "Dear God, what a disaster."

"Assorted pieces of several chariots and carts, about fifty bronze projectile points, spearheads mostly, along with four-hundred-and-seven oracle plastrons out of the original thousand-and-twenty-two. We have all the skeletons, of course, the soldiers wanted nothing to do with those, and a few of the smaller jade sculptures."

"A thousand-and-twenty-two oracle bones?" echoed Bergdorf, his eyebrows arched.

"Yes," said Weiskopf. "The soldiers destroyed many of them, and we had to leave hundreds on the ground when the train started again. However, I kept the most important one with me, and it's still safe."

"One...and that one is...?" inquired Bergdorf, sarcasm sharpening his tone.

"I'll tell you everything after I've confirmed the translation. It requires at least two further verifications by specialists, although I'm confident of it, myself."

"Spare me your scholarly caution," Bergdorf snapped. "Just tell me what's so important about it. Don't forget I'll have to face the governors over this. I need everything I can get if I'm to come anywhere close to redeeming myself."

An angry retort sprang to Weiskopf's lips, but with an effort he bit it back. There was some truth in what Bergdorf was saying. The university governors would have many questions to ask him. His interview would not be a pleasant one, even if he was concerned only with saving his own skin.

"I have every expectation it will confirm the battle of Mingtiao as an actual historical event, and that General Chang was not a mythical figure, as has customarily been thought."

Bergdorf said, "That won't go far towards placating the governors."

"I am sorry, *Herr* Professor," said Weiskopf, although he felt no responsibility for what had happened in China, nor any need to apologize for it.

Bergdorf sighed again.

* * *

Aaron Weiskopf was not the sort of man who paid great attention to politics. His world was his work, and the objects he found and studied filled that world with fascination. What they told him of life in ancient China was more important to him than the demagogic harangues and hate-filled rantings of Germany's new masters. By late 1933, Germany was being remolded and refashioned around him, but he took little or no notice. He rode a tram to his office at the university at the same time each morning and returned home at the same time each evening. An unmarried man, his only family was a half-brother in Stuttgart with whom he seldom ever spoke. He employed a cook and housekeeper, and after her excellent dinners he relaxed with his Meerschaum pipe, a book, and his collection of gramophone records, predominantly Mozart. He almost never listened to the news or read a newspaper, and consumed as he was by his research, and isolated by his insular existence, the changes in Germany overtook him like an unforeseen tidal wave.

The previous year, a clique of German aristocrats, alarmed at the surging popularity of Adolph Hitler, had persuaded eighty-five-year-old President Paul von Hindenburg to run for re-election. This he did, and defeated Hitler in a runoff. But Hindenburg was ill, and the Nazi party knew the collapse of the tottering Weimar Republic was only a matter of time. Twice that year, von Hindenburg dissolved the Reichstag in hopes of stemming the rise of National Socialism, but the moves served only to further destabilize the political situation, add to people's fears of civil war, and strengthen Hitler's position. In March of 1933, two weeks after Weiskopf's departure by ship for China, Hindenburg, reluctantly succumbing to the vehement pressure being placed on him from all sides, appointed Hitler Chancellor of Germany.

Now, it was August the second, 1934, and Hindenburg was dead. After a lavish funeral, which included as impressive a display of German military might as anyone had seen in many a year, Adolph Hitler declared the positions of Chancellor and President were merged, and he appeared before the Reichstag flanked by his lieutenants, and was proclaimed Germany's Führer. Parliamentary democracy was at an end.

Weiskopf took barely any notice of these ominous events or the social disorder which accompanied them. The anti-Semitic laws and civic ordinances promulgated thus far by the Reichstag and the city of Leipzig had not touched him to any great extent, and although he was aware of them, he tended towards a somewhat fatalistic attitude. He had fought for Germany in the war to end all wars, sustained a shrapnel wound at the Somme, and lived through the years of turmoil and hyperinflation that followed Germany's defeat. He remembered the days when it took a wheelbarrow-load of money to buy a loaf of bread. What could be worse than all that, he asked himself.

When the new laws were pointed out to him, he merely shrugged.

"Such things have come and gone in the past, and they will do so again. Nazism is a fashion, a fad, as far as I can see, and Germany will soon tire of it."

By chance one day, he came across a copy of a leftist newspaper discarded in the hallway outside his office, and, stooping to retrieve it while muttering words about untidiness and carelessness, the headline, *Germans Awake*, attracted his attention.

The German people, the front-page article declared, *must awaken and see Hitler's vacuous jingoism for the dangerous threat it really is. Nazism is far more than spectacles, parades, and the sound and fury of hysterical party rallies. Hitler is a megalomaniac who will destroy Germany and her high traditions of art, music, philosophy, and literature. Hitler is not the friend of the people; he will enslave the people.*

He finished reading, and folding the paper, he carried it into his office. Hitler has no monopoly on jingoism, it seems, he thought, wryly, as he dropped the paper into the wastepaper basket by his desk. Everyone is taking the Nazis far too seriously. Far too seriously, indeed.

He had not heard the sound behind him of a door being softly closed as he entered his office.

What he and the rest of Germany did not know at that particular moment was that the Nazi leaders were meditating the creation of a slate of laws to be propounded at a party rally the following year in Nuremburg. Those laws were to herald a latter-day reign of terror unexampled in human history. The tempest was soon to be unleashed, and Aaron Weiskopf did not see the storm clouds boiling up over Germany, blotting out the sun.

161

By early October of 1935, Weiskopf had completed his paper on the Mingtiao oracle bone — it had grown into a somewhat larger project than he had at first envisioned when he thought about it in China — and he submitted the manuscript to the prestigious archeological journal which had published his work for many years. To his great surprise and undeniable irritation, it was refused, politely enough, but without explanation.

"I don't understand it," he complained to Bergdorf during one of their increasingly rare meetings. "The findings are extremely significant. The evidence irrefutable."

"Yes, yes, I'm sure it's all very fine," said Bergdorf, in a distant tone of voice, suggesting he had more important things to do elsewhere, "but things are difficult these days. There are new laws people cannot ignore. You must surely understand."

But Weiskopf did not understand, and voiced his frustration to Schilling, who stared at him, stone-faced.

"Aaron, open your eyes and look around yourself. You've heard of the book burnings while we were in China, haven't you? They're still going on, you know."

"Young hotheads," scoffed Weiskopf. "Ardent young minds misdirected, that's all."

"Don't be too sure," said Schilling. "*Reichsminister* Goebbels made a speech extolling the death of anti-German intellectualism."

"What on earth is *anti-German intellectualism?*" Weiskopf demanded, but Schilling said nothing, contenting himself with an unwavering stare. Comprehension dawned on Weiskopf. Goebbels meant *Jewish* intellectualism.

He said, "Look Eduard, I'm a sinologist and archeologist. My work has nothing whatever to do with politics, let alone this so-called anti-German intellectualism, and it certainly has nothing to do with my being Jewish."

Schilling sighed and chewed his lower lip for a moment.

"Must I spell it out for you, Aaron? Even you must be aware Hitler now governs without the Reichstag. He has been given virtually unlimited power to do as he thinks best. As of last month, all Jews are deprived of their citizenship and all the rights associated with it."

"Yes, yes, I've heard about the Nuremburg laws," said Weiskopf, testily, "but I don't see what they have to do with my research or the publication of my paper."

"The laws declare you are a non-German."

"I'm as German as anyone else," said Weiskopf. "My family has been here for six centuries, and why should nationality matter, anyway? My paper should be judged on its scholastic merits, not on my ancestry, my citizenship, or anything else."

Schilling was silent for a moment, then in a harsh voice, he said, "Well, other things are now more important in Germany than scholastic merit, and perhaps that's a good thing just at this time."

Weiskopf was thunderstruck. It seemed his friend actually believed what he was saying. How was it possible? He knew Schilling admired Hitler as a strong leader, but did he also subscribe to Nazi dogma? It was hard to imagine.

"So," said Weiskopf, "*who* a man is has now become less important than *what* he is."

"Yes," said Schilling, with a shrug, "I suppose you could put it that way."

Weiskopf stared at his former assistant, wondering if he ever really knew the man, but Schilling spoke again, this time in a conciliatory tone.

"Look, Aaron, I know it all seems a little heavy-handed sometimes, but you must admit Germany needs a leader, a man who will get things done. People need jobs. Germany needs a strong, well-equipped army, a powerful navy, and a modern air force. The Versailles Treaty is crippling us, and we've lost the Rhineland which is rightfully ours. Once Hitler has put these things right, things will settle down. You'll see. But in the meantime, he's got to have a free hand, or we won't get anywhere at all. He has to take control of our economy, and, frankly speaking, the Jews, particularly the financiers, wield far too much power over the rest of us. Hitler is merely trying to rectify the imbalance. Just give him a little time."

"Ha," grunted Weiskopf. "So, you want to give him time, do you? Time to take away your citizenship as well, perhaps? Listen, Eduard, for what it's worth, I say the best thing Germany could do would be to rid herself of Adolph Hitler and the Nazis right now, not wait for things to *settle down*, as you so quaintly put it."

"I'm only trying to explain things to you for your own good, Aaron," said Schilling, before turning and walking away without waiting for a reply.

After several further submissions and rejections, the paper was finally published as a feature article in a tourist magazine in Düsseldorf called *Mysteries of the Orient*, the publisher of which was more than pleased to list the distinguished Dr. Aaron Weiskopf as one of its contributors. Photographs of the plastron appeared in the text, but to Weiskopf's bewildered consternation, the article achieved instant oblivion, even amongst his colleagues. Unknown to him, however, a copy of the magazine somehow made its way to the University of Oxford where it found a comfortable place on a dusty shelf in the Bodleian Library and slumbered there in peaceful obscurity, its significance unrecognized.

But its publisher was not left in similar peaceful obscurity. Within a month of the article's appearance, he was attacked by ten members of the *Hitlerjugend*, the Hitler Youth, who smashed his windows and his presses, and beat him senseless in front of his terrified staff as recompense for what they called his *love of Jews*.

The very distinction Weiskopf had attained as a scholar had now turned him into a marked man, but as yet he knew nothing of it.

* * *

"What on earth do you mean, *dismissed?*" demanded Weiskopf, a month later, gaping at Professor Bergdorf in utter incredulity.

The two men stood in the corridor outside Bergdorf's large office — he had not invited Weiskopf in, saying the matter he wished to discuss would not take long.

"It's out of my hands," he said, his voice impatient. "It's an order from Berlin. Jews are to be dismissed from all university faculties throughout the Reich immediately. I received the directive from the governors this morning. Surely you can appreciate I have no choice. You're lucky to have stayed on as long as you have, but you must be aware of what's going on. This can't have come as a surprise to you. In any event, kindly remove your personal possessions from your office, and leave the campus at once."

Weiskopf was dumbstruck. "But —"

"There's nothing more to be said, *Herr* Weiskopf," Bergdorf interrupted harshly, pointedly omitting Weiskopf's professorial title. "Vacate your office by tomorrow evening at the very latest." After a perfunctory nod, he added, "Good day."

Bergdorf strode into his office, and then, turning to face Weiskopf, he hesitated for a moment before saying, "Good luck to you."

Weiskopf was about to make one final, utterly useless protest, but he was left staring impotently at the closed door in front of him. He asked himself, was this revenge? Was Bergdorf actually sacking him because of the catastrophe in China two years ago? True, he had been furious at the time, and he had been embarrassed in front of the governors, but they had not held *him* responsible. They had, however, commended Weiskopf for his handling of the situation, which had not improved Bergdorf's frame of mind, but surely, he was not so small a man as that.

No, he thought wearily, as he left the building. Bergdorf was right. It should not have come as a surprise. There had been many warning signs, but he had not taken them seriously. He had been too complacent, too trusting. Jews had been dismissed from the civil service, from banks and large corporations, even from symphony orchestras, which caused several of the smaller ones to all but disappear.

He walked across the green lawns of the campus to his office in a daze, his mind unable to encompass what had just happened. The sun shone, birds sang, but all was lost on him. His thoughts were in a turmoil.

How can it be, he asked himself, that this great university, the university of Friedrich Nietzsche, could behave this way? How can this place, the very home and hearth of unfettered thought, of creativity and open inquiry, now turn its back on me because I am a *Jew*? My friends, my colleagues…it is sheer madness. And the words of Nietzsche himself then came unbidden into his thoughts.

Insanity in individuals is something rare — but in groups, parties, nations, and epochs it is the rule.

As he crossed the ancient cobbled quadrangle fronting the building housing his office, he caught sight of three of his students and hailed them.

"I am sorry to tell you, gentlemen, I am leaving the university," he said, striving to keep his voice calm. "I —"

"It's about bloody time," one of them interrupted, his tone coarse and full of malice.

"We no longer learn from Jews," sneered another. "Jews have nothing to offer to Aryan Germans but cultural degradation and racial contamination."

He stared at the young men, three of his best and brightest students, noticing for the first time they each wore an armband emblazoned with a swastika. They had not come to see him for two weeks or more, but that was not untoward. They were all engaged in research of their own, and he had thought nothing of their absence.

Bowing his head to hide the stricken expression on his face, he turned away, the final words of the third student reverberating in his ears.

"Dirty Jew!"

166

He spent the rest of the day packing up his office into cardboard boxes, and the following day carrying them one by one to his flat by tram. Most of his books and files were already at home, since the bulk of his work on the Mingtiao oracle bone had been done there in the evening when he would not be disturbed, but by the time he was finished, he was exhausted. Dropping the last box onto a pile in his study, he told *Frau* Kempner, his rotund and gray-haired long-time cook and housekeeper, he was more than ready for his supper.

"It smells wonderful," he said, in eager anticipation.

"It's your favorite," she said. "Beef stew and dumpling." She seemed less talkative and cheerful than usual that evening, but he was too hungry to think much about it.

She served him an excellent meal as she always did, but after giving him his coffee in the sitting room, she stood before him twisting her apron in her hands like a nervous child.

"What is it, Marta?" he asked, after lighting his pipe. "You look very worried about something."

"Oh, *Herr* Professor," she said, tears beginning to stream down her round cheeks, "I cannot work for you any longer. I must tell you goodbye. I will not be here tomorrow morning."

Weiskopf was stunned. He put down his pipe and stared at her in disbelief and consternation.

"But why, Marta? What has happened?"

"I am so sorry," she whispered, sniffing, and dabbing at her face with a lace-edged handkerchief. "They tell me I must not work for a…a Jewish person."

"Who tells you this?" he demanded, but Marta Kempner only shook her head.

"Goodbye, dear Aaron." She crossed to where he sat and kissed his forehead. She had never done such a thing before, and he was startled. He opened his mouth to speak, but she shook her head again and hurried from the room. He heard the door close behind her as she left the flat.

They tell her, he thought, bitterly. As if I didn't know who *they* are. The Nazis are poisoning this nation. True German culture is shamed by this bigotry and hatred, this twisted so-called patriotism and love of country. I don't belong here any longer.

I don't belong here any longer!

And in that instant, he was struck by a brilliant shaft of determined resolution. He decided, as he sat there in his own comfortable sitting room in Leipzig, that he would leave Germany. The strength of his conviction brought him to his feet, and he paced around the room.

"I shall leave everything," he said aloud. "I will take only the Mingtiao bone and one small suitcase. I shall pack this very night and take passage from Bremerhaven as soon as I can. I shall go to England, or perhaps even America. I can continue my work there. I shall go to the bank tomorrow and withdraw money for the exit visa; then I can obtain the forms I will have to complete. If my country will no longer have me, I shall go elsewhere."

He knew, strictly speaking, the Mingtiao belonged to the university, not to him, but he dismissed the thought as the university had dismissed him.

Bergdorf and the governors owe me that much.

The following morning, he arose early, made his own breakfast — something he had not done for more than twenty years — and prepared for his visit to the bank. As he reached for his coat, there came without warning a fearsome hammering on his door, and a harsh voice demanded he *open up*. Bewildered, he did so, and was confronted by four men in black raincoats standing in the corridor.

"Weiskopf?" one of them demanded, as the four of them pushed past him into the flat. He was a tall, heavy-set man with a bull neck and dark eyes as cold as stones.

"I am *Professor* Weiskopf, yes," he answered, defiance now beginning to supplant his initial surprise and confusion. "Who are you, may I ask, and what right have you to force your way into my home?"

168

"Gestapo. You are under arrest for sedition and anti-German activities."

Indignation was now added to defiance.

"I have done nothing," he declared. "Nothing whatsoever. I am a scientist, and I take no interest in politics."

"Really," sneered Bull Neck, as the other three laughed. He took a step closer. "Do you deny being in possession of an anti-government publication?"

Weiskopf opened his mouth to protest, but the man held up his hand.

"Don't bother to say anything, you traitor. You were seen taking it into your office."

"Yes, and I threw it away," said Weiskopf. "It was inflammatory nonsense."

"But you read it, didn't you? And you didn't destroy it as you should have. As a true German should have. But you aren't a true German, are you? *You're a Jew.*" He fairly spat the last words.

"I am not a man of political views," Weiskopf protested again. "These things mean nothing to me."

"Is that so? Well, answer me this, then. Did you or did you not say to one of your colleagues that the best thing for Germany would be to get rid of Adolph Hitler and the National Socialist Party?"

Weiskopf tried to speak, but no sound came. He stared, aghast. Schilling was responsible for this. Eduard Schilling, his colleague. His heart sank. How was it possible? There had been stories of Nazi sympathizers denouncing friends and neighbors, even family members, but, like so many other stories he had heard, he dismissed them as exaggerations or deliberate fearmongering. Now, the deadly reality of it stared him in the face. The four men glared at him menacingly, and with a supreme effort he retrieved what dignity he could.

"I deny —"

"Shut your mouth, Jew," shouted one of the others. "We're going to search this place. You stay where you are. If you try to run, we'll shoot you down. Understand?"

169

Weiskopf no longer recognized the world around him. His urbane, ordered life, all that was familiar, had fled. No longer defiant or indignant, he was terrified, and his knees no longer supported him. Sinking into a chair, his hands trembling, he watched the four men ransack his small flat, emptying drawers and cabinets onto the floor and flinging his books off their shelves. One man tipped out the small, leather suitcase he had already packed and seized the Mingtiao oracle bone.

"He was getting ready to make a run for it, all right," the man shouted, as he held up the plastron. "What the hell's this old bone thing?"

"Be careful," said Weiskopf, fear for the oracle bone outweighing fear for himself, "that's nearly four thousand years old, and very precious."

"And you were going to steal it, weren't you?" the Gestapo man snarled, waving the bone in Weiskopf's face. "Just like any other thieving Jew."

"Please be careful with it," Weiskopf begged.

"Maybe I'll just smash it, shall I?" taunted the man, laughing, but the bull-necked one, who appeared to be in charge, delivered a crisp order which silenced him.

"I don't know what the damn thing is, but don't damage it. All works of art and antiques confiscated from Jews must be sent to Berlin. The *Reichsmuseum* will look after it."

"What about all these notebooks and things?" asked one, and Bull Neck shook his head.

"No, not that sort of stuff. Just leave it."

"So, we take this?" said the man holding the oracle bone. "The Jew says it's old."

"Yes, whatever the hell it is."

"Give it to me, please," Weiskopf pleaded, trying to reach around Bull Neck and jostling him as he did so.

"Don't touch me, Jew," shouted Bull Neck, and with a full swing of his thick arm, he drove his fist into Weiskopf's face. He staggered backwards, blood pouring from his nose. One of the others took hold of him, preventing him from falling, and pinned his arms behind his back.

"All right," he laughed, "let's teach the teacher a lesson, for a change."

The three other Gestapo men took turns punching Weiskopf in the face and stomach and clubbing him with the butts of their pistols. The beating was accompanied by crude insults and coarse laughter, but before long unconsciousness delivered Weiskopf from his torment. He descended into merciful oblivion and knew nothing more.

* * *

Dr. Aaron Weiskopf, eminent professor of archeology and distinguished scholar, was never seen again. He simply disappeared. Like so many others who were taken, he existed thereafter only as a name and number on a list of many names and numbers carefully recorded, duly filed, and promptly forgotten. His neighbors remarked on the disappearance of *Herr* Dr. Weiskopf, but in the end, most agreed he had been taken for resettlement.

"Well...he was a Jew, after all," they said, with knowing nods, "and resettlement is what happens to Jews nowadays, isn't it?"

Everyone had heard there were special areas being set aside for Jews, pleasant places of their own where they could live and work without influencing the lives of German citizens or debasing the purity of the Aryan race. No one seemed to know exactly where those idyllic places were — except that they were somewhere in the east — but apparently the Jews were very happy there. Wherever they were, however, the resettlement was an excellent and humane solution to the Jewish problem. A good idea, they agreed. A very good idea, indeed.

Part Four
London, England 2015 - 2016

Chapter Fourteen

On a chilly day in November when the watery sunshine was doing precious little to warm the damp city, a tall, strongly built man of sixty-two strode into the front entrance of Scotland Yard, the headquarters of the London Metropolitan Police Force, on Victoria Embankment. He had gray hair — now a little thin on top — a round face with deep-set, bright blue eyes, and a wide mouth which looked as if it were always about to break into a smile.

"Good morning, sir," said the duty constable. "Nice to see you again. How's retirement treating you?"

"It's not all it's cracked up to be," Foy said, shrugging. "Tell DS Stuart I'm here, will you?"

"Mr. Foy's here," the duty constable said into his headset microphone. He listened for a moment, then said, "You can go straight up. Here's your pass."

Foy had not been in this building, and it took him some time to find Stuart's office. In Foy's day, the headquarters were located elsewhere and known as New Scotland Yard, but now the metropolitan force was housed at its original location, and the *New* had been dropped. After obtaining directions, Foy rode the lift up to the fourth floor, and crossed a squad room, waving to the people who recognized and greeted him. He knocked on the office door and entered without waiting for a response.

"Hello Bill," said Stuart, "glad to see you."

"I doubt that, Harry," grunted Foy, seating himself. "You know why I'm here."

"Old time's sake?" Stuart ventured, sitting down behind his desk. Foy could see he was wary, and he sensed tension in the air.

"Very droll," said Foy. "You know damn well why I've come, Harry. I want some action on the Terry Preston case."

"No more than I, Bill," said Stuart, his accent thickening, "but as I've told you, we've nowhere to go with it for now. It's regrettable, but from time to time cases do go cold. You had your fair share of them in your time, did you not?"

For all his anger and frustration at the lack of progress in finding his nephew's killer, Foy knew a confrontation with Harry Stuart was not the solution. He was no great admirer of Stuart as a policeman, but he pushed those thoughts out of his mind. He and Stuart had not been the best of mates when Foy was on the force, but if he was to do anything useful now, he needed Stuart's approval if he could possibly get it. His Plan B involved moving forward without Stuart's cooperation, but that could be very messy and unpleasant, to put it no higher. Taking a deep breath, therefore, he reset his sails and tried again.

"Look, Harry," he said, in as contrite a voice as he could muster, "I'm sorry if I was out of line when I called the last time. I haven't come to shout at you and bang my fist on your desk. I'm not here to pick a fight."

"I'm very glad to hear it," said Stuart in a voice as dry as long-dead leaves.

"I want to help. You know, a fresh pair of eyes? A different perspective, perhaps? Terry was the only nephew I had, and my sister died when he was born. I feel I owe it to her, and Terry, to see what I can do here. You know my marriage didn't work out, and I suppose I always regarded

173

Terry as the son I never had. I want justice for him, that's all. It's not complicated."

Foy waited. He wondered if he had become too maudlin or melodramatic, but it was truly how he felt. He watched Stuart's face, but his expression was unreadable.

After a few moments Stuart sighed, and said, "I suppose I can't blame you, Bill, but you've been retired nearly three years now. You can't expect to just stroll back in as if you'd never been away."

"Why not?" asked Foy, beginning to remember what it was about Harry Stuart he disliked. The man was a plodder. He could never see the big picture. As he waited, he could not help remembering the way Stuart had slithered out of the blame for mishandled evidence in a murder case many years ago. Foy had been made to carry the can for that one, and he was sure Stuart had not forgotten it either. He put that thought firmly out of his mind.

That was then, this is now.

What he was asking for was not unreasonable in his view, nor was it unheard of, so why the hell was Stuart tap-dancing around it and worrying about how long he had been away? Two years and ten months was nothing. He had spent years on the force; picking up the threads of this investigation would not be difficult.

He doesn't want me around at all, I'll bet. He's afraid I might get somewhere when he hasn't.

Stuart, perhaps also attempting to avoid confrontation, moderated his tone as well, saying, "Bill, I understand where you're coming from, and I sympathize, but I can assure you we're still active on the case. We haven't let it go over the side, although, as I told you, leads are thin on the ground just now."

In the pause that followed, Foy tried to decide what his next move ought to be and was about to speak when Stuart forestalled him.

"How's this for a compromise? I'll undertake to give you regular updates. You know, sort of progress reports. Any time we get anything to go on, I'll make sure you know about it, and what we're doing. How does that

174

sound? I probably should have been doing that all along, anyway," he added, in an apologetic tone.

It's a bit lame, Foy thought. He still wants to sideline me, leave me as a spectator without any involvement.

He decided to take a firmer stand, although he knew it would put paid to any idea of peaceful coexistence. He hesitated for a moment, but the thought of Terry's killer walking the streets and living his life with impunity impelled him to take the step. It was time for Plan B.

He said, "Look Harry, perhaps I should have a word with Ollie Drake."

The anticipated explosion came immediately. Stuart's face reddened with anger, and his eyes blazed.

"Now how did I know you were going to say that?" he snapped, his accent becoming its thickest as it always did when he lost his temper. "Just you listen to me, Bill. Don't you go blabbing to Drake, or anyone else, d'you hear me? Don't you dare go off pulling strings and having quiet words behind people's backs, especially mine. You were famous for that sort of little trick, and it made you damned unpopular with a lot of people."

Certainly, unpopular with you, Foy thought.

"I want this case solved, Harry," said Foy, getting to his feet. "I want a result, and if you won't let me help, I'll have to talk to someone who might be more receptive. I'm sorry. I was hoping this would be easier."

Stuart stood up as well, his face like thunder, and shouted at Foy as he turned to go.

"Bill, don't you dare do it. You come back here...*now*!"

Foy strode out of the office, leaving the door open behind him.

* * *

Upon seeking an appointment with Deputy Assistant Commissioner Oliver Drake, known as Ducky Drake when

175

he was not in the room, Foy learned he was away for the rest of the week at a law enforcement conference in Los Angeles, and his personal assistant had been instructed not to put anything into his calendar for the two days following his return. The next three days were already fairly full, so, "Would next Friday afternoon do?" the assistant inquired. Fuming at the delay, Foy had no choice, and arrived at Drake's office punctually at four o'clock on the appointed day. He found the deputy assistant commissioner looking pale, haggard, and decidedly the worse for wear.

"It's the bloody jet lag," he said, in answer to Foy's solicitations. "I've never been able to deal with it. I haven't slept properly since I got back. I keep waking up every hour or two. And Los Angeles is a nightmare of a place. I don't know why anyone lives there, for God's sake. Unbelievable traffic, freeways with I don't know how many lanes with none of them going where you want." He paused. "Anyway, that's enough about all that. It's good to see you, Bill. How've you been, and what's brought you here?"

Oliver Drake was nearly fifty-five, and had come up through the ranks, though few knew quite how or why. His usual view of good management was that everyone should be kept happy if at all possible, and he was not known as a man who liked making tough decisions. There had been both surprise and a good deal of consternation when his promotion was announced. Foy recalled the occasion as he glanced around Drake's large, well-appointed office, noting it to be much more imposing than the one occupied by Harry Stuart which looked very spartan by contrast.

Being as careful as he could to avoid implications of incompetence on the part of Stuart or his team — no use in getting off on the wrong foot — Foy told Drake what he wanted, and why. Drake listened without interruption, and then nodded.

"I see what you mean, Bill, but what about Detective Superintendent Stuart?"

"I want to help," Foy said, avoiding a direct answer but doing his best to sound positive. "I hope Harry will realize

176

that. I mean…well…Terry Preston was my nephew, Ollie, and it's been over a year since he was killed."

"Yes," Drake said, with a sigh. "Nasty business, the whole damn thing."

Foy sensed silence was in order, and as he watched Drake's tired face, he saw his features begin slowly to brighten.

"You know, Bill," Drake said, with what sounded very like actual enthusiasm, "your idea may be more helpful than you realize. Let's go down and see Stuart straight away and get the ball rolling. After that, I can do the paperwork on your temporary reinstatement."

"I don't want any pay for this, Ollie," Foy put in, hastily. "I'm not after money here."

"No," said Drake, "but if you're to do a proper job, you'll need a warrant card and some sort of official existence." He got to his feet and came around his desk, his hand outstretched. "Welcome back, Detective Inspector Foy."

When Drake broke the news of Foy's reinstatement to Stuart a few minutes later, the atmosphere in Stuart's office all but crackled as though electrically charged. Stuart sat behind his desk, arms folded, and his face as hard and cold as a marble statue. Drake appeared oblivious to it all, however, and forged ahead with effervescent cheerfulness.

"I'm sure you'll agree an experienced helping hand wouldn't come amiss at the moment, Harry, and who knows, Bill might just stumble onto something new. Which is not to say you and your team haven't done a splendid job up to now, of course."

Foy winced. Stop where you are, Ollie, he pleaded silently. This is not the direction to go in.

Stuart said nothing, but words would have been superfluous. Foy could feel and see his reaction. He'd gone over Stuart's head, and Stuart had warned him against it, but his determination to return to the force to work on Terry's behalf had overridden all other considerations. He just hoped Stuart would come around in time, although he was not overly sanguine about the possibility. As he looked at Stuart now, he thought he looked like Vesuvius must have looked just before it blew up and buried Pompeii.

I think he'd like to bury me, he reflected.

"In fact," Drake was rattling blithely on, clearly pleased with the proposal he was about to present, "Bill's offer of assistance is most timely. I've been trying to find a way around a little human resource shortfall we're experiencing just at the moment, so I'm bringing Bill back and making him the lead investigator on the Preston case. I —"

Bloody hell, said Foy to himself, taken completely aback. That's never been the idea. Harry's going to have a conniption.

And Harry did exactly that, making no attempt to conceal his fury.

"*Lead?*" he interrupted Drake. "With all due respect to DI Foy's experience, sir, he's only going to be a temporary addition, a sort of advisor, isn't he? I hardly think it's reasonable to give him the lead."

"Yes, of course, he's a temp," Drake said, his voice almost cajoling, "but his being here gives me an opportunity to use you, Harry, for something else. Something very important."

Suspicion closed over Stuart's face like the drawing of a curtain, and he said warily, "What might that be, sir?"

"Well, Harry," said Drake, with renewed vigor, "I want you to spearhead the new community relations program Whitehall's been on at us about. I'm sure you're aware of it. I think you're just the man to get it moving."

Foy winced again. The entire episode had gone pear-shaped. He had not expected to be handed the case at Stuart's expense, and he could see nothing but trouble on the horizon. If he told himself the truth, he had never been much looking forward to working with Stuart, but he had also to admit having the lead on the case would give him far more independence than he had dared to hope for.

He and Stuart shared one thing in common, however, and that was an intense and abiding dislike for community relations programs; both of them believing that while they were probably a necessary evil, they kept policemen away from the more important work of investigating crime and nicking villains. Stuart himself had put it very well some years ago.

"Relating to the community is all well and good, but protecting it is what we're really supposed to be doing."

"Now," Drake was continuing, "Bill will need some people with him, won't he? I'd suggest we let him have Detective Sergeant Fielding and Detective Constable Mahajan. That all right with you, is it, Harry?"

"Yes, sir," said Stuart, his voice clipped, his features rigid.

What else can the poor bugger say, Foy thought.

"Well," said Drake, standing up and rubbing his hands together like a schoolmaster congratulating his class, "this is all excellent. I'll leave you to it, shall I? Harry, pop up and see me on Monday morning, will you? We'll need a chat about this community relations business. Must keep Whitehall happy, you know. Cheerio, and once again, Bill, welcome back."

"I don't give a damn about bloody Whitehall," Stuart exploded, as soon as Drake had gone.

"I didn't know he was going to do that, Harry," Foy said, quickly. "I honestly didn't. I —"

"Shut up," Stuart growled, his expression one of undiluted rage. "Don't give me that. I'm sure you set the whole bloody thing up. You've made me look like an idiot in front of my department."

"That was never my intention, Harry," Foy said. "All I wanted was to —"

"And you can drop the *Harry* stuff, d'you hear? You've been reinstated at your previous rank of detective inspector. Well, I'm a detective superintendent, and don't you forget it. You may be lead, but you're in my department, and that makes me your governor. Got that, have you? I want regular reports on what you're doing and what you're finding out, if anything. I don't want you swanning about all on your own and talking to Ducky Drake whenever you like. I'm your superior officer, and if

179

there are reports to be made on the case to the people upstairs, I'll be the one making them, not you. You fit in exactly where you're supposed to. Is that abundantly clear? You are *not* an independent entity."

"Understood," said Foy, with a nod, anxious to show willing. Drake's move had completely altered the landscape and he knew he would have to tread carefully until he knew where he was.

Stuart leaned forward across his desk and glowered at Foy. "Understood, *sir.*"

Chapter Fifteen

On Monday of the next week Stuart introduced Foy to the department, and briefly announced his reinstatement. The introduction was perfunctory, and he spoke tersely as he explained that Foy's reappearance was due to a decision by senior officers. It was clear from their expressions that some of the detectives in the room were uncomfortable. They shuffled their feet and looked at the floor, and only acknowledged Foy with brief nods. He wondered if he could ever get them all on side but decided to concentrate on the two people who would actually be reporting to him.

Stuart assigned him a miniscule office — an unexpected bonus, cramped though it was — telling him he was lucky to have one at all. Foy proffered his thanks, to which Stuart replied, "Wasn't my idea. Ducky said I was to find you a place to hang your hat."

Not much room to hang anything else, Foy said to himself.

The technical people appeared as if from nowhere bearing phones and a computer, set it all up, gave him various and sundry account numbers and a password, before vanishing as quickly as they had come. Foy then brought in a few personal items for his desk and settled in as best he could.

All these preliminaries took the best part of the morning, so after lunch he called Fielding in. He knew Fielding and was happy to have him to work with.

"Well, Sergeant," he said, "I remember you when you were a new constable in uniform. You've come a long way, and I'm pleased to see it."

"Thank you, sir," said Fielding, a little stiffly, but Foy could understand his reticence.

He's probably thinking about the phone calls I made to him months ago, Foy thought. I don't think I was too polite to him. It'll take a bit of time for us to get used to each other, he decided, and made up his mind to do his best on that score. He also reminded himself he had to try to get along with Harry Stuart as well — not because he liked Stuart, God knows he certainly did not — but simply because it would make life easier if he and Stuart were not in a constant state of confrontation. He was not hopeful, however.

Foy requested Fielding to get him all the notes, recordings, and whatever else was in the Preston file.

"I want to review everything and get up to speed as quickly as possible."

"Let me know if I can help, sir," said Fielding.

Foy saw an opportunity to let the sergeant take the lead. "Well, perhaps there is something you can do. You've been active on the case, so at this point do you have any personal intuition or a hunch about who killed Terry Preston? I'm a great believer in following up on people's hunches. Evidence is one thing, but a competent investigator's interpretation of the overall picture can sometimes be the key to solving a case."

Fielding looked pleased to be consulted in this manner, but he had nothing to offer. He shook his head and said, "I'm afraid not, sir. I wish I had. You'll see what we've got and what we've done when you get the file, but, basically, we haven't been able to make any real progress. Leads have just dried up one at a time, not that we ever had much to go on in the first place."

Stuart said the same thing, Foy thought, and he was obviously right. Aloud, he said, "Well. I'll review the file and see if I can come up with anything."

"I'll make sure you get everything, sir," said Fielding, standing up.

Foy had one more question.

"Who is *Mahajan*, by the way? I don't recall hearing the name."

"Ah yes, sir," said Fielding. "Detective Constable Ms. Neeta Mahajan. She's rather famous around here."

"Oh? Why so?"

"You'll understand as soon as you see her, sir." Fielding grinned and went out without further explanation, leaving Foy wondering what he may have meant.

The material was duly delivered, some of it in hard copy, most on a USB stick, and Foy spent the rest of the afternoon and most of the evening absorbing everything he could. He had to agree with Stuart and Fielding that things were pretty thin.

All right, he said to himself, I have to start somewhere, so what do we know, and what don't we know?

Turning to his computer, he created a file called *Items*, and made a list. To begin with, it was clearly established that Terry Preston had been killed elsewhere before being dragged into the alley and dumped. There was no evidence to indicate where he was actually killed, but the post mortem conducted by a Dr. Alison Crane concluded he had been shot at close range with a small caliber handgun. There was no information on the time the body was left in the alley; the only reference to it came from a very unreliable local resident who thought he heard a car. Not much help, but the working assumption was it was probably the night he was murdered. Killers usually wanted to be rid of their victims as soon as they could.

Next, Michael Barrow, the last person known to have seen the victim alive, appeared clean. Terry left his flat in the early evening to go home, probably by bus. There was no evidence Barrow had seen Terry again at any time that night. Barrow left Britain early the following morning, and his presence in France was attested to by his friends who met him off the Eurostar in Paris. That information having been provided in a statement to the French police.

Staring at what he had written, Foy murmured aloud, "Come on, Terry, what happened to you that night? Where did you go? Who did you meet?"

183

He typed *Motive* and searched for references before typing *Not robbery*. The only thing stolen was Preston's mobile phone, which had gone inactive on the night of his death.

Why just the phone, Foy mused. You leave money, you leave his watch, but you swipe the phone. The killer must have known there was something on it, otherwise why take it? A text, an email, a photograph? What? So, unless the killer was a homicidal maniac who collects mobile phones, he must somehow have known what was on Terry's phone.

He was a friend of yours, wasn't he, Terry?

Foy rummaged through the piles of material on his small desk, cursing under his breath as a wad of papers slipped onto the floor with a crack like a pistol shot, and found the phone records. What was the last thing Terry did with his phone? Yes, here it was. It appeared the last use of the phone had been an email to a Donald Willard in Oxford, a professor apparently, but although there was an attachment, there was neither subject nor message. And, he recalled from the notes, Willard had told Fielding he had not received that email. Was that true? Why would he lie? Perhaps he really did not receive it, in which case it took them nowhere. On the other hand, Foy thought, Willard may be implicated. He was out of the country when Terry was killed, but that did not mean he was not somehow involved.

"Terry, Terry," he muttered under his breath, "what were you up to, lad?"

He reread Fielding's notes on his telephone interviews with Willard, and the professor had indeed asserted he did not receive anything from Preston the night of the murder, or for several weeks prior, come to that. Fielding's notes included a personal observation that he believed Willard was *totally reliable*.

As he sat there in his cramped office, bathed in the pool of light spread by the desk lamp, ruminating on what he was learning about the death of his nephew, Foy slowly became aware his eyes were very tired and he had a slight headache. He glanced at his watch and saw with a shock it was nearly nine o'clock. He rubbed his eyes and straightened his back, finding he was stiff as well.

That's enough for one day, he decided, and left the Yard, bidding a goodnight to the duty constable as he went. He stopped for a quick bite of supper in a pub around the corner from his flat in Bexleyheath, and then went home to bed.

* * *

Foy was at his desk by eight the following morning and turned his attention to the matter of Barrow's stolen car. On the face of it, there seemed to be no connection between Preston's murder and the theft of the car, but this particular theft was a little out of the ordinary, and it set him thinking. Cars were pinched in London every day and twice on Sundays, Foy said to himself, but very few of them ended up being set on fire in a field so far from the city. Vandals might steal a car and set it on fire just for the hell of it, but fire had another use, it destroyed evidence. Evidence of murder, perhaps?

But Barrow wouldn't have had time to shoot Terry, dump him in the alley, drive to Peterborough, torch his car, and then somehow get back to London in time to catch his train. Unless...unless...he wasn't acting alone.

Seeing the theft investigation was being tracked by Neeta Mahajan, and wanting to meet her in any case, he called her in, watching with considerable interest as she seated herself on one of the plastic chairs in front of his desk. He remembered what Fielding had said about her being famous and he now understood why.

My God, she's absolutely stunning.

Neeta was a slim woman in her late twenties. She had a flawless, olive complexion with an oval face and high, sculptured cheekbones. She wore a blue sweater which emphasized her perfect curves, and white slacks. Foy had to discipline himself not to stare.

After a brief exchange of greetings, during which she showed a careful reserve but a friendly smile which displayed perfect white teeth, he asked her to check on where things stood with the investigation into Barrow's stolen car.

"Will do, sir." She had large, wide-set eyes, fathomlessly dark, and lustrous ebony hair drawn back from her face and secured in a tight bun at the nape of her neck. Looking at her, Foy wondered how many ardent young hopefuls there were lining up to seek her companionship.

"How long have you been a Detective Constable, Neeta?" he asked, conversationally.

"Four years, sir, but I'm taking my sergeant's exams as soon as I can." She flashed him a dazzling smile. "Fingers crossed, eh?"

Neeta was obviously of South Asian heritage, yet her speech betrayed no vestige of it. The contrast between her appearance and her pure cockney accent startled Foy. It seemed so utterly incongruous, and yet such apparent contradictions were all around him in the Britain of the twenty-first century. He, himself, had once worked on a case with a detective inspector named Stan Mitchell, who was of Jamaican descent born and raised in the green valleys of south Wales. Foy had been charmed, if a trifle bemused, by his lilting Welsh voice. Stan had never called him Bill, only *Boy-o*.

"I'm sure you'll be fine," Foy said, coming back to Neeta's examinations, "but I hope they don't transfer you after you pass."

"So do I," she said, "but you know how things go around here."

Yes, Foy thought a little sourly, I certainly do.

Neeta stood up with a lithe and graceful movement and left Foy's office, making room for Fielding who had appeared at the door a moment earlier.

Fielding looked at Foy, then at Neeta as she turned down the corridor, before saying, with a grin, "I'm afraid she's too young for you, sir."

Foy said nothing. At least he didn't tell me I was too old for her, he thought, wryly.

The remark was rather impertinent, coming from a junior officer, but he decided to overlook it. Impertinent it may have been, but it was damned perceptive. He had been lamenting the fact that Neeta was only a young detective constable. He sighed quietly.

Ah, well...

"Anyway," Fielding added, sitting down, "she's spoken for, more's the pity. Lives with some lucky sod in Narcotics."

"What've you got?" Foy asked, relegating Neeta Mahajan to the realm of pleasant fantasy.

"Nothing yet," answered Fielding. "I just wondered if there was anything you wanted me to do."

"As it happens, there is," said Foy. "I want you to set up a time for us to go and have a little chat with the good Professor Willard in Oxford." Then, seeing Fielding's puzzled expression, he went on, "I know you interviewed him, but only by phone. I think a face-to-face talk might be useful. Your notes refer to a message Terry sent him, which he says never got to him. Could be many reasons for that, I suppose, but it's worth another look. It appears that one of the last things Preston did before he was killed was to try to contact Willard, and that makes him a potentially significant person. He also may be able to help us draw up a better picture of what sort of private life Preston had. I knew him when he was just a youngster, but we were not in touch very often as he grew older, and I know nothing of his life at Oxford."

"Will do, Guv." Fielding nodded, rose, and went out.

Neeta Mahajan re-appeared later in the afternoon to report she had been able to get the entire file on the Barrow case. It had been shelved as unsolved theft and vandalism.

"The whole thing was put to bed a month after it happened," she said, and Foy nodded; it was as he

187

expected. Just one more annoying, petty crime the police really didn't have time to investigate fully. There was nothing about it to suggest it merited special or extended investigation — it certainly didn't appear to be a terrorist act or a threat to national security — and so with everything else there was to do, it soon joined the ranks of the forgotten.

"Barrow was informed things were shutting down," Neeta was saying. "His insurance company finally paid up, and that, apparently, was that. Do you really think there might be a link to the Preston murder?"

"I don't know," he answered, exhaling a long breath, "but it's worth thinking about, in lieu of anything else at the moment."

Foy pored over the file, reading and rereading, going through every action taken, all the evidence collected — which was scanty at best — and all the interviews conducted. It did seem thin, he reflected, but the following morning, after a good night's sleep, he went at it again. By ten o'clock he had finished, and he had found something. It wasn't much, he reflected, but there was at least one concrete step to be taken.

"If someone swipes a car," he said to Neeta, "then sets fire to it after a joyride a few miles up the motorway, how does that person get back to London? One assumes the thief wouldn't want to hitchhike. So, if the thief's a Londoner, he or she must have had an accomplice, and there must have been another vehicle involved somehow."

"Good point, sir," said Neeta, "but what if they stole the car to get home? I mean, what if they live in Peterborough or thereabouts?"

"Well, okay," Foy conceded, "but nicking a car in London, driving it north, then setting it on fire in a field outside the city seems like a complicated and rather risky way to get home."

Neeta acknowledged this with a slight, but ever so elegant tilt of her glossy head, as Foy consulted his computer, saying, "There's a note here about the bloke who

188

reported the burning car. Said he and his girlfriend were out for a picnic."

"Right," said Neeta, with a suggestive smirk, "a picnic. Past midnight in the dead of winter."

"Yes, that's what I thought." Foy allowed himself a grin. "But here's the point. He said he thought he saw a blue van in the vicinity at the time, but it appears that wasn't fully followed up, or if it was, there's no record of it."

"I'll get on it, sir."

"Good. And you'd best let everyone know what we're up to as well. I don't want to tread on anyone's toes. I've got no solid reason for reopening this investigation. There's no actual evidence it's connected to the murder."

Chapter Sixteen

The day Foy and Fielding drove to Oxford was clear, sunny, and surprisingly warm for a late autumn day. Drake had placed a car at Foy's disposal, and Fielding, who obviously liked to drive, covered the distance in an hour and ten minutes, a miraculous achievement in view of the apocalyptic traffic jam they encountered almost as soon as they left the Yard. It seemed everyone in the city and surrounding counties had decided to drive to Oxford at that very time. Maintaining a smooth and constant speed wherever possible — which was very seldom — he maneuvered the car through the traffic in a seemingly effortless manner. Occasionally, he would address drivers in other vehicles, a habit Foy at first found a trifle irritating, but as time went on it struck him as rather funny.

"I've always liked to drive," said Fielding, as he guided the car expertly around a slow-moving lorry, and then, to the lorry driver, he added, in a conversational tone, "Just stay where you are, chum. Let me get by, and then you can do whatever you like."

"Did you take advanced driver training?" Foy asked, and Fielding nodded as he slowed to a halt at the end of a line of vehicles which appeared to extend into infinity. Moving off again after about five minutes, he got behind a red Toyota driven by a white-haired gentleman well into his senectitude, trying to make a right-hand turn.

"Get on with it, then, Grandad," Fielding muttered to the white-haired gentleman, before observing, "There are some people who shouldn't be on the road, sir."

Their appointment with Professor Willard was not until two o'clock, but thanks to the traffic, they arrived at half past one, starving hungry. They found a congenial-looking pub called *The Admiral Hawke*, where Foy gratefully downed a pint of his favorite Guinness, while Fielding confined himself, with a resigned scowl, to Ginger Ale. After a quick sandwich, they made their way to the venerable old building in St Aldate's, close to the even more venerable Bodleian Library, which housed Christ Church College.

"Marvelous city, this," Foy said, looking at the soaring spires and broad expanses of manicured lawn. "The whole place simply exudes history. Just think of all the great scholars and thinkers who've studied and taught here. Sir Thomas More, Erasmus, Roger Bacon, John Wycliffe. It's amazing, don't you think?"

"Yes, sir," answered Fielding, looking not at all amazed. "Pretty traditional, though. I was interested in a more modern approach."

So much for Oxford, Foy thought. "Did you go to university?"

"Exeter," Fielding replied. "Bachelor of Science in Criminology."

"Good for you. Wish I'd had the opportunity."

"It wasn't so much of a requirement in your day, was it, sir?"

"No, not really," said Foy, "and I'm not all that ancient, you know."

"Sorry, Guv," Fielding said, grinning.

Professor Sir Donald Willard, Ph.D. and God only knows what else, proved to be an elderly but energetic gentleman of over seventy, still serving as a senior member of the faculty of oriental studies, as well as a professor in the school of archeology. He was quite tall, slightly stooping, very lean, with a sandy moustache and bright, sharp, little eyes. He wore a nondescript light brown jacket with leather patches at the elbows, which Foy thought was well on the way to being shabby, but it completed the image of a man perfectly suited to his surroundings. He looked as if he belonged right where he was, in his study in

Oxford. In fact, Foy could not imagine his being anywhere else in the world.

Willard greeted the two detectives with almost Dickensian formality.

"Do come in," he said, ushering them into a large, wood-paneled room. "Can I offer you something? A cup of tea, perhaps? A scone? We have the most excellent scones."

"No, thank you, sir," said Foy, looking at the long lines of bookshelves and noting that a great many of the books had Chinese characters on their spines. The tall window in the far wall admitted pale shafts of sunshine, and the scene struck Foy as the epitome of what he imagined the Oxford academic world to be. Very formal, a trifle old-fashioned and fussy, a little musty, and rather remote. Willard seated them in deep armchairs at the end of the study opposite his enormous desk and settled himself on a sofa.

"Now, how can I help you?" he asked, in the sort of voice he probably used when talking to bewildered undergraduates.

Foy began by explaining their mission and reminding Willard of the phone call he received just over a year ago regarding the death of Terry Preston.

"Ah yes, yes," said Willard, frowning and turning down the corners of his thin mouth. "Young Preston. What a sad thing that was. He was one of my most promising doctoral students, you know. I believe it was you, Detective Sergeant, who telephoned me, wasn't it?"

A professor he might be, thought Foy, but absent-minded, he's definitely not.

"That's right, sir," said Fielding, "but now we're wondering if you can tell us anything about Terry Preston as a person. His interests? His friends?"

"His interests were China and his research," said Willard, massaging his bony jaw. "That's all I know about it, and as to other features of his life, I'm afraid I can't tell you anything." He regarded them gravely for a moment or two, then said, "I know he liked to play chess, if that helps at all."

"Was he popular with the other students?" asked Foy. "With other faculty members?"

"Indeed," said Willard, in an earnest voice, clearly keen to help. "He was a very pleasant young chap, totally committed to his research. He would have been a distinguished scholar, had he lived."

"So," said Fielding, going back to the initial question, "there's no one you could identify who bore Mr. Preston any sort of grudge or ill-will? No one with whom he had quarrels or disagreements?"

"No," said Willard. "Apart from the usual divergence of views one sometimes has with one's colleagues on scholarly matters, Terry could not be described as unduly competitive or intellectually aggressive in any sense of the word. If his colleagues disagreed with him, as I did myself sometimes, he listened, considered, and made his own decisions. And when he wished to point out a flaw or inconsistency in someone else's thinking, he did so with utmost respect."

"A model scholar, then," Foy observed.

"Yes, that does describe him, I'd say," agreed Willard, with a sad smile. "I still miss him."

"Do you know if he had a girlfriend?" asked Fielding, and Willard raised his sandy-colored eyebrows.

"Good God. I've no idea. I certainly wouldn't know anything about that sort of thing."

"So, you couldn't hazard a guess as to whether he was gay or straight?" Fielding persisted.

"No, I most certainly could not," said Willard, with some vehemence. "I suggest you take that up with his friends or his parents."

"His parents both predeceased him," said Foy. "I'm the only living relative he had. He was my nephew."

"Oh, dear me," said Willard, a look of sympathy and consternation clouding his narrow face, "I'm so sorry, Inspector."

Foy inclined his head in acknowledgement, before saying, "The few friends we've been able to identify have been interviewed. Terry seems to have been something of a loner, so we were simply wondering if you had any insights."

"None, I'm afraid," said Willard, and then, obviously anxious to change the subject, he asked, "Are you sure you wouldn't like some tea?"

"Quite sure, thank you, sir," said Foy.

"Professor Willard," said Fielding, "there's one issue which might have a direct bearing on this case, and it concerns the email Terry Preston sent you the night he was killed."

"Oh, yes," said Willard, nodding. "I remember your mentioning that when we spoke on the telephone."

"Have you, by any chance, come across that message since then?"

"No," said Willard. "I would have saved it had I received it."

"Do you still have a folder for Terry's messages?" asked Foy, hopefully. One more search might be useful, he thought.

"No," said the professor, with a shake of his head. "I eventually brought myself to delete it. It was difficult to do, you see. It seemed to be the ultimate recognition of the finality of Terry's death. The irretrievable end."

"I understand, sir," said Foy, and was about to continue, when Fielding unexpectedly broke in.

"Excuse me, sir. Sorry to interrupt, but I've just had a sort of brainwave. May I ask, Professor Willard, how often you check and clear your Junk Mail folder?"

"Oh, my goodness," said Willard, with a deprecatory laugh, "almost never, I'm afraid. I haven't time to go through all that rubbish. People telling me they want my help to invest millions of pounds, and heaven knows what else. I used to review the folder years ago, but so much trash comes in these days I tend to let it all go into Junk and then just delete the lot at some point. I haven't time to do anything else with it."

"And when was the last time you did that?" Fielding asked, and Foy, realizing what Fielding was getting at, almost held his breath in anticipation.

194

Good for Fielding. This could be our last chance, and we might have missed it.

"A long time ago," said Willard, after a short pause. "I can't really remember."

"Well, sir," Foy put in, "would you mind letting us have a look now? Sergeant Fielding is right. We know from the phone records the message had no subject or text content, only an attachment. There's a good chance your mail filters would have junked it."

Foy and Fielding looked at Willard's computer monitor as he opened his email and called up the Junk Mail folder.

Willard asked, "What date was it?"

"Just search *Preston*, sir, if I may suggest it," said Fielding. "I daresay that will be quicker. There's likely only one message…if it's there at all."

"This may be a long shot," muttered Fielding, as Willard initiated a search. There was a short pause before a single message appeared in the *Results* pane.

"That's it," said Foy, crisply.

"By Jove," said Willard. "Thank God it's still here. Just let me open the attachment." He manipulated the mouse and they all waited.

"Come along, come along," Willard chided in a schoolteacher voice. "Honestly, gentlemen, I sometimes think this system is as old as the university itself."

The three men stared at the image on the screen when it finally emerged — a yellowish, oval-shaped object, cracked and partly covered with an incised inscription.

"Goodness me," said Willard, obviously startled. "I wasn't expecting anything like this."

"What on earth is it, sir?" Fielding asked.

"It's a *jiagu*," said Willard, staring intently at the screen.

"A what?" asked Foy.

"A *jiagu*," Willard repeated. "Commonly known as an oracle bone."

"I think I've heard of those," said Foy, "but I'm not sure I know exactly what they are. I do know what an oracle is, though."

"You're probably thinking of the famous Greek one at Delphi," said Willard, smiling, "and there are similarities in that both the Delphic oracle and the Chinese oracle bones sought to answer questions, usually about the future. The *jiagu* mainly date from the late Xia and throughout the Shang Period. Roughly the late eighteenth century to the early ninth century before the common era."

"That's quite a stretch of time," Fielding observed.

"Indeed," said Willard. "Many thousands of these bones have been found in excavations of sites from that period. The customary material used was either the scapulae of oxen, or, more usually, the plastrons of turtles, which is what we see here." He gestured at the screen. "The oracle bones were a form of pyro-divination, or pyromancy, which is to say divination through heat or fire. The method was to heat a metal rod, usually bronze, and press the end of it onto the bone so that the expansion thus caused would result in a pattern of fine cracks on the surface radiating from the point of contact. You can make some of them out in the photo." He pointed, and then continued. "The priests, or shamans, who were often women, by the way, then interpreted the pattern and thereby answered the questions asked…well, hopefully, anyway."

"I see," said Foy. "But if there are so many of these things around, why would Preston send you a picture of this one? Was it just for fun, do you think, or is there something special about it?"

"Perhaps there is," said Willard, his reserved manner beginning to give way to surprising animation as he studied the screen. "You see, the thing about oracle bones that makes them so interesting and useful to us is that both the questions *and* the answers were inscribed on them, and those texts have become a primary source of information on the Xia and Shang Periods. Now…somewhere around sixteen hundred BCE, the Xia king, Jie, was defeated by the king of Shang, variously called Da Yi, Tang, or Tian

Yi, depending on your source, in a decisive battle at a place called Mingtiao. In a dreadful thunderstorm, according to tradition."

"Excuse me, sir," Fielding interjected, "I thought China had emperors, not kings."

"Ah, yes," said Willard, warming to his work, "so it did, but not until later on. You see, from about four-hundred-and-seventy-five BCE to two-hundred-and-twenty-one BCE, there was a long, but sporadic civil war known as the Warring States Period. One of those warring states was the state of Qin, and in the end, it was Qin which emerged triumphant. The ruler of Qin was the famous Qin Shihuang, the one who buried the terracotta army, which I expect you've heard of. Upon uniting the warring states into one unit, he added the syllable *di* to his name, making it Qin Shihuangdi, which means *Yellow Emperor of Qin*. The word *Qin* gave us the name *China*, and ever since the Qin Dynasty, China has had emperors. Prior to that, rulers were called *wang*, which means *king*."

"Fascinating," said Fielding, "I —"

"Could we get back to the oracle bone in the attachment, please?" Foy said, more as a statement than a question. "You said it had some sort of significance, perhaps."

"Oh yes, yes," said the professor, his excitement returning immediately. "As I was saying, the Shang king defeated the Xia at the battle of Mingtiao somewhere around sixteen hundred before the common era. There are a great many myths and legends surrounding the battle, and some scholars dispute the question of its ever having taken place, but I think, from what I can see on the bone we have here before us, the inscription actually mentions Mingtiao and asks questions about a battle. In addition, one of the legends of the time has concerned a great general supposedly named Lord Chang, who, it's said, commanded the Shang army side by side with King Da Yi himself. I think I can see a reference to him on this bone, and if I'm right, historians and archeologists will be delighted, let alone those people hunting Nazi treasure."

"I beg your pardon, sir," said Foy, startled. "What on earth have the Nazis to do with it? I thought they were only interested in the Ark of the Covenant and the Holy Grail and that sort of thing."

"You're quite right," said Willard, nodding, "they did go looking for those things, bless their little pointed heads, but they also stole works of art and antiquities for their private collections and for the great museum Hitler was going to build in Linz. As you no doubt know, the search still continues for such stolen treasures. Now, about twenty-five years ago, an archeologist and a colleague of mine named Dr. Gerhard Martins died and left his papers and books to the University of London where he'd been teaching since he fled Germany in early nineteen-thirty-six."

I hope all this is getting us somewhere useful, Foy thought, as Willard continued, "Now Martins earned his doctorate at the University of Leipzig, and in nineteen-thirty-three he went to China to assist at the excavation of Da Yi's tomb, a dig directed by a Dr. Aaron Weiskopf, a very eminent sinologist of his day, also from the University of Leipzig." Willard paused for a moment, and then, perhaps catching sight of the look on Foy's face, raised a hand and said, "It's all right, Inspector, there is a point to my little homily, and it's as follows. Aaron Weiskopf was arrested, and his house looted by the Gestapo in late nineteen-thirty-five, shortly after the promulgation of the Nuremburg Laws which deprived Jews of their rights. Martins told us that Weiskopf, alas, disappeared forever at that time, and it was his arrest and disappearance that convinced Martins he could no longer stay in Germany. Now, when Professor Martins' papers were catalogued, they discovered a notebook from the Da Yi excavation in which Martins wrote an account of Weiskopf's discovery of an oracle bone which appeared to confirm both the battle and the existence of Lord Chang. There was also a photograph of Dr. Weiskopf holding an oracle bone."

"I don't wish to sound too much like a heretic, sir," said Foy, for whom Chinese history held little fascination, "but why are those two things so important?"

"Well," answered Willard, with something like an apologetic smile, "I suppose in comparison to global warming or nuclear proliferation, they have no importance at all, but to those such as I who are attempting to understand the rise and fall of past civilizations, they are very significant. And, who knows, if we learn about the rise and fall of past civilizations, we may be better equipped to understand the here and now."

Well, I'm trying to find a murderer in the here and now, Foy said to himself, but decided not to say so just then. Willard paused in case there was further comment, and then resumed his narrative.

"Martins' notes say that once back in Leipzig, Weiskopf kept the bone on display in his office until he was dismissed from the university in the Jewish purges. From what I can see, this might well be that very oracle bone."

"And the treasure hunters?" asked Fielding.

"But don't you see, Sergeant?" Willard rejoined. "If I'm right about this oracle bone, and it *is* the one Weiskopf found and kept, it means at least one stolen piece came to England at some point, and if one, why not others as well?"

"But it sounds as if you're not quite sure it is the one," said Fielding, and Willard shook his head.

"No, I'm not. You see, Weiskopf never published a syllable about the find in any scholarly journal in Germany or anywhere else. Perhaps he couldn't by that time, who knows, but what that means is that we don't have his original translation of the inscription, nor any record of what the bone looked like. Dimensions, and all that sort of thing. Now, in Professor Martins' papers, the archivist in London did find a letter from Weiskopf to Martins saying he had found a publisher, but he didn't say who or where. In any event, no one knows of any such publication, so we're at a dead end."

"Are the bones relatively easy to translate, sir, if one knows modern Chinese?" Fielding inquired, and Willard shook his head again.

"No. The characters used on oracle bones aren't simply a form of ancient Chinese from which today's characters directly descend. They're unique to the bones themselves, and I'd have to see the real thing to be absolutely certain of what it says. The photo attachment we've got here isn't large or clear enough. It's a thousand pities Terry didn't write a message with the photo telling me where he saw it."

"I'll say," Fielding declared. "If we knew that, we might have a good line on who killed him."

"Dr. Willard," said Foy, sitting forward in his chair, "it occurs to me that perhaps we might learn something from the photo you were sent. I mean, there might be something distinctive in the background, or some such, that might help us determine where the object was when Terry took its picture. Would you be willing to email it to Sergeant Fielding?"

The attachment was evidence in a murder investigation, surrendering it was not optional, but it seemed to Foy that requesting it was more in keeping with the circumstances.

"Oh, by all means," said Willard, and, taking Fielding's address, had it done in a moment. Twenty seconds later, Fielding's phone played the opening four notes of Beethoven's fifth symphony to acknowledge receipt.

"I daresay that when the image is enhanced," Fielding pointed out, "the inscription will probably be much easier to read. I'll make sure you get a copy, sir."

"That would be marvelous," Willard enthused. "Thank you so much. I shall wait for it with the keenest of interest."

After a few more general questions about Willard's whereabouts for the next few weeks, and how he could best be contacted, the two detectives took their leave.

"Interesting old chap," said Fielding, driving out of Oxford. "I hope they can sharpen up those inscriptions for him. It seems really important to him."

"I'm more interested in what else might be in that image," said Foy, "if anything. It's the only solid thing we've got to work on at this point."

"Well," said Fielding, "Willard said it might have been stolen during the war, and so if we can ever find it, it should be returned to its rightful owner, probably the University of Leipzig, I suppose. But more than that, given the only thing nicked off Preston's body was his phone, it's a safe bet that image was what the killer hoped to retrieve and destroy. The bone's location was what needed to be concealed, not its historical significance, which I suspect the killer neither knew nor cared about."

"Yes, I agree, but I wish we knew exactly when Terry had seen it. We know when he sent it to Willard, but he may have actually taken the photo some other time, perhaps days before."

"I doubt it, sir. Willard was very excited when he saw it, so I would think Terry was as well. I suspect he knew the significance of the inscription and sent the photo as soon as he saw the bone. According to the time of receipt showing on Willard's computer, it was sent at least two hours after Michael Barrow says Terry left his flat."

"Right," Foy said, nodding. "Plenty of time for Terry to have seen the bone somewhere else."

"But the Nazi treasure thing is an interesting new angle, don't you think?" Fielding said.

"Could be." Foy was noncommittal. Hunting Nazi plunder was all well and good, but he was after a murderer, first and foremost.

* * *

"So," said Superintendent Stuart, morosely, "you really think this old Chinese bone thing is somehow significant, do you?"

Foy had stopped by the super's office to provide an update, but Stuart was evidently in no mood for speculation.

"It may be," Foy said, his tone carefully neutral. He had no desire to commit himself. "I don't know yet."

"I don't see how it could be," Stuart said, skepticism writ large on his face.

"I'm not sure myself," Foy admitted, "but I'm looking at everything that comes along and ruling out nothing for the time being."

"And has Mahajan got anywhere with Barrow's stolen car? That sounds like a wild goose chase to me. The thing's been well investigated already. I think you're wasting her time."

Stuart's arrogant dismissiveness infuriated Foy. He's bent on belittling everything I'm doing, he thought. He'd rather see me discredited than catch the killer. Suppressing the urge to strike back, he decided he would answer the question and ignore the rest.

He said, "Not yet, no."

"So why d'you think there's a connection between it and Preston's murder? I can't see one."

"I don't know that there is a connection," said Foy, as calmly as he could. "That's what I'm trying to establish, one way or the other."

"All right, all right," said Stuart, with an elaborate sigh. "Go on then, get on with it, and be sure you keep me fully informed."

Foy left Stuart's office, feeling the superintendent's malevolent eyes boring into his back as he went, and squeezed himself into his own cubbyhole where he reviewed the notes of Stuart's interview with Michael Barrow. He had done this several times already, but he tended to work on the principle that there was always the chance something had gone unnoticed. There could be a point missed, a question unasked, some follow-up overlooked, or a small thing which might prove significant beyond its size. He was pondering it when Neeta Mahajan tapped on the door and entered, wearing a purple dress and looking as stunning as ever.

"I tracked down the witness, sir. His name is Brian Shaw, and he says he's pretty certain he did see a blue van leaving the vicinity of the burning car and going at a good clip."

"The file doesn't say much about that," said Foy. "What else did he say? Does he remember anything about the van? Make, model, that sort of thing?"

"He doesn't know anything like that, I'm afraid."

Foy muttered, "Damn."

"But I'll do a follow-up. He hasn't been interviewed in a long time. He might recall something now he'd not mentioned first time around."

"Good," said Foy.

Neeta went her graceful way, and Foy returned to the file on Barrow's interview. Barrow had no form, not even a parking ticket, but as he scrolled through the report, Foy came across something that needed checking, something which should have been seen before. It was exactly the sort of thing he was looking for.

"Sloppy work, Superintendent Stuart," he said, under his breath.

Part Five
Austria, Germany, and England 1945 - 2001

Chapter Seventeen

Gefreiter Peter Bretz, twenty-two years old and wearing a dirt-stained gray uniform of the *Heer*, the army of Nazi Germany, swore violently as the rear wheels of the lorry he was driving spun on the icy, snow-covered road. The vehicle slewed sideways, threatening to leave the road altogether. The gears crashed and ground together as he shifted down and fought the steering wheel to regain control.

"I said a lorry was no good to us in muck like this," he growled. "I told them we needed a half-track. We'll be lucky if we don't end up going over a cliff."

"Stop whining, Corporal," snapped thirty-year-old *Leutnant* Konrad Schumacher, who sat in the passenger seat. "Keep your mind on your work, and your mouth shut."

Schumacher brushed flecks of gray ash off the front of his trim, clean uniform, and immediately lit another cigarette.

"Just where are we going again, *Herr Leutnant*?" came the voice of *Unteroffizier* Manfred Hoven, from his place on a narrow jump seat squeezed into a cramped space behind the lorry's front seat; a space made all the more uncomfortable by the presence of a tarpaulin-covered wooden crate wedged in next to where Hoven sat perched, his knees almost under his chin. He was barely twenty, and already a sergeant, but his uniform was as creased and grimy as Bretz's. With the Thousand-Year Reich stumbling towards its chaotic and conflagrant death, the *Wehrmacht* barely had the resources to feed its men, let alone provide new uniforms for soldiers who could not afford to buy their own.

"*Althaussee*," said Schumacher, adding, as he exhaled a cloud of slate-blue smoke into the lorry's cab, "and I can tell you something else as well. These American cigarettes are a hell of a lot better than what we get from our commissariat, when we get any at all, that is. Made with dried horse manure, those, if you ask me. I have an uncle on Himmler's staff, and he sends me the American ones. They're the only decent thing about the goddamn allied invasion. Crazy name for them, though, *Lucky Strike*. What the hell's that supposed to mean?"

"I've never heard of *Althaussee*," grumbled Bretz, nursing the lorry around a sharp bend in the icy road which brought them to the side of a frozen lake, barely visible through the snow and fading light of late afternoon.

"All right," said Schumacher, consulting his map, "we're where we should be. The village is just ahead, but about halfway up that mountain in front of us."

"You mean, we're going up?" Bretz was incredulous. "In this snow, we're going *higher*?"

"Just keep going," said Schumacher, before lighting another cigarette.

The three soldiers had driven from northern Germany, escaping ahead of the advancing allied armies with barely a day to spare. Before leaving, however, Schumacher had ordered the lorry driven to a warehouse well outside Berlin used for storage by the Reich Museum where the crate now sitting next to Hoven was loaded into the cab.

"What's that?" asked Hoven. "I don't have much room now."

"You'll find out in due course," Schumacher grunted, "and in the meantime, get in and shut up."

Ordered by a senior member of *Reichsmarschall,* Hermann Goering's personal staff, to carry out their orders or face a firing squad, they drove with all speed to Nuremburg, the spiritual heart of National Socialism and the site of Adolph Hitler's most grandiose and extravagant party rallies, where they reported to an address *Leutnant* Schumacher had been told to memorize before they left Berlin. The address proved to be that of an ordinary-looking, if somewhat seedy, old beer hall on the southern outskirts of the city, but what they found there was anything but ordinary. The street was filled to capacity with lorries of every size, and there were heavily armed soldiers everywhere. After being billeted in the very draughty attic of a nearby house, Bretz and Hoven waited while Schumacher reported for orders.

"It's chaos in there," he told them when he returned six hours later. "There's paperwork everywhere, and a lot of civilians getting in everybody's way. There's an SS Major General in overall command, I think. This is top priority. Anyway, I've got a list of the stuff we're supposed to take, and once it's loaded, we'll be on our way."

"It'll be dark in less than an hour," Bretz protested.

"That's the idea," Schumacher said, pulling out a pack of cigarettes.

It was past midnight and bitterly cold when they finally left Nuremburg. Under *Leutnant* Schumacher's careful supervision, the lorry had been loaded with crates taken up from the vast network of tunnels beneath the ancient city. Many dating from medieval times, these abandoned watercourses, drains, and beer cellars were now being used for very different purposes as the allied air forces methodically and remorselessly pounded Nuremburg into shapeless heaps of rubble. While some underground caverns were serving as air raid shelters for a few lucky citizens, the rest were declared off-limits, guarded, and sealed behind bullet-proof doors installed well before the war began. For many years, those restricted, steel-reinforced tunnels had been used by high-ranking Nazis and the Berlin *Reichsmuseum* as safe storage depots for artworks, antiquities, and plundered treasure, but now, with Germany sinking to her knees, emptying them and saving their contents had become imperative.

After Nuremburg they kept off the main roads as much as possible and travelled only at night with masked headlights. They hid wherever they could in the countryside during daylight hours catching what sleep they could, until they got beyond the reach of American and British air patrols whose vengeful, swooping fighters attacked and harried anything that moved. Exhausted, they at last gained the region of southeastern Austria known as the *Salzkammergut*, a rich landscape of rugged mountains, shimmering crystal lakes, and small, centuries-old farming villages.

It was not, however, for what could be seen that the Nazi leadership valued the *Salzkammergut*, but for what could not. For many hundreds of years, the region had been a treasure-store of salt — vast deposits of it — left by the evaporation of primeval oceans untold eons ago. These thick salt beds were ultimately buried by the ceaseless action of erosion and deposition, only to be thrust upwards when the mountains of the *Salzkammergut* were born amid colossal tectonic convulsions as the earth's crust fashioned itself anew.

An indispensable commodity for the preservation of food, salt mined from deep within the bowels of those mountains became a lucrative economic mainstay of the Hapsburg Empire throughout the many centuries of its hegemony in Europe. But since the 1930s the mines, by then long-disused, had become equally essential to Nazi Germany; not for what could be taken out of them this time, but for what could be put in.

"When we get to *Altaussee*, or whatever it's called," Bretz said, peering intently into the rapidly gathering darkness as he guided the lorry ever upwards, "what are we supposed to do there?"

"What do you think we're supposed to do?" asked Hoven, sarcastically. "We unload the stuff in the back, then get the hell out of here. Correct, *Herr Leutnant*? Why else have we dragged it all the way from Germany to the arse-end of Austria?"

Ignoring their comments Schumacher blew out another billowing pall of smoke from his Lucky Strike and said, "There's the village up ahead, I think. When we get there, look for a large house flying the German flag."

A few minutes later, Bretz halted the lorry outside an edifice set against the side of a hill with a flight of wooden steps leading up to the front entrance. Built in the Austrian style, the house was square with a steeply pitched roof, its brown wood siding accentuated by white window trim. Picking his way up the snow-covered steps, Schumacher pounded on the door with his fist. As the other two soldiers watched from the lorry, the door was opened by a small man wearing a dark suit and waistcoat. Taking a long, ornately carved Tyrolean pipe from his mouth, he exchanged a few words with Schumacher, nodded, and closed the door. As Schumacher climbed back into the lorry, the man reappeared wearing a long overcoat and fur hat, still with his pipe clenched in his teeth. Descending the steps, he made his way along a narrow pathway dug out of the deep snow to a black Daimler parked under a wooden shelter at the side of the road.

"He won't get far in that," snorted Hoven, and then shut his mouth on a curt order from Schumacher.

"Follow him," said Schumacher, pointing.

"I will if I can see him, *Herr Leutnant*," muttered Bretz.

Schumacher barked, "Just do it, Corporal. That's an order."

"*Jawohl, Herr Leutnant*," Bretz answered crisply, the word *order* having had the desired effect.

For twelve tense minutes Bretz followed the black car still further up the mountain through the steadily increasing wind-driven snowfall, the lorry's wheels frequently spinning and sliding. All too aware of the danger of going off the road and down into God-knew-what below them, even Schumacher was silent. He sat next to Bretz, lighting each new cigarette with the butt of the old one, and holding his peace. The only words spoken came quietly from Hoven who held onto the back of Schumacher's seat with a white-knuckled grip as Bretz wrestled the steering wheel to control a sickening slide which brought them perilously close to the abyss on their right-hand side.

"Dear Jesus." It was a reverential request for salvation, not blasphemy.

Bretz breathed an audible sigh of relief when at last the black car, which appeared to have had no difficulty, drew up in front of a building solidly constructed of thick concrete with a flat roof, deeply domed with snow. The wall facing them was windowless, the only opening being a long horizontal machine-gun slit which gave the appearance of a malevolent grin. A gate in the form of a single wooden pole painted alternately red and white barred further progress, but it swung upwards to allow them through; the guard in his heavy overcoat presumably recognizing the driver of the lead vehicle.

The road wound up a gentle hill for some fifty meters more, and the two vehicles then drew up at another concrete blockhouse similar to the first but much larger, guarded by a squad of heavily armed soldiers of the *Heer*. Illuminated by the yellow glare of lights mounted atop tall concrete columns, four men stood before what appeared to be a heavily plated steel door set directly into the rock face which rose into the snow-filled darkness above. They came smartly to attention as soon as the driver of the car emerged and beckoned to the lorry.

"All right, you two," snapped Schumacher, "listen carefully. The crate we brought from Berlin in the back here, the one labelled *Antiquitäten*, stays right where it is. It's not to be unloaded with the other stuff from the back. Is that absolutely clear? Just leave it alone. Don't talk about it to anyone, don't mention it at all. I have special orders for it, and that's all you need to know."

"What's —" Bretz began, as he opened the door of the cab, but Schumacher turned on him, angry-faced.

"Shut up, and do as you're ordered, unless you want a boot up your backside."

Bretz paused a moment, shrugged, and got down as Schumacher did the same. Then Hoven, with a good deal of cursing, wriggled his way into the front seat before joining the other two outside in the snow.

"It's damn cramped in there."

"Well, here's your chance to work off the stiffness, Sergeant," said Schumacher, clapping Hoven on the shoulder with mock joviality.

Bretz flung aside the heavy canvas flaps at the rear of the lorry, and the lights revealed the interior to be filled to the roof with wooden crates of all sizes, none of them more than half a meter deep.

The small man with the curly pipe hurried up. He was about fifty, with a narrow, sharp face and thinning, gray hair.

"Come along now," he said, in an officious tone of voice. "We must have these crates inside as soon as possible. This cold and damp is dangerous for the paintings. I greatly wish better care could be taken when transporting them, but I suppose it's the best we can do at the moment."

"Paintings?" echoed Bretz, eyebrows raised. "We did all this for a load of paintings?"

"Of course, paintings," said the small man with the weasel face, impatiently pulling the pipe from his mouth. "What did you think they were, you imbecile, grand pianos?"

Sticking the pipe back into his mouth, he hurried away, shouting to the guards to unlock the door, and as he went, Schumacher said, "His name is *Herr* Karl Zieber. He used to be a restorer of old paintings. He was more-or-less a nobody until he joined the Party. Then, in nineteen-forty-three, the Führer ordered this salt mine converted into a storage depot for works of art Germany wanted to save for future display. The Führer placed Zieber in charge of everything, and now he thinks he runs the Reich...pompous little clown."

"And who decides what paintings to keep?" asked Bretz, handing down a large crate to Hoven and one of the soldiers who had come to help.

"I couldn't tell you," said Schumacher, "but somebody does, somewhere. Maybe Zieber himself, who knows? I was in Paris in the summer of forty-two when they burned a whole pile of paintings someone decided not to keep."

"What were they?" grunted Hoven, passing a heavy crate to another soldier.

"God knows," Schumacher snorted. "Idiotic stuff. You couldn't tell what the hell they were supposed to be. People with square faces, and everything in crazy colors."

"No wonder no one wanted them," said Bretz from the depths of the lorry.

"Just keep moving," said Schumacher, his communicative mood evidently evaporating. "They've unlocked the door and *Herr* Zieber wants this stuff inside. He's got Party connections at the highest level and upsetting him could get us all a free ticket to the Russian front, so get going."

With the aid of more soldiers, the wooden crates were carried into the mine and then sent down a lift into the heart of the mountain which, according to Zieber, was called the Teinberg. When the lift doors opened, the men found themselves in an enormous cavern carved out of the native salt. Electric lights with broad metal shades were strung down the middle of the roof, illuminating endless stacks of crates, boxes, and trunks of all sizes. It was a vast underground warehouse, its floor, roof, and walls of ancient salt from an immemorial sea. Here and there large pillars of salt, irreverently referred to as *Lot's wives*, had been left by the miners as supports for the roof.

"I thought Lot had only one wife," said Bretz, chuckling, as they began to unload the lift, but a sharp rebuke from Schumacher stifled any response.

"Don't upset *Herr* Zieber," he hissed. He wanted to get this job done as soon as he could and get away from this

211

place with the crate left hidden in the lorry. He had no interest in anything else.

"Good God," said Hoven, looking around him for a brief moment. "There must be hundreds of things down here."

"Thousands, actually," said Zieber, with expansive pride. "Tens of thousands. This place is huge, and more than seven hundred years old. I explored it myself several years ago, before the war began, when it was nothing more than a derelict old mine. Do you know there's a painting down here that's been in the miners' chapel for three hundred years, and it looks as if it was finished only yesterday? Think of that. I told the Führer about it immediately, and he was very happy. He congratulated me and shook my hand. Yes, the Führer actually shook my hand. We've been storing art treasures here ever since then." Zieber paused, and then, raising his eyes as though to heaven, he said, "I have the Führer's complete trust."

"Why store paintings in a place like this?" Bretz asked, handing one of the smaller crates off to Hoven.

"Safe from air raids, of course," Hoven said.

"That's not the reason at all," said Zieber, impatiently. "It's because of the salt."

Bretz and Hoven looked at him blankly, while Schumacher, seemingly uninterested, put a cigarette between his lips and fished a box of matches out of his pocket.

"*Stop!*" shouted Zieber. "Don't you *dare* light that cigarette."

"Why not?" asked Schumacher, clearly irritated at receiving so peremptory an order from a civilian, even an important one.

"Do you want to start a fire?" snapped Zieber. "Are you completely ignorant? Put that cigarette away immediately. These masterpieces are beyond price. Smoking is strictly forbidden down here. Didn't you go to school? Can't you read the signs?"

Schumacher had not even noticed the signs, and he was feeling the need for nicotine. Not only did he resent

Zieber's attitude and tone, he was angry at being so openly criticized and insulted in front of his two subordinates. Grudgingly, he remembered his own advice about not upsetting *Herr* Zieber, and abandoned his cigarette. He snapped an order to Bretz and Hoven to hurry up. He was now even more impatient to see the last of this place and the bumptious *Herr* Zieber.

Stay calm, he told himself. Just stay calm. You're going to be a lot richer than that little rat when all this is over. What's one lousy cigarette compared to that?

"*Herr* Zieber," said Hoven, seeing the fury in Schumacher's eyes, "what were you about to say about the salt?"

Zieber turned to him. "What?"

"We were asking why the paintings are stored here."

"Ah, yes," said Zieber, his weasel-like features brightening a little. "The conditions we have here are unique, ideal for the preservation of paintings, because the air is absolutely dry. Totally desiccated. All the moisture, every scrap, has been absorbed by the salt. There is no mold, no mildew. Nothing. No rats, no mice, no ants, no worms. I told the Führer about it, and he shook my hand. Did I tell you that?"

"That was a great honor," said Hoven, in a sarcastic tone Zieber missed entirely.

"It was indeed," said Zieber, swelling with pride once again.

"What will happen to them all?" Bretz asked, carrying one of the last crates out of the lift and setting it down where Zieber indicated.

"Be careful," he snapped. "That's an Amstel."

"A what?"

"Not a *what*, you troglodyte," said Zieber, with exaggerated patience, "a *who*. Can't you read the label? Jan van Amstel was an early sixteenth century Flemish Master. A leading figure of the renaissance in northern Europe. Didn't they teach you anything in school? That painting is one of Amstel's finest, and was a gift to Germany from a prominent family in Warsaw."

"You were about to tell us what will happen to the paintings, *Herr* Zieber," Hoven intervened, saving Bretz from further castigation for his apparently limitless ignorance of fine art.

"Yes," said Zieber, in the tone of voice a child might use when about to reveal a secret. "Adolph Hitler intends to show the world the Third Reich is a nation of high culture, a place where great art is valued and appreciated by all citizens."

"How is that to be done?" asked Bretz, as he and three other soldiers carefully set down the last crate, a large, heavy wooden box labelled simply *Miscellaneous Seventeenth Century Italy, Netherlands.*

"What number's that one?" asked Zieber.

"Forty-three."

Zieber consulted his list, checked off the number, then continued his story.

"Have you ever heard of something called the *Special Operation Linz*?"

Bretz and Hoven shook their heads.

"Well," said Zieber, in his I've-got-a-secret voice, "it's a stupendous idea. There's to be a great museum and art gallery built in the city of Linz, the Führer's birthplace. There will also be opera houses, theatres, and even a huge cinema. It has been planned since long before the war, and Albert Speer, the Reich's greatest architect, is working closely with the Führer to design its buildings and grounds. It will be grand and glorious, the finest center of its kind in the world, containing the greatest art treasures known to man. What we are doing here is carrying forward the special operation by collecting items which, after proper adjudication, may be selected for display. People from throughout Greater Germany and far beyond, will come and marvel at its magnificence. When they see it, they will come to understand the grandeur of the Fatherland."

"But we already have many museums and opera houses," said Hoven, straightening his back after moving a small crate to where Zieber pointed with his pencil.

214

"But none like these will be," said Zieber, after checking his list again. "You see, Germany is far more than a mere country, Germany is a civilization, and this museum complex will show that to the world. It is to open in nineteen-fifty, and," he added, in a smugly supercilious tone, "I am to be its Director-General, reporting to no one but the Führer."

"Nineteen-fifty?" Hoven echoed.

"Yes," Zieber snapped. "Nineteen-fifty, when we have crushed the Slavs, the Zionists, the Allies, and everyone else who's trying to destroy the Third Reich."

The steel lift continued its up and down activity and was unloaded under Zieber's vigilant eye. Each case, box, and crate, was checked off on his list until Bretz came down with a final load.

"That's all of it, *Herr* Zieber. The shipment is unloaded."

Zieber looked at his list, frowning, and muttering numbers under his breath.

"No," he said, at length, in a decisive voice. "There's one more. Number eighty-six. It hasn't been brought down. It's listed as *Antiquities*. The paintings all came from the Nuremburg storage depot, but number eighty-six is listed as coming directly from the Reich Museum. Do you men know anything about that?"

Schumacher gazed impassively as Hoven and Bretz shook their heads.

"This is everything, *Herr* Zieber," Bretz repeated, lamely. It was not convincing.

My God, thought Schumacher, in a sudden panic, I've got to take over. I can't rely on those two idiots.

He said to Zieber, "Let me go up and have a look." His unusual animation and apparently cooperative manner made Zieber stare in surprise. Since being ordered not to smoke, the lieutenant had stood in morose silence.

Without waiting for an answer, he entered the lift, and pulled the metal gate shut. He shot Bretz and Hoven a narrow, meaningful glance as the lift began to move. Zieber looked up from his list in time to see Schumacher's shiny leather boots disappearing upwards out of sight.

As they waited, the only sound came from Zieber, who read and re-read his list, muttering, "Yes, there's definitely one missing. Definitely."

The lift at last returned Schumacher, boots first this time, to the underground storage gallery. He pulled back the folding gate and emerged, shaking his head, and looking the very image of mystification.

"I'm very sorry, *Herr* Zieber, but *Gefreiter* Bretz is quite correct. The lorry is empty. Everything we brought has been unloaded. There must be some sort of clerical error. We were never given anything from the Reich Museum."

He did not choose to add that he had arrived at ground level just in time to distract a young private about to investigate the lorry's cab.

"Just a final check, *Herr Leutnant*," the man had said, coming smartly to attention and saluting.

"Never mind, *Gemeiner*," snapped Schumacher, "*Herr* Zieber has ordered me to do that, so I'll take responsibility. Get back to your post."

"Yes, *Herr Leutnant*." The soldier, looking a trifle crestfallen, saluted again, and turned away, while Schumacher sighed quietly in vast relief. He didn't give a damn about the paintings, but he wanted what was in that last crate, and that inquisitive private could have wrecked the entire plan.

He went through the motions of examining the lorry, looking into the cab, then into the back, before smoking a hurried cigarette to settle his nerves and re-entering the mine.

"I don't understand it," said Zieber, making a peevish, clicking noise with his tongue. "This has never happened before. I'm responsible for all the items listed. If something is missing, I must be able to explain it to Headquarters. What will they think of me now? There were several ancient artifacts in it, ceramics as well, according to the inventory. They are very valuable. It's my duty to report that it didn't arrive. There will have to be an investigation."

I need to deflect this, thought Schumacher. I signed for that crate in Berlin, and the receipt was filed. The war's going to be over very soon, but I don't want this old goat making trouble for me before it does.

"*Mein Herr*," said Schumacher, in a tone of earnest reassurance, "this is not your fault at all. The situation in the north is utterly chaotic. None of us here doubts Germany will ultimately triumph, but at this precise moment we're fighting for our very lives. Berlin and Nuremburg are both nothing more than piles of bricks. I'm afraid a single crate of artworks is a small matter."

"Not to me, *Herr Leutnant*," said Zieber, stone-faced, as he stood, list and pencil in hand, amongst the piles of crates and boxes. "Not to me. There is no excuse for carelessness, no matter the circumstances. Laxity can never be tolerated."

"*Leutnant* Schumacher is quite right, *Herr* Zieber," said Hoven, in an attempt to mollify the agitated Director. "The fighting is monumental. Mistakes are regrettable, but at this time, understandable."

Good for you, thought Schumacher. Maybe you're not such an idiot after all.

"*Ach!*" was Zieber's only retort.

"I've an idea," said Schumacher, apparently eager to help. "You said the crate was labelled *Antiquities*, whereas everything in our consignment was labelled *Paintings*. Nothing was more than a few centuries old, I believe. I have a suspicion the missing box was actually part of a completely different shipment, bound for some other storage depot. Somewhere they're keeping much older items. I'd be willing to bet it was never meant to be here at all. Some clerk in Berlin or Nuremburg or God-knows-where just didn't know the difference and probably didn't care."

Zieber considered this possibility, a frown sharpening his features even further, clearly still most unhappy. Eventually, however, he sighed loudly, reluctantly drew a line through number eighty-six, and wrote *Missing* beside it.

He said, "I daresay you're right, *Herr Leutnant*. Somebody probably did just make a stupid mistake in all this temporary upheaval. It's unacceptable, all the same, and I don't like it."

"Of course, it is," said Schumacher, firmly. "It's reprehensible."

After riding the lift to the surface and exchanging formal thanks and farewells with Zieber, Schumacher, Bretz, and Hoven emerged from the mine tunnel to find the air still and deathly cold. The sky was clear, save for some ragged clouds hanging close to the mountain-tops away to the south. The snow-mantled world around them was rendered a pale silver-blue by a full moon, and the surrounding peaks of the *Salzkammergut* rose into the deep purple of the night sky like shining, silent sentinels.

"Thank God it's stopped snowing," said Bretz, getting behind the lorry's wheel. "I wasn't looking forward to going back down that hill in the snow."

Schumacher reflected that for his purposes, falling snow was preferable, but not actually vital. It will work either way, he said to himself as he climbed in beside Bretz.

"Pardon me, *Herr Leutnant*," said Hoven, contorting himself with a grunt into his cramped place behind the front seat, "but what are we supposed to do with that crate you hid?"

"Do we take it somewhere else?" asked Bretz, steering the lorry onto the snow-covered, narrow road down the mountainside towards the village, "or are you keeping it, like the others we stored in the barracks for you?"

"I'll let you know," answered Schumacher, his mouth a thin line. "Damn, no more cigarettes." He patted his pockets and snorted in disgust.

Without taking his eyes off the road, Bretz rummaged in a pocket of his crumpled uniform and tossed Schumacher a somewhat squashed half-empty pack.

"Here, these are French. See if you like them, *Herr Leutnant*."

"I had a French whore in Paris once," said Schumacher, leering, "I liked her."

The lorry, restricted to its lowest gears, ground slowly downwards, Bretz ignoring Schumacher's periodic demands he speed up.

"I'm doing my best, *Herr Leutnant*," he muttered at one point as he negotiated a sharp bend.

"All right, all right," snapped Schumacher. "Just get on with it."

As he smoked cigarette after cigarette, Schumacher scanned the road ahead, grateful for the moonlight after all. They had passed a particular place on their way up; a perfect place for his purpose.

Where the hell is it? Ah...there. Good.

"See that spot up ahead, *Gefreiter*? There's room to pull off the road. Stop there."

"Sir?"

"You heard me. I said pull over."

Bretz, frowning, steered the lorry off the road, pumping the brakes to avoid a skid, and nursed it to a stop.

"All right," said Schumacher, "leave the engine running and get out. You, too, Hoven."

As the two bewildered soldiers stood in the snow, Schumacher came around the front of the lorry, drawing his Luger. Without a word, he levelled the weapon at Bretz and fired, the bullet taking him squarely in the chest and killing him instantly. With an incredulous shout of *Jesus Christ*, Hoven dived for cover behind the lorry, slipping and stumbling as he went. His curse was cut short as Schumacher's second shot found its mark and he fell, striking his head on the edge of the lorry's rear bumper.

Schumacher, satisfying himself the two men were dead, dragged them to the opposite side of the road and rolled them into a gully well out of sight of any passing vehicle.

Okay, he thought, looking around. With any luck it'll snow again soon, and they won't be found until spring, if then, and no one will give a damn by that time anyway. Germany will be done for, *kaput*, but not Konrad Schumacher, oh no. He's looking after himself, by God. Anyone who doesn't take advantage of this war is a fool, and I'm no fool.

* * *

Sergeant Hoven opened his eyes and looked cautiously around in the moonlight before slowly sitting up. He was alone, he was freezing cold, and his head hurt like hell. He found himself in a snow-filled gully below the level of the road, and the weight he felt on his legs was the dead body of Corporal Bretz, whose eyes stared up at the night sky, as cold and sightless as pieces of glass. Hoven tried to push the corpse off, but as soon as he moved his left arm, a paralyzing pain ran down from his shoulder to his wrist like a river of liquid fire, and he yelled aloud at the unexpected shock. Gingerly, he felt his shoulder and found his uniform sticky with blood, much of it beginning to congeal and freeze. Gritting his teeth, he explored the wound and concluded there were no bones broken. Using only his right arm for leverage, he wriggled out from under Bretz's body and staggered to his feet. He had no idea how long he had been unconscious, and his brain felt as thick as porridge as he tried to understand why he was there and how he had come to be wounded. He shook his head in an attempt to clear his thoughts, but that exercise only intensified the thunderous pain. He squeezed his eyes shut, but it made no difference. He had no choice but to stand still for a minute or two until the throbbing eased a trifle. He dug back into his reeling memory as best he could.

Were we attacked? What the hell happened? We were in the lorry, and the Leutnant *told Bretz to pull over. We got out...and then...No, we weren't attacked. It was Schumacher! He shot us both. Bretz is dead, and he must have thought I was, too.*

"I'll kill that bastard," he muttered aloud. "I'll kill him, by Christ, I will."

The snow was deep, and it made the climb out of the gully difficult. Hoven slipped and stumbled several times, pain racking his left arm and shoulder. In spite of the bitter cold, he was sweating profusely, and the pounding in his head made him feel sick. The white world swam before his eyes as he fought his way up the slope, gritting his teeth against pain and exhaustion. Nearing the top at last, his breath rasping in his throat, he felt he was about to lose consciousness. His legs seemed unable to support him a moment longer.

No. Not far now. You can do it. If you don't make it to the road, you'll die out here, and that's just what Schumacher wanted. Keep moving.

And then he was there, staggering onto the side of the road, gasping from weakness and utter exhaustion. The moonlit snow offered some pale light, but he could see no one anywhere. Then, as he stood swaying and fighting to catch his breath, he became dimly aware of a sound which grew slowly louder. He saw two narrow shafts of light appear around the bend in the road to his right. A car. Someone was coming.

Some remote part of Hoven's swirling brain, numbed though it was by pain and cold, told him to get into the road and wave the vehicle down. Staggering forward, he put his foot squarely on a patch of ice and fell onto his left side, his full weight landing on his wounded shoulder. With a yell of agony, he passed out.

Chapter Eighteen

Now it was June of 1945. The war was over in Europe, and the Thousand-Year Reich had been laid waste, smashed and devastated, after a mere twelve years. Adolph Hitler, the twisted megalomaniac who had sowed the wind and then reaped the whirlwind, died in his *Führerbunker* in Berlin by his own hand, as did several of his blood-witted henchmen throughout Germany. Red Army divisions, seeking a terrible revenge for the atrocities visited on the Russian people, rampaged across the eastern half of Germany, pillaging, raping, killing whom they wished, wherever and whenever they wished. The Western Allies, led by the United State and Great Britain, were somewhat more restrained in their conquest, but many evil deeds were nevertheless done. Germany lay prostrate before her vanquishers, her cities razed to the ground, her armed forces, once the scourge of Europe, brought down. The German people waited for their conquerors to decide their fate. There was little else they can do as the Allies divided up their country.

In the chill of an early June evening in that time of waiting, a mother and her daughter sat in the cellar of their bombed-out house in Munich. They huddled together by a small fire over which they were boiling two small potatoes in water salvaged from the radiator of an abandoned car. The mother was about forty with fair hair, now long and unkempt, an oval face and pale gray eyes. Her daughter, seventeen, had her mother's oval face and fair hair, but her eyes were a penetrating green. Both were thin, their faces gaunt and haggard. Starvation and fear had made them both older than their years.

The girl spiked a potato out of the steaming water with a fork, examined it critically, and said, "All right, I think they're edible, but God knows how they'll taste."

"That water smells vile," said her mother, wrinkling her nose. "I hate to think what's in it."

"Don't worry, *Mutti*," said the girl, "the boiling will have killed the bugs."

"It's the oil and grease I'm talking about," her mother retorted.

"We've eaten a lot worse," said the girl, grimly, "and we're lucky I was able to steal these two potatoes in the first place."

They ate the meager meal slowly and in silence. They had been living in the cellar since the end of April when one of the last daylight air raids of the war delivered a five-hundred-pound high explosive bomb into the back garden of the house across the road, obliterating it and killing everyone inside. The blast devastated the houses close by, and the mother and daughter, forced to stay in the house because the bomb shelter was full, were dug out of the wreckage of their home by neighbors who had survived.

"I've got you, *Frau* Schumacher," a man said, as Hilda felt herself being pulled gently but firmly out of the rubble, a splintered piece of wood lacerating her leg as she came, causing her to scream in pain.

"Where's Ellen?" Hilda shouted, coughing the plaster and brick dust out of her throat, oblivious to the blood running down her leg.

"Your daughter is safe," said the man. "She isn't hurt...just a scratch or two, thank God."

There was nowhere for them to go, no shelter or sustenance to be had; local government was virtually non-existent. Munich's venerable old city hall, the *Rathaus*, was a heap of rubble, but most of the officials had fled in any case. They had been clever enough to realize they could not hope to pretend to know nothing about the huge concentration camp near Munich on the outskirts of the village of Dachau, and so they had taken what plunder they could carry and simply vanished. The populace was therefore left to its own devices, and so, with the help of neighbors, a small portion of the cellar of the Schumacher house was cleared out and made roughly habitable through the addition of a makeshift corrugated iron roof. With donated clothes, a few blankets, and other necessities, along with what could be salvaged from the ruins of the house, Hilda and her daughter eked out a precarious existence.

"Hitler said no bombs would ever fall on Germany," said Hilda, swallowing the last morsel of potato and leaning back in a tattered and creaking armchair which had graced the family's sitting room in happier times. She sighed and shook her head with an expression on her face of bewildered disbelief. "There was a time, you know," she went on, looking at her daughter, yet not seeing her, "when I thought Adolph Hitler was our savior. I thought he would restore Germany's greatness, her pride in herself." She paused for a moment, and then focused her gaze directly on Ellen. "And now look at us."

"Hitler took everything from us," said Ellen, almost in a whisper, pulling a threadbare blanket around her thin shoulders, "including Papa. How could that soldier have just shot him like that? It still terrifies me."

Images of that fearful night were never far from Hilda's mind, but her daughter's words conjured them up yet again. Her memory took her on a caliginous journey back to a day in late February when she, Ellen, and her husband were sitting at home together in peaceful silence. Ellen reading, Hilda sewing the torn sleeve of a blouse — there were no new clothes to be had — and Konrad smoking contentedly in his customary easy chair by the fire. There had been no air raid that day, and one was not expected that night. It was said the full ferocity of the Allied air forces was turned on Berlin, Frankfurt, and the industrial cities of the Ruhr, so the Schumacher family was spending a congenial evening at home, instead of a cramped and frightening one in a bomb shelter. Konrad had somehow managed to obtain a month's leave — an almost unheard-of privilege with the war going as badly as it was

224

— which offered a precious respite from worry for his wife and daughter. Hilda remembered being puzzled that he never wore his uniform when he went out. He had been proud to wear it when he became a lieutenant, and all the more so after receiving his Iron Cross, but he shrugged off her questions.

"I'm on leave. I want a break from the army for a while."

When Schumacher came home to a rapturous welcome, he brought several boxes and crates with him which he hid in the cellar, flatly refusing to divulge what they contained.

"The war can't last much longer," he said, "and we'll need these when Germany has been defeated, as I'm afraid she will be all too soon. Then I'll show you, but for now it's best you don't know anything about them."

"All right," said Hilda, with an amused smile. "I'll let you keep your little secret."

The evening's familial serenity was abruptly disturbed by a knock on the front door, making Hilda start and look up from her sewing.

"Who on earth can that be at this time of night? It's nearly ten o'clock."

"I'll go," said Ellen, jumping up.

"If it's someone for me," called Konrad as she left the room, "tell then I'm not in." And to Hilda, he added, "I just want to be left alone."

Hilda heard a man's voice as Ellen opened the front door, and at that instant, Konrad leapt from his chair.

"Jesus, it can't be. He was dead. I saw him."

Before Hilda could even speak, a man burst into the room, his left arm in a sling of stained white cloth and a semi-automatic pistol in his right hand. His shabby, faded uniform was torn in several places, and he stared at Konrad with a malicious scowl. He was dirty and unshaven, but triumph and hatred glowed in his eyes. Hilda screamed in terror at the mere sight of him, as her husband lunged towards a cabinet on his right where he had stored his luger.

225

"Stay where you are," the intruder snarled, raising his pistol.

"Konrad," said Hilda, finding her voice, "who is this?"

"He's my Sergeant, Manfred Hoven."

"The man you thought you'd killed." Hoven levelled his pistol. "And now I'm going to kill you, *Herr Leutnant* Schumacher."

"Now look, Sergeant," Schumacher stammered, "I...I can make all this up to you. Just give me a chance to explain. You remember all those crates I collected, don't you? Well, in the cellar here, there's —"

"Shut up," Hoven shouted, and then called over his shoulder, "You, in the hall, get in here, *now*."

Ellen, white-faced and trembling, edged into the sitting room, never once taking her eyes off Hoven as he stood with his gun pointing at her father.

"Ellen, come here," said Hilda, and she went to take her mother's outstretched hand just as the clock on the mantel chimed ten, its mellifluous, gong-like tones drifting gently into the room, as though attempting to soothe the harsh atmosphere.

"Don't worry, *Frau* Schumacher," Hoven said, still staring at her husband. "It's not you I've come for. It's your miserable, murdering husband."

"In the cellar here —" Schumacher tried again but got no further.

"You killed Peter, you bastard," growled Hoven. "My cousin. He was supposed to get married next month, settling down once the war's over, and you killed him. Shot him down like a dog, and you thought you'd killed me, too, didn't you?"

"I didn't know he was your cousin," said Schumacher. "I swear I didn't."

"If old man Zieber hadn't come along, I'd have died as well, just like you wanted."

"How did you find me?" Schumacher asked, unbelieving, and Hilda remembered wondering why the hell that mattered. He was here, wasn't he?

"Easy," sneered Hoven. "Zieber's wife was a nurse in the last war. She patched me up, and as soon as I was fit enough, I told them I should go to a military hospital, and they agreed. Zieber even drove me there. I only stayed a few days, just long enough to sweet-talk one of the nurses into telling the *Bayern Regionalkommando* she was your sister. They told her you were on leave, and then the Red Cross provided your address after I told them you'd been killed, and I wanted to visit your family. Nobody questioned anything. These days no one has time." He laughed mirthlessly.

Schumacher blurted, "Sergeant —"

But Hoven interrupted. "I slept in barns and hitched rides all the way from Austria. I even stowed away on a couple of trains. They were both staffed, and I nearly got blown up, but it was worth it, by Christ. Putting a bullet into you was all I thought about, night and day, and now I'm going to do it."

"Listen to me," Schumacher shouted, desperation in his voice. "I can make you rich. I'll give —"

Hoven fired his pistol four times, the shots thunderous in the confined space of the small room. The two women clung to each other, screaming, as the impact of the heavy caliber bullets flung Schumacher backwards over a chair and onto the floor. Hoven turned without a further word, the screams following him as he left the house.

The image of her husband's blood staining the carpet still vivid in her mind, Hilda sat quietly in the battered armchair for a few moments, looking at her daughter. The air in the cellar was chilly and damp now the fire had gone out, but she paid no attention. She had remembered something; something that had escaped her until now.

"Ellen," she said, at last, "do you recall what your father said to Sergeant Hoven just before he shot him?"

"No. I just remember the four shots."

"Yes," said Hilda, "but after your father told him about those boxes he'd hidden, he said, *I can make you rich.* I've only thought of it now."

"Well, what did he mean?"

"I don't know, but I think we should try to find those crates. I hadn't thought much about them until now, but I'm suddenly rather curious to see them."

"If we clear away a little more of this rubble," said Ellen, "perhaps we can find them. Two or three of them seemed quite heavy. I mean, it took two men to carry them into the house."

"They could have been blown to shreds for all we know," said Hilda, then, after a pause, she sighed and said, "Anyway, I haven't the strength to do it now."

* * *

The years following the war saw Germany partitioned. Thanks to the European Recovery Program — the Marshall Plan — which had opened a cornucopia allowing billions of American dollars to flow into western Europe, reconstruction was transforming West Germany. Many high-ranking Nazi leaders and the senior staff officers of the *Oberkommando der Wehrmacht*, the High Command, had been executed in 1947 following the Nuremburg trials, and the world was being scoured for other war criminals as nations hastened to extirpate the abomination that had been the Third Reich.

In Munich, Hilda and Ellen Schumacher now lived in a large house once owned by a wealthy and notoriously anti-Semitic industrialist, who, as a prominent member of the Bavarian wing of the Nazi party, had been able to use inmates of Dachau as slave laborers in his munitions factories, and had hanged himself rather than face prosecution. They wore the best clothes money could buy, they had a car and chauffer, and frequented the best restaurants and nightclubs. Hilda, although a very attractive woman, remained aloof from all would-be suitors, contenting herself with managing the Schumacher family's business and fortune, a task she performed with assiduous care and conspicuous success. When asked about the

228

business, she would say only that the firm bought and sold *household ornaments, knick-knacks, and such.*

However, this easeful and prosperous existence lay in an undreamed-of future when, in early July of 1945, Hilda and Ellen received word they could leave their ruined house and move into a temporary shelter erected for displaced and homeless families. Hilda refused point-blank.

"We're not leaving here," she told Ellen, "at least, not until we dig out those crates and see what's in them. If there's anything of value, we're not leaving it to the damn scavengers."

In spite, therefore, of entreaties and direct orders from the newly-minted municipal government, the two women had continued to camp in the cellar of their crumbling house, but once food became more readily available, and their strength returned, they set to work clearing away the dense pile of broken bricks, splintered wood, and plaster shards which covered the place where, to the best of their estimation, Hilda's late husband had hidden the five mysterious crates. Refusing all help, they worked little by little, moving the debris out to the road where it was eventually collected by work gangs largely composed of German prisoners of war. At first, they had to carry everything by hand, making the pace grindingly slow and exhausting, but after a few days, a sympathetic British soldier scrounged them a somewhat dented old wheelbarrow, with which Ellen went back and forth time and again as the cellar was gradually emptied.

At last, on a hot afternoon in early August, Hilda heaved aside a large broken plank and whooped in triumph.

"I think we've found them, Ellen."

A few minutes' more work exposed the end of a wooden crate, and Hilda grasped the handle.

"Dear God, it's heavy. Give me a hand."

The two women coughed and gagged in the cloud of plaster and brick dust which rose as, grunting with the exertion, they hauled a box about a meter square out of the rubble. Brushing away the few remaining fragments of debris, Hilda examined the crate.

"There's a padlock on it," she said, "but the box isn't damaged as far as I can see. It's very solidly built."

"Does it have a name on it anywhere?" asked Ellen. "I mean, can we just assume it's ours?"

"It's in our cellar," said Hilda, grimly. "That makes it ours."

"What can possibly be in it?"

"Who knows?" answered her mother, straightening, and wiping away a bead of perspiration creeping into her eyebrow, threatening to sting her eye.

"We have an axe," said Ellen. "It's not very sharp, but we might be able to split the lid with it."

"No," said Hilda, "it might damage whatever's inside. We'll have to see if we can find something to break the lock with. Mind you, we don't want anyone asking us what we need it for."

"Let's worry about it tomorrow, shall we?" Ellen said. "I'm dead tired for now."

The following morning Ellen disappeared for an hour and returned bearing a long steel crowbar.

"Where did you get that?" demanded Hilda, but Ellen merely shrugged.

"Ask me no questions, and I'll tell you no lies. That's what you and Papa always used to say, isn't it?"

"Did you steal it?"

"No. The workman said I could take it."

"Ellen —" Hilda began, but her daughter interrupted, her temper flaring.

"We needed a crowbar to open the box, so I got one, all right? I got it the same way I got most of the food we ate when half the city was starving. What did you expect? I couldn't buy it, could I? We don't have any damn money."

"You told me you stole the food," said Hilda.

"I did, some of it, anyway," Ellen said, "and I got the rest however I could. There was little enough as it was, and we didn't want to starve to death, did we?"

Hilda looked at her daughter, wondering what the world had done to the innocent teenager who loved jigsaw puzzles, school, and spending hours with her collection of books. She tried to expunge the images rising in her thoughts of Ellen giving herself to lustful, uncaring men in return for the meager scraps of bread, potato, and sausage on which they had subsisted until the International Red Cross and other food aid agencies finally came to Munich. A fearful thought struck her like a physical blow.

"Ellen," she said, horror in her voice, "you're not —"

"Pregnant?" Ellen interrupted. "No, *Mutti*, there's no danger of that. There are lots of things men like which don't make babies."

Hilda wrapped her arms around Ellen and held her tightly. She could think of nothing else to do, no words to say.

"It's all over now, *Mutti*," Ellen said, quietly, "and look at us, we're alive and well, aren't we?"

Hilda hugged her again, her eyes brimming with hot tears as she realized her daughter was comforting her when she, herself, could not speak for sorrow and anger. Sorrow for Ellen, and anger for herself. She had been a fool. Ellen always said she stole their food, and she believed her. She never asked too many questions, simply accepted Ellen's vague explanations. Perhaps it was because she suspected the truth and was afraid to hear it spoken. The thought consumed her with remorse and self-contempt.

"We'll win our own war," said Ellen, with a wan smile. "We'll survive, *Mutti*."

A lesson for life, Ellen thought bitterly.

"Yes, we shall," she said, with firm resolve, "and the first step is to use your splendid crowbar to get the lock off this box and see what's in the damn thing."

Setting the end of the long steel bar into the hasp of the lock, Hilda leaned on it with all her weight until the lock flew apart with a loud snap and she all but lost her balance, dropping the bar onto the cement floor with a reverberating clang.

"That was a spectacular effort," said Ellen, grinning.

Removing the last few bent fragments of the broken lock, Hilda lifted the heavy lid and the two of them peered inside. Whatever was there was covered by a folded piece of gray cloth which Hilda pulled off and dropped onto the floor, revealing the interior of the crate to be divided into several compartments by vertical wooden slats. On the left were about half a dozen narrow slots each containing a painting, but the right side of the box formed a single large compartment filled with cloth bags. Ellen lifted the paintings a little and looked briefly at each of them.

"These aren't large," she said, "but they look very old. I'll bet we could sell them."

Hilda was not listening. She had opened one of the cloth bags and was staring at what it contained.

"My God, Ellen," she finally managed to whisper.

Ellen carefully replaced the last painting before turning to her mother, an expression of concern on her face.

"What is it, *Mutti*? You've gone pale."

"Look," said Hilda, holding out a handful of gold coins. Ellen stared, dumbstruck.

There were twelve bags in all, most containing 500-mark gold pieces dating from the reign of Kaiser Wilhelm and the First World War, but there were also gold Louis from France, as well as coins from Holland, Russia, Britain, South Africa, and even a few twenty-dollar pieces from the United States. The two women looked through them all in breathless amazement.

"There's a fortune here," whispered Hilda, as if someone might somehow overhear. "It's no wonder your papa kept it a secret. If anyone had ever found out what he'd done, he'd have been shot, and us along with him, probably."

"But we didn't know," protested Ellen.

"They'd have shot us anyway," said Hilda, shrugging, her eyes fixed on the glittering hoard in front of them. "I don't know where or how your papa got all this, but you can be certain it wasn't honest. He was a lieutenant, not a field marshal."

"What do you mean?"

"I mean that when a field marshal takes possession of a treasure, everyone shrugs and says nothing, because they daren't. But if a lieutenant takes a treasure, they call for a firing squad. Your papa told me many stories about such things."

"He stole it?" Ellen looked aghast. "Papa wouldn't do that."

"Oh, for God's sake, girl," Hilda snapped, "do you think some kind soul just gave all this to him? He always told me the war would make us rich. He said if people are clever enough to do it, they take advantage of wars and come out of them ahead of everyone else. This is obviously what he meant." She gestured towards the open crate.

Ellen stared at the bags of coins. Gold was a treasure, a commodity beyond the dreams of avarice. Many people had given up their gold jewelry in the cause of Nazi victory, an act Adolph Hitler once called *heroic sacrifice*, declaring it would be *recompensed a thousand-fold when Germany has crushed her enemies*. Those who had any jewelry left were now selling or pawning it wherever they could — usually for a fraction of its true value. The occupying forces administration in the western zone was doing its utmost to stabilize the German currency, although the mark was still widely distrusted, but to have gold in a form and quantity such as they saw now was dizzying. All life and living for Hilda and Ellen had changed the instant that crate was opened. The squalid existence, the fear and indignity they had endured, all passed at one stroke into unqualified oblivion.

"And this is only the first box," said Hilda, almost reverentially. "There are four more, as I recall."

Over the next few days, Hilda and Ellen, working quietly and as casually as they could to avoid attracting undue attention, unearthed the other boxes and pried them open. Two held paintings and more coins, the third held some thirty gold ingots, each about half the length of Ellen's forearm, along with eight large bags of gem-encrusted gold and silver jewelry, but the last was different altogether.

"This one's labelled *Antiquitäten*," said Ellen, as they prepared to break the lock. "I wonder what's in it."

"We'll soon find out," said Hilda. "Come on."

The final crate contained neither gold, nor jewels, no paintings or coins. Instead, the two women found ancient-looking stone carvings, five ceramic jars, two large shallow bowls of heavy, cobalt-blue glass, and a flat piece of what looked like bone with mysterious marks scratched into its cracked surface. Each piece, except the bone, was accompanied by a written statement of age and provenance. The piece of bone was tagged simply, *China*.

* * *

In 1948, Ellen fell passionately in love with a handsome American soldier who told her he came from a place in Texas with the improbable name of Amarillo, of which neither Ellen nor Hilda had ever heard. This young man stayed just long enough for her to become pregnant before bidding her a fond farewell and telling her he was being *rotated stateside*, whatever that meant. He said he was going back to his wife in Texas, although he had always promised Ellen he was not married. Ellen was devastated and Hilda was furious, but their complaints to the American authorities availed them nothing.

"Well now, Private O'Connor just may be the father of your child, Miss Schumacher," drawled the liaison officer they were finally able to speak to, "but there ain't no proof of that, y'see, no proof at all. And so, we can't go holdin' up his rotation just on your say-so. I mean, for all I know, you might've had a whole bunch o' boy friends."

By 1955, therefore, Gabriella, Ellen's daughter, was seven, and away at a Swiss boarding school. Ellen was twenty-seven, a strikingly beautiful blonde woman, tall, slim, and elegant, who loved night life and the company of men, although she showed no inclination whatever to marry any of them. Hilda Schumacher had died of tuberculosis in 1952, after creating the organization over which Ellen now presided with dictatorial inflexibility and authority.

Immediately after discovering the treasure of the five boxes in their cellar, Hilda sold the jewelry on the black market. A dangerous proposition, but one she carried off with courage and sheer bravado.

"We need cash," she told Ellen, "before we can do anything else, and we have to get it from people who won't ask questions."

The underworld of post-war Munich was flourishing. Hilda had no trouble finding it, although she never told Ellen exactly how she did so. To the surprise of the men she did business with, she proved herself more than their match in toughness and poker-faced, cold-eyed negotiations. She earned grudging respect, and made connections in Munich and beyond which she, and later Ellen, would use to their advantage.

Armed with a Spanish passport procured at considerable expense from a master forger in Madrid, and two ordinary-looking suitcases with false bottoms, Hilda made several irregularly spaced trips by train to Switzerland where she opened accounts at various banks. The employees of those banks happily accepted the gold coins, advised upon their storage, potential sale, or exchange, and all without asking any questions, awkward or otherwise. The paintings were also sold on the black market through Hilda's carefully cultivated connections, but the gold bars presented a somewhat different problem.

"They're very heavy," she told Ellen. "I can't manage them."

"Can you take them one at a time?" Ellen suggested, but Hilda shook her head.

"If I did that, it would take far too long, and require too many trips. I've already done a lot of travelling, and the last thing I want to do is get on somebody's watch list."

Ellen saw the point. Travel on Hilda's Spanish passport was relatively easy, but records were always kept as part of the continuing hunt for Nazi war criminals still at large, so an alternative had to be found. Eventually, after several months of discreet inquiries amongst people who had a vested interest in keeping secrets, Hilda was

contacted by a Berliner who told her that in return for a
certain commission he and his associates would smuggle
the ingots into Switzerland in a single load, following
which they could be transported to a bank of Hilda's
choice.

"So, I give you the gold, and you disappear with it,"
she scoffed at the man who identified himself only as Willi.
"Do you take me for an idiot?"

"My dear *Frau* Schumacher," Willi said, with polished
urbanity, "in times such as these, the reputations, if not the
very lives, of businessmen such as I, depend on absolute
trustworthiness and integrity. My associates and I are
highly experienced in operations of the kind you require.
We have, in fact, been active for many years."

"You mean you worked for Nazis," she said, but Willi
said nothing, contenting himself with a smile that would
have made him look like the Mona Lisa had he been a
woman.

Hilda was well aware that Switzerland was under
increasing pressure to reveal the nature of its business
dealings with the Third Reich. Thus far, the Swiss were
standing firm, but there was always the chance they would
ultimately be somehow forced to open their books. Hilda's
accounts were numbered, not named, but she was
nevertheless concerned for the safety of the coins she had
already lodged beneath the sidewalks of Geneva and Zurich
and had therefore resolved to sell the bullion if she could,
rather than store it.

"Here's another idea, Willi," she said. "I assure you I
have no interest whatsoever in what your network did, or
did not do, for Germany's previous government, but there's
talk that at least some high-ranking Nazis have made their
way to South America."

"I have heard those rumors also," said Willi,
guardedly. "Go on, *Frau* Schumacher, but understand I
admit nothing."

"Of course," said Hilda, smiling as sweetly as she
could. "Now let's suppose those stories are true. Just
suppose. Is it not possible that those...persons...will

require at least *some* financial support in their new homes in South America?"

"It is possible, yes." Willi nodded slowly.

"Then perhaps, if the price is right, you would be willing to buy the gold I have and ship it to South America...if that's where those people are, of course. I am willing to ask a reasonable price which will allow you to make a fair profit."

"That could be arranged, I think," said Willi. "If I could know how much gold you have, and the price in marks you would ask?"

"Not marks, for God's sake," Hilda declared, shaking her head. "American dollars, or there's no deal. The money has to be deposited to an account in Madrid under a name I shall give you when the time comes. You get the bullion only after I have the deposit confirmed."

An agreement was ultimately reached after some grim-faced negotiations. Hilda journeyed to Madrid to set matters in train, and within three weeks the ingots were gone, and Hilda's cash reserves had markedly improved.

"You lost some money doing it that way," said Ellen.

"Not very much," said her mother, "but it was worth it to have it done quickly and at no risk to us."

The paintings had not been easy to sell and produced very little revenue. The well-publicized plundering of Europe's art treasures by the Nazis had made most prospective buyers reluctant to purchase paintings which might well be later identified as stolen property. Demand, therefore, was sluggish, and prices low. Hilda did the best she could and was happy to have them off her hands.

That left only the crate-full of antiquities, the contents of which were of precisely no interest whatever to anyone Hilda approached. She wondered why her late husband had bothered with any of it. Amongst those men with whom she now worked, the demand was for hard currency, jewelry, and precious metals. All of which yielded a healthy and speedy return on investment. Ancient artifacts of stone and glass and ceramics held no such promise.

"Dump them," she was advised by one of her new associates. "No one will ever buy them. Not now. Take my word for it."

It was with some surprise, therefore, that a solution to her problem was found in the person of an enterprising museum curator in Bonn. This official, an anthropologist and archeologist, was supplementing his salary through the judicious selling of artifacts and antiquities long buried and forgotten in the storage vaults of his museum. Working on the theory no one would ever notice these undocumented disappearances, the gentleman in question was enjoying considerable success. Through this energetic and well-connected man, therefore, Hilda discovered a high demand for antiquities amongst certain shadowy segments of society; a demand neither she nor her associates in Munich ever dreamed existed. She had obtained the curator's name in 1948 from a fence in Hamburg to whom she sold a diamond and ruby brooch, and who she contacted regarding the old ceramics in box number five. She found there were people all over the world willing to pay handsomely for ancient artifacts and artworks to enhance their private, usually illicit, collections. The curator, by name *Herr Doktor* Max Brandt, was more than willing to help.

"There are wealthy people everywhere, *Frau* Schumacher," he told her, "who know little or nothing about antiquities, but accumulate them as status symbols, as ways of showing off their supposed refinement and good taste, neither of which they usually possess. They are arrogant, conceited fools for the most part, and they will buy from both legitimate and illegitimate sources. Anything to get what they think they want. Anything to impress their equally ignorant friends."

With Brandt's help, paid for through a substantial commission on sales, the contents of the antiquities crate were swiftly disposed of. The most gratifying of the sales being the heavy glass bowls which Brandt declared were Roman, dating from the first century of the common era.

"I know just the customer for these," he told Hilda, "and he will pay whatever we ask. He is obsessed by all things Roman. He says he is sure he is descended from Julius Caesar. I am sure he's quite mad."

The curator was as good as his word. To Hilda's astonishment, the two bowls fetched a staggering price from the Roman *aficionado*, a millionaire collector in Genoa, and the episode prompted her to open a new line of business. With help from her Munich network and advice from Brandt, she began to acquire antiquities — usually stolen by petty thieves who had no idea of their value — at absurdly low prices, and sold them to collectors throughout Europe and sometimes beyond. She guaranteed complete secrecy, and this soon established her reputation. Going one step further, however, she also guaranteed each piece as genuine, and sought out fences and intermediaries who could be relied upon to provide items of high quality and sound provenance. The secure word of Hilda Schumacher became legend in the dark and dangerous trade in smuggled and stolen antiquities; a legend greatly fortified by the whispered story she had once caused an Italian supplier to be beaten to death by four chain-wielding Mafia thugs in the front room of his house in Sienna. It was said he had lied to her concerning the authenticity of a purported Etruscan amphora, and the deception had caused her severe embarrassment — not to mention financial loss — so she exacted a swift revenge. The post mortem stated there were almost too many broken bones to count. This tale, along with similar stories and rumors, combined with her business acumen, resulted in Hilda's becoming known in the trade as *Athena*, the beautiful Greek goddess of ancient times, the patron of wisdom, war, diplomacy, and commerce, amongst other things. By the time of her death in 1952 Hilda's vast and complex network was referred to with increasing frequency as the Athena Syndicate, and it soon grew to a position of unassailable preeminence. And yet, thanks to Hilda's planning and organizational skills, no one knew precisely how the syndicate actually operated. Hilda controlled it, but no one knew how. Her only confidant was Ellen.

Chapter Nineteen

Throughout the rise of the syndicate, Ellen, her mother's faithful assistant and devoted pupil, watched, listened, and learned. She found the work alluring, fascinatingly dangerous, and fell in love with the money it brought in and the resulting luxury in which she and her mother lived. She imbibed not only her mother's skill and determination, but also a double measure of her ruthlessness and vindictive temper. When Hilda died of tuberculosis, probably contracted during the many months of privation during the war, Ellen was more than ready to take command and did so with zeal and enthusiasm. In 1954 she moved the headquarters of the operation to West Berlin, it being clear by then that Stalin had given up his efforts to unite the city under communist rule. She preferred the night life of Berlin to that of Munich, and soon thereafter the syndicate expanded into a truly global enterprise.

From time to time throughout these years, efforts were made to sell the mysterious flat bone from crate number five. A turtle plastron, aged to a pale yellow, cracked, and with its surface marred by columns of scratches looking to the uninitiated eye like meaningless graffiti, was apparently of no interest to anyone, no matter how old it might be or where it might have come from. Its label had said it was Chinese, but the specialists Hilda turned to for an assessment of its value had no expertise in Oriental artifacts, and so it remained something of an enigma.

"Just hold onto it for now," Brandt advised. "Someone may turn up who's interested in it. It doesn't look like much, and that's part of the problem, I think. I mean, it's hardly to be called beautiful, is it? A shabby old piece of bone?"

So, shortly after moving to Berlin, Ellen had a rosewood stand made for it and displayed the bone in her house.

"To remind me of our days in Munich in that God-awful cellar," she said, "and to see I don't forget how much I owe to Papa."

In fact, such a souvenir was unnecessary. Ellen never forgot her father or the hideous way he died, and with the help of a contact in Berlin, she found a private investigator and commissioned him to find his killer.

"I want a man who can be persuaded to keep quiet and do the job without attracting attention," she explained, and was then given the name of Erich Richter. His background was exactly what she was looking for. She interviewed *Herr* Richter, a sturdily built man of perhaps forty-five, with small, blue eyes set close together under bushy brows, and was satisfied he was the right man. Two months later, he reported the killer's name was most probably Manfred Hoven.

"As far as I could find out," *Fraulein* Schumacher," he said, "Hoven was a sergeant in the army, assigned to special duty with your father."

Ellen nodded, saying, "Yes, I think I remember my father calling him *Sergeant*, but were you able to find out what work my father was doing?" She recalled how many times he had refused to divulge, even to his family, the nature of his activities during the last few months of the war.

"I'm sorry," papa would say, with an apologetic smile. "I just can't tell you."

"Yes," said Richter. "He was in command of one of several small secret units assembling and transporting artworks and other valuables to storage facilities in Austria and elsewhere."

That explains it all, thought Ellen. Papa helped himself along the way, just as *Mutti* said.

242

"Hoven's cousin, Peter Bretz," Richter was continuing, "served in the same unit, but he vanishes from the records in early nineteen-forty-five and is listed as presumed killed. Hoven was wounded, but he disappeared from a military hospital in Austria. The hospital records describe it as a bullet wound but say nothing about how or where he received it. I did manage to find out he hadn't been in a combat unit since early nineteen-forty-four on the eastern front, so God knows how he got shot. Anyway, he was ultimately posted as a deserter in March of nineteen-forty-five."

"Do you know what happened to him after that?" Ellen asked, and Richter shrugged, pulling down the corners of his mouth.

"The trail's cold, dead. If the Russians got him and shipped him to the east, he probably didn't survive. Most didn't, you know."

That's a pity, Ellen reflected. I was looking forward to having him killed, or better yet, killing him myself.

"I tracked down a doctor who was on the hospital staff, and he vaguely remembered Hoven," Richter went on. "Apparently Hoven claimed not to remember how he'd been wounded but told anyone who'd listen he intended to kill his commanding officer."

"Then why wasn't he arrested?" Ellen asked.

"Most of the staff thought he was just off his head. Shell shock, or something. There was a lot of that, so no one took him seriously."

"Well, they damn well should have," snapped Ellen, and Richter smiled.

"You don't know what it was like in the army in those days, *Fraulein* Schumacher. Men just wanted to get home alive without being captured by the Russians. Many were bitter, demoralized, and angry. They believed they'd been betrayed by the high command and their own field officers. They were convinced that if things had been handled properly, Germany would have won the war. With that sort of talk flying around, no one paid any real attention to a man raving about shooting a lieutenant."

They were sitting with glasses of wine in the elegant sitting room of the house in Berlin, and Richter sipped his wine while he waited for Ellen to respond. She appeared to be deep in thought, so he put down his glass and continued.

"The doctor did say that at one point Hoven accused this unnamed lieutenant, presumably your father, of shooting his cousin."

Ellen nodded, taking up her own wine glass.

"Yes. That's what he shouted at my father before he shot him."

"Then that would explain Bretz's undocumented death, I suppose," said Richter, and Ellen nodded again, remaining silent for a few more moments, somewhat disappointed the search had led nowhere in the end. Her father had stolen treasure others had stolen before him, and now she was rich, and he was dead.

As she ruminated on this, Richter's eyes wandered around the large and ornate room.

"That's a peculiar-looking thing," he said, catching sight of the oval plastron in its place on the mantel above the carved stone fireplace. "I wonder if those scratch marks actually mean anything."

"They probably do," said Ellen, absently, "but I'm not interested in them just now. I have something else I want to discuss with you."

"And that is?" asked Richter, his bushy eyebrows raised.

"First of all, I'd like to know if you can travel freely. What passport do you carry?"

"I'm not sure that's any of your concern, *Fraulein*," said Richter, in a level voice. "In my profession —"

"I'm making it my concern," interrupted Ellen, sharply.

After a pause during which Richter was obviously weighing his options, he said, "I have several passports in several names which I am not prepared to divulge. No doubt you can understand why."

"Can you get in and out of the Eastern Zone?"

"Certainly."

"Good," said Ellen. "That's all I wanted to know."

"Is that what you wanted to discuss?" asked Richter, still cautious, still wary.

"No," said Ellen, calmly, "that was merely my first point. My second is to tell you that I know who you are, Albert Schmitz. I also know you were a major in the *Totenkopf* Brigade, and commanded SS guards at Bergen-Belsen, where the prisoners called you *The Jackal*."

"Then I'm afraid you're very much misinformed," Richter said, angrily. "Where did you get that nonsense?"

"It's not nonsense, *Herr* Schmitz, and I'm not misinformed," said Ellen, casually finishing the last of her wine. Richter made to speak again, but she held up her hand.

"Don't bother, *Herr* Major Schmitz, or plain *Herr* Richter, whichever you prefer. Do you seriously think I'd employ you without finding out everything I could about you first? I have to protect myself, you know. You came highly recommended, but my contact knew all about you. It's his business."

Richter, brought up short, said nothing. He stared at Ellen with narrowed, calculating eyes.

"But don't worry," she went on. "That bit of your past is of no concern to me. I don't care what you did, or where you did it. We'll use your new name and leave it all at that."

"What are you after, *Fraulein* Schumacher?" Richter asked, still eyeing Ellen with undisguised suspicion.

"What I'm most interested in is the work you did before the war. I understand you were a petty criminal, in and out of jail for fighting, assault, and so on, but burglary was your real specialty, and you were very good at that...very good indeed. Am I right?"

"If you say so." He shrugged.

"I do say so."

"You seem to have learned a great deal," said Richter, bluntly. "However, I assume you have some sort of proposition for me, so I suggest you get to it. I've had just about enough of your version of the Spanish Inquisition."

She liked his forthrightness; it appealed to her own straightforward nature, but she had to be very sure of him. If he was the right man for the job she had in mind — an entirely new venture — then all would be well, but if not, it could prove fatal to the syndicate. She needed to know he could be controlled. Could he be relied to obey orders? Yes, she decided, he could. He would have learned all about that in the SS, she reminded herself, with a wry, inward smile. Trusting her instincts, she took the plunge.

She asked, "Are you aware of what I do for a living, *Herr* Richter?"

"No, I'm not," he answered, his eyes still narrowed and still wary.

Ellen shot him a penetrating stare which clearly said, *you're lying*. Richter returned the look for a moment before lowering his eyes.

"I'm told you're the brains behind the Athena Syndicate."

"That's correct," she replied, "but don't imagine you can tell that to anyone. Certainly not the police."

"Why not?" asked Richter, with a smirk, "There may be a reward."

"Don't get cute with me," she snapped, menace in her voice. "Remember what I know about you."

"Well," said Richter, "you know about me, and obviously I know about you. I'd say that makes us even."

"Not quite," said Ellen. "If the police find me, I may go to prison for a few years. If they find you, you die."

It seemed Richter had also come to a decision, for when he spoke again, it was in a calm, business-like voice.

"All right, *Fräulein* Schumacher. I believe we both understand the situation, so I suggest we get to the details. I am prepared to listen to whatever it is you have to say."

"Very well," said Ellen, with a quick smile, "no more Spanish Inquisition."

Richter grinned, visibly relaxing as he accepted Ellen's offer of more wine. She refilled their glasses and settled back in her chair feeling she had been right about *Herr* Richter. The crackling tension in the room had disappeared.

He was now attentive, at ease, and comfortable. So comfortable, in fact, she felt his gaze wandering over her slim frame, from her more than shapely legs to her rather well-filled blue silk blouse. She felt like telling him she knew what he was thinking, and he didn't have a hope in hell, but turned to business instead.

"So, here it is," she said, taking a sip of the very fine red wine, of which she was so proud. It was far better than anything available on the open market. "I've been contacted by a man in Argentina, a very wealthy man, who wants a Roman statue. Marble. Preferably a representation of a gladiator, but that's not essential. A trusted associate of mine in Bonn gave him my name. The connection is completely secure."

"I know absolutely nothing about Roman statues, *Fraulein* Schumacher," said Richter, spreading his hands and smiling in self-deprecation. "Marble or otherwise."

"Don't worry. That's my department." And after another sip of wine, she resumed. "Now usually, I go looking for something a client wants. I find it wherever I can, buy it, and then sell it on to the client."

"So, I've heard," said Richter, a note of unmistakable admiration in his voice. "And I hear you drive a damned hard bargain, to boot. But I assume that's not working in the case of this Argentinian fellow."

"Very perceptive of you," Ellen answered. "Open market or black market, there isn't a statue like that to be had anywhere at this moment, and, believe me, I've looked."

"But you don't want to disappoint your filthy rich Argentinian client, correct?"

"Correct," said Ellen, nodding. "I've offered to procure a statue for him as soon as one becomes available, but he says he isn't willing to wait, nor is he willing to buy from anyone else. He says he won't trust any other supplier."

"It must be gratifying to have so high a reputation," said Richter, somewhat dryly, "but if you have nothing to sell him at the moment, he's out of luck, isn't he?"

"Look," said Ellen, lighting one of her favorite black Turkish cigarettes, and fixing Richter with a level gaze, "when I buy a piece and sell it, the profit margin is usually fairly modest. It's satisfactory, but it could be a lot better. I've been doing very well so far, of course, but as I get more and more orders, it's becoming harder to find items to buy, and a prompt response to orders is my trademark now. I don't just fill a showroom with things and wait for customers to walk in; I give people exactly what they say they want. I go out and find it somewhere and do it faster than anyone else. I ask no questions, and my clients appreciate that."

"Where is all this leading *Fraulein*?" Richter sounded more interested than impatient.

"As you can tell," said Ellen, lighting another cigarette, "I'm not overly squeamish about where I obtain the items from. I want to minimize my costs and protect my reputation. That's just good business."

"So, what's the solution?" inquired Richter, wine glass in hand. "If you can't find the sort of statue this guy wants, what can you do?"

"Well," said Ellen, exhaling a stream of pungent smoke towards the ceiling, "thanks to my associate in Bonn, I have found exactly what he wants."

"Excellent," Richter said. "Then why are you telling me all this?"

"I've found it, but it's not for sale."

Richter put his glass down on the rosewood end table at his elbow and regarded Ellen from beneath his bushy eyebrows.

"So, you want me to steal this statue for you. No middleman. Is that the idea?"

"Precisely," said Ellen, pleased she had not misjudged *Herr* Richter. "The...shall we say... *business*...of my associate in Bonn gave me the idea. I'm thinking that when I receive an order for something I can't buy, I find it elsewhere, acquire it, and fill the order. I may not have to steal it every time, but it will enable me to specialize in one-of-a-kind specimens. This gentleman in Argentina wants a Roman statue of a gladiator, but what if someone wants a very particular Roman statue, perhaps one of a certain age or by a particular sculptor? See what I mean?"

"Yes, I'm getting the picture, *Fraulein*," Richter said, nodding.

"I know there are clients out there willing to pay a lot more than I charge now, and all the more if I can fill specific orders. Millionaires in South America, Panama, Hong Kong, the States, you name it. I'd go even more international than I am now."

"No doubt," said Richter, in even greater admiration, "but how do you plan to track down these special pieces? I can steal them if you want, but I can't find them. I don't know how."

"My contact in Bonn can find what we need. I can offer him three times what he makes at work now, including his little business on the side. He'll be my research department."

"Sounds perfect, but do you think he can really do it? I mean, find all these obscure things?"

"I'm sure of it. He's already found a statue for us, as I said."

"Wow," exclaimed Richter. "Who is this guy?"

"You'll never know," said Ellen, shaking her head, "and he'll never know who you are. That's the way it works. I'm in the middle of the operation. Everyone else is around the outside, and no one knows anyone but me, unless I allow it for some particular reason."

"Fair enough," said Richter, unperturbed, "but a minute ago you said *us*, *Fraulein* Schumacher."

Ellen ground out her cigarette in a large, red onyx ashtray.

"Yes, *us*. I want you to head up what I might call my acquisitions department. You can hire other men as you need them but remember you're responsible for them. One slip and they're out, and so are you. I'm willing to start you at forty thousand American dollars per annum."

"Jesus." Richter nearly dropped his drink. "Forty thousand."

"There are three conditions," said Ellen, holding up three fingers. Richter looked at her inquiringly.

"Yes?"

"One. Don't you ever let me down or mess me about. If you do, the police will immediately be told all about your past life. Two. There will be no unnecessary violence. No violence at all, if you can possibly avoid it. I'm not running a free-for-all for half-witted thugs. If it's necessary to teach someone a lesson or collect on an unpaid debt, I'll take care of it, but I don't want people harmed simply because you're relieving them of something they own. Understood?"

"And three?" asked Richter, nodding.

"Don't get caught."

"Of course," he said, grinning, "I might have guessed. But," he said, after a short pause, "I can see a problem. You said you were operating internationally, and wanted to expand even further, right?"

"Right."

"When you buy something on the open market, you can ship it anywhere legally, but if it's stolen property, you can't just send it off the way you do now."

"You're quite right," said Ellen. "At the moment, I use a trucking company that operates within Western Europe. Up to now, the smallest part of the business has been to ship beyond Europe, but the big money and the richest collectors are overseas, as I said. So, in addition to professional thieves, we'll need professional international smugglers in our employ. Now, I've heard there's more than one network still operating that smuggled people and their possessions overseas after the war. Is that correct?"

"Yes. I could contact one or two of them for your consideration, if you like. They're damn good at what they do, I can assure you of that."

"No," Ellen said. "I don't want to deal with that sort of gang. What I want is to hire the people to work for me directly, not retain an independent organization I can't keep track of."

"Okay," said Richter, "if you're willing to pay well, you can recruit your people from those networks."

"So, why aren't you in South America or elsewhere?" Ellen asked, putting out her latest cigarette, and Richter shrugged.

"I'll take my chances here. So far, so good, and I'm very careful."

"I'll just bet you are," said Ellen, with a grim smile, "and I need you to stay careful, *Herr* Richter. Very careful indeed."

Richter inclined his head in understanding.

"You've been planning all this out, designing it. I can tell it's just what you love to do, *Fraulein* Schumacher. Nothing escapes you. Am I right?"

"Now we can go for the really big stuff," Ellen said, satisfaction in her voice. She ignored Richter's question, although her mind registered the accuracy of his assessment. She did love to plan, to design, but it was not done for enjoyment alone. She did it so that she could feel she had total control of her life, her future, and, most importantly, her very destiny. The war years, the bombs, the murder of her father, the Munich cellar, the hunger, and what she had done to find food, had all taught her the meaning of helplessness, desperation, and the paramount need to be self-reliant. She remembered those lessons; they were inscribed on her soul.

"The multimillion-dollar stuff," she affirmed, with a decisive nod.

"Naturally," said Richter, smiling.

"And our Argentinian multimillionaire will be our first project. He's Client Number One."

"Well," said Richter, "speaking of that Argentinian plutocrat, I have another question. If he has so much money, why doesn't he just buy himself a statue on the open market?"

"Good question," said Ellen. "For one thing, statues of the size he wants don't often come up for sale, and as I told you, he's not prepared to wait until one does. It seems patience is not one of his virtues. However, those aren't the main reasons. What we shall call his *business interests*, require he keep a very low profile. We are in a position to act as his agents, and he knows he can trust us. He knows what he wants, and he wants it now."

"Then let's give it to him," said Richter.

"Champagne?" asked Ellen, heading for the drinks trolley by the window, and Richter smiled in agreement.

She filled a crystal flute for him, but before seating herself with her own drink, she retrieved the oracle bone from the mantel and slid it into a drawer.

"Now I know for certain what dear old Papa was up to, I think perhaps I should keep this thing out of sight. God knows where it might have come from or who might be looking for it now."

* * *

So it was that two weeks later, a large marble statue of the Roman god Mars, dating from the first century before the common era, disappeared from a pseudo-classical temple built on the grounds of the palace of the former Grand Duke of Mecklenburg-Schwerin, in north-east Germany, well inside the Eastern Zone. The final report of the investigating officer of the civilian police force of the German Democratic Republic would later read, in part — *The thieves left no trace of themselves whatsoever. No evidence could be gathered as to how they obtained the statue or transported it off the island on which the palace is built. No suspects were apprehended, and the statue has not been recovered. The nature of the theft strongly suggests it to have been the work of a highly professional organization, but no clues to its identity could be found.*

Two months after the theft, a moving company delivered a large wooden crate to a certain facility in Buenos Aires, where the manager caused it to be sealed in a strong vault with a heavy combination padlock he had previously received in the mail with instructions and payment from an anonymous source. Two days later, another crew of six men appeared in a lorry, their foreman opening the lock using a combination he had been given over the phone by a voice which did not identify itself. A day after that, a large statue of Mars was being proudly displayed in the foyer of the palatial and well-guarded mansion of Señor Carlos Méndez, leader of one of Argentina's most powerful and savage crime families. In due course, two million cleanly laundered American dollars were circuitously transferred to a particular Swiss bank account, fees and commissions fully paid.

And, exactly as Richter had envisioned, *Fraulein* Ellen Schumacher sat like a contented spider at the center of her carefully woven web; the only person able to forge these disparate events into the highly organized operation they comprised. The test had been successful, and she smiled to herself as she lit another black Turkish cigarette, there in her comfortable sitting room in West Berlin.

Chapter Twenty

To say the Athena Syndicate prospered would be an understatement. It grew, it burgeoned, and expanded over the succeeding years into a worldwide operation employing many people — the actual number known only to Ellen Schumacher. Professor Brandt, Head of Research and nearly eighty, had seven investigators working for him by 1965, all specialists in fine art and antiquities, all highly qualified, and all seduced from their legitimate occupations by the financial rewards offered by the syndicate. Brandt and his team created a broad network of contacts which penetrated not only the world's greatest museums, auction houses, and galleries, but also government Ministries of Culture, or their equivalents, in many countries of Europe and beyond. When enough money was on the table, information was soon forthcoming on *objets d'art*, whether publicly or privately owned. Once the location of a required piece was established, Richter's thieves moved in, objects disappeared, and were smuggled out of their home countries to be delivered to clandestine buyers who displayed them discreetly or gloated over them in secret. Vast fortunes were paid for these services, allowing the syndicate's numerous employees to enjoy comfortable, and in some cases, lavish, lifestyles.

Not surprisingly, the thefts did not go unnoticed. Police forces everywhere investigated them, but the men and women Richter recruited were highly skilled, very resourceful, and left no traces. Their *modus operandi* was always different; no pattern ever emerged for investigators to recognize. The aid of Interpol was often enlisted, and although numerous files were opened, no connections between them were ever established. The name, *Athena Syndicate*, was heard with increasing frequency from paid informers and small-time fences, but discovering what it was, or where it was controlled from, proved elusive. Arrests were made from time to time, but they were always worker ants who never knew the size of the nest, let alone who, or where, the queen might be. Couriers who never knew the name of the person who hired them, lorry drivers who had no idea what they were actually carrying and could not even identify the person to whom a delivery was to be made. None came even remotely close to exposing the syndicate as a whole. Ellen kept very few written records, and even they appeared innocuous, offering no hint of their true meaning. The work of the syndicate was kept safe in her encyclopedic mind. No one, not even Richter, who knew more than most, knew the whole picture. Ellen saw everyone as cogs in her machine, and it was not necessary for them to know why they were turning, or what effect their turning might have on any other cog in the machine.

"It's like the SS," she told Richter one day in answer to his question about an operation. "If you don't need to know, you will never be told."

He grinned and shrugged. When it came down to it, he was making far too much money to care about the fine points.

The West German police had no reason to suspect that the glamorous Ellen Schumacher, the *habituée* of exotic nightclubs and sophisticated restaurants, was living her lavish life well outside the law. She was known to be independently wealthy with no need whatever to work, and those concerned with such things openly speculated that her wealth probably emanated from post-war profiteering or wartime plunder, or perhaps both, but nothing could ever be proved. Her late father's military records were known, but the paper trail ended with the stark, uncompromising word, *Gefallen* — killed in action — so nothing further could be revealed from them. In the numerous searches conducted by governments, civil, and military organizations for what was often described simply as *Nazi treasure*, many clues pointed to connivance on the part of the Swiss, and strenuous efforts were made to trace the routes by which ill-gotten gains made their shadowy way to the vaults of Zurich and Geneva, but there was no success. The Swiss financiers, safe within their thick-walled banks and wood-paneled offices, maintained a sepulchral silence. They collected their fees, balanced their ledgers, and went home to sleep the untroubled sleep of those who had convinced themselves they had a clear conscience.

And nor was Ellen's notoriety confined to Berlin. The society columnists and gossip-mongers throughout Europe fairly trembled with expectant excitement whenever rumors began swirling about regarding her possible marriage to this Italian Count or that Greek industrialist. If she turned up in Cannes or St. Tropez on the arm of a French millionaire, there were photos and speculations in *Paris Match*, and if she attended a performance of Parsifal — she loved the music of Richard Wagner — at the Bayreuth Festival with a high-ranking West German politician, *Der Spiegel* made considerable haste to publicize the event. At forty, she was as incandescently beautiful as ever she had been. The socialites longed to know why she had not married, but she remained silent and aloof. A tabloid newsmagazine in Munich dubbed her *die Eiszapfen* — the Icicle — and asked how it was that a woman could be so well known, and yet remain a mystery, but it was that very mystery she cultivated. No one was ever permitted to get too close, no one became a confidant, and although occasionally, and in utmost secrecy, she allowed a man into her commodious and luxurious bed, sex was all she shared — never love, and certainly never secrets. Her life itself was a secret, and her liberty depended upon its remaining so.

In 1966, encouraged by an increasing demand for Oriental, especially Chinese, art and artifacts, she expanded into Asia. This she did with considerable care, for although she had learned a great deal about western classical and Egyptian antiquities, she knew almost nothing about the cultural history of Asia. She needed expertise. Armed only with a name provided by one of Brandt's researchers, her agent in London arranged to put her in touch with a former high-ranking member of the Royal Hong Kong Police, now resident in Britain. She met this man, Andrew Hamilton by name, in a Greek restaurant just off Oxford Street in the heart of London's shopping district.

"Is there something I can do for you, Miss Schumacher?" he asked, after preliminary small talk.

"Perhaps," she said, using the English she had worked so hard to learn, "and perhaps I can do something for you, Mr. Hamilton."

Hamilton raised his eyebrows. He had a fleshy face with a ruddy complexion, and his once-muscular body had run to flab. Ellen knew his age to be fifty-two.

"Tell me," said Ellen, conversationally, "why on earth do you have such a lousy job? A bouncer in a squalid little knocking shop in Soho calling itself a nightclub."

Hamilton shrugged. "It's a paycheck, but what —"

"Could it be because it's the only job you could get after your release from prison?" she interrupted. He opened his mouth to reply, but she forestalled him with a wave of her hand. "Five years in Dartmoor, I believe, wasn't it?"

"What the hell's your game, lady?" Hamilton growled.

"It must be especially humiliating considering the amount of money you have in banks in the States." She smiled at him.

"I've had enough of this," he snapped, throwing down his napkin and pushing his chair back.

"Stay where you are, Mr. Hamilton," she said, coolly. "I can help you gain access to that money, if you like."

"How?" he asked, his tone cautious.

"Never mind how," she answered, "but there's a price to it."

"I thought so," said Hamilton.

"I don't want money," she said, after a short pause during which she finished her lamb souvlaki, "I want information and contacts. I know you still have them."

257

Hamilton, immediately attentive, was only too happy to hear more. "If you help me get my money —"

"Your money?" Ellen interrupted, straight-faced. "You mean the money you took as bribes in return for looking the other way when you were in the Hong Kong Police. That's why you ended up in prison."

He looked at her, and she finished, "I know a lot about you, you see."

Hamilton downed the last of his red wine and shrugged. "There was never any high-level stuff. No political games. They were all petty criminals. It would have cost a fortune to prosecute them all. I saved Her Majesty the time and trouble."

"How much have you got squirreled away?"

"About three million."

"Three million doesn't sound very petty to me," she observed.

"Well, call it what you like," Hamilton said, "as long as I get it back. What do you want from me?"

She told him, and he nodded.

"I can put you in touch with several international triads operating out of Hong Kong with ties to Singapore and Taiwan. Will that do for starters?"

"Quit your job," she said, after a momentary pause for thought. "You and I are going to Hong Kong."

"I don't have a passport, and they'll never let me in even if I did," he protested.

"Don't worry about that," Ellen said, as she waved at a waiter for the check.

* * *

Ellen and Hamilton flew first class from London to Hong Kong's Kai Tak Airport, and under Hamilton's guidance she made the necessary arrangements. Hamilton himself, supplied by Ellen with a false passport and forged citizenship documents identifying him as a native-born

South African, made himself sufficiently indispensable that she made him her lieutenant for Asia and set him up in a fine flat in North Point overlooking Hong Kong's teeming harbor.

"I trust no one will recognize you," she said one evening at dinner in the Wanchai District of Hong Kong Island.

"No," he said. "It's ten years since I was on the force. Almost all the senior people I worked with have moved on or retired, and the beat constables wouldn't know me from Adam."

"You know what I do and what I need," she told him. "Get me agents I can rely on who will be able to assist my acquisitions people when the need arises."

"Don't worry," he said. "I can get the agents easily, and when it comes to what you so quaintly call *acquisitions*, I know the Chinese organizations as well as anybody. They can get you all the stuff you can use. They've got real specialists."

"Do your job, keep your mouth shut, and everything will be fine," she told him. "With salary and commissions, you'll do very well."

"And you will too." Hamilton raised his glass.

"Just so," she said, nodding, "but don't you ever let me down. If you do, you'll regret it severely. Understand?"

"I do indeed," Hamilton replied, with a grim smile. "But what about my money in the States?"

"Right," she said. "I trust the holding accounts you have aren't in your real name?"

"Of course not," he said. "I invented a person named Guy Vickers."

"Okay," Ellen said, finishing her red bean soup. "I'll get you the documents you need to get into the US and access the accounts under that name. How and when you do that, and what you do with the money afterwards is up to you."

* * *

"I wish we could get into Mainland China," Ellen said to Hamilton, one day in the winter of 1968 in Berlin, whither he had been summoned for a reporting and planning session. "There's a Sinophile in France who's richer than God and he wants a Buddha statue from the Forbidden City."

"Good grief," said Hamilton, "why bother? We can get one for him from temples in all sorts of places far more interesting than that."

"That's what I told him," said Ellen, "but he's fixated on the Forbidden City. He'll pay whatever it takes. Whatever we ask. What are the chances?"

"Look," said Hamilton, "I've just told you how well we're doing in Asia. The network's fully in place and completely reliable. We got you the Ming vase from the museum in Singapore, the Shang bronze wine vessel from Taiwan, and all the other acquisitions ordered. In my view, there's no reason to take unnecessary risks. Tell this Frenchman it's not possible."

"I don't like turning clients away," she said, her chin lifting in defiance. "It can damage our reputation."

"All right, then," said Hamilton, "I'll arrange to acquire a Buddha from somewhere, and you can tell him it's from Beijing."

Anger blazed in Ellen's eyes, and her cheeks reddened perceptibly as she snapped back at him.

"Absolutely *not*. The provenance of every piece is guaranteed. That's the only way we operate. You've always known that, so stop being an idiot. My mother once had a supplier in Italy killed because he falsified a statement of authenticity."

This was a side of the Athena Syndicate Hamilton had been unaware of until now, and he retreated rapidly.

"I want to keep this client," Ellen said, in a tone that brooked no denial, "and I need you to tell me it can be done, not give me half-baked little tricks. There's a lot of money at stake on this one."

"All right, all right," said Hamilton, hastily, clearly anxious to spread calming oil on the decidedly troubled waters he had inadvertently stirred up. "Sorry."

Ellen lit a black cigarette, her fingers still trembling slightly. Hamilton had turned out to be a good and useful man, of great value to the expanded syndicate, but he had a habit of losing sight of the important, but less tangible, aspects of the operation. She gazed at him through a haze of aromatic smoke, "So, how long's it going to take to do what this client wants us to do?"

Hamilton did not answer immediately. He sat back in his chair, chewing his lower lip meditatively for nearly a full minute while Ellen smoked. Impatience was not a vice for which she was famous; she preferred her food well chewed and properly digested.

At last, Hamilton said, "To begin with, I'm not certain there is a Buddha statue in the Forbidden City, and even if there is, I don't know if it's accessible enough to be extracted successfully. What does Research say?"

"This one's got them up a tree," said Ellen. "They really don't know. China's a closed shop. I'm told no one knows for sure what's happened to many of the galleries and museums since nineteen-forty-nine. We do know a good deal about the Imperial collection that was taken to Taiwan, but Research confirms there isn't a statue there that comes directly from the Forbidden City. It seems if we want one as ordered, it will have to come from Beijing."

Hamilton considered this for a few moments, the said, "All right, let's assume for sake of argument that there is, and we can get at it. We then have the problem of getting it down the whole length of China and over the border into Hong Kong."

Ellen remained silent. She knew when to speak and when to listen.

"I think I can get someone to check it out," he went on, "but it's tricky in China at the moment."

"I gather there's a certain amount of upheaval," she said, lighting another cigarette.

"That's putting it mildly," grunted Hamilton. "Some say the country's going to hell in a basket. Large portions of it are in a state of virtual anarchy. Mao calls it the *Great Proletarian Cultural Revolution*. I call it a bloody disaster."

"So, what's it all about?"

"Well," said Hamilton, clearing his throat quietly, "it all goes back to a thing Mao called *The Great Leap Forward*, which he proclaimed in nineteen-fifty-eight. The big idea was to make China an industrialized society able to compete with developed nations within the space of five years."

"Sounds a little far-fetched," Ellen observed.

"It was, and it didn't work. There was economic chaos. Millions of peasants built blast furnaces anywhere they could and produced lousy iron that was liable to shatter if you dropped it. Rural life was totally disrupted, and the result was three years of raging famine. Tens of millions starved. They were called *The Three Bitter Years*."

"I'm not surprised," said Ellen, "but what's that got to do with what's happening now?"

Hamilton raised a forefinger, saying, "I'm coming to that. The whole Leap Forward thing was such a debacle Mao's popularity fell off the graph and he was no longer regarded as the infallible leader he once was. By nineteen-sixty-three he needed a way back to power, and the Cultural Revolution is it."

"How?"

"Well," said Hamilton, "it was a huge risk, but it proved to be a brilliant political move. He proclaimed China's troubles were the fault of antisocial revisionists in the central government. Men like Deng Xiaoping, who has now disappeared into the ether. Mao called on students to remove all such figures from government and reject all the elements of the old culture. By nineteen-sixty-five the whole idea had caught on, and the Red Guard were being formed with the help of Mao's wife, no less. Literally tons of old coins have been melted down, artifacts and manuscripts destroyed, universities and high schools are shut, the countryside is being collectivized, and God knows what else is going on. And as for Mao, he's never been so popular as he is now."

"So, it worked."

"It certainly did."

"Very clever of him," mused Ellen. "Very clever indeed. But does all this help us get a Buddha from the Forbidden City, or just make it more difficult?"

Hamilton pursed his lips in thought, then said, "I'm not sure. I need to see what connections I can make. It's not easy to get into China at the moment, but it's not impossible, and there's still a good deal of communication with Hong Kong. The Hong Kong and Shanghai Banking Corporation is still very much a going concern, for example. No matter what seems to happen in China, money in the right hands can still work wonders."

"Well, let's see if we can use these upheavals to our advantage?" Ellen persisted, and Hamilton nodded, smiling.

"My thoughts exactly."

Hamilton departed immediately for Hong Kong, and three weeks later he was back in Berlin. Ellen clearly saw the glint of enthusiasm and excitement lighting his eyes.

"This will be our first operation in China," he said, "and the potential for growth is enormous. Everything's in place. All I need is your go-ahead."

"One thing at a time," she said. "What did you find?" She had never let mere emotion influence her judgement, and she was not about to start now. She had always been the epitome of patience and caution. She was in every way the Icicle.

"There is a statue, all right," he reported. "It's in a shrine in what used to be the private apartments of the old Empress Dowager, right in the heart of the Forbidden City. It's a fair size but it should be easy enough to move. All it needs is an ordinary hand-cart."

"But can we extract it?" Ellen asked. Knowing the item was there was only half the story she was interested in. The ability to move it was irrelevant if it could not be got out in the first place."

"Yes, we can," said Hamilton, nodding vigorously, "and here's how we propose to do it. The Forbidden City is closed to the public at the moment, but soldiers of the People's Liberation Army go in from time to time to make sure everything's okay. We'll get a squad of six good men to wear PLA uniforms and make a sort of unscheduled inspection. The guards at the entrance are just young kids basically, the hardened troops are off in the hinterland somewhere, or just hanging about in their barracks. Things are not organized at all these days, and a small troop of men showing up unexpectedly won't be a surprise. Nothing out of the ordinary, really."

"You mean they'll just walk in?" Ellen asked, doubtfully. "It sounds a bit like wishful thinking to me."

"They'll have bogus orders," said Hamilton, "but it's highly unlikely they'll be stopped. No one will have the authority. They'll go in, get the statue, and then carry it out the way they came in. The whole operation hinges on doing it all right under people's noses. We'd never get away with it if we tried a night raid, or something daft like that."

Ellen was dubious, but Hamilton seemed very sure of himself. She was used to working in Europe, to setting everything up herself, knowing all the details, but China was new ground for her. However, she reminded herself that the five operations conducted with Hamilton and the Hong Kong agents had been total successes. She thought of how much she had charged for the Tang Dynasty ivory carving of Guanyin, the Goddess of Mercy, they had extracted from an antique dealer's vault twenty feet below the man's showroom floor in Kowloon. If the situation in Beijing was as Hamilton described it — and God knows he should know — then she felt willing to take the chance. And this client was prepared to pay more than handsomely.

"There's one more thing," said Hamilton, as though reading her mind. "On the day we plan to move, there's to be a huge Red Guard rally in Tiananmen Square, right by the Forbidden City. Mao's going to speak. It'll be pandemonium with bedlam and hysteria thrown in for good measure. No one's going to notice a small group of soldiers, especially since they'll be acting quite openly and confidently. No sneaking about."

Ellen weighed the risks. There were uncertainties, but that was nothing new. Hamilton was convincing. She made up her mind, took the plunge, and agreed.

Nothing ventured, nothing gained.

"But don't you dare let me down," she growled, throwing Hamilton a threatening glance, and grinding her cigarette into the marble ashtray more as if to kill it than put it out.

* * *

She need not have worried. When Hamilton saw her six weeks later, he was jubilant.

"In and out," he exulted. "Smooth as a baby's bottom."

They were sharing a private dinner in a small salon adjacent to the large main dining room in the Berlin house, and Hamilton was regaling her with the story of the operation.

"Go on," she said, taking up her champagne flute.

"There's not much more to say, actually," said Hamilton, spooning up the last of his French onion soup. "The six of them moved through the crowd without trouble and got into the Forbidden City by the main entrance, as planned. There was only one young soldier there on guard, so called, and he was perfectly terrified at the sight of those six barging in as if they owned the place." Hamilton chuckled. "They crated up the statue and brought it out. No drama at all. The rally was even more deafening than I expected…a total melee. Excellent cover."

"All right," said Ellen, very relieved, "but how did they get it out of China?"

Hamilton was prevented from answering by the appearance of a steward bearing steak and lobster with roasted vegetables. He anointed the lobster with melted butter before departing with a small bow and a muted *bon appetite*.

"You keep a remarkably fine table," said Hamilton, looking at his steaming plate and grasping his knife and fork purposefully.

"Finish the story, please," said Ellen, a slim note of asperity in her voice. The China operation had never been far from her mind in the past weeks. Along with the work in Hong Kong, it represented a new way of doing business for the syndicate and for her; a sort of arm's length system she was not yet wholly used to.

"Well," said Hamilton, after a mouthful of filet mignon, "since they all looked and behaved like soldiers, they commandeered a military lorry from a depot near Tiananmen and drove south as fast as they bloody well could. They were stopped once, just outside Changsha, by a gang of over-zealous Red Guards, but they claimed they were on PLA business. What with their uniforms and conditions being so chaotic, they got away with it easily. In fact, you know, I doubt anyone's noticed the statue's even missing. At any rate, they eventually got it to a place called Juhai, just over the border from Macau. Security's a little slacker there than at the border with Hong Kong. Once into Macau, and I don't know exactly how they did that except that it cost five thousand US dollars, the rest was simple. I got the crate onto a fishing boat and across the estuary to Hong Kong. A lot of those ocean-going junks do a little unregistered business on the side, no questions asked."

"There were rather a lot of people involved in all this," said Ellen, a trifle dubiously. "More than I usually like, quite frankly. I hope they're all reliable, and remember it's on your head, if they're not."

There was no mistaking her meaning, but Hamilton was unperturbed.

"Absolutely reliable," he said, wiping his mouth after a bite of buttered lobster. "The Hong Kong people are all into so many things they'd end up in the clink for the next hundred years if they ever got nicked. Silence keeps them safe. The pseudo-soldiers in China know enough to take their money and shut up. If they ever talked, they'd find themselves stapled upside down to the wall of a hut somewhere in the deserts of Inner Mongolia, or dead, which is more likely. No one will say a word. It's as tight as the proverbial drum."

"Let's hope you're right," said Ellen, delicately lifting a lobster tail from its protective shell, her meaning once again clear.

"We took the crate to a safe house on Lama Island in Hong Kong harbor," Hamilton went on, "hid it there until we were sure it was safe to move it, and then hired an ordinary little sampan to get it to the mainland. The harbor's full of them, and it attracted no attention at all. It was duly delivered to our contact at the Port Authority who had it put aboard the freighter to Bordeaux, and the rest you know."

"Yes," said Ellen, nodding. "The client knows the shipment is on its way, and he's highly pleased. Our agent in Paris is arranging for final delivery." She raised her champagne glass and added, "Here's to the future in China."

Chapter Twenty-One

In 1966, Ellen's illegitimate daughter, Gabriella, who insisted on being called Gabby, reached the age of eighteen, and left her school in Switzerland fluent in English, French, German, and Italian. Gabby had grown into an extremely attractive young woman, having her mother's elegant frame and full bosom, but her American father from Amarillo had granted her a darker complexion, hazel eyes, and curly brown hair. The truth concerning the source of her family's wealth having been concealed from her for obvious reasons, all Gabby knew was that her mother ran a company with some connection to the world of fine art and antiquities. Gabby was in love with her mother's luxurious lifestyle, her chauffeur-driven car with its deep leather seats, her sparkling nightclubs on Berlin's trendy *Kurfürstendamm*, and her expensive clothes. She had enjoyed that lifestyle herself during school holidays and was very anxious to enjoy it on a permanent basis as soon as she could. Ellen, however, had other ideas.

"Gabby," she said one evening, as they sipped their after-dinner liqueurs, "have you thought about going to university?"

"No," she answered, in some surprise. "Why would I go to university? You tell me you have a successful business, and I want to learn about it and help you run it." She paused for an uncertain moment and then added, "If you want me to, that is."

"Well, I do want you to," said Ellen, "but for you to be of real help, you need more training."

"In what? Business? Commerce? That sounds positively sterile to me."

"No," said Ellen, smiling. "Our business doesn't call for that kind of training. I can teach you whatever you need in that line. Mostly investment and money managing. But we do need another kind of expertise."

Ellen could plainly see Gabby's lack of enthusiasm, although her record at school amply demonstrated her intellectual capacity. Apart from her obvious linguistic talents, she had received other glowing reports, especially from her art teachers. She drew and painted well, they said, had a natural gift for design, and showed considerable interest in the history of art. It's perfect, Ellen reflected, but she has to go further.

"What I'm thinking," Ellen went on, choosing her words with infinite care, "is that you could go to Paris to the Sorbonne, and study art history."

"*Paris*," exclaimed Gabby. "Really?"

"Yes," said Ellen, seizing her advantage. "We'll find you a lovely flat, and you'll have a decent allowance. But you mustn't fritter your time away, understand? I want you to stick with it. I want you to graduate with a background in art history and prehistory. Europe, Greece, Rome, Egypt, and even Oriental art. It'll be tough slogging, and you need to know that right from the start."

"Paris," echoed Gabby. "It'll be wonderful. What did you say I should study?"

"Oh God," breathed Ellen, hoping she had not created a monster, and then went through it all again.

"Well," said Gabby, "that does sound a lot more interesting than business studies and all that dreary stuff. And I'll be living in Paris." Her eyes shone.

"You will be *studying* in Paris," said her mother, with firm deliberation and a severe look.

"Yes, yes," said Gabby, finishing her cognac, "but if I'm studying there, I'll have to live there, won't I?"

Ellen said nothing, but as she swallowed the last of her own drink, she trusted she had not made a dreadful mistake.

True to her word, she provided Gabby with a well-furnished flat in the fifth *arrondissement*, close to the Sorbonne on the left bank of the Seine, and a handsome allowance; even a small car. All this on the promise Gabby would attend assiduously to her studies, keep her marks high, and not waste her substance in riotous living, as did the biblical prodigal.

"This is heaven, *Mutti,*" she enthused, spinning about in the middle of her new sitting room, her arms out. "Look at me, everyone, I'm living in Paris."

"Remember our agreement, my girl," Ellen said, before she kissed Gabby and climbed into the taxi which was to take her to the airport for her flight back to Berlin.

"Yes ma'am," Gabby answered, with a mischievous grin and mock salute.

* * *

"I hope I've done the right thing," Ellen said to Richter, a few days later. "If she lets me down, I swear I'll send her to a convent."

Richter chuckled, saying, "I'm sure she'll be just fine. She's a smart girl, and beyond that, she's got plenty of good common sense."

"Hmm," said Ellen, still uncertain. "I trust so."

"And," Richter added, "she knows which side her bread's buttered on, or at least she will do very soon. When she sees what most of her fellow students have to survive on, she'll realize how well off she is."

"I'm glad you think so," said Ellen, from behind a veil of pungent Turkish tobacco smoke, "but she's barely nineteen. At nineteen I was sure I knew everything."

"So was I," Richter agreed, "but I think she'll quickly see she doesn't…just like we did."

As it transpired, Richter was correct. Gabby emerged from her first-year finals with excellent marks and came home in triumph for the holidays.

"I'm proud of you," said Ellen, hugging her daughter.

"You were worried, though, weren't you?" Gabby said, with a teasing grin.

"Not at all," said Ellen, putting every ounce of sincerity she could into her voice.

"Not much, you weren't."

"Oh, all right," Ellen confessed. "When you were in Switzerland, you were in a protected and controlled environment."

"Controlled, you say?" Gabby blurted, laughing. "That wasn't a school, it was a penal colony."

"I imagine it was, a bit," Ellen said, with a rueful smile, "so I suppose that's why I wondered about when you got out on your own…"

"I know," said Gabby, "you pictured me hanging about with a crowd of hippies, dressed like a scarecrow with unwashed hair, and high as Everest on some chemical or other."

"Well, I —"

"Of course, I tried that," said Gabby, matter-of-factly, and Ellen stared in horror.

"*What*?"

"Yes," said Gabby, nodding. "I'm really angry about what the Americans are trying to do in Vietnam, so I joined the protest movement. There's a lot of what you'd call *hippies* there, and I tried to be like them at first. I even tried acid. That's LSD to you, I suppose."

"*Gabriella!*" Ellen almost shouted in a mixture of shock, anger, and fear. She had seen many news reports about what was commonly called the *drug culture*, and she knew what LSD could do to people's brains. "How could you be so stupid? That stuff…" Her voice trailed off as she struggled for words she could not find.

"It's all right, *Mutti*, it's all right," Gabby said, in a soothing voice. "I tried it once, that's all, and I had a horrible trip."

"You didn't tell me about any trip," said Ellen, wondering what was coming next. "Where did you go?"

"Nowhere, silly," Gabby said, laughing. "When you say you had a bad trip, it means the LSD gave you a really bad time. Not enjoyable, the way it's supposed to be. You know, not fun or interesting, or anything like that at all.

271

After I dropped it, it was worse than a nightmare. The whole world was spinning all around me in crazy colors, and it wouldn't stop, no matter how much I screamed. And then I began to fall."

"Fall?" Ellen was appalled. "Fall where?"

"Just falling. Forever. Everything rushing by me, getting darker, and then blindingly bright. I know I screamed and screamed, but the more I screamed, the faster I seemed to fall. I was totally hoarse by the time it was all over."

"Dear God," said Ellen. "How long did all this last?"

"No idea."

"And you did this only once?"

"Once was enough," said Gabby, with conviction. "Somehow I ended up under the kitchen table. Don't know how I got there."

"What happened then?"

"I threw up all over Alain."

"And who's Alain, may I ask?"

"Alain Montpellier. He's in two of my art history classes. He's a bit of a creep, actually. He gave me the stuff in the first place and goaded me into trying it."

"Serves him right, then," growled Ellen.

"Anyway," said Gabby, "the whole thing going on with Alain and his crowd just put me off, so I hooked up with a group of others who were protesting the war on the basis of the historical research they'd done. That all made a lot more sense to me. I've written several articles on the origins of the war and American involvement in it since the French left. They all got published." This last news she delivered with something akin to smugness.

Ellen gazed at her daughter with a mixture of pride and admiration tinged with a certain mystification. When Ellen was about Gabby's age, she and her mother had been struggling to stay alive in the rubble of their shattered house in Munich. Hunger and desperation had forced her to get on her knees for lecherous toads and pleasure them in return for a few shriveled potatoes, or a loaf of stale bread, or once, she remembered, for a goddamned crowbar. Now,

272

she reflected, here was Gabriella, bright, beautiful, and self-possessed, having all the money she needed, as well as security and a place to live. True, Gabriella had never known her father, but at least she had not seen him shot to death before her eyes. She realized that the crowbar she had obtained all those years ago from that smelly laborer had opened many doors as well as those five wooden crates.

"Well done, Gabby," she said, giving her a hug. "Good for you. I only wish your grandparents could see you now." She held out her hand to her daughter, and said, "Now, let's go out for dinner and celebrate your grand marks, and your being home for a while."

"A splendid notion," said Gabby, smiling, "but I nearly forgot there's something else I want to tell you."

Now what, Ellen wondered. "Yes?" She hoped she didn't sound nervous.

"I found out what that old bone thing is. It's a Chinese oracle bone."

"A what?"

"An oracle bone. From the bronze age. Three thousand years ago or so. I found a reference to them in one of my art history books. They're a great source of information on life in those days."

Ellen listened as she explained how the bone was created and used.

"I can't read the characters, of course," she finished, "but I know a professor in Paris who can. If you like, I'll take it back with me and get it deciphered. At least then you'll know what it's all about."

"What's it worth?" Ellen asked, her eyes narrowing, thinking less of selling it than of assuring its safety.

"Dunno," said Gabby. "They're not exactly rare. There's been thousands of them dug up over the years. Most of them are in museums, I suppose."

"I think I'll just keep it," said Ellen, as they prepared to leave the house. "I don't really care what it says. Your grandmother gave it to me, and it reminds me of my parents and of those times in Munich. Whenever I think of it, I realize how lucky we are."

"You should display it," said Gabby, closing the door behind them, but Ellen said nothing. The time was not yet right.

* * *

In 1974, Gabby turned twenty-five, and had begun to play an important role in the running of the syndicate. She had gone from strength to strength in Paris, eventually graduating with a bejeweled academic record amid earnest pleas from her professors that she stay, and begin post-graduate work immediately. Ellen sat in the audience to watch her receive her degree, and in spite of her resolution never to think of Gabby's father, she could not help wondering where he might be at that moment. Was he still alive? Did he ever think about the young German girl he had occupied while he was occupying Germany? He knew Ellen was pregnant when he left, but did he care, then or now? Probably not.

Well, you lose, she thought, as Gabby stepped off the platform, a radiant smile on her face. You can't see your lovely daughter and appreciate what she's accomplished. Too bad for you, you creep. I hope you're having a sad little life in Armadillo, or whatever your stupid hometown was called.

As Ellen had discovered, Gabby's university life was by no means a cloistered existence. After her experiments with drugs and the brief fling with the awful Alain, she found numerous friends with whom she travelled extensively during the holidays. The phone calls and postcards home rapturized about the museums, the galleries, and the monumental, silently brooding ruins she visited. The Colosseum in Rome, the Acropolis in Athens, and the Blue Mosque and Topkapi Palace in Istanbul.

Her love life certainly did not end with Alain; rather, it became a whirlwind. It seemed to Ellen that she attracted boyfriends as a brilliant flower attracts hovering, hungry hummingbirds, but she was not in the least surprised. With astonishing regularity, Gabby told her about the procession of young hopefuls with whom she was involved, but she was at all times reserved, never wildly passionate or starry-eyed. She remained in perfect control. Her usual comment was that this or that young man was *nice*, or *really good-looking*. Occasionally, one of them might be *very nice*, but never more than that. Ellen was pleased at her lack of impulsiveness, her natural caution and self-possession. They augured well for the future, but would Gabby change as she grew older, Ellen wondered. People often did. Would she decide she wanted a husband, children, perhaps? Would she find a man, marry him, and leave home?

Well, she told herself. Gabby may not love any of her boyfriends, but she does love luxury, so let's hope there's never a man who comes along one day who's very nice, really good-looking, *and* rich.

"I only hope she'll sign onto the business before she becomes too independent," Ellen murmured as she sat smoking, a discarded book on the sofa beside her. "So much depends on how I introduce her to everything."

She stubbed out her cigarette and lit another.

"What if she'll have nothing to do with it all after she knows what it is?" Richter had once asked, and Ellen replied that she would trust Gabby to be discreet and keep her mouth shut, while she, Ellen, continued managing the syndicate on her own.

"She'll want the money to keep coming," Ellen added, a trifle wryly. "and I presume she wouldn't want to see her mother thrown in jail for several decades."

"Risky, though," said Richter, frowning. "Damn risky." And Ellen had been forced to agree.

So, with Gabriella's studies complete, her diploma proudly framed on the wall, and she showing no signs of wanting to pursue an academic or domestic career, Ellen confronted the task of explaining the nature of her business to her daughter.

With infinite caution, Ellen began to unfold the story, starting with Munich and the five bounteous crates of stolen treasure.

"So, there it is, my dear," she finished. "That's what the Athena Syndicate is, that's the family business, and the reason we are able to live as we do."

Gabby was silent for a time. To Ellen's initial relief, she did not leap from her chair in righteous indignation shouting that her mother was a common criminal or declaring in horror that the money they lived on was ill-gotten. There was no, *Mother, how could you*, which she had been half expecting. Ellen chewed her lower lip, hardly daring to breathe, as the silence extended into eternity.

"So," said Gabby at long last, "you steal what's been ordered. Well, I suppose that makes reasonable sense. Apart from paying off your thieves, there's very little up-front expense. There's a higher margin of profit. Right?"

"Precisely," said Ellen, exhaling, as she wondered what might be coming next.

"Athena," Gabby mused. "That makes sense as well, given who she was."

"It wasn't my idea," said Ellen. "People we worked with in Munich started calling it that. Mainly because of how your grandmother did business."

"I wish I'd known her better," said Gabby. "She sounds like a powerful lady."

"And then some," said Ellen, allowing herself a smile.

And now for the big question. This has all gone better than I'd hoped.

She said, "So now you know, Gabby. Our money is in various tax havens and secure banks throughout the world, and our gold is in Switzerland. I can tell you all about that later, but it must be obvious to you by now that I run what amounts to a criminal organization. Theft, smuggling, corruption, and all. We do our best to see no one gets hurt, but I daren't tolerate any fooling around or anyone who tries to operate by themselves at the syndicate's expense. If anyone goes rogue, we get tough because we have to protect ourselves." She paused for a long moment before

276

asking, "So…are you interested in coming on board, or shall I go on alone? If you'd rather not be involved, I'll understand, but you'll have to promise not to go blabbing all this around. If it ever comes to it, I'll swear you never knew anything."

"You give me a good allowance now," Gabby said, "but if I go to work for you, will I get more? A cut of the profits, or something?"

Is it going to be nothing more than sheer greed, Ellen asked herself?

She said, "Of course. You'd be a partner."

"Then let's get started, shall we?"

Chapter Twenty-Two

The syndicate suited Gabby perfectly. She absorbed everything Ellen told her, quickly learning the names of those in the network she would be dealing with and putting her expertise and linguistic skills to effective use. She appeared to have no qualms whatever about the illegality of the operation, and soon began to make her mark.

"All right," said Richter, now nearly sixty, but still active as Head of Acquisitions, "your instincts were correct. Gabby is doing very well indeed."

"Yes," said Ellen, "I'm very pleased. She's looking after all the Asia operations now, and since her visit to China, she's got a lot better sense of what's there and how we might get at some of it if we need to. She and Hamilton work well together, and the Far East network is expanding into Vietnam, Cambodia, Laos, and Thailand now the war's over. She's also picking up Mandarin Chinese, no less. I'm really quite impressed."

"She's her mother's daughter," said Richter, smiling. "And by the way, Hamilton's just put me onto a couple of new people who can assist with acquisitions almost anywhere in Asia, including India and Japan."

"Good," said Ellen, nodding, and lighting a black cigarette, "but I'm afraid there's some bad news to go along with all this good stuff. Old Brandt died in hospital in Bonn yesterday. He'd been ill for a few weeks, I understand."

"Sorry to hear that," said Richter. "He was a close friend, wasn't he? He helped your mother as well."

"Yes, he did. He was just doing a bit of petty thieving from his museum when she met him, but he died a multimillionaire, thanks to his research for us."

"I'll bet he did," said Richter, with a chuckle. "Did he have a family to inherit it all?"

"Not that I know of."

"So, who's going to head up Research now?" asked Richter. "Faber?"

"No," said Ellen. "I don't think so. He's good, but he's not a forward planner. He thinks no further than the job at hand, and once that's done, he just waits for the next assignment."

"Not much of a self-starter, as they say nowadays," said Richter.

"No."

"Got someone else in mind, have you?"

"Well actually," Ellen said, "I'm thinking of moving the whole research division here to Berlin. "It was all right having it in Bonn while Brandt was alive because he was on top of everything. I didn't have to worry. Now, I think I'll have to keep a much closer eye on them, and I can't do that at a distance unless I travel all the time, which I don't want to do. I like living in the London flat as a home base, but I'm here a lot of the time on other business, as you know, so having Research close by makes better sense than leaving them in Bonn."

So it was, then, that the late Professor Brandt's team of six researchers, whose proud boast was, *If it exists, we'll find it*, moved, all expenses paid, to Berlin where they set up their new offices in three rooms in Ellen's large house. In a fourth room, Gabby could be found hard at work in several languages any time of the day or night checking, verifying, and expanding the provenances and histories of items on order. From a spacious office on the floor above, Richter choreographed his acquisitions teams wherever in the world they happened to be needed. Ellen retained over-all control of the syndicate's finances, and in particular, she looked after the delicate business of shipping and delivery to her wealthy but well-concealed clients. Those clients were known only by numbers; she alone knew their names and made purchase agreements with them.

"Shipping and delivery are the weakest links," she told Gabby. "There's so much that can go wrong when it comes to moving these things across international boundaries, let alone across whole oceans and continents. And even if that's done smoothly, the piece still has to be safely delivered to the client without any possibility of our being connected to it. Ideally, the piece should just materialize on the client's doorstep one day, so to speak, without anyone ever appearing to put it there."

"Like magic," said Gabby, grinning.

"Exactly," said Ellen, with a laugh. "I'm working on it."

And thus, the syndicate prospered. Items were ordered, acquired, shipped, delivered, and paid for, all according to the principles and procedures Ellen had laid down, based on what she learned from her mother and passed on to her daughter. Then, in 1977, on what had until then been a placid evening at home, Gabby put down her glass of sherry and calmly delivered a piece of news to her mother which was as unexpected as a thunderclap on a cloudless day.

"You've fallen in love with *who*?" Ellen demanded, incredulous, after Gabby had unburdened her soul.

"Irwin Becker," Gabby repeated, "and we want to get married as soon as we can."

Ellen knew her daughter lived a full — some might say frenzied — social life, but she had never once shown any sign of wanting to marry any of the numerous and ardent young men who paid her court. As far as Ellen was aware, since Gabby began working for the syndicate, there had never been anyone who qualified, even remotely, as a particular boyfriend, and yet, seemingly out of the void, had come this declaration of love for a co-worker from the research division, of all places.

"But...but, " Ellen struggled for words, hastily putting down her own glass to avoid spilling it in her agitation, "how...when...?"

"Oh *Mutti*." Gabby could not help laughing at her mother's discomfiture and confusion.

"We met when Research moved in here. We've been seeing each other for a long time. We understand and love each other, and we want to make our lives together." And seeing the blank look of astonishment still on her mother's face, she added with a grin, "Love and marriage are not uncommon occurrences, you know."

Ellen continued to stare, and Gabby laughed again.

"It's all right, Mother dear. I'm twenty-eight. I'm a long way from being a child or a hormone-addled teenager. I know my own mind."

Ellen had to agree with that. She had watched Gabby step into her position with the syndicate, confident of her skills, self-assured, and self-aware. She relied on her, felt comfortable asking her advice, and her knowledge of art and antiquities was invaluable. And Becker was an excellent man, compendious in his knowledge, holder of a doctoral degree in art history and museology. She relied on him with equal confidence. So, here came the vital question.

"Will you both want to leave the syndicate, Gabby? I mean, will you want to start some sort of legitimate business, or an illegitimate one, for that matter?"

"Not at all, for heaven's sake. We'd never get into a situation that pays as well as you do, and besides, we both feel part of the syndicate. We aren't about to just get married and waltz off on our own."

Ellen's relief was boundless, and having established this positive view of the future, she happily turned her attention to the matter of giving Gabby a wedding West Berlin's high society would remember for many and many a year.

* * *

281

The wedding was a triumph of the highest order, and, true to their word, Gabby and Irwin stayed with the syndicate. They bought a large flat near Ellen's house, and moved into it after a month-long honeymoon at a luxury resort in Pattaya Beach, Thailand. Ellen saw with pleasure how radiantly happy her daughter was, and having privately, confidentially, and in great detail, described to Becker exactly what she would do to him if he failed to treat his new wife properly, she settled into her new and solitary domestic existence. Gabby and Irwin worked together as harmoniously as it appeared they lived together, and the syndicate progressed as it always had. Ellen's reputation for being able to acquire virtually anything ordered gave rise to more and more specialized requests from a smaller, but wealthier, clientele. Prices in the millions were routinely charged. The formidable mother-daughter partnership became ever stronger and was in no way weakened by Gabby's announcement in late 1978 that she was pregnant.

"Next August, around mid-month," she said, in answer to Ellen's question. "You're going to be a grandmother."

"The mind boggles," said Ellen, in mock seriousness, before hugging her daughter and telling her she was thrilled. "How wonderful," she whispered. "How very wonderful indeed."

Privately, in the weeks that followed, she was somewhat concerned about Gabby's ability to handle her work and a newborn baby as well but reminded herself there were plenty of nannies and *au pairs* who could be hired to help at home. And besides, she reminded herself, working mothers are everywhere these days.

Apart from a month or so of mild morning sickness, Gabby sailed through her pregnancy in radiant good health, but the baby arrived some two weeks earlier than anticipated while Ellen was in London. She had gone there to hold discussions with three muscular young men who had been engaged to persuade a recalcitrant client in Gloucestershire to pay what he owed for a Ming Dynasty vase acquired with considerable difficulty from a museum in Taiwan. Appearing at the meeting in a wig, horn-rimmed glasses, and heavy makeup, they had no idea what she actually looked like. They never knew her name, nor how the debt had been incurred. All they knew, or cared about, was that the gentleman in question owed a great deal of money, and once it was paid, they would receive a very handsome commission.

"Scare him to death," she said. "Threaten him or his family with whatever you like. Smash some chinaware or something if you think you need to, but don't hurt anybody. He can't pay if he's in hospital, and an assault would attract the attention of the police, which can't be allowed to happen. Is that perfectly clear?"

Apparently, it was. They glanced at one other, nodded, and Ellen went back to her luxury bijou hotel in Mayfair where she got out of her disguise, showered, and went to bed, well satisfied. When in London on business of that sort, she never used her flat in Russell Square as a base. She wanted no possible connections to be made.

"Gabby's in the delivery room now," Irwin told her at two o'clock the following morning after the telephone had jarred her out of a deep sleep. It took a moment for her to assemble her wits before she could speak.

"Already?"

"Yes. At first, they thought the contractions were false, or maybe something else altogether. Anyway, once they got her to hospital, they saw what was happening, and off she went."

"Any word at all?"

"Nothing so far. I wish someone would tell me something. I'm going crazy here. I'll call you as soon as there's news."

"All right," said Ellen. "I'll get the first flight I can. I'm on the way, and for God's sake don't be so worried. Women have babies all the time. She'll be just fine, you'll see."

"Right, yes," said Irwin, clearly unconvinced. "See you later."

Landing at Berlin's Tempelhof Feld, Ellen went straight to the hospital, where she met Irwin Becker in a maternity waiting room that smelled faintly of antiseptic and plastic furniture. He was unshaven and wore a haggard expression which was more than mere fatigue and worry. Ellen felt a stab of alarm and fear.

"A long night?" she asked, trying to put aside her premonition. "How's Gabby? Is it a boy or a girl?"

"It's a girl," he answered, but without a trace of excitement in his voice. Ellen saw the distress in his eyes and sensed the worst.

"What's happened?" she demanded. "Is it Gabby?" Desperation rose.

"No," said Becker, in a flat, expressionless voice, "she's fine. Actually, the delivery was fairly easy."

"Then what's —?"

She was interrupted by the arrival of a small, white-coated man in his late fifties, balding, and avuncular-looking. He appeared from a room on their left, through a door Ellen had not even noticed.

"Oh," said Becker, distractedly, "this is *Herr* Doctor Grossman. *Herr* Doctor, this is Gabriella's mother."

"Ah, yes," he said, shaking Ellen's hand, "I am very sorry this has happened."

"I haven't told her," Becker interposed.

"Oh, I see."

"Told me *what?*" Ellen snapped, now thoroughly frightened and giving way to anger. "What's going on here?"

"Dr. Grossman is a pediatric ophthalmologist," said Becker. "He was called in when…that is, to confirm—"

"*Frau*…er?" The doctor raised his eyebrows.

"Schumacher."

"Yes, *Frau* Schumacher," said Grossman, and then, in a gentle but business-like voice, he went on, "We are very sorry to say the baby has been born with a rare condition known as bilateral microphthalmia. It means that both eyes are smaller than they should be and are much malformed."

Ellen stared at the man in wordless horror.

"The fact is," Grossman said, "the child cannot see, and will never see. In all other respects, however, she is perfectly healthy."

For a dreadful moment, Ellen thought she might be sick. The walls of the austere room closed in on her, spinning and whirling. The framed print of a Bavarian landscape on the wall appeared to be rushing towards her, and she squeezed her eyes shut. Becker caught her elbow as she swayed backwards and lowered her into a chair.

"Are you all right, *Frau* Schumacher?" The doctor put his hand on her shoulder.

For a full minute she could say nothing as her churning stomach slowly reordered itself while her mind tried to grasp what she had heard.

"Are you saying there's nothing to be done?" she finally managed to whisper. She still felt dizzy. "Nothing at all?"

"Nothing, I'm afraid. I am so very sorry."

"No surgery?"

"No. No correction is possible. The structure of the eyes, you see…" His voice trailed away.

Ellen squeezed her eyes shut again for a moment, as her thoughts flew to Gabby.

"Does my daughter know?"

"I told her before she saw her baby," said Grossman. "It was imperative to do so. To allow her discover it herself was out of the question. The shock would —"

"What happened? What did she say?"

"She insisted on the baby's being brought to her, and she has her still."

"Have you seen them both?" Ellen asked Becker, and he nodded, his face gray and pinched.

"Dear God," breathed Ellen, "my poor, precious girl." And then, turning to Becker, she grasped his hand. "Irwin…I don't know what to say."

"*Frau* Schumacher," said Grossman, "why don't you go in and see Gabriella and the child? I think she would want you near her just now. Gabriella is…very strong. I know of women who utterly reject babies born blind. They

285

thrust them away, abandon them to adoption. But, your daughter…well, you should see for yourself."

He held the door open for them to enter the small room where they found Gabby sitting up in bed in a white hospital gown, the baby in her arms.

"*Mutti*," she said, smiling, "you came so quickly."

Gabby seldom called her Mama these days, and Ellen's eyes brimmed with tears.

Becker kissed Gabby on the forehead, muttered, "I need to go to the washroom," and disappeared.

"Irwin's really upset," said Gabby, staring at the white door which had closed behind him.

"Well, yes," said Ellen, thinking how lame her words sounded.

"I hope he'll come around," said Gabby, biting her lower lip.

"I'm sure he will," said Ellen. "Try not to worry."

"Her name is Sylvia, *Mutti*," Gabby said, looking down at her baby. "Isn't she beautiful?"

Is this simple denial, Ellen asked herself, or is she afraid even to think about it?

Ellen steeled herself and looked at the tiny, pink little being in Gabby's arms. Set in its round, rather pudgy face, were two, miniscule eyes, shriveled, and without light. Ellen compressed her lips, feeling her chin tremble.

No…no. I can't cry. I mustn't.

"Gabby —"

"I know, *Mutti*," Gabby interrupted. "I asked all the questions. There's nothing they can do. Dr. Grossman said perhaps a virus or something like rubella might cause it, but there's no direct evidence of that. Basically, it's a genetic aberration. It's not anyone's fault. Sylvia is my…our…lovely daughter, and she'll do whatever she wants to do as she grows up. I'll…we'll…make sure of that."

Ellen looked at her daughter, wondering where she found the fortitude for such composure and determination, and as she watched, Gabby bowed her head. Tears fell onto the blankets swaddling the child.

"My poor little Sylvia," she whispered. "My poor, sweet little girl."

* * *

By the time Sylvia Becker was twelve, the Berlin Wall was gone, Germany had been reunified, and the Union of Soviet Socialist Republics was a thing of the past. Millions rejoiced. The Athena Syndicate now had access to Eastern Europe and was making inroads into Russia and the other countries of the former Soviet bloc as new economic realities provided opportunities for the accumulation of personal wealth. The times were turbulent, and the syndicate took advantage of that turbulence wherever and whenever it could.

Gabby was raising Sylvia alone. Irwin's reaction to his daughter's disability had been one of revulsion, anger, and bitter resentment. Feelings he turned on Gabby, accusing her of somehow being the cause of Sylvia's blindness. He had as little to do with the child as he could, and never told anyone he had a daughter.

"She is our child," Gabby told him one night when Sylvia was five. "Ours, Irwin. Yours and mine together. She needs a father and a mother. How can you turn your back on her as you do?"

It was past midnight. Becker had come home staggering drunk, as he did more and more frequently. Leaning on the back of a chair, he stared at her, glassily.

"Our child?" he mumbled. "Are you telling me I had anything to do with creating that freak?"

"How dare you call her that?" Gabby shouted in towering fury.

"Because that's what she is," retorted Becker, before stumbling away to the single bedroom he had been using for almost four years. Gabby heard him vomiting in the bathroom.

A firm of expensive lawyers speedily completed the divorce, Gabby obtaining full custody of her daughter on the evidence of her husband's alcoholism and her demonstrated ability to provide for Sylvia's future well-being. The property they jointly owned was sold, and Gabby moved with her daughter into Ellen's home, the house she had lived in since her return from Switzerland as a seventeen-year-old. This arrangement provided Gabby support and greater opportunities for Sylvia to interact with other people as she grew up.

"I'm concerned that Irwin won't keep his mouth shut," said Gabby, but Ellen told her not to worry.

"I have explained what will happen to him if he does anything stupid. I have also given him a sum of money and he has accepted my humble suggestion that he emigrate to the States and disappear. He also agreed to change his name and we are giving him new documents and passport. He is about to become a Mr. Harvey Schultz."

"You must have terrified him," Gabby said, grinning.

"Oh, I certainly did," Ellen agreed, gravely.

The syndicate's network of agents in the United States was given Becker's new name, and six months later it was reported to Ellen that Harvey Schultz had been shot and killed by police in Portland, Oregon, as he tried to flee after robbing a convenience store.

"Problem solved all by itself," Ellen observed.

* * *

Sylvia progressed well, and the two older generations watched with pride. She became adept in the use of a white cane, made great strides in reading braille, but, to Gabby's disappointment, refused the option of replacing her tiny eyes with natural-looking prosthetic ones. She insisted instead on wearing dark glasses.

"My eyes may look funny," she declared, "but they're mine. People don't have to look at them, but I want to keep them. Besides," she added, on one occasion, with a mischievous grin, "these glasses make me look mysterious."

"But, Sylvia," Gabby said, "with those black glasses, you don't look as pretty as you really are."

"I look like myself," she retorted, "and that's how I want to look."

"She has a mind of her own," said Ellen. "Much like her mother."

Gabby shook her head as she watched her daughter navigate across the room and out into the hall. Sylvia had inherited her grandmother's blonde hair and was already displaying an elegance of form and movement which distinguished her from the other girls at the school for the blind in Berlin. She was popular with everyone, and her teachers were impressed.

"She's a most intelligent and gifted girl," said one of them to Gabby at a Sports Day when Sylvia was seventeen. "She reads German and English braille, speaks English fluently with only the slightest German accent. She has also grasped the use of braille for the study of mathematics, which is not easy, and she has an excellent memory. We hope she will one day find good employment, although I am afraid, she is a little hot-tempered sometimes."

"As to employment," said Gabby, balancing a coffee cup in one hand and a small piece of chocolate cake in the other, "I'd like to have her working with me in our family business after she completes university."

"Oh, well," said the teacher, a brisk, gray-haired woman of over fifty and tending towards a certain rotundity, "if I were you, I would hesitate to give Sylvia the impression she can attend university. Very few totally blind people do, you know. Especially girls. I'd be more inclined to steer her towards some sort of secretarial or clerical position. A job which is somewhat repetitive that she can master more easily."

Gabby opened her mouth to respond, and the teacher hurried on.

"I'm sure she would qualify for entrance, *Frau* Becker, but post-secondary studies are very arduous, you understand."

"But you, yourself, said she's very intelligent."

"Oh, my word she is. That's why she would make an excellent secretary. Or she could train as a basket weaver or a maker of wicker furniture, you know. I'm sure she would be brilliant."

"If Sylvia wants to go to university," Gabby said to her mother later that evening, "then I think she should have the chance. I think that teacher is much too over-protective, and perhaps a little behind the times. It was all I could do not to pour my coffee all over her head."

"That's all well and good," said Ellen, her customary black cigarette between her fingers, "but you don't want to set her up for failure. I mean, there will be a lot of reading and so forth. You know that yourself. And no doubt there are all sorts of obstacles we don't even know about. Are textbooks available in braille?"

"Not generally," Gabby admitted, lighting her own cigarette, "but we can hire people to transcribe the books she needs. I know we can hire readers as well, so she can have books read aloud to her."

"It's a lot to ask," said Ellen, shaking her head. "It sounds daunting to me."

"She reads braille almost as fast as I read print," said Gabby, exhaling a stream of smoke. "You've seen that yourself."

"That's true," Ellen agreed. "It's phenomenal."

"She wants to study history," said Gabby, and Ellen laughed.

"That's your influence. All those trips you've taken her on to Greece and Rome and wherever else."

"Well, you certainly influenced, or should I say *manipulated*, me, Mother dear," said Gabby, smiling and raising her wine glass in Ellen's direction.

"It was all in aid of our business," said Ellen, inclining her head in acknowledgement. "There was always a higher purpose."

"So, going back to Sylvia," said Gabby, "if anyone can be successful, she can, so if university is what she wants, then that's what she shall have."

"All right," said Ellen, stubbing out her cigarette. "I just hope it doesn't prove a disappointment." She paused a moment, then added, "To both of you."

And so it was, that in 1998, just after her nineteenth birthday, Sylvia began university. Through braille, audiobooks, readers, technological aids, and stoic determination, Sylvia earned her degree, and Gabby watched with immeasurable pride in November of 2001 as one of her professors guided her across the platform to receive her diploma. She had been using a guide dog for several years by then, but it was not allowed onto the platform at graduation. The audience applauded enthusiastically, and Gabby overheard murmurings about how wonderful it was that a blind girl could obtain a degree. But an older gentleman in the row behind gruffly observed that it should not be permitted.

"Academic standards should not be diluted," he growled, "in order to make it possible for helpless people to receive a pseudo-education. And now they pretend to give her a degree just to make her feel good. It is a farce, and the university should be ashamed of itself."

Sylvia's grandmother was not present, however. Two months before, Ellen had been sitting in the entrance foyer of an investment firm in New York with which she had been doing business for several years. She neither saw nor heard the aircraft that struck the building, killing her instantly.

Part Six
London, England 2015 - 2017

Chapter Twenty-Three

"What the hell are you talking about?" Superintendent Stuart snapped, his Glaswegian accent rich and round.

Inspector Foy had asked to see Stuart in his office, but the meeting was not going at all well.

"I've looked through the notes on the interview you conducted with Michael Barrow," said Foy, "and I'm wondering about follow-up."

"What d'you mean, follow-up?" Stuart's glittering eyes betrayed his anger. "Barrow was clean. There was no point in wasting time on him."

"He said he left for Paris early the morning after Terry Preston was at his flat, the morning after he was killed," said Foy, renewing his efforts to sound reasonable. "I didn't see any reference to that ever being verified."

"The French police checked his alibi. He did go to Paris." Stuart stared at Foy in open hostility.

"Yes, but there's no information as to when he got there or when he left. And when he did leave, where did he go? Did he come back to London, or did he go somewhere else first?"

"I wasn't about to tell the French police how to do their damn job," said Stuart, his accent thickening even further. "And in any case, there was nothing to link Barrow to the murder. Who cares if he came back to London or went to Timbuktu?"

"For God's sake," Foy burst out, "Barrow was the last person to see Terry Preston alive. He's the obvious first place to start. We need to know everything we can about what he did, where he went, how long he stayed, and how many times he went for a piss after he got there."

"How dare you?" growled Stuart between clenched teeth. "You waltz back in here like the high king of mucky-muck, talk to your pals upstairs, get yourself re-instated, and then presume to sit in judgement on the rest of us. Who the hell d'you think you are?"

"I'm trying to get at the truth," said Foy, "that's all. Once we've found Terry's killer, I'll be gone. You'll never have to see me again, which I'm sure you'll appreciate."

"Too right I will. Roll on the day."

"But until that happy day," Foy persisted, calming his voice to a more level tone, "I want to let you know I'm going to check out Barrow's version of his movements the day after Terry died. I'm also looking into the witness who thinks he saw a blue van leaving the site of Barrow's stolen car. There may not be any connection between the theft of the car and Terry's murder, but we won't know until we look, will we?"

"All right, please yourself," said Stuart, morosely. "Send someone out to talk to the witness, but make sure the original investigators know."

"Already done," said Foy, "and I've got Neeta Mahajan on it. I think she's a damn good young detective."

* * *

Two days later, Neeta Mahajan came into Foy's office, lowered herself gracefully onto one of the uncomfortable plastic chairs, and crossed her long legs.

After a brief exchange of routine pleasantries, she said, "I talked to that bloke about the blue van, sir. I must say I don't think he's very reliable. Doesn't seem sure about what he saw. He'd be destroyed if he ever got into the witness box."

"Well hopefully we won't need him to do that," said Foy. "Could he give you anything useful?"

"Perhaps," she said. "He says he saw two men in the van, and he thinks, I stress *thinks*, the van had writing on the side."

"And does he *think* he remembers what the writing said?"

"He *thinks* it said *Bell Brothers*."

"Bell Brothers…what?" asked Foy. "Plumbers, undertakers, rocket scientists? What?"

Neeta shook her head, her long ebony hair, on this occasion left loose, swaying gently.

Damn me, thought Foy, as he looked at her in her white blouse and gray slacks. Where the hell were you when I was twenty-five? Yes, I know, he answered himself, you weren't born yet. God, I must be really old.

"And you've checked out *Bell Brothers*, I assume," he said, reestablishing his focus with some difficulty.

"Of course, I have," said Neeta, with crisp efficiency. "There are firms of that name in Stockport, Bristol—"

"Okay, okay," said Foy, holding up his hands. "Sorry. I'm sure you've done your homework, but does the name get us anywhere?"

"Not actually, sir, no," Neeta conceded. "In fact, all things considered, I couldn't find out anything beyond what they turned up in the initial investigation."

"So, we're no further ahead on that front," said Foy, in a gloomy voice.

"Not for the moment, sir, but I'll keep at it. I'm nothing if not persistent, you know."

* * *

Mike Barrow watched as Lombardi guided Sylvia Becker to her desk and waited until she sat down before stretching out on the carpet beside her chair. She reached down, found his left ear, and gave it a scratch.

"Good boy."

Lombardi tossed his golden head as if to say, *think nothing of it*, or, *just doing my job*, then licked her hand with his big, wet tongue.

Barrow said nothing. Sylvia began all conversations. You spoke only when spoken to.

"So, Mike," she said, "the bronze is on its way, is it?"

"Yes. The *Gdansk* sailed from Felixtowe yesterday. Due in Shanghai in two months, making a few stops on the way."

"The client is very anxious about his order," said Sylvia. She wore an emerald green dress, quite short in the skirt, and Barrow thought she looked as stunning as ever. Except for those damn dark glasses, he said to himself, not for the first time. Why on earth does she wear them?

As he looked at her, he wondered whether it was because she actually had no eyes, and he found the thought disturbing. She's so gorgeous, he said to himself, and as his thoughts dwelt on this as his eyes dwelt on her, he became aware she was talking to him.

"They hid the statue very well," he said, in answer to her question. "It'll be fine."

"Let's hope so," she said, unsmiling.

Barrow waited. Sylvia had asked him to come to Germany, so something else must be up. He seldom met her in her Berlin office, but it was as well-furnished as her London one — expensive hardwoods, deep upholstery, and elegant accent pieces and accoutrements.

"We have a new client," she said. "Referred by client eight-five-six. He wants the gold ruby ring worn by Catherine the Great at her coronation."

"Excuse me?"

"You heard. The client found out about it somewhere but isn't sure it's still extant. Research thinks it is, however."

"If it's in a museum or private collection in Russia," Barrow said, "we may have trouble getting hold of it. I think our agent in Moscow's dodgy."

"I know," said Sylvia. "I'm working on a replacement, and then I'll probably have to shut Vladimir up permanently. Maximum response." She paused to light a cigarette, and then resumed. "Fortunately, however, the ring isn't in Russia, it's in England... At least, Research says there's a gold and ruby ring reputed to have belonged to Catherine. It's not absolutely certain she wore it at her coronation, but the client's satisfied with it."

"So where is this ring?"

Sylvia deftly balanced her cigarette on the edge of an ashtray, and then moved her hand across her desktop until she found a sheet of heavy paper which she pulled towards her. Her fingers swept smoothly across the raised braille dots.

"Research says it's in a private house, so it's another job for the twins."

She always referred to Richard and Graham, her London-based acquisitions men, as *the twins*. They undertook virtually all European assignments with Barrow acting as liaison in most cases. This structure represented a change from the days when Gabriella ran the syndicate, but Sylvia had felt it necessary. Erich Richter, the former manager of European acquisitions, had retired in 1990 to an easeful life with his family in South America, and died in 2011. Andrew Hamilton, Richter's opposite number in Asia, had met a most unpleasant end in 1992 when a victim of his double-dealing as a Hong Kong policeman finally caught up with him and tortured him to death in a variety of very imaginative ways. At the time, Ellen Schumacher had been unsuccessful in finding trustworthy replacements for either of them, so she took over the work herself and trained Gabriella as her assistant. After Ellen's death, Gabriella Becker stepped into overall command of the syndicate, including the organization of acquisitions. Sylvia, who seemed to enjoy that particular aspect of the syndicate's operations, had retained it for herself as well when she assumed control of the organization as Gabriella's health declined.

A real matriarchy, Barrow reflected, before hastily returning his attention to Sylvia.

"Apparently," she was continuing, "the current owner of the ring obtained it by inheritance. The family has a long history of employment in the British diplomatic service, and one of the ancestors picked the ring up while he was Ambassador to the court of the Czar in the mid-nineteenth century. The client who wants it is Russian by birth, but now lives in Indonesia, believe it or not. Once we have it, we'll decide on delivery. Hopefully, we can use the engagement ring procedure, but it depends on how soon you can get it out of the country after it's been acquired. If the theft attracts a lot of police attention very quickly, we'll do it another way. We have an agent in Jakarta who we've used many times, so I don't anticipate any significant difficulties with the handover."

"Okay," said Barrow. "Where is it?"

Sylvia provided the address, and Barrow flew back to London where he gave the twins their orders. Sylvia, having no desire to leave any sort of paper or electronic trail, insisted on verbal communications only when it came to acquisition operations. It slowed things down but was much safer. A careless phrase in an email or text message which afterwards fell into the wrong hands, could well be disastrous. She was the fourth generation CEO of the syndicate, and not only did she sincerely respect that responsibility, she also harbored a desperate fear of arrest. Incarceration was anathema to her since it would mean the loss of the multimillion-dollar net worth she regarded as indispensable to all normal life. The privations of prison would be utterly intolerable, and to avoid them she ran the syndicate in an inflexibly autocratic fashion beyond even that of her dictatorial predecessors. She insisted on absolute control and unquestioning obedience.

As a nineteen-year-old on holiday with friends in Italy, she had been raped by a local farmhand, ten years her senior. Terrified and humiliated, she told no one until she discovered she was pregnant. Gabriella's rage was indescribable. After sending Sylvia away to a facility in the Netherlands to have the pregnancy safely terminated, Gabby hired two specialists from the Corsican mafia who travelled to Italy, shot the rapist in the head in front of his wife, and departed, each pocketing a handsome fee. Sylvia never forgot the lesson she learned on that occasion. Money can make any problem go away, make anything right, and she wrapped herself snugly in the vast fortune the syndicate continued to provide as though it were a warm blanket.

Five days after Barrow's conversation in Berlin, the twins, disguised this time as Roman Catholic priests, joined a party of sightseers on a guided tour of Hazelton Park, a stately home in Kent. The owners of the house proudly displayed more than two centuries' worth of treasures which marked out their long association with British foreign policy, and in a solidly built glass cabinet, the twins saw the ring they were looking for. That night, a set of bolt-cutters was employed to sever the thin bars across a first-floor window, and the closed-circuit surveillance cameras recorded the progress of two hooded figures as they dashed through the house, alarm klaxons shrieking. They smashed the glass cabinet which housed the ring and were gone in a heartbeat.

Later that day, Barrow, using his forged Dutch passport in the name of Jan Vandermeer, boarded a flight to Soekarno Hatta International Airport, Jakarta, Indonesia, with the ring in a velvet box in his carry-on backpack. Counting on the news of the theft not yet being widespread, he was prepared to explain it as an engagement ring for his soon-to-be *fiancée,* but he was unchallenged by the humorless security staff at Heathrow. After the fourteen-hour flight he emerged bleary-eyed from the airport into the sweltering heat and clinging humidity of Java and found a taxi that did not look as if it would fall apart before reaching the city. He checked into a blissfully cool air-conditioned five-star hotel on Jalan Thamrin, showered and changed into lighter clothes. Discovering that he was ravenously hungry, he decided a meal was in order, but a tropical storm was by then raging over the city sending great peals of crackling thunder rolling across the lowering sky accompanied by blinding rain, so leaving the hotel was out of the question. Accordingly, he headed for the Indonesian restaurant on the second floor where he enjoyed a feast of *nasi goreng* followed by a plate of sweet mango, papaya, and *rambutan*. Too tired to do anything else, he returned to his room and fell asleep immediately he lay down.

After breakfast the next morning he put some items into a plastic bag, wrapped the small velvet box in newspaper and taped it thoroughly. Tucking the little parcel into his pocket, he left his room. Outside, the concierge, through the use of a deafening whistle, attracted a taxi for him out of the maelstrom of traffic on Jalan Thamrin and after squeezing himself into the back seat he gave the driver the name of a large department store about fifteen minutes away.

"And turn on the air-conditioning, for God's sake," he said, but the driver, a wrinkled old man of indeterminate age, smiled a cordial gap-toothed smile saying, "Not work, but everything okay, I keep windows open."

It was like riding in a moving furnace, and the small car was filled with the acrid stench of diesel exhaust as it proceeded slowly through the dense traffic.

It was the longest fifteen minutes of Barrow's not uneventful life.

As he sat perspiring and gasping in the stultifying atmosphere, Barrow noticed the meter was not working either, and the prune-faced old driver offered another cordial smile and said, "It is dead, sir."

"I know Jakarta very well," said Barrow, "so I know how much the fare should be."

That was a lie, but the trick usually worked whichever city the taxi happened to be in. Unwilling to risk a cheap trip, the driver muttering morosely in Bahasa, then smacked the meter sharply on one side, instantly and miraculously restoring it to life and function.

Once at the store, Barrow found the men's washroom and entered a stall where he applied the disguises from the plastic bag. After dropping the bag into the rubbish bin, he left the store with its teeming throng of noisy shoppers and hailed another taxi. To his vast relief, both the air-conditioning and the meter worked, and he asked to be taken to a flea market called the Jalan Surabaya, a twenty-minute trip through Jakarta's teeming streets. Arriving at the market, a long row of stalls lining one side of a narrow road, he mingled with the reams of tourists and local folk seeking a bargain on everything from suitcases to old brass instruments and souvenirs of the Japanese occupation, most of them manufactured quite recently in local workshops. Counting along the row of narrow stalls, the heat and humidity threatening to melt him into the dusty pathway, he arrived at number twenty-three. The owner, a white-haired old man with two broken front teeth, seeing a possible sale, accosted him immediately.

"Many fine and rare antiques here, sir. Excellent price for you."

The dark interior of the narrow stall was airless and smelled of the dust which lay thickly over the shabby ceramic bowls and jars which the owner declared to be genuine specimens of ancient Chinese porcelain.

"Many from Ming Dynasty, sir," he proclaimed. "Some, like this one, are from Tang Period. Very, very old." He held up a chipped blue bowl, and Barrow snorted.

"If that's Ming or Tang, I'm Genghis Khan."

The proprietor, somewhat deflated, took the clove cigarette from his mouth after half-suffocating Barrow in a pall of its sweet-smelling smoke.

"Good price," he said again, albeit with much less enthusiasm. No doubt he was thinking Barrow was going to be an awkward customer.

"No thanks," said Barrow. "I'm not here to buy. I have a gift for you from Athena."

"Ah," said the old man, looking furtively around, before beckoning Barrow behind a curtain so threadbare as to be almost transparent at the far end of the wood-sided

300

stall. The cramped and odiferous space held a cane stool and a three-legged card table, its legless corner resting on the cracked rim of a tall ceramic jar. The table bore an ancient metal thermos flask, a cup half full of cold coffee, and a large tin ashtray heaped with ash and cigarette butts. The heat inside the confined space made Barrow's head swim.

"Here," he said, handing over the small box.

It weighed virtually nothing, and the round-backed old man took it with a quizzical expression on his brown face.

"What is it?"

"Never you mind," Barrow snapped. "Just take it to the address you were given. Don't let anything happen to it, and don't breathe a word to anyone, or you're a dead man."

"Payment?" asked the stall-owner, extending a yellow-stained hand, his eyes narrowed, his expression cunning. Barrow's mention of *Athena* had evidently removed the veneer of his glib chatter revealing a quite different man of business.

"Here. As agreed." Barrow handed him an envelope containing a thick wad of American dollars, fixing him with a threatening stare. "That parcel must be delivered by tonight, understand? Tonight. When you deliver it, you'll get the other half of your fee. But if it's been unwrapped, all you get is your throat cut. Got that?"

"Of course, tonight," said the man, his cigarette bobbing up and down between his thin lips as he spoke.

As he rejoined the milling crowds thronging the market, Barrow reflected sourly that the motionless, wet air outside offered precious little refreshment after the feted and claustrophobic little stall, piled to its low ceiling with grimy pots. He had no idea whether the address given the little man was that of the client or yet another intermediary. Sylvia managed all such arrangements, and secrecy was absolute. He, Barrow, did not even know the name of the stall owner with whom he had just been doing business, but so rigid was the syndicate's structure and discipline he had no doubt the parcel would be delivered as required.

By this time, he was in desperate need of a shower and a glass of exceptionally cold beer, but he had one final task to complete. He needed to become someone else.

Walking the length of the market he casually turned the corner and strolled unhurriedly along a deserted side street lined on either hand by small, concrete houses with red-tiled roofs. He was looking for a particular thing, and within a hundred yards he came upon a rubbish-filled vacant lot overgrown with ragged banana palms, clumps of high razor-edged grass, bamboo, and vines. The entire place stank of rotting garbage and wet vegetation and it was exactly what he wanted. Doing his best to ignore the putrid air, he shouldered his way into the undergrowth until he was invisible from the road and then tore off the false moustache he had put on in the store washroom. He threw it and his sunglasses into a tight stand of bamboo before pulling off his red t-shirt, revealing the blue one he had been wearing underneath. Rolling the red shirt into a ball, he thrust it under a pile of litter, at the same moment releasing the air trapped in his bursting lungs. Unknowingly, he had been holding his breath. The stench assailed his stomach as well as his nose, and after a cautious look around, he emerged from the thicket, taking care to avoid several small heaps of feces deposited there by some of Jakarta's large population of homeless people. He stood for a moment looking up and down the street as though he were lost, then shrugged and sauntered back to the market.

After wandering about for a quarter of an hour pretending to be a tourist, resisting all attempts by persistent stall-owners to sell him things he didn't want, he hailed an orange taxi to return to his five-star hotel on Jalan Thamrin. The odor of the garbage heap lingered in his nostrils, combining with the driver's cigarette smoke as the car crawled through the dripping heat and tumultuous traffic. Barrow, anxious to be back at his hotel before the onset of the afternoon rains, sat confined in the cramped back seat thinking that if he did not get that beer soon, the only viable option would be to give up and die.

Since the attentive men and women who guard Britain's shores might find his returning from a Muslim country, or indeed any country, after only one day's stay somewhat suspicious, Barrow flew to Bali and spent a pleasant week at a beach-front resort. All part of the job, he told himself complacently, working on a plate of *nasi goreng* with its fried rice, chicken satay, and spicy peanut sauce. As he ate, his mind wandered, in fact went directly, to the darkly attractive young woman in the hotel's spa with whom he had an appointment that evening for a massage.

"With happy ending?" she asked, smiling, and he smiled back.

And two days before he tore himself away from his Balinese paradise and the young woman in the spa, Sylvia Becker was informed by circuitous means via a small brokerage house in Guernsey, that two million American dollars had been deposited into a bank account she maintained in the Cayman Islands under the name of a shell consulting company calling itself *Hilda Incorporated.*

* * *

"The image enhancement your people came up with was most helpful," said Professor Willard, shaking hands with Sergeant Fielding and Inspector Foy as they stepped into his capacious office. "I was most impressed."

"We came as soon as we got your email," Foy said, as they seated themselves. "What can you tell us?"

"Well," said Willard, "I wish I could tell you who killed poor Terry, but, of course, I'm afraid I can't. However, from an historian's point of view, the bone tells us a great deal. As I had hoped, it confirms the battle of Mingtiao actually took place, and Lord Chang to be a real person."

"And I know those items were important," said Fielding, for whom the only interesting history was that of the London police forces going back to the first six men nicknamed the *Bow Street Runners* in 1749.

"Oh, yes," said Willard, "very important indeed."

"So," said Foy, "it definitely appears that Preston saw this oracle bone somewhere, took a photo of it, and sent it to you on the night he was killed. Do you have any idea why he would have done that?"

"I'm sure it was because he knew I'd be interested in it. He would have been able to read it, you see."

"But he sent no message."

"Terry and I had developed a friendship that complimented our professional relationship," said Willard, "and doing something like that was just like him. I expect he intended to come and see me straight away to explain everything." Willard paused for a moment, his face grave. "I miss the talks we used to have."

"I'm sure you do," said Foy, "and I want to catch his killer. Can I ask if you have any idea at all about where he might have seen this oracle bone?"

"None whatsoever, I'm afraid," said Willard. "Until now, I didn't know it even existed, and nor did anyone else, so far as I know. I couldn't begin to conjecture where he saw it, except to say it wasn't in a museum."

"Why do you say that, sir?" Fielding asked.

"Well," said Willard, "the photo shows it sitting on a sort of wooden stand on what looks like an open shelf. A museum, even a small or obscure one, would never display it like that."

"So, it could have been in a private home," said Foy, "and given its historical significance, we can safely say that if the bone's existence were to become generally known to sinologists, you would hear about it. Correct?"

"Oh yes," said Willard, inclining his head for emphasis. "There's no doubt of that."

"So," Foy persisted, "why is the current owner keeping it a secret?"

"Probably doesn't know what it actually is," said Fielding. "Might simply be a souvenir or some such. Perhaps acquired a long time ago."

"And I wonder, then," Foy mused aloud, "if Terry had time to take a photo, did he also have time to explain to the owner why he was doing so?"

An answer was impossible, and there followed a short silence before Fielding changed the subject.

"Professor Willard, we're wondering if you'd consider doing Scotland Yard something of a favor?"

"By all means," Willard answered, "especially if it might help find Terry's murderer."

"We're doing all we can, sir," said Foy, then immediately wished he hadn't. Willard was offering to help, and now was not the time to be defensive.

"Of course, you are," said Willard, with grave politeness. "I didn't intend to imply otherwise."

"We appreciate that, sir," said Fielding, perhaps seeing that Foy was squirming a little, "and here's what we're thinking. Preston's flat was thoroughly searched after his death. That's routine, as you can imagine. The search didn't turn up anything useful in terms of actual evidence or leads, but there was a hell of a lot of stuff on his computer, and also a very large amount of paper. Notes, some handwritten, many typed and printed out, and also quite a lot of photocopied articles, and so on. Some of it's in Chinese, as well. It's all sealed up in the evidence room and we trolled through it all as best we could, but the oracle bone wasn't an issue at the time because we didn't know about it. But even if it had been, none of us would have known what to look for. So…we're wondering if you'd be willing to go through it…all of it…and see if there's anything there that might suggest where he found the oracle bone."

"Yes," said Foy. "All we're saying is that perhaps he knew of its existence before the night he sent you the image. We can't tell when he actually took the photo, because there's no date or time on it. Perhaps it was taken well before he was killed. We assume his killer was aware he'd sent you the image. He, or she, might even have known where and when he took it."

"But, good God," said Willard, in sudden animation, "why kill him, or anyone, over an obscure artifact of interest to only a handful of scholars who happen to be fascinated by the doings of kings in ancient China?"

"Well put, sir," Foy said. "That is clearly the central question now."

"But if Terry *was* killed because he saw the bone," said Willard, "doesn't that put my life at risk, as well?" Willard's expression had turned very somber.

"We thought of that, sir," said Foy, "but it seems to us to be highly unlikely Terry was killed solely because he saw an ancient artifact, important though it might be historically. We're working on the assumption there was much more to his death than that."

"But the murderer did take Terry's phone," Willard pointed out, still dubious.

"Sure," said Foy, "but remember it was more than a year ago, and there may well have been other reasons for taking it, reasons we don't yet understand. There's no cause for alarm in our view, sir."

"Dear me," said Willard, nervously furrowing his brow. "This is all rather awkward."

Foy understood his feelings. Murder, mayhem, and personal peril formed no part of Willard's staid and circumscribed academic life. He now found himself in a new and alien world as far removed from normality as the earth is from the stars. Foy sought for words of reassurance.

"You did receive a photo of the bone, assuming that artifact is somehow a factor in Terry's death, but you can't tell anyone where it is now, or where it was at the time. Put bluntly, sir, you do not represent a threat to the murderer. You know nothing, and the murderer will have realized that long ago."

Foy waited in some suspense as the professor considered the position with a grave and thoughtful expression. He pursed his lips and frowned again, making his thin face appear even narrower.

"Yes," Willard said, at long last, his face clearing, "I'm sure you're right."

"So, Professor Willard," put in Fielding, his tone not over-hasty, "coming back to the material in Terry's flat…?"

"Certainly," said Willard. "I'm ready to help if I can."

"Excellent. Thank you very much, sir," said Foy, feeling a powerful sense of relief. The search may reveal nothing whatever, but the possibility could not be overlooked.

"Not at all, Inspector, and now can I offer you a cup of tea?"

* * *

"Just suppose," said Fielding, as they left the building, quite full of weak tea and shortbread biscuits, "that Preston's seeing the bone was, in fact, the sole reason he was killed. Does that tell us anything?"

"In what sense?" asked Foy.

"I'm only thinking of Willard's question about why anyone should be killed just because they saw an old Chinese bone, and it occurs to me that a plausible reason could be that it was stolen from somewhere."

"Could be," agreed Foy, as they approached their car. "Follow that up, will you?"

Foy returned to his office and began to compose in his mind the update he would soon have to give Superintendent Stuart.

"Yes, come in," he said, in answer to Neeta Mahajan's request for a quick word, and glad to stop thinking about the Super. "What've you got?"

"Well, sir, it occurred to me that perhaps our witness, uncertain as he was, might have mistaken the name on the van…assuming there *was* a name, that is,"

"And?"

"And so, I tried some variations on the theme of *Bell*. There's only five vowels, thank God, so I came up with Ball Brothers straight away, and it so happens there's a

307

firm of movers in St. John's Hill, not far from Clapham Junction. I gave them a shout, and guess what? One of their smaller vans, blue in color, was pinched on the very night in question. That night being the night after Preston was shot."

"Well, well," said Foy, "and what else did you discover, pray?"

Neeta smiled her incandescent smile.

"The van was found abandoned but undamaged, so nothing more was done about it. The Ball Brothers were happy to have it back, but I went through the investigation notes anyway. There was almost nothing to them, but I found something that might just help."

"Good," said Foy, "we could use a break about now."

It might make Stuart happier, but I doubt it.

"Ball Brothers has a strict policy against smoking in their offices, on the job, or in their vehicles, but a cigarette butt was found in the stolen van."

"DNA?" Foy asked, trying to keep the eagerness out of his voice, but suspecting he hadn't.

"Tests and checks were run at the time," said Neeta, "but there were no hits. I had Forensics run the profile again, and they got a match this time."

"Well done, you," said Foy. "Now, perhaps, we're getting somewhere."

"Let's hope so, sir. The match was to a Carl Weber, flat three-zero-eight, Foxstall Court, nineteen-twenty-seven Laurel Close, Maida Vale. Born in Germany in nineteen-eighty but has lived in the UK for the past twenty years or so. And…he's got form. Disturbing the peace, a grievous bodily harm, and he got eighteen months for possession of controlled substances for the purpose of trafficking. He was also a prime suspect in an unlawful confinement investigation in Newcastle, but they couldn't get enough on him to prosecute."

"A small-time gutter-creeper, then," observed Foy. "Unsavory little git."

"Basically, yes, but there was a strange note in his file that he'd come briefly to the attention of Interpol over a murder investigation in Colombia, of all places. That's all it said, though, *come to the attention of,* so I assume the thing came to nothing as well."

"Sounds like a charming chap," said Foy. "Is any of that recent?"

"He got out of the clink two years ago, after twelve of his eighteen months, and there's been nothing since then except for the stolen van with his fag-end in it."

"Were his prints anywhere in the van?" Foy asked, and Neeta shook her head.

"No, sir, only Ball Brothers' employees."

"Well," said Foy, standing up, "care to take a drive to Maida Vale?"

In the garage, Neeta announced she would take the wheel, if that was all right, and Foy made no objection. After only a few minutes on the road, however, he concluded she was either a trained Formula One driver, or a woman with a well-developed death wish. She was the antithesis of Sergeant Fielding, but at least she didn't talk to the other drivers.

"Where did you learn to drive?" he asked, as the car weaved in and around the other vehicles on the road, constantly changing lanes.

"Here," she answered, cheerfully, "but I drive in Kolkata whenever I go back to India to see my grandparents." She gave him a mischievous sideways glance. "I assure you, I'm perfectly safe, sir. If you don't watch out for yourself in Kolkata, you die."

"I can believe it," Foy said, with utmost sincerity. He did not much like driving, although he was very competent. Since his retirement he had grown used to buses, taxis, and even the maelstrom of people crowding onto the Tube, and he preferred those modes of transport to the frustrations of London's crowded streets and frenetic rush hours which always seemed to him to last most of the day.

Once in the affluent streets of Maida Vale in the west of London, Neeta's driving became somewhat more sedate, and with the aid of the car's GPS, she soon drew up outside Foxstall Court. Shutting the car door behind him, Foy looked up at the building. A late nineteenth century edifice, built plain, dour, and as imposing as a Victorian governess. Once, perhaps, it had been a private home, but had long since been turned into expensive mansion flats. It crossed Foy's mind to wonder how Carl Weber, by all accounts a petty thug, could afford to live in such salubrious surroundings.

"Who says crime doesn't pay?" Neeta asked, obviously sharing his thoughts.

The building had no electronic security, but a liveried porter at a reception desk in the foyer admitted them on sight of their identification, and they made their way to the third floor via a wood-paneled lift with highly polished brass doors. Finding number eight, they knocked, and after once more showing identification, were admitted to the flat by a short, thick-set man with long, dark hair and a jaw as square as a brick, who confirmed he was Carl Weber.

Introductions were made, and Foy, whose long experience had taught him to study a suspect's expression, noted Weber's close-set eyes fixed themselves firmly on Neeta Mahajan and never wavered.

"I don't know anything about any stolen van," Weber said, a trace of German in his voice. "I contacted Ball Brothers when I moved into this flat, and I got a lift round here with the furniture. That's the only time I was ever in one of their vans, and that was over a year ago."

"Tell me, sir," said Foy, "when you were in the van on your way here, did you smoke?"

"I dunno. Maybe. What of it, anyway?"

"A cigarette butt was found in the stolen van with your DNA on it," said Neeta.

"Then I suppose I did smoke, didn't I? Smoking's not a crime."

"You have a very nice flat here, sir," said Neeta, *a propos* of nothing, but perhaps trying to knock Weber off balance.

"Thanks," said Weber, devoid of sincerity.

"May I ask what you do for a living?" said Foy.

"I don't have to work," said Weber, "not that it's any of your business. I got a large inheritance form my uncle. Satisfied?"

"Not quite," said Foy. "Where did your uncle live?"

"Germany. Frankfurt, to be precise."

"And when did he pass away?"

"I don't know," Weber snapped. "When I was a little kid. I don't remember him at all. The money was left in a trust fund which I got when I was twenty-one."

"And your uncle's name?" Foy inquired, his tone perfectly neutral.

"Schneider," said Weber, exasperated. "Don't know his first name. I told you, I don't remember him, and I'm getting tired of all this crap."

The questions continued, but Weber held fast to his story. His explanation was plausible enough, but given his previous form, Foy was very much disinclined to accept it. In the end, they collected all the details they could about Weber and his move with Ball Brothers and left the flat.

"Check it all out with the movers," said Foy, as Neeta guided the car away from Foxstall Court.

"I'll get on it, sir," she said. "I don't trust Weber one little bit with his fancy flat and expensive bits and pieces, and did you notice his watch, by the way?"

"His watch?"

"Yes. Solid gold bloody Rolex with diamonds for numbers. Cost half the national debt, that did. I'll see if I can check on his dear departed uncle as well. The old geezer must have been filthy rich, if he ever existed."

They sat in silence for a time, Foy marveling at the ease with which Neeta negotiated her way through the churning traffic.

"I suppose the van story could be true," he said, eventually, his voice betraying his skepticism "But if we assume he did steal Barrow's car and torch it that night, the question is *why*. I mean, why would he pinch a car and set it on fire just to get his jollies? He doesn't look the type to me. I'll just bet there's some sort of connection between Weber and Barrow, and all we have to do is ferret it out."

311

There followed a few more minutes of silence before Neeta said, almost to herself, "Traffic's bad this evening."

"And speaking of Barrow," said Foy, as though she had not spoken, "let's see what's happening with that worthy gentleman, shall we?"

He touched a speed dial on his mobile, waited a moment, and then spoke. "Fielding? Foy. What did you find out on Barrow?" He listened, then said, "Right, go and confront him with that, and then set me up with someone in the Paris force I can talk to about his alibi. Something's not right here, and I want to find out what it is."

Foy consigned his phone to the darkness of his inside pocket, and said to Neeta Mahajan, "So I'd better go and let Superintendent Stuart know what's going on, hadn't I?"

"I hear he's loving the community relations work, sir," she said, smirking.

"Oh yes, I'm sure he is," said Foy. "I'm very sure he is."

She drove them back to the Yard, and Foy went up to see Stuart, who received him with all the warmth of a winter's day in Novosibirsk. Foy brought him up to speed on the stolen van, the cigarette butt, and the DNA trail to Carl Weber.

"My feeling is there's a connection between Weber and Barrow, but at this precise moment, I can't pinpoint it."

"Around here these days we work on evidence, not feelings." Stuart's words were clipped, his tone deliberately condescending. "Your privately-held personal *feeling*," and here he injected exaggerated sarcasm into his tone, "is about as much use to anyone as a rubber flagpole."

"I'm working on it," said Foy, ignoring the insult, "but on another subject, we may have found a chink in Barrow's armor."

"Barrow?"

"Yes. He was the last person to see Terry alive. It appears he didn't leave for Paris on the morning after Terry's death as he told you he did when you interviewed him. I had Fielding check his story. He took the Eurostar from St. Pancras International at eight o'clock at night, not first thing that morning. I've sent Fielding to see him again and get the facts." He was about to add *this time* but decided against it; warned off by Stuart's reddening face as he folded his arms and glared across his desk.

"I resent that implication, Foy."

"Harry," said Foy, trying to keep a reasonable tone, "or *sir*, if you insist. Contrary to whatever you may think, I haven't come back for the express purpose of making a fool of you, or anyone else. As I've told you repeatedly, my only concern is to find my nephew's murderer. To do that, I have not only to break new ground if I can but go over the old as well. It's standard operating procedure, and I know you're well aware of that."

Stuart sat silent for a few moments, stone-faced, and then gave a non-committal grunt.

"Can I take that as an *okay*?" Foy asked, but Stuart made no response.

"If there's nothing else, Foy," he said, in a crisp tone of dismissal.

"Well, just to complete the report, you should also know I intend to ask the police in Paris to re-interview the couple who provided Barrow's alibi on the basis of his first incorrect statement. I'd like to know when they say he arrived."

"Oh God," said Stuart, rolling his eyes. "Not content to question our competence, you don't trust the French police either. I'm sure they'll be happy about that."

"It's nothing of the kind," said Foy, feeling his own anger beginning to rise. "It's just more of the old ground, that's all. It's been some while since they were questioned, so I want to see if they stay consistent. It's a tried and true technique, and since Barrow has changed his story, it might throw them off balance."

"Don't you dare try to tell me my business," snapped Stuart, banging his fist on his desk. "Now…I asked you if that was all."

"Yes," said Foy, standing up to go, unable to stifle an audible sigh, "that's all."

"And keep the reports coming," Stuart shouted after him as he opened the office door. "I want to know every single, solitary move you make, d'you hear me?"

Chapter Twenty-Four

The breeze that rattled the bare branches of the trees by the curbside lifted Sylvia Becker's long, blonde hair off her shoulders as she walked with Lombardi at her side towards the house her family had owned since the war, where her mother still lived, and where she stayed whenever she was in Berlin. A morning walk was a ritual for her. She found it allowed her to think, to plan, and prepare her mind for the day. Wearing a long coat against the chill of the cloud-shrouded morning, she held the handle of Lombardi's harness in her left hand and kept her right deep in the voluminous pocket of her coat. She held her head erect, her eyes, concealed behind her dark glasses, saw nothing, yet guided by Lombardi, she walked as purposefully and directly as any sighted person. Lombardi steered her unerringly around a pair of cyclists who had dismounted and become engaged in an animated conversation in the middle of the broad sidewalk. The two young men stopped talking and watched as she passed.

"Too bad you can't see what hot-looking guys we are," jeered one. "You don't know what you're missing, sweetheart."

"Get screwed," Sylvia called over her shoulder, and the two cyclists gaped in shock, staring as Lombardi guided her to the front door of the house and brought her to a halt. She unlocked the door, and with a command of *forward* to Lombardi, the two disappeared inside.

"Stand, wait," she said, and Lombardi, doing as he was told, watched as she took off her coat and hung it on an ornate brass hook by the door. The entrance hall they were now in was well-lit and spacious with a slate floor and a large centrally placed pedestal table of milk-white, flawless Carrara marble. The table bore a tall vase of Bohemian cut crystal laden with fresh flowers replenished each morning by Sylvia's express instruction. Dominating the far wall opposite the door was a large painting, an original Picasso, acquired by Sylvia's grandmother in 2000, a year before her death on nine-eleven. As was her habit, Sylvia paused for a moment to savor the fulsome fragrance of the flowers before turning to the dog waiting patiently at her side.

Stooping to remove Lombardi's harness, Sylvia said, "Dismiss," at which the dog, now officially off duty, vanished in the direction of the kitchen where a bowl of water was always waiting. She trailed her hand along the left-hand wall until her fingers found the button for the lift installed when Gabriella could no longer manage the stairs. In truth, she had no need to navigate in this manner; she had been brought up in this house, and knew every one of its halls, corridors, and rooms. However, as a very little girl, barely understanding the nature of her disability, her mother had taught her to find her way using the walls for guidance, and the technique became a habitual reminder of her mother's abiding love and steadfast support.

The lift's polished doors opened, and Sylvia was conveyed to the upper floor and her mother's rooms. She stepped confidently into the sitting room where Gabby sat reading, a blue knitted shawl around her shoulders in spite of the room's warmth. She looked up, smiling, as Sylvia entered.

"Good walk?" she asked in German, her voice rasping and harsh from the emphysema which clogged her lungs.

"Yes, thanks." Sylvia felt for the large sofa, settled herself, and snapped, "Coffee."

"Freda isn't here yet," said Gabby, and Sylvia made a clicking, exasperated, noise with her tongue.

"Well, where the hell is she? Honestly, Mother, I wonder why you bother to keep her on. She's hopeless."

Before Gabby could answer, a short woman of about sixty entered the room. She was very rotund, wore glasses as round as she was, and had her iron-gray hair drawn severely beck into a tight bun at the nape of her neck.

"Back from your walk, *Fraulein* Becker?"

"Obviously I am," said Sylvia, impatiently, "and I want my coffee."

"Yes, *Fraulein* Becker, at once."

"You shouldn't speak to her like that," Gabby chided, after Freda left the room. "She looks after me very well, and this job is all she has since Wilhelm died. They had no children. She is alone."

"Yes, yes, I know the story." Sylvia leaned back on the deep, leather sofa and crossed her legs with a voluminous sigh. "But I find her far from efficient."

"Wilhelm was one of the best acquisitions men we ever had in Europe," said Gabby.

"Oh, yes he was," snorted Sylvia, "when he was sober, which wasn't all that often. Freda would have been comfortably off if he hadn't drunk his money away."

"Yes, he was a problem sometimes, but he was very valuable to us, notwithstanding."

Barely able to finish the sentence, Gabby dissolved into a prolonged fit of coughing and choking which racked her whole body, leaving her gasping for breath, her face gray and her eyes staring. She groped for the oxygen mask at the side of her chair and put it over her nose and mouth. Sylvia waited until her breathing became less labored.

"I take it Freda still doesn't know I had to have Wilhelm killed?"

"Of course, she doesn't," said Gabby, setting the mask aside, her voice hoarse, "and you had no choice, anyhow. There was too great a risk of his talking too much as his drinking took over his life."

At that point, Freda entered carrying a tray bearing a cup and saucer, a small cut-glass jug of cream, and a silver coffee carafe. Placing it on the low table in front of Sylvia, she said, "Your coffee, *Fraulein*. Allow me." She filled the cup, added a dash of cream, and set the cup on the table within Sylvia's reach. "There you are. It's at twelve o'clock. Will there be anything else?"

317

"No. Lunch at the usual time, and see the rolls are fresh today. Yesterday's were like sawdust."

"Yes *Fraulein*. I'm sorry."

Freda withdrew, and Sylvia, leaning forward, moved her right hand slowly across the tabletop until she located the cup. She took a sip, then said, grudgingly, "Well, there's one thing to say about Freda. She makes a good cup of coffee."

"Sylvia," said Gabby, "you usually go straight to your office when you come back from a walk, but here you are. What's on your mind?"

Sylvia put down her cup and sat silent for a few moments. This was the usual prelude to her raising a problem, so her mother waited, her breathing still labored. Sylvia lit a black cigarette.

"What is it, Sylvia?" Gabby croaked. "You know I don't like you smoking. I don't want you to end up like me."

Sylvia ignored the remark. She liked to smoke.

"I don't know if this will lead to anything awkward," she began, exhaling a stream of aromatic blue Turkish smoke towards the ceiling, "but do you remember just over eighteen months ago, Mike Barrow went and shot a friend of his because he saw that old Chinese oracle bone we kept at home for so long? It was just before I sold it to a client in France."

"Yes, I do," wheezed Gabby. "You got Carl to sort it out."

"That's right. Everything seemed fine, the whole thing died down. Mike was questioned and things got a little tense, but his story and alibi held up. I thought it was all over and we'd dodged the bullet, so to speak, However, Mike has been questioned again, and a day or two ago a couple of detectives showed up at Carl's flat and began to grill him. He says all they wanted to know about was the company he used when he moved, and there were no difficulties. But what worries me is that Carl's not all that bright when it comes to this sort of thing. I mean, he doesn't think on his feet very well. Mike's okay, but Carl's

318

doubtful. I wouldn't have kept him with us, except he's very good at logistics. He's even handled a couple of overseas maximum response cases, including getting that bastard in Colombia for me. He's completely reliable for that sort of work."

"How did you find this out?" Gabby asked.

"Carl let me know immediately they left his flat."

"Why would they want to know about his movers?"

"I have no idea. It's so bizarre, but that's what makes me afraid something somewhere, may have gone sideways."

"This is a time for patience and a steady nerve," Gabby declared, after a pause. "Carl's got to hang about long enough for the police to check him out thoroughly, otherwise it will arouse suspicion. I'd say two days, and then he should disappear for several months. And I do mean disappear. Russia, South America. Somewhere he can't be traced. He'll know how to do that. They had no evidence against him in the first instance, so I doubt they'll find any this time."

"What if he's questioned again?" Sylvia asked, grinding out her cigarette as if she were trying to kill it.

"You make sure you get to him first," said her mother. "Rehearse everything if you have to. As many times as it takes until you're sure of him."

"I was thinking of something less time-consuming," said Sylvia.

"You mean…what do you call it…*maximum response*?"

"I'm considering that option, yes."

"Are you certain it can be done cleanly?" Gabby took up the oxygen mask again and inhaled several rasping breaths.

"Yes. I know a Serbian woman who's excellent. A real single shot professional. Uses a heavy caliber hand gun."

"Maybe so," said Gabby," clearing her throat noisily, "but Carl's death would only give the police a reason for investigating him more thoroughly. You never know what that might turn up."

"True," said Sylvia, nodding, "but it's likely the police would concentrate on finding his killer, which they'll never do, rather than looking into the stolen car thing."

"Well," said Gabby, nodding, "it's your decision, but consider all the ramifications of whatever choice you make. Weigh the relative risks. You're usually very cautious and thoughtful, Sylvia. Be so now."

After lunching with her mother — the rolls warm from the oven — Sylvia excused herself and went downstairs to her office. There, seated at a large teak desk inset with brass strips at the edges and corners, she listened to several reports from the research department and dictated her comments using her computer's voice recognition software. She answered three heavily encrypted emails, frequently consulting the open Internet and various databases — some on the Dark Web — everything being routed through the syndicate's heavily fortified private server.

Midway through the afternoon, Sylvia heard the gentle padding of Lombardi's paws on the think carpet and the metallic jingle of his collar as he trotted into the office. She held out her hand.

"Hello, my handsome friend. What are you up to, eh?"

The golden dog licked her hand with his very large, very wet tongue, then stretched out beside her chair where he soon began to snore quietly. His presence always calmed her thoughts, and by evening she had decided what to do about Carl Weber. The unexpected appearance of the police at his flat, and the connection which might well be made between Carl, Barrow's car, and the death of Barrow's friend had placed her in a risky position. It had been complete and utter stupidity on Barrow's part to kill his friend, but it seemed the matter had been safely handled. Now it was clear something was still happening, but what was it? Carl had not been questioned previously, so why now, and why about his movers? It made no sense. She pondered these things, together with the overriding question of whether or not Carl could be relied upon. If he were suddenly confronted with new evidence, it could easily catch him off guard, and that could be disastrous.

There must be new evidence, she said to herself. Something must have turned up to link him with Barrow's car, but what could that be, and if it implicated him, why didn't they arrest him there and then? I can't prep him for every possibility, for God's sake.

At six o'clock, as she was dictating a message about a tenth century Russian icon of the Virgin Mother to someone in Prague code-named Stefan, Freda knocked before putting her head round the door.

"Dinner in half an hour, *Fraulein* Becker. Will you be joining your mother?"

"Dammit, Freda," Sylvia blazed. "How many times have I told you to allow me time to pause the dictation after you knock, instead of just barging in and screwing everything up?"

The color fled from Freda's round cheeks.

"I'm sorry, *Fraulein*, I —"

"All right, all right," Sylvia interrupted. "Tell my mother I'll join her at six."

"Yes, *Fraulein* Becker," said Freda, in little more than a whisper. "Thank you."

Freda closed the door as soundlessly as she could, and Sylvia went back to her dictation after deleting Freda's voice.

Stupid woman.

And before going upstairs for dinner, she called Mike Barrow with a coded summons to come to Berlin the following morning.

* * *

Barrow arrived at the house at ten-thirty the next morning, having paid a bin-full of the syndicate's money for a flight at short notice. Freda answered his knock, greeting him warmly in accented English.

"Where's Medusa?" he whispered, making Freda giggle, then try to look repentant.

321

"In her office, *Herr* Barrow. She said to send you straight in."

"Are there many snakes in her hair this morning?"

"Yes, I'm afraid so." Freda could not stifle another giggle.

"Then we shall all be turned to stone," he said, with great solemnity.

"It's about time," Sylvia growled, as he entered the well-appointed office, feeling his feet sink into the thick carpet. He remembered that carpet only too well. He had been responsible for shipping it to Germany from Shanghai whence it had come as a bonus to Sylvia from a client in grateful appreciation for her services in supplying a certain bronze statue. Her brusque words contrasted with Lombardi's effusive greeting, and Barrow scratched his jaw.

"Hello Lombardi. How are you?"

He settled himself in a deeply upholstered leather chair whereupon the dog immediately turned around and presented his hindquarters to be scratched, bumping himself against Barrow's legs in encouragement and eager anticipation. The ritual of welcome thus completed, the dog resumed his station by Sylvia's chair.

"The flights were crowded, Sylvia," Barrow said, "and I had to wait forever for a taxi from Tegel. I'll be glad when the new airport's finished, if it ever gets finished, that is."

"Our agent in Istanbul has been in touch," Sylvia said, without preamble, ignoring Barrow's remark, "and we need to move very quickly."

"What's up?"

"Client one-four-six-nine has been wanting a specific item for over two years, but there's been no way to fill the order until now."

"What's he want, for God's sake," Barrow asked, "an Egyptian mummy?"

"If that's all it was," said Sylvia, "we'd have done it in two weeks. No, the client is a woman, actually, and she wants a set of Sumerian cuneiform clay tablets with the Gilgamesh on them."

"The what?"

"The Gilgamesh," Sylvia repeated, an impatient barb in her voice. "You did go to school, didn't you? It's a Sumerian epic poem whose earliest versions date from the Third Dynasty…about two thousand BC or thereabouts. Bronze Age Mesopotamia. I presume you know where that is."

Barrow said nothing. He knew when to keep silent

Sylvia was continuing, "Our client is interested in a later, more complete version, from somewhere about the thirteenth or twelfth century BC. Three sets of tablets like that are known to exist, all of them in museums in Iraq or Syria."

"And how do we get hold of one?" asked Barrow, slightly nervous of the answer. "That part of the world is either blowing itself up or being blown up by someone else. I don't recall ever hearing we had an agent anywhere there, and you surely don't expect the twins to drop in and pick a set up."

If he could have clawed back his words, he would have done so immediately, but they were out, and he cursed his impetuosity. It was not that Sylvia had very little sense of humor, it was that she had almost none at all.

"Don't be stupid," she snapped, slapping her hand on the top of her desk with a sound like a pistol shot, making Lombardi jump. "I may be blind, but I'm not an imbecile."

She paused. Barrow waited. Was the silence ominous, or merely for effect? He could usually tell, but this time he was not sure.

"We have the tablets already," she resumed, her tone more neutral, and Barrow breathed a quiet sigh of relief. His comment had been trivial, but Sylvia's mercurial temperament was not to be trifled with.

"A supplier in Istanbul approached our agent there and showed him one tablet, saying he could provide a complete set for twenty-five-thousand Turkish lira, just under five thousand American dollars. Obviously, the supplier had no understanding of what he was selling. Apparently, the tablets had been smuggled into Turkey after being looted from a museum in Ramadi by soldiers of the Islamic State. After hearing of it, I negotiated an inclusive price with our client that will give us an enormous profit. It's payable on delivery, of course, and the client's now looking forward to seeing her new treasure." Another pause, and Barrow thought, *here it comes.* "That's where you come in," Sylvia finished.

"Right," said Barrow. "Have we bought the tablets already?"

"In a heartbeat, and everything's complete," said Sylvia, nodding. "Our agent in Istanbul has the tablets in safekeeping. What you have to do is pick them up and have them delivered to the client."

"And the client is where, exactly?"

"Madrid. Not difficult. I'm told the soldiers who sacked Ramadi and looted the museum left such a hell of a mess the theft hasn't even been properly reported yet, which is good news for us. It means no one will be on the lookout for the tablets. You can pack them in an ordinary briefcase and go by train. Security's a lot tighter since the attacks in Paris and Brussels, so make sure you have a good story if the tablets are found during a search."

"I'll take care of it," said Barrow. "I'll use my Paul Ellis documents. They've never been a problem."

"Just do as you're told," said Sylvia, her voice cool again, "and get the job done on time."

"And I make the handover the same way I did with the Romanov pearls for the last client in Spain, do I?" asked Barrow, trying to overlook the implied threat in Sylvia's words. He had heard it many times before, but it still had the power to unnerve him. From time to time he made direct contact with the lower echelons of a delivery network as he did in Indonesia, but he had never set eyes on any of the syndicate's people in Spain. Only once had he ever handed merchandise directly to a client's representative, and that had been the time he delivered the oracle bone in France.

"Never mind that now," said Sylvia, tartly. "You'll get handover instructions once you check in with me from Madrid."

It was always the same. Sylvia alone made contact with her network, acting as a go-between for deliveries. If she ever made notes, they were in braille, and were burned once final payment had been made and the file closed. Barrow knew Carl Weber usually handled that little chore. The files on clients, contracts, prices, and dates of transactions were in Sylvia's laptop, deeply submerged and encrypted through a program designed uniquely for her by a Dark Web hacker in Pakistan who thought it was for the Taliban, his customary employers.

Sylvia herself was an enigmatic figure for the majority of syndicate staff who knew of her, but nothing about her. She was the puppet-master, the remote presence who, unseen, dominated everything and everyone. Only a select handful of syndicate staff had ever met Sylvia, but as her most experienced *transport manager*, as she called him, Barrow worked directly with her. He knew Carl and the twins, but no one else. Sylvia often spoke of the research department, yet Barrow had no idea where it was, nor who he, she, or they, actually were. He would have been surprised to learn they worked in a section of the Berlin house he believed to be closed off and disused.

"Well, I think that's all for that," said Sylvia, but Barrow interposed.

"Hang on," he said. "How many of these tablets are there, and what's their condition?"

"It's a unique find," said Sylvia. "The later Gilgamesh is on them, as I said, but there are a number of other poems as well, some of them unknown until now. There are thirty-one tablets, and the Istanbul agent says they're fragile, but not brittle or crumbling. If we couldn't transport them, he wouldn't have bought them, cheap as they were."

"Terrific," said Barrow, and Sylvia actually chuckled. He stared at her, unsure he had heard properly.

"They're quite small," she went on, "and they'll be well packed when you get them. Just don't drop your briefcase."

"When do I —"

"That's all for that one," Sylvia interrupted. "Now for item number two."

"There's more?" Barrow was still trying to get his head around the concept of carrying several million dollars' worth of fragile clay tablets in a briefcase from Istanbul to Madrid. He had ghastly visions of arriving in Spain only to find his briefcase full of dust. Sylvia would pursue him to the gates of hell and beyond to exact a terrible revenge.

With that image in his mind, he did not particularly relish the thought of having a second operation to worry about, but he knew of old, objections were useless. They would be met with an angry tirade, all of which would amount to his being told to remember who he was, who made the decisions in the syndicate, and if he forgot that, he was a dead man. Her recent ephemeral flash of good humor did not signal an Ebenezer Scrooge-like change of character.

"Yes," she said, "there is more. Client one-nine-zero-eight lives in Mexico. She has a passion for all things oriental and has more money than God. On a recent visit to China, she went to a museum in Jinan and saw a pearl and emerald necklace which once belonged to the Empress Wu."

"Never heard of her," Barrow said.

"Her full name was Wu Zetian," said Sylvia. "She seized power in the late seventh century, creating a brief hiatus in the Tang Dynasty. She was the only female ruler of a unified Chinese empire in all its history. I've always admired her, as a matter of fact."

I'm not surprised, Barrow thought, as Sylvia returned to the subject of the Mexican client.

"She wants the necklace she saw and will pay whatever we ask."

"That'll be a local acquisition job, then," said Barrow, and Sylvia nodded.

"Our agent in Beijing has contracted with the necessary human resources," Sylvia continued, "and the raid will take place shortly. Once the merchandise is acquired, I'll let you know, and we'll use the Panamanian Embassy again. Our contact there will ship the piece out of China in the diplomatic bag. He never charges very much, so it's the best way to do it. Then it's only a quick job for you to pick it up in Panama City and take it to Mexico. I'd use the Mexican Embassy in Beijing if I could, but our person there has been transferred to Lima and I haven't been able to recruit a replacement so far."

"Will I be able to do that after the Madrid shipment?" Barrow asked.

"You let me worry about the timing," said Sylvia. "You'll be told what you need to know when you need to know it. I'm flying to China tomorrow morning for a meeting with the agent."

* * *

Two weeks later, at eight o'clock in the evening, while Michael Barrow was quietly celebrating the safe handover of a briefcase full of undamaged clay tablets with a solitary drink in the bar of his Madrid hotel, a man on the other side of the world was buying an admission ticket to a museum. The man was about twenty-five, wearing an orange T-shirt and baggy brown trousers. The museum was the Shandong Museum on Yaojia Street in the Lixia District of southeast Jinan, capital city of Shandong, China's easternmost province. Entering the museum, he meandered through the spacious galleries, pausing frequently, ostensibly studying the artifacts in their glass cases, but his eyes were not on the displays. He soon caught sight of what he was looking for. Two guards in smart green uniforms and peaked caps at the far end of the gallery.

Good, he said to himself, catching the eye of one of them who nodded almost imperceptibly.

As he moved amongst the exhibits, he looked as innocuous and unremarkable as any other visitor, and since the museum was closing shortly in any case, there were very few people in the gallery.

Perfect.

After about five minutes he turned aside and went into the public washroom where he entered one of the stalls and locked the door. Dropping his baggy trousers, he untied two pieces of string which held a length of steel pipe against the outside of his left thigh. Refastening his belt, he pulled a ski mask from his pocket and put it over his head. Pausing for a moment to slow his racing heart, he cautiously opened the door a crack and peered out. Seeing no one, he made for the door of the washroom, and after catching a deep breath, he burst out into the gallery.

Turning to his left he pelted into a display hall adjoining the main gallery and headed for a row of display cases against the far wall. Two or three visitors stared at him in bewilderment as he raced by them, but he paid no attention. Coming to an abrupt halt, his shoes squeaking on the linoleum floor, he brought the steel pipe down onto the glass top of a display case about half-way down the row, smashing it to smithereens. A second later he had reached into the shattered case, seized the object inside, and dropped it into his pocket. The entire episode had taken less than half a minute.

Immediately, an alarm siren began to shriek, and a bell nearby leapt into life with a harsh, deafening clang. There were only three visitors in the hall, and they fled for the doors in panic. A woman screamed as two security guards ran into the gallery. Drawing their pistols, they shouted, "You there. Halt. Stay where you are."

The masked man, his escape route blocked, stood still, and then raised his hands in surrender.

With shouts, curses, and kicks, the would-be thief was dragged into a guardroom off the main gallery, and the alarms fell mercifully silent, their cacophonous clamor seeming to hang in the air even after it had ceased. The last of the terrified visitors rushed from the building and a crowd of curious spectators, attracted by the noise and tumult, began to collect outside. The excited mob spilled onto the road, and blaring horns contributed to the general commotion.

Under cover of this brawling chaos, the thief, his mask and weapon discarded, was cordially ushered out of a small side door by the guards who had apparently apprehended him only a few minutes earlier. He was now dressed in different clothing and carried a plain plastic shopping bag. Three weeks before, when the plan for the robbery was explained to him, he was assured the guards would be well paid in advance, and they had certainly acted as anticipated. The man walked calmly out into a narrow lane leading away from the main street and into a park with well-tended flowerbeds and clipped shrubbery. Mingling with the people enjoying the late afternoon sunshine, the man strolled across a broad expanse of grass to join a group of people at a bus stop. Several buses, each belching thick, black clouds of noxious diesel smoke and crowded with passengers, drew up in quick succession, and he boarded one of them. He disappeared with his shopping bag in the direction of Jinan's main railway station where he had been told a foreigner would pay him and take the shopping bag from him.

That night, the television news reported that a man had stolen a valuable piece of ancient jewelry from the Shandong Museum on Yaojia Street. After his arrest, the thief unexpectedly drew a gun and escaped. The jewelry had not been recovered. The police were investigating. The museum guards were commended for their gallant attempt to prevent the robbery.

At eleven o'clock in the morning of that same day in Berlin, Sylvia Becker received a call on her mobile phone. After listening for a moment, she said, "Thank you," and then placed a call of her own to Mexico.

Chapter Twenty-Five

"I finally tracked Barrow down," Fielding said, seating himself in front of the desk in Foy's miniscule office. "He seems to travel a good deal."

"And what's his story?" asked Foy. "Why did he tell you he'd left in the morning when he'd left at night?"

"Claims it was a simple mistake," said Fielding. "Many apologies. Says he goes to Paris a lot, has friends there, and just got confused. He was as smooth as a baby's bottom. Didn't even blink."

"Hmm," said Foy, in a skeptical tone. "What d'you think?"

"Plausible enough excuse, I suppose…"

"But…?"

"I think he could be lying. I don't think he was expecting the question, if you know what I mean."

Foy nodded. "Right, then. What have we now? Barrow, who now seems unable to tell what time of day it is, and Weber, who wants us to believe he left a fag end in a moving van when he moved house. Neeta's checking that out, by the way, along with his sources of income."

"Oh, that reminds me," said Fielding, looking down at his notes, "I dug into Barrow's income, but I couldn't get very far with it. He's obviously got a good source of revenue, but I think it'll take some work, and perhaps a court order, to uncover everything."

Foy grunted. "I trust Barrow less and less. He's bent. I can feel it, and so's Carl Weber, if it comes to that."

"Well, let's hope the good Professor Willard turns up something in Preston's papers."

"Right," said Foy. "Follow it up immediately if you hear from him."

* * *

Sylvia Becker flew Business Class through a stormy sky from Berlin to London, with Lombardi curled up in front of the vacant seat next to her she had purchased for him. The flight was far from smooth, but, oblivious to the swooping gyrations of the aircraft — gyrations which caused many passengers to clench their teeth and wish they had not eaten so much for lunch — Lombardi snored gently until jolted from his slumber by the landing. Amongst the first passengers to disembark, Sylvia was met by a representative of the airline who greeted her with stiff formality.

"Good afternoon, Ms. Becker. Nice to see you again. I trust the flight was comfortable."

"Not particularly," she retorted, in an offhand manner. "I assume you heard the weather report."

"I'm sorry," he said, apparently feeling the need to apologize for his company's inability to control the weather.

"There should be a car waiting for me," Sylvia said.

"Can I carry your laptop bag for you?"

"No."

With Sylvia's one hand on his elbow, her other on the handle of Lombardi's harness, and her laptop slung on her shoulder, the young man conducted her without a further word through the teeming throngs of people, the tumult of innumerable foreign languages, and the labyrinthine series of twists and turns that is Heathrow Airport, to the Rolls Bentley which awaited her in its permanently reserved parking place. The chauffeur, a good-looking dark-skinned young man in his mid-twenties, sprang out as she approached and opened the back door. The two men exchanged meaningful glances as Sylvia, ignoring them as if they were both inanimate objects, addressed herself to the dog.

"Inside Lombardi. Good boy. Go on."

The dog climbed in obediently and Sylvia followed without a further word to the young man from the airline, who appeared not to expect it in any case. He simply turned and walked away as the chauffeur closed the car door with an expensive-sounding thump.

"Russell Square, Ms. Becker?" he asked, getting behind the wheel.

"Yes, and get a move on, will you? The damn flight was delayed and I'm late."

She was unable to see the driver grinning as he put the Bentley into gear and moved smoothly away.

Sylvia sat back in the wide, soft seat and lit a black cigarette, her mind occupied with the particular problem which had brought her back to London several days before her expected return. She knew what she was going to do; the question was how best to do it, and when.

The Bentley slowed to a stop, ensnared in a tangled knot of cars and lorries.

"Sorry," said the driver over his shoulder. "An accident, perhaps."

He had been Sylvia's chauffeur since she bought the Bentley three years ago, and was at her beck and call all day, every day, for which availability she paid him handsomely. He enjoyed other perks as well, however. Quite frequently she invited him into the house to provide certain additional services not usually found in a chauffer's job description, but which he performed with commendable zeal and skill. As he waited for the traffic jam to unravel, he glanced over his shoulder, admiring Sylvia's elegant form, her long and very shapely legs casually crossed, and her fair hair falling loosely about her shoulders. She was a stunner, all right, except for those dark glasses, although he knew why she wore them. Sylvia took off her glasses, along with everything else, before they climbed into her commodious and comfortable bed. He saw her eyes were small and shriveled, the wrinkled lids almost completely closed. Once in bed, of course, he had other things to occupy his attention; Sylvia being eager, demanding, and very vocal in her encouragement and enthusiasm. He often wondered if the people in the next door flat could hear, but he was too busy to worry about it, and afterwards too exhausted to care.

Fifteen minutes later, the car drew up outside a building which bore the marks of careful restoration and renovation, newly re-pointed brickwork, fresh paint, and the latest in energy-efficient windows.

"Will you be needing the car later, Ms. Becker?" the driver asked as he opened the rear door for her.

"No," she answered, following the dog from the car and onto the sidewalk, "you can have the rest of the day off. But," she added, grasping the handle of Lombardi's harness, "don't go too far away. I may call you this evening."

"I can come any time, Ms. Becker," said the driver, and he meant it.

The car purred its expensive and elegant way down the street as Sylvia spoke to the golden dog waiting at her side.

"Lombardi, find the door."

The dog, his tail wagging happily, guided her unerringly to the front door, where she entered five digits into the keypad after finding the dimple on the number five. As the door buzzed, she pulled it open, saying, "Lombardi, forward."

Crossing the tiled foyer, replete with its potted shrubs and flowers, Lombardi found the lift and he and Sylvia rode up to the third floor, where, without further instruction, he guided her to the door of her flat, a carved slab of blackwood with highly polished bronze fittings.

Once inside, she removed Lombardi's harness and dismissed him. The dog trotted away and flopped down on a large, soft pillow, stretching out with a long groan of utter contentment.

Sylvia trailed her hand along the wall as she walked down the hallway and turned left into her office. Easily finding her desk, she booted up her laptop, going straight to her email Inbox. After the device burrowed through the interwoven layers of encryption, the computer read aloud the first message.

Client confirms order number 67389.

"Excellent," she murmured, under her breath. "That's what I wanted to hear. Now I can let Bucharest know."

She dictated a text message to her phone to someone she called *Samuel*, inviting him to come to London for a long-overdue visit if he could spare the time. She added that she had two box seat tickets for La Traviata at Covent Garden, and would love his company.

"It will be a wonderful opportunity to get caught up," she finished.

Accordingly, a day later, Samuel, having correctly interpreted the coded message to mean *come immediately,* sat before Sylvia's desk, revealing himself to be a short, dark-haired woman of about fifty, by the name of Anna.

"So, the job's on, is it?" she said, sipping the excellent white wine Sylvia poured for her.

"Yes," said Sylvia, resuming her seat behind the desk and running her hand across the top to find a safe place for her own glass. "If your contact at the National Museum is still in need of money, I think we'll be all right, but if not, I'll make other arrangements."

"He certainly is," Anna answered. "His mother is still incapacitated, and he can't afford her care. They wouldn't keep her in hospital, so she's had to go into a private nursing facility, and his insurance barely covers half the cost. He's absolutely desperate."

"Excellent," said Sylvia. "Hopefully, the old bat won't recover very quickly."

"There's no danger of that," said Anna. "The problem is she might die."

"Fingers crossed, then," said Sylvia, raising her glass, "and here's to a long and expensively decrepit life to her."

"How do we get the thing out of the country?" Anna asked. "The two tourists trick again?"

"I think so, yes," said Sylvia, nodding slowly and choosing her words. "I'll let you know in two...no, three days…before they arrive in Bucharest. That should give you ample time to be ready. Is that okay?"

Anna nodded, and Sylvia snapped. "I said is that okay?"

"Sorry," said Anna, hastily, "I nodded."

"Well that's no good to me, is it?"

Anna took another mouthful of wine before saying, in a firm tone of voice, "We may need a lot of money, and in view of the danger, I'll have to raise my fee."

"We can provide the money," Sylvia said, after a long pause, "and as for your fee, we'll discuss that later. You know damn well I never pay in advance, anyway, so don't dice with me now."

"No, no," said Anna, "I just —"

"Leave it," said Sylvia, in a harsh voice. "Go back and start working on this. I want to know things are in place by the first of the week. Clear? This is a big one, and I don't want it screwed up. The piece in question is unique and hugely valuable."

* * *

Bill Foy, his ear to the phone, beckoned Fielding into his office and pointed to a plastic chair, as he said, "All right Superintendent. Yes…yes…as soon as I can."

Foy replaced the phone, his expression one of resigned weariness and vexation.

"DS Stuart is wondering why I haven't given him a report in the last few days. Wants to know what we're all up to."

"Well, sir," said Fielding, "I might just have something for you to tell him."

"Praise God. What is it?"

"I had a call from Willard this morning, and he asked me to go down and see him. Said he'd found something very interesting amongst Terry Preston's papers. You recall we asked him to go through them and see if there was anything he might turn up that we'd missed."

"Right," said Foy, nodding. "And I take it he did."

"I drove down straight away, per your instructions. Just got back."

"What's he come up with?"

"It seems Preston had found an article about an oracle bone in an obscure German journal even Willard hadn't heard of. It must have been the publication Weiskopf referred to in his letter to Martins but didn't identify. Willard told us about it some time ago."

"I remember," said Foy, nodding.

"It was more a popular magazine, actually. Hardly a scholarly journal at all. Terry only had a photocopy of the article with a note of the date of publication. It's pre-war, of course."

"If it helps us," said Foy, in an acerbic tone, "I don't care if it was handwritten on toilet paper before Stonehenge was built."

"Not quite that bad, sir," said Fielding, with a grin. "Willard doesn't speak German, but he recognized the article because it contains several pictures of the bone. It's definitely the one Preston found and photographed."

"All well and good, if you're an historian and China wonk," said Foy, "but it doesn't seem to help us much in the here and now."

"Hang on, sir," said Fielding, "there's a little more. You remember Willard told us Weiskopf had disappeared around nineteen thirty-five or so, and it was later confirmed he'd been arrested when Jews were being purged from the universities after Hitler came to power?"

"Yes," said Foy, "but where does that get us?"

"Well," Fielding answered, "Willard was all excited about the article, and took it upon himself to do some more digging, no pun intended. Willard, via one of his colleagues, has found out from someone at the University of Leipzig that Aaron Weiskopf had a half-brother who emigrated to the US after the war. His son apparently became an archeologist and China wonk at Princeton University."

"And?"

"Willard actually tracked him down. He's retired now, but Willard asked if he knew anything about the oracle bone. He didn't, but he got interested and said he'd follow it up."

Foy, beginning to wish Fielding would get to the point, said, "What did he find, if anything?"

"The current Dr. Weiskopf, Saul, by name, by the way, went and looked through a load of old family photographs in case anything might turn up, and found a photo of Aeron W. with some of his greatest finds, including an oracle bone."

"Where's this leading, Sergeant?" asked Foy, now impatient. "If I go into all this with DS Stuart, he won't be impressed. I need something solid that promises to advance the investigation."

Nodding, Fielding quickly resumed. "Saul W. sent Willard a copy of that photo, and Willard got a pal of his to enlarge it. Although it's blurry, Willard confirmed it's the bone in question. The younger Weiskopf told Willard that all Aaron's artifacts had been confiscated when he was arrested."

"Willard told us that already," said Foy. "He got that from Martins."

"Yes, sir, but Saul from Princeton remembered his father saying that all Uncle Aaron's artifacts and so on were taken to the *Reichsmuseum* in Berlin. That was official policy at the time."

"So," said Foy, "that old bone is actually Nazi plunder, and Terry found it somewhere here in London. Is that it?"

"It would appear so, yes, sir."

"This thing gets worse and worse," muttered Foy. "Now we're looking for stolen loot from eighty years ago. Stuart's going to have a conniption."

"I don't know if it'll lead anywhere," Fielding admitted, closing his notebook and standing, "but there are several places where we could check that out. I mean, if the bone is, or was, part of a larger cache of stolen art or antiquities, there may be other people out there who know about it and may be looking as well."

"It's a long shot," said Foy, "but do what you can. Use my name as your authorization if you have to use Interpol or anything like that. Keep me informed, in any case."

Chapter Twenty-Six

A week after her meeting with Anna, Sylvia Becker, still in London, received a coded message from Bucharest that all arrangements were now made.

She texted Graham and Richard, giving them one hour to be in her office, and having learned the hard way that it was extremely unwise to keep Sylvia waiting, they were both sitting in front of her desk in just under fifty minutes.

"All right," she said, as Lombardi, out of harness, rested his golden head on Richard's knee requesting attention, "it's Romania this time, and you'll be the two tourists again."

"What size vehicle do we need?" Richard asked, scratching Lombardi's head, to the dog's evident delight.

"Just a car," said Sylvia. "The item is not very large. It's a gold chalice dating from the time of Vlad the Third. You may know him as Dracula."

"*Dracula*?" Graham burst out. "You're joking."

"I don't joke," said Sylvia, in a voice to congeal the blood.

"Sorry," muttered Graham, breaking the brittle silence which followed Sylvia's rebuke.

"For your information," Sylvia went on, in a tone of the purest condescension, "Vlad the Third was the son of Vlad Dracul, and was, therefore, called Vlad Dracula. He was a member of the House of Draculeşti, and a Prince of Wallachia in the fifteenth century."

"Is that where we have to go? Wallachia?" asked Graham. "I've never heard of it."

"No," said Sylvia, sighing. "You're going to Bucharest. But for your further edification, Wallachia is a region of Romania, north of the Danube, and south of the Carpathian Mountains."

"Oh," said Graham, clearly not much enlightened.

"Vlad was famous for his cruelty to his subjects and his prisoners of war," Sylvia continued, "who he liked to impale on high wooden stakes. Hence, he's sometimes known as Vlad the Impaler."

"Sounds like a really nice bloke," said Graham, but Richard was all business.

"Okay," he said, "but what's all that got to do with the chalice thing we're acquiring? What's the deal?"

"There's a traditional belief," said Sylvia, "that Vlad placed a solid gold chalice in every village and town and boasted that his subjects were so afraid of him, no one dared steal even one of them. The chalice you'll be acquiring is said to be the only surviving specimen."

"And it's how big?"

"About fifteen inches high, and about eight inches in diameter at its widest," said Sylvia. "It's in the standard shape of a pedestal cup with a circular base about six inches across. And it's heavy. Solid gold. Understand?"

The twins confirmed they did understand.

"You'll tell me when you're three days away from Bucharest. Then, when you arrive, there'll be further instructions. What's different this time is that no burglary is required. Our agent will leave the chalice at a certain place, you'll conceal it in the car, and drive back here. Delivery to the client will be arranged afterwards, and you don't need to know anything about that. Clear?"

"Leave it to us," said Graham, as the two rose to go.

The following day Richard hired a car using an alias and a forged driving license, while Graham went shopping. Later, they and the car were transported at high speed to Paris via the Channel Tunnel. They drove to a small village to spend the night in a bed-and-breakfast using different names and telling their hosts they were schoolteachers on holiday. Driving into the open countryside next morning after a sumptuous breakfast of rolls, diverse cheeses, butter, and homemade fruit preserves, Graham found a little-used narrow track leading into a deciduous forest. Once out of sight of the main road, he and Richard unpacked the tool kit Graham had purchased and set to work on the car. Graham, originally a mechanic by trade, detached the cover from the rear portion of the console between the two front seats and measured the cavity beneath.

"Perfect," he announced, letting the metal tape snap back into its case. "Lots of room."

He reset the cover in its brackets, minus the screws, allowing for easy removal when required, and all was done.

They spent the rest of the day touring the countryside, taking pictures, stopping at roadside cafés for lunch and dinner, before finding a hotel where they registered using a third set of identifications. The desk clerk seemed surprised they took two rooms, but merely shrugged, saying, "As you wish, gentlemen."

The hotel, once a private chateau, offered large, somewhat drafty rooms, decorated in pseudo eighteenth century style with bogus period furniture, and acrylic instead of cut crystal in the chandeliers, all of which needed dusting.

"This is supposed to be Louis the Something-or-other style, is it?" asked Graham, as they mounted the wide, curving staircase to the first floor.

"More like the Reign of Terror, if you ask me," grunted Richard, fitting the archaic key into the lock in the door of his room and turning it with a loud clank.

* * *

After two more days playing tourists in and around Paris using various identities and documents, along with simple disguises, Richard and Graham heard from Sylvia that everything was ready.

"You should be in Bucharest in three days," she finished. "It's just under fifteen hundred miles."

341

Sharing the driving, the miles unrolling behind them, they made it easily, and checked into the hotel Anna had recommended. At the time they were settling into their comfortable rooms, however, Anna, herself, was trying to make sense of the chattering voice on her mobile phone. The voice was that of her contact at the National Museum, and the man was almost incoherent with fear and distress.

"It's gone. The chalice is gone."

"Calm down," she snapped. "What do you mean, *gone*?"

With an effort, the man controlled his trembling voice, and said, "When I came to work at noon, it had disappeared. I found out it has been loaned to the Smithsonian in America. It is to be there five years."

"Damnation," growled Anna, seeing her commission evaporating. "Hell, and damnation."

"What about my money?" asked the distraught voice on the phone. "I must have it. I must pay the nursing home."

"No chalice, no money," said Anna. "That was the deal all along."

"But…but…what is to become of my mother?"

"Ask someone who cares," Anna snapped, "and don't ever contact me again, understand?" She heard an anguished wail as she terminated the call.

Anna phoned Sylvia immediately.

"The contract is cancelled," she said. "I can't supply the merchandise after all. I'll explain later. You'd better tell the shipping company."

"We're scrubbed," said Graham, dropping his mobile phone into his pocket. It seems the merchandise is no longer available."

"So, this whole thing has been a colossal waste of time," said Richard, morosely. "All this tourist crap and driving across Europe…all for nothing."

"Looks like it," said Graham. "We're ordered home."

"Well, we aren't leaving tonight," said Richard, "and we haven't come all this way just to sit around in our hotel

342

rooms. I don't know about you, but I need some excitement."

"Relax," said Graham. "This is a great opportunity to sit back and do nothing, for once. And don't forget, Atilla the Hen is picking up the tab at this very nice hotel."

"I'm sick of acting like a limp-wristed schoolteacher prancing about taking pictures of cathedrals. If this was a real holiday, I'd be in the pubs. I'd be finding girls"

Graham grinned and announced he was going to bed, leaving Richard to his own devices.

"Good idea," Richard grunted. "There's nothing better to do, anyway. But I think I'll go for a walk first. Get some fresh air. It'll help me sleep."

"Okay," said Graham, "but mind how you go, and don't get into any trouble. Stay out of the boozers and stay away from the hookers."

"Yes, sir," said Richard, mimicking the voice of a small boy in trouble at school. "I'll be on my best behavior, sir. Honestly, I will. I promise, sir."

Leaving Richard in the lobby, Graham rode the lift up to the eighth floor of the elegant hotel and reached his room. Settling gratefully into the large, soft bed, he wondered idly what had happened to the merchandise — Vlad's gold chalice. Why was it no longer available? Had someone got to it before them, or had someone in the system simply got cold feet? Well, whatever the explanation, it was Sylvia who gave the orders, and she expected them to be carried out. She had ordered them to come home, so home they would come.

In spite of his conjecturing, he soon fell asleep, but his rest was brief. He was dragged up from the depths of a sound slumber by a commotion in the corridor outside his room. Thrashing his way out from under the voluminous eiderdown duvet, he sat up, wondering what the noise was all about. Curiosity finally overcame him, and, padding barefoot across the room, he cautiously opened the door an inch and peered out. Half-a-dozen policemen were gathered around the door of a room some twenty feet away down the corridor, and Graham recognized one of the front desk clerks as he inserted a keycard into the lock. It was Richard's room.

* * *

"It all checks out, sir," said Neeta Mahajan to Foy, over a cup of tea in the Scotland Yard canteen. "Weber did move house, just as he said, and he got a lift round to the new place in the Ball Brothers' moving van carrying his furniture. The driver even remembers asking him to put his fag out."

"And that was definitely the van that was stolen?"

"Yes, that was easy to confirm. I've mined all the records concerning Barrow's car, and I can't think of anywhere else to turn. The bloke who saw the van leaving the area didn't get a look at the driver or anything else useful."

"Damn and blast," growled Foy. "That means we can't tie the theft of the van into the theft of Barrow's car, although my instinct says there has to be a connection. The question is, how the hell to prove it."

"Well," said Neeta, "assuming Weber did swipe it and use it to get away after torching Barrow's car, he'd have had an accomplice. One man can't drive two vehicles."

"You astound me, Neeta," said Foy, in a gloomy voice. He drained his cup before declaring with a grimace, "God, this tea's terrible."

"I wish I had better news," said Neeta.

"Not your fault," said Foy, with a shake of his head. "You did all you could. We're back at square one, and that's all there is to it, I'm afraid."

"The Super won't much like it, will he, sir?"

"Stuart? No, he certainly won't," Foy said, with a long sigh, "and I suppose I'd better go and tell him. Get it over with."

"D'you mind my asking why he's got it in for you, sir? It's not my business, I know, but…" She let her voice trail off.

Foy hesitated. He knew he could trust Neeta, that wasn't the problem. It was just that as he thought about the episode now, it seemed so much like harrowing up the past, opening an old wound, and he was not at all sure he wanted to do that. Moreover, once Terry's murderer was apprehended, he would be gone from the Yard permanently, and the whole thing wouldn't matter then. However, Neeta would still be there working with Stuart, and if Stuart ever got an inkling she knew about the incident, she could be in a vulnerable position. On the other hand, he reflected, she's strong enough to take care of herself, and she is working with me now, so she probably has a right to know the background.

He exhaled a long breath.

"It's a long time ago. Stuart and I were both Inspectors. There was a chap called Charlie Stafford we were after for murdering his girlfriend with a hammer. Stuart, who's slightly senior to me, and I, were leading the team on it, and I finally collared Stafford one night when Stuart just happened to be off duty. I got a commendation for it. Stuart resented the fact I didn't call him in so he could share the arrest, but in fact there hadn't been time to do anything but go straight in and get the bugger before he did a runner. Stafford walked away free, though. The trial judge ruled a key piece of evidence Stuart had collected to be inadmissible because it had been improperly obtained. Stuart managed to pin it all on me, and I could never prove otherwise. The commendation was withdrawn, which was no surprise. That's why he's now a Super, and I stayed an Inspector until I retired. Stuart took the view that as his junior I should be the one to carry the can. He knew I was watching every move he made after that, so he made life as difficult as he could for me. He wanted me chucked out so he could stop looking over his shoulder all the time to see where I was."

Neeta said nothing, merely shaking her head in disbelief.

"It's all over and done with now," said Foy. "I don't really care any longer. It was every man for himself in those days, and some of the other things that went on were far worse than what happened to me. Everyone knows Stuart won't rise above his present rank, and he knows it too." Foy grinned before saying, "And, of course, he now has the honor of looking after community relations, doesn't he?"

"Indeed, he does," Neeta agreed, with a discreet chuckle. "More tea, sir?"

"God, no."

With a smiling, "Good afternoon, sir." Neeta left him and Foy returned to his office. Notwithstanding his status as a reinstated temporary officer, he was responsible for the routine paperwork which abounds in all bureaucracies, particularly those supported by the taxpayer. This was the worst part of the job in his view, but with an inward groan he admitted he could put it off no longer — the accumulation had reached critical mass Turning to his computer, he set to work passing a remarkably tedious afternoon dealing with expense claim forms, travel documents, meal vouchers, and all the other administrivial things considered vital by the luminaries in the accounts department. By five o'clock he was done, but as he sat contemplating the final completion of these Herculean labors, his mobile phone chimed.

"Foy speaking."

He listened, then said, "All right, we'll pull the bugger in and sweat him for a while. I'm on my way. Arrange for backup and be ready to go as soon as I get there. And well done, Constable Mahajan."

Chapter Twenty-Seven

In Bucharest, Graham was in crisis mode, and for all he knew, he had precious little time to act. He had no idea why the police should want to get into Richard's room, but whatever the reason, it was not a good sign. Where was Richard anyway, he wondered. He could hear the voices of other guests and peremptory orders being issued telling everyone to go back into their rooms and stay there. He glanced at his watch. Eleven-forty-five. What the hell was going on?

He wasted no time in speculation, however. Working swiftly but without panic, he flushed his disguise materials down the toilet, false goatee, false moustache, and small wig. Next, he ripped out the picture page from each of his three forged passports, tore them into the smallest fragments he could, and flushed them away as well. The passports themselves were not so easy, but he managed to shred them and dispose of them in a similar fashion. Finally, the shards of his three false driver's licenses disappeared into the sewers of Bucharest. He dropped onto the bed, sweating from tension and concentrated effort. He heard the policemen talking and shouting to one another but could not understand what was being said. He knew it was only a matter of time before they found Richard's disguises and forged documents, and in fact he was a little surprised it was taking them so long. Syndicate protocols strictly forbade the use of hotel room safes since they could be opened by staff if it were deemed necessary, so other hiding places were prescribed. There was, however, only a limited number of those, ingenious though they were, and Graham knew the inevitable would eventually occur. In less than five minutes, he heard loud shouts of triumph amongst which he was able to discern the word *paşapoarte*.

"Christ," he muttered, "that's done it."

He was so knotted with tension that when his phone rang it sounded to him as if all the bells in hell had gone off at once, and he leapt from the bed as if he'd been kicked. After asking for *English, please*, an apologetic voice asked him if he would be so kind as to get dressed and come down to the hotel lobby. Rousing himself, got his clothes on, had a last quick look around the room to be sure he had overlooked nothing, steadied his nerves, and then, taking with him the passport he had used at check-in, he headed for the lift.

It was the syndicate's rule that when he and Richard arrived in a city where they were to undertake an acquisition or receive a previously acquired piece, as in this case, they should check into their hotel separately, each using passports from different countries. Accordingly, Richard, who spoke French, had used his Belgian passport, while Graham presented a British one in the name of Brian Astell. Later, they staged a *chance* meeting in the hotel bar.

Upon reaching the lobby, Graham saw other guests milling about, many of them angry, shouting questions at hotel staff, themselves bewildered and confused. The police officers were organizing the guests into a line and questioning each individual. As they approached Graham, he saw they had one of Richard's passports.

"Do you know this man?" demanded a policeman in heavily accented English, and Graham studied the photo.

"Not really," he said. "I met him this evening in the bar."

The officer called to a young woman Graham recognized as one of the serving staff in the bar and spoke to her. She looked at Graham, and then spoke to the policeman, nodding.

"You're coming with us," he said. "We have some questions for you."

Graham was hustled out of the hotel into the dark street, and after a short drive at high speed to the accompaniment of a shrieking siren, he found himself sitting on a straight-backed hard wooden chair at a metal table in a small interview room at the General Directorate of Bucharest Police, a fortress-like edifice with barred windows on the *Calea Victoriei*. The room was without windows and smelled faintly of some sort of disinfectant. There was a mirror on the wall to his left, which he assumed was two-way, and he had no doubt appraising eyes were on him. Opposite him, in a more comfortable chair, sat the arresting officer, a swarthy and dark-haired man of about forty wearing a humorless and hostile expression that matched well his imposing uniform. Between them on the table lay a false moustache, two bottles of hair dye, a pair of glasses with plain lenses, and several passports.

"Mr. Astell, the girl at the hotel says you spent several hours in the bar with this man," he looked down at one of the passports, "Michel Tours, and yet you say you hardly know him."

"I told you," said Graham, doing his best to look bewildered, "we met in the bar, that's all. We had a few drinks and chatted."

"What about?"

"Soccer, mostly."

"Soccer?"

"Yes. It turned out we were both very keen on following the qualification rounds for the world cup. You see, I think some of the African teams —"

"Never mind," snapped the policeman. "Did Tours tell you anything about himself? What he did, where he'd been recently?"

"No, he didn't."

The questions went on and on. Did Mr. Astell know anything about the disguises found in Tours' room? No, he didn't. Can Mr. Astell explain the existence of all these passports? No, he couldn't. Was Michel Tours his real name? Yes, as far as Mr. Astell knew.

As time wore on, it seemed to Graham that he was wearing the policeman down, rather than the other way around. The man relaxed visibly and gradually became less aggressive. Graham, therefore, ventured a question of his own. He knew he would have to tell Sylvia what had happened, but so far, he didn't actually know.

"Look," he said, "I have no idea why I'm here. I've tried to help you all I can, but what's Michel done? Is he here under arrest?"

"He is," answered the officer. "He got into a drunken fight outside a bar not far from here. He half killed the man he was fighting, then he got snotty with the officer who broke up the brawl. Because of that, he was brought in and thrown into the drunk tank for the night, but when he was searched, we found he was carrying two passports, one from Spain and one from Belgium."

"Dual citizenship?" Graham asked in all innocence, although he knew the answer.

"The names on the passports were different," said the officer, his eyes narrowed, "and that led us to search his hotel room where we found all this stuff and more phony documents. We now strongly suspect he entered Romania using false documents, and that is a serious crime. In any event, he will be charged with disturbing the peace, public drunkenness, and assault causing bodily harm."

Graham shook his head in apparent wonder, but as he did so he felt his own forged passport burning a hole in his shirt pocket. They had looked at it when he arrived at the Directorate, but thankfully had not run it through the system. It was as good a forgery as money could possibly buy, but a check on the number would have resulted in his own immediate arrest. All he wanted now was to get out of there.

"Well," he said, "I'm very sorry I couldn't help you further. I better be more careful who I talk to in bars from now on."

The officer regarded him critically for several moments before finally snorting a brusque laugh.

"All right Mr. Astell, I'll arrange for someone to take you back to your hotel. Please don't let this little incident mar your stay in Bucharest."

It was nearly dawn when Graham at last walked back into the hotel lobby. The night staff had gone, so no one gave him a second glance as he got into the lift and went up to his room. Walking in, he saw immediately that the police had been there before him. There was mess everywhere. His suitcase had been tipped out onto the floor, and its lining torn out. They had pulled apart the bed, leaving the duvet flung over a chair. Drawers were left half open, and the pockets in his spare pairs of trousers were all turned inside out. In the bathroom he saw they had squeezed all the toothpaste out of its tube and squirted the shampoo out of its bottle into the bath. They had even gone through all the pictures in his camera, and he thought wryly how bored they must have been by it. Endless street scenes, cathedrals, and churches from half of northern France. He was sure they would have taken Richard's camera, and hoped to hell no one would notice he had many similar photos, and some identical ones, and put two and two together. He was overwhelmingly grateful for the syndicate's rule that when two or more operatives were playing tourists, they were never to take photos of each other. A picture of Richard in his camera…he shuddered at the thought.

Dead tired, he tidied up as best he could and replaced the duvet. Flopping down onto the bed, he tried to sort out his whirling thoughts. At first, all he could do was thank God, or any other deity who might by chance be listening, that he'd had time to destroy his disguises and spare forged documents, but gradually he turned his mind to the question of what to do next. The syndicate was in jeopardy, to put it no higher, and he had to tell Sylvia Richard was in storage in Bucharest's central slammer. Everything might have been fine if Richard had not been idiotic enough to be carrying two of his passports, a practice strictly forbidden by syndicate protocols. And on top of that, he'd gone and got drunk. Sylvia was going to go berserk.

God, he thought, exhaling a long breath, what a bloody, bloody mess. He got wearily to his feet and extracted a can of beer from the mini-bar. As he did so, he noticed for the first time three empty cans on the dresser.

"Those buggers," he said aloud. "I'll have to pay for those."

He downed his beer nearly all at once, feeling suddenly desperately thirsty, and then steeled himself for the call to Sylvia.

For the rest of his life, Graham would remember that call. He had said Sylvia would go berserk, and so she did. Her fury defied description.

"That moron," she blazed. "Suppose he talks, what then?" She paused, and Graham could hear her breathing hard. He thought he could hear her grinding her teeth as well, but he couldn't be sure.

"What came over him?" she shouted. "What was he thinking?"

"I wish I knew. I wasn't with him. I don't know exactly what happened."

"I can tell you," she almost spat the words. "He wasn't thinking at all. And as for you," she added, "you get the hell out of Romania and try to do it without getting yourself arrested. Our only hope now is that Richard obeys orders and keeps his mouth shut."

Graham gathered his things, checked out, and, abandoning the car, made straight for Bucharest's Henri Coanda Airport. He flew back to London as Brian Astell without incident, and faced Sylvia in person later that day, finding her rage undiminished. He explained the situation in complete detail while she sat, her palms flat on the desktop, with her lips compressed. Her whole body was rigid, and when she finally spoke, her voice was harsh and abrasive.

"Why the hell did you let him get to a bar? You might have known he'd get drunk."

"He's got drunk before, Sylvia. Many times, in fact. I didn't tell you because he never got into trouble. Never."

Sylvia raged at him. "Do you mean to tell me you knew he had a drinking problem and you kept it to yourself? You...you," Words failed her, and Graham sat silent, cowed by the sheer intensity of her incandescent rage.

"My God," she growled, venomously, "I don't believe it, I really don't. This could cost us everything...*everything*...you know that, don't you? And all because of a drunken brawl."

Graham judged it best to continue holding his peace.

"Richard has to be silenced," Sylvia went on, still furious, but now as though she were thinking aloud. "I can't trust him, and now they have his passports, they'll be all over him to explain who and what he is." Then, seeming to remember Graham was there, she asked, "Can they tie him to you?"

"I very much doubt it," Graham said. "If they manage to trace his movements prior to reaching Bucharest, they'll soon find out he was traveling with someone, but they have no idea who I really am, and I trashed all my fake identification except for my Astell passport. I used that to get home and destroyed it as soon as I got to London. All according to the rules. Even if the Romanian police find out Astell doesn't exist, they still can't trace anything to me."

"Well, that's good news for a change," she said, morosely, "For a minute I thought you were going to tell me you came home under your own name."

"No, of course I didn't," Graham said, trying unsuccessfully to keep the irritation out of his voice. "I used the proper entry and exit protocols. I was Brian Astell going into Romania, in Bucharest, and when I left. Neither of us carried genuine documents. We never do, you know that."

Sylvia often seemed to proceed on the basis that everyone who worked for her was a half-witted idiot, and Graham resented it this time more than ever. Yes, this was a crisis, a dangerous crisis, but it was not of his making. He had obeyed the rules, Sylvia's rules, in everything he had done throughout the operation, especially when it went off the rails. He was not about to let her impute blame to him just because he happened to be sitting in front of her at that particular moment.

"According to all the driver's licenses and passports I used," Graham finished, "the real me never left this country at all, and Brian Astell the tourist came and went as expected."

"And just what do we do if Richard identifies you?" The question was rhetorical, but Sylvia's voice was more than menacing. Graham was well aware of what she was probably thinking. She sat silent for almost a full minute before telling Graham to go home and lie low until he received further instructions.

"Meanwhile, I have to figure out what we can do about that imbecile in Romania. I think Samuel has contacts in the police and elsewhere in Bucharest and can organize what we need."

Graham pretended not to hear. Sylvia had never tipped her hand in that way before. He had heard Samuel's name mentioned once before in connection with syndicate operations in the countries of the former Soviet Union, but he knew nothing more about him. Sylvia must really be beside herself to let that name slip in the present circumstances.

* * *

"How did you get onto this, Neeta?" Foy asked, as she drove them towards Maida Vale, followed by a second police car and a van.

"I didn't, Guv," she answered, smoothly rounding a corner, and then neatly avoiding a parked lorry. "I got a call from the Ball Brothers' van driver, who said he'd thought of something that wasn't right...sort of didn't fit, he said. I'd told him earlier we'd found the fag end in his van, but he'd suddenly remembered that when he asked Weber to put out his cigarette, he hadn't dropped it on the floor, he'd chucked it out the window."

"And he was sure about that?"

"He said so."

"Well good for him," said Foy. "It's too much of a coincidence that Barrow's car is stolen and torched right after Terry was killed, and now we know Barrow didn't go to France when he said he did. There would have been plenty of time for him to arrange to lose his car, so to speak. Once we have a chance to sweat Weber for a bit, we may be able to find a connection. I'm still suspicious of Barrow. There's just something about him I don't trust."

The vehicles drew up outside Weber's building, and with fully equipped constables stationed at the main entrance and rear doors, Foy, Neeta, and two more constables took the lift up to Weber's flat. Loud knocks on the door, and repeated calls of *Police*, elicited no response, and when Foy tried the door, he found it unlocked. They stood to one side as Foy slowly pushed open the door with his foot, calling, "Mr. Weber, Metropolitan Police. We'd like to talk to you."

"This is weird," said Neeta. "Why go out and leave the door unlocked?"

Foy put a cautious eye around the door and said, "He hasn't gone out. He's here, and he looks very dead."

Foy called in the Scenes of Crime investigators, the police pathologist, Dr. Crane, and all the other specialists who attend at the site of a murder. They arrived carrying cases of equipment and at once settled down to their work. After a quick look round for himself, which revealed nothing of consequence, Foy left them to their work, and they drove back to the Yard.

"Well, well," sneered Stuart, two days later. "So, you finally found a decent suspect, and you let someone get to him first. Well done."

Foy battled a monumental urge to drag Stuart across his desk by his tie, and then throttle him with it, but he won the fight and merely continued his report as if he had not heard the taunt.

"Scenes of Crime said the place was clean. No prints except for Weber's own. It was a professional piece of work, and they timed it perfectly. The occupants of the flats on either side, as well as those above and below, were all away at work, and those that were home elsewhere in the building heard nothing. The gun would have been silenced in any case, I daresay. A single shot to the head from fairly close range, according to Dr. Crane's postmortem, and no match on the bullet which ended up in the opposite wall. It was a forty-five. Blew Weber's head half to bits."

"Struggle?" Stuart asked. Foy shook his head.

"Weber most likely knew the killer and let him, or her, in. I've got someone checking to see if we have any matches to that MO. Forty-five, single shot, but nothing so far."

Stuart leaned back in his chair and regarded Foy with an amused expression.

"So," he said, his voice laden with patronizing condescension, "where do we go from here, I wonder? You've spent a lot of time going over all the old ground, as you so quaintly put it, found one person who might have helped, and he's killed right under your nose."

"We're not at a dead end quite yet," said Foy, seething. "We've still got Barrow to check out, and I'm very suspicious of him."

Stuart uttered a derisive snort. "You and your suspicions. I've told you we work on evidence these days, not suspicions."

"There's a team working on the Weber murder," said Foy, rising. He knew if he stayed much longer there would be a monumental row. "They're reporting to me. I also told Neeta Mahajan to send Weber's fingerprints to Interpol and follow up with them as necessary."

"And just who set all that up?" snapped Stuart.

"I did," Foy called over his shoulder, as he left the room.

Back in his own office, Foy sat for a few minutes just staring at the top of his desk, scratched and chipped as it was, turning over the situation in his mind. He had to admit it was not especially encouraging, but there was one possibility, small, but promising. If his speculation was correct, and Weber knew his killer, then if that killer could be found there was a chance, he or she could lead them to whomever Weber worked for. If that revealed a connection to Barrow, there might be a resolution at last. Weber was topped by a professional, and someone had to have hired him, or her. Everything depended on finding Weber's killer, but he had assigned that case elsewhere to avoid Stuart's accusing him of neglecting the case he was reinstated to solve. He therefore felt unsure of what to do next. Of one thing he was totally convinced, however, and that was that Stuart was sitting in his office like a praying mantis just waiting for a reason to recommend his removal. He, Foy, needed results, and he needed them quickly, but where the hell were they to come from, just at that moment?

He became aware of a tentative knocking on the window in his office door and looked up to see Fielding.

"Got a minute, sir? Can I have a word?"

As Fielding sat down, Foy could see from the light in his eyes he was anxious to share whatever news he had.

"It's about the oracle bone, sir," he began. "As you know, there are a lot of people hunting for Nazi loot these days. They're in Germany, the US, and elsewhere, but there's a foundation here in London that funds some of them on a private basis. They procure donations from various sources, including Israel as well as the local Jewish community."

"What's it called?" Foy asked.

"The Saint Anthony International Art Recovery Trust, or AART for short."

"I've never heard of them."

"Saint Anthony was born in Lisbon in the twelfth century and died in Padua."

"Bit before my time," Foy observed.

"He's the patron saint of lost things."

"That's appropriate," said Foy. "I take it you've been in touch with these good people?"

"Yes, sir. They have a huge database of their own, but they also keep tabs on many of the other like- minded organizations and share information back and forth with them. I went along to their offices in Notting Hill, and spoke to the executive director, Sir Alan Westbrook. He got his knighthood a couple of year ago in recognition of the work he does, and he was most helpful. He told me the only helpful thing the Nazis are famous for is keeping the most exacting records of everything they did, legal, illegal, and outright barbaric. Westbrook described it as a sort of perverted obsession."

"Sounds about right, but where does this take us?"

"So, Westbrook found a reference to some of Professor Weiskopf's artifacts having been sent to the *Reichsmuseum* from the University of Leipzig."

"Yes," said Foy, nodding, "I remember Willard telling us about that as well."

"Right," said Fielding, "but now we have an idea of what happened to them. Westbrook found out they were sent to Austria at the end of the war when the Nazis were busy trying to hide everything. Those artifacts were in a crate with a consignment of other antiquities, but the records indicate that crate never got to Austria. It was reported missing by the bloke who managed the salt mine where it was supposed to be stored. I can't remember his name."

Foy was again about to ask what this was leading to, when Fielding, perhaps noting the expression on his boss's face, said, "There is a point to this, sir."

"I'm glad," said Foy. "What is it, particularly?"

"The shipment to Austria was in the hands of a small troop of soldiers commanded by a certain Lieutenant Schumacher, who didn't survive the war. Westbrook didn't know what happened to him, but about ten years ago, several medieval paintings went on sale by auction in Vienna. They were part of an estate and were listed as having been bought in nineteen-forty-seven in Switzerland. These paintings were recognized as having been looted from a Dutch art gallery, and it turned out they had been in the crate that went missing."

"So," said Foy, "it would appear this Lieutenant Schumacher pinched the crate, and someone started selling the stuff in it later on."

"Exactly right," said Fielding, "and I think that person could well have been Schumacher's widow, Hilda."

"Sounds feasible," agreed Foy, "but that was a long time ago, and we still don't know for sure the oracle bone was in the missing crate. And even if it was, we don't know what happened to it afterwards."

"That's true, sir," said Fielding, "but there's a fair chance it was in the crate, and I thought anything we could do to trace it might be useful."

"So, it might indeed," said Foy, impressed. Fielding was a bright young man, showing good initiative. If his investigations into this affair bore fruit, it would mean sure promotion for him.

"So," Fielding was continuing, "when I told Westbrook the oracle bone might well be a crucial piece of evidence in a current murder inquiry, he offered to follow up and see if he could find out anything further about Hilda Schumacher on the theory she might have sold it along with the paintings. He said he'd get back to me."

"Excellent," said Foy, the tedious and insulting interview with Stuart now forgotten.

Chapter Twenty-Eight

Sylvia Becker, her long blonde hair streaming water, stepped out of the shower and felt for the large, soft towel on the rail to her left. Drying herself vigorously, she hummed quietly. She was happy. She dried her hair before dressing in blue slacks and white blouse. It had been a very good night. Her driver had been in excellent form as usual and had energetically propelled her to several ecstatic climaxes before groaning with pleasure at his own. Such sensuality never failed to leave her feeling invigorated and powerfully alive, but in addition to sexual repletion there was much else to be pleased about that morning. Carl Weber was expertly silenced, and the Romanian situation seemed under control. All syndicate operatives were under her personal standing order to say nothing about the syndicate if arrested or reveal any names, and so far, it appeared Richard was doing as he was told. According to Anna's sources he had divulged nothing apart from an agreed-upon story created for such an occasion but which up until now had never been used. After resisting interrogation for a reasonable length of time he had finally appeared to crack and tell the police he was a small-time thief and kept disguises and false documents to help him get away. He staunchly maintained he had committed no crime in Bucharest apart from the brawling — and they had charged him with nothing else — so everything looked good.

Lombardi, anticipating the morning walk, was sprawled in the hallway by the front door as she approached, and, jumping up, he walked into the harness she held down for him as he had done countless times before, his tail flailing enthusiastically.

She opened the door and said, "Out we go, boy. Forward."

The walk was pleasant. She felt the sunshine on her cheek and listened to the traffic, which she sensed was very light that Sunday morning. The air smelled clean at that hour, and she filled her lungs, breathing deeply, adding to her feeling of well-being and confidence. As Lombardi guided her back into Russell Square towards the house after the customary half-hour circuit through the streets, Sylvia's phone announced an incoming call.

"Yes?"

Anna's voice was breathless with wild agitation.

"I must see you at once. I am already on my way to London."

"What's going on? What's happened?"

"I can't tell you on the phone. I'll be there as soon as I can."

"Damnation," Sylvia growled under her breath, her buoyant mood gone.

Five hours later, Sylvia poured Anna a stiff tot of whiskey and delivered it to her, telling her to calm down and get hold of herself. Anna had always been unemotional and reliably pragmatic; Sylvia had never seen her like this. She downed the drink and drew a deep breath.

"It's Richard."

"What about him?"

"At first," she said, in a more business-like tone as the alcohol took hold, "it appeared his story was holding up well. The Directorate decided to forget about charging him with illegal entry to Romania because they realized they couldn't actually prove it. They were going to fine him heavily for the fight and the injuries caused, confiscate all his false documents and expel him from the country, but all that's gone to hell now."

"What's changed?" Sylvia demanded. She had thought the Richard problem solved, and she hated surprises with a passion. Her strategy in the syndicate's business was to avoid them at all costs.

Anna continued, "It seems that somehow the case came to the attention of Romanian State Security. God knows how. They threw his burglar story out. They've revived the illegal entry charge, which, unlike the Bucharest police, they say they *can* prove."

"Damnation," Sylvia muttered, through clenched teeth. "That's all we need."

"There's worse, I'm afraid," Anna went on, after a deep sigh. "They're now holding him indefinitely on suspicion of conspiracy to commit an act of terrorism."

"*What?*" Sylvia was aghast. "They can't do that. He's committed no crime except for disorderly conduct, or whatever they want to call it."

"They can do it," Anna said, spreading her hands palms up in a gesture of helplessness which Sylvia could not see. "These days, tensions are so high, and Romania is determined to avoid the sorts of things that have happened in France and Spain, and here in London, for that matter. State Security has wide powers of detention and interrogation."

"God blast Richard," Sylvia exploded. "I can't be sure he'll resist really heavy stuff. He's good, better than Carl Weber was, but…"

Anna waited, then said, "If they think terrorism is involved, who can say what will happen? Things could get very rough."

"He's a British subject…," Sylvia began to say, then realized as she spoke that appealing to the British Embassy for assistance would be absurd. Richard was carrying passports from several countries, none of them the United Kingdom, and apart from that little awkwardness, the danger to the syndicate would be enormous if Richard had to explain himself to British officials.

"That's no help," said Anna, evidently sharing Sylvia's thoughts.

Sylvia ground her teeth in monumental fury. Her fingers trembling, she lit a black cigarette, trying to settle her jagged nerves.

"Richard, a terrorist," she said, with a mirthless laugh as she exhaled a stream of smoke. "The only thing he knows about bombs is how to blow open a safe."

The involvement of the Romanian Security Service had magnified the crisis a thousand-fold. They would be in touch with their counterparts all across Europe and beyond as they investigated Richard's background; the mere mention of the word *terrorist* would cause a major alert. And to make matters worse, if that were possible, they had a list of his numerous aliases. Meticulously careful as she and the syndicate had always been, so intensive an inquiry might detect a weak link somewhere. Sylvia had never faced this level of threat before, and it unsettled her to an unaccustomed degree, but she had been the syndicate's guiding hand too long to surrender now. She settled her raw nerves, suppressed her anger, confronted the problem, and made a decision.

* * *

A week after his visit to the Saint Anthony International Art Recovery Trust, the AART, Fielding announced he had something to report, and Foy suggested they go out for lunch.

"I need a break from the office," he said, as they walked to a small sandwich shop two streets away from the Yard. The noise of the traffic was ever-present, and pedestrians thronged the pavements as always, but before long they were safely ensconced at an inconspicuous corner table in an establishment called — no doubt with an eye to the tourist trade — *Ye Olde English Tea and Crumpet Shoppe*. Their lunch was delivered to them by a dark-skinned young woman with a powerful South Asian accent and a broad streak of purple in her hair. She was further

363

ornamented by multiple piercings through her lips, nostrils, eyebrows, and chin, several of them decorated with tiny silver charms. As he watched her go, Foy observed, "All stapled up like that, you'd think she was afraid her face was going to fall off."

"Not particularly old English, is she?" Fielding asked, grinning.

"It's enough to put you off your food," Foy grumbled.

"Not nearly enough to put me off mine, Guv," said Fielding, taking firm hold of a large Cornish pasty. "I'm bloody starving."

"So," said Foy, "you've got something from the Saint Anthony people, have you?"

Swallowing a mouthful of pasty, savoring its rich meat and vegetable filling, Fielding said, "Yes, although it actually came from one of the German organizations they work with. It appears that after the war, Hilda Schumacher began to live life very large in Munich. It's known she bought and sold artworks on the black market as well as the open one, but she had a hell of a lot of money right from the start. Things were pretty chaotic at the time, and she took advantage of it."

"So perhaps her husband had been helping himself, as we suspected," said Foy. Fielding nodded, his mouth full again, and Foy waited, attending to his own lunch, a sizeable steak-and-kidney pie.

"That's right," said Fielding, eventually. "Now, it appears she never tried to sell artworks known to have been stolen, that is, famous pieces that everyone was on the lookout for, so no one paid much attention to her. She sold jewelry for the most part, none of it traceable to concentration camps or anything like that. The authorities went so far as to make sure of that, and, of course, a lot of people needed money in those days. There were all kinds of wheeling, dealing, and manipulation going on, and Hilda Schumacher was just one of the many."

He paused for more pasty, remarked on how excellent it was, and then continued.

"The family moved to Berlin in the fifties, and Hilda's daughter, Ellen, took over when Hilda died. She lived an extravagant life as well, and the West German Police regarded her as dubious to say the least. They strongly suspected her wherewithal was based on Nazi treasure, although there's no indication of any Nazi Party affiliation in the family. Anyway, nothing could ever be pinned on her."

"Another dead end, then," said Foy, working diligently on his pie.

"Maybe not," said Fielding, after a swig of pale ale. "The West Germans noted a rather interesting thing happening over the years."

"Which was?" Foy put down his glass of stout.

"A marked and steady increase in thefts of art objects and antiquities. Thefts from private homes, museums, even one from a former royal palace. They were all professional jobs, but one or two arrests were made. In each case, the story was the same. Instructions and payments always came from an anonymous source. No one knew anything beyond that, so the masterminds could never be found."

Fielding swallowed the last of his pasty before continuing.

"Now, Ellen Schumacher had a daughter named Gabriella. There's no word of a husband, by the way, but Gabriella inherited all the money when Ellen was killed in New York on nine-eleven."

"And do we know where they keep all the money?" asked Foy, pushing aside his empty plate.

"No, we don't. Presumably buried in Swiss banks, maybe in the Caymans, or the Channel Islands."

Fielding finished his pale ale, signaled the well perforated server for another round, and resumed the narrative.

"Interpol says Gabriella's still living in the Berlin house, but her daughter, Sylvia, divides her time between that house and a place here in London. I checked it out but couldn't locate anything until I found out that Gabriella got herself married to, and subsequently divorced from, a bloke named Becker."

"And from whom did you discover that? Interpol again?"

"No, sir, nothing so grand. The German police. Public Records, and all that. Your basic stuff."

"Simple enough," said Foy, grinning. He was pleased with Fielding's tenacity. The way he'd begun with a single piece of information and carried it forward from one step to the next in a logical progression. Exemplary.

"Yes, sir. So, I checked again on Gabriella Becker, and she does have a flat in London all right. Russell Square, to be precise, which passed into her possession on the death of her mother, Ellen Schumacher."

"Okay." Foy tried not to look at the decorated server as she delivered their recharged glasses and removed their lunch plates. "You know," he said, as she left, "I'll bet she can pick up the wi-fi in here with all that stuff stuck in her face."

"Gabriella Becker still holds title to the flat, but Sylvia Becker pays all the bills. Interpol has been trying for years to get something on the Becker family. There's all sorts of snippets and bits, but nothing on which they can actually build a case for issuing a warrant. Whatever they're up to, they've insulated themselves damn well. Brilliantly, in fact."

"All right, then," said Foy, after a mouthful of his second pint, "what have we got now, exactly? There's the apparent possibility that the oracle bone was part of a shipment of antiquities which may have been appropriated by a minor German officer who may have had his hand in the till. We also have a series of female descendants of the said minor officer who are filthy rich and perhaps live outside the law, but no one knows for sure. That's quite a collection of uncertainties, maybes, and perhapses. However, we do know there's been an undue increase in thefts of art works and antiquities. Interpol and the German police are highly suspicious, and we probably should be as well. Is that about it?"

"Yes, sir." Fielding sipped his ale and nodded.

"But," continued Foy, "we still can't trace the oracle bone."

"There's one thing I forgot, sir," said Fielding. "When it comes to thefts of *objets d'art*, Interpol says they keep tripping over a name. Not a person, a thing. But they can't get a handle on it. It's apparently a very well-concealed clandestine organization, or whatever it is, without any connections to known gangs or other such operators."

"And what's the name they keep tripping over?"

"The Athena Syndicate."

* * *

They took Richard to the *Palatul de Justiție* on the *Splaiul Independenței* in Bucharest in a dark green, windowless steel van escorted by two motorcycle outriders. He had been assigned an attorney who proved to be neither use nor ornament, and he had resigned himself to at least a year or two in a Romanian prison on the illegal entry charge. He tried not to think about what might happen if they nailed him as a terrorist, and when he asked about it, his so-called attorney helpfully told him that was exactly what they intended to do.

"But," he protested, "it's purely circumstantial. I'm guilty of nothing except illegal entry and possession of false documents. I'm prepared to admit to that."

"That is enough to build a case against you for conspiracy," his attorney answered politely. "Romanian law would allow for such a prosecution."

"They'll bang me up 'til bloody doomsday," he said, angrily, and the attorney merely shrugged.

"Perhaps, yes."

As he sat handcuffed to the steel bench against the side wall in the darkness of the van's interior, Richard felt the vehicle turn a corner. Abruptly, the tires screeched as the brakes were slammed on, flinging him sideways, his wrists

367

being wrenched by the handcuffs. He yelled in surprise and pain. Settling himself upright once more, he heard shouting and wondered what was going on. His heart beat faster at the sudden thought that Sylvia might have staged a rescue for him. The back door of the van was thrown open with a loud, metallic clang and bright sunlight poured in. Richard shut his eyes against the dazzling glare, and so did not see the policeman in motorcycle uniform who leapt in, put a pistol to his head, and fired.

Witnesses later reported one motorcyclist, who appeared to be a policeman, covered the van driver and his partner, while the second entered the van and a shot was heard. The two motorcyclists then sped away in opposite directions. It was all over in less than a minute.

The news media in Romania reported the brazen killing, and speculated that the prisoner, whose actual identity was not yet known, must have been a gangster, murdered by his comrades to silence him. The police officers driving the van swore they believed the motorcyclists to be fellow policemen, although they did not know them. In Berlin, Sylvia and her mother shared champagne, and in Bucharest, Anna received a substantial fee.

* * *

Back at Scotland Yard, Foy entered his office in a pensive mood. He could not shake off the feeling he was close to cracking the case, but soberly reminded himself he'd had that feeling before, and it had not been correct. However, it seemed to him entirely too coincidental that Weber should fall victim to a professional hit man just as he, Foy, was closing in on him. There had to be something there, he was sure of it; tantalizingly close, almost within his grasp, yet remaining elusive.

Then, of course, there was the constant irritation of Superintendent Stuart. Publicly, Stuart was pushing hard for progress, but Foy knew he had no real interest in seeing results. The longer the investigation went on without observable progress, the better Stuart liked it. At some point, when he judged the time to be propitious, he would approach Commissioner Drake with a recommendation Foy be removed. The investigation would then be quietly shifted into the background where it would languish in the cold once files once again, and Stuart's reputation would no longer be in jeopardy.

Foy contemplated telling Stuart about Fielding's work on Nazi art thieves, but quickly decided against it. Thus far, what Fielding had found was not truly germane to the case, interesting though it was. Stuart would simply ridicule him for what he always called Foy's *wild goose chases dressed up to look like genuine investigations*. He would tell him, as he had before, to make an arrest or just bugger off back into the wilderness and leave the police work to those properly able to carry it out.

"My God," Foy muttered under his breath, "I really think he'd let Terry's killer walk away just to protect his self-important little image."

And his assessment was correct.

* * *

Unbeknownst to Foy, Stuart had already prepared a lengthy report on Foy's performance — or, more exactly, his lack of it — since his reinstatement. He had sent this condemnatory document upstairs to Deputy Assistant Commissioner Oliver Drake, accompanied by a recommendation that Foy's tenure at the Yard be terminated forthwith, and control of the Preston murder investigation returned to Superintendent Stuart. Drake read, re-read, pondered, and worried himself almost to distraction over it. Harry Stuart was obviously very unhappy with things, and one might easily conjecture Bill

Foy was equally so. That circumstance troubled Drake, he was never happy if he thought others were unhappy.

However, there was a deeper side to Commissioner Drake, one which most of his colleagues were unaware of. His reputation as a weak and ineffectual leader was not wholly deserved. He went about his work quietly; there were no trumpets or drums, and what people did not hear about, they did not talk about. On many occasions over the years, Drake had made cogent and crucial decisions which proved his worth. It was those decisions, in spite of their not having come to general notice, and although some of them went against his fundamentally pliable nature, which had been marked by his superiors and which resulted in his promotions. This situation, Drake ultimately concluded, was going to be another one of those occasions, and after a period of what his closest associates privately called *dithering*, he made up his mind.

He summoned Stuart to his office, and Stuart appeared with alacrity, assuming, no doubt, he was about to hear good news.

"You've spent a great deal of time preparing this, haven't you, Harry?" Drake held up the report.

When Stuart entered the office, he had worn the smug expression of a man expecting to be congratulated, but Drake's opening gambit took him somewhat aback.

"I…I thought you ought to know what was going on, sir," he said, trying to recoup his confidence and gain some momentum. "It is, after all, a matter of the most effective use of resources."

"Oh, is it?" Drake asked, with apparent innocence. "And here's me thinking it was a matter of getting a long overdue result on a murder case. Silly me."

"Well," blustered Stuart, "yes, sir, of course —"

But Drake cut him short. "A murder case, which, I believe, you'd had virtually no success in unlocking. Correct?"

Drake watched calmly as Stuart, now completely off balance, thrashed about for a response. It was obvious Drake's attitude was totally unanticipated.

"The case was still under investigation when DI Foy first came to see me, sir," he said.

"Nonsense," said Drake, stone-faced.

"I beg your pardon, sir…"

"I said *nonsense*, Harry. You'd let it go as cold as a dead fish. I receive reports on all active cases, as you well know, and the Preston murder had disappeared from that list, hadn't it?"

"Well," said Stuart, uncertainly, "I suppose other priorities might have arisen, so I —"

"Dropped it," Drake finished, and Stuart's chin came up in defiance.

"The case was *not* dropped."

"Then tell me this," said Drake. "At the time Bill Foy arrived to offer his help, who was assigned to the case, hmm?"

Stuart hesitated, and Drake could tell this little scheme of his was not going at all as planned.

"There was no one, was there, Harry?"

Drake, almost unrecognizable to Stuart as the smiling and affable character he had seen — or thought he had seen so often before, now fixed him with an unwavering stare. Stuart faltered before managing to retrieve some dignity.

"It is my considered opinion, sir," he said, returning the stare, "that retaining the services of Inspector Foy is deleterious to the department, and the management of the investigation."

"Deleterious to you, you mean," said Drake, who, although speaking severely, was in complete control of his temper. "You're afraid Bill will succeed where you failed."

"I did not *fail*, as you put it, sir," said Stuart, his accent thickening as his anger grew. "The case was still under investigation, as I said, and in my view, Inspector Foy has got no further in the time he's been here. Moreover, while he has been here, he has monopolized the time of two valuable officers, Detective Constable Mahajan and Detective Sergeant Fielding."

At this point, Drake, ignoring Stuart's last remark, changed direction so abruptly Stuart looked baffled. He stared at Drake, open-mouthed, as the commissioner said, "Did you seriously think no one knew you had it in for Bill Foy ever since that chap walked away from his murder charge? I, and many others, certainly knew. You were far from subtle about it, I'll tell you. It was as plain as day. We all had our suspicions it was you, not Bill, who buggered up the evidence. We weren't all born yesterday, you know. There was nothing we could do, but we let Bill know we were on his side if ever he needed us. He was too much of a professional to tell tales, so he left it alone after a time, and the higher-ups never heard the truth. But what goes around, comes around, Harry, and you'd do well to remember that."

Stuart sat dumbfounded. Drake saw him struggling desperately for an appropriate retaliatory reply, but none was made. Drake waited, watching expressions of anger and incredulity following each other across Stuart's face.

"So," said Drake, standing up behind his desk, "I'll decide when Bill Foy goes, and until then, he stays and gets on with it. And," he added, tossing Stuart's report back to him, "you can take this piece of malicious rubbish and shred it. If I hear of it getting any further than this, I'll raise hell and prop the lid up, is that clear?"

* * *

Stuart left Drake's office, seething with rage at both Drake and Foy. He felt stung and bitter. He had been humiliated, and, what was worse, that old murder case had come back to haunt him after all these years. He thought it had been forgotten. He saw clearly that he no longer could hope for promotion. He was a marked man. It was hard to believe Ducky Drake, of all people, was in a position to make or break his career. Unbelievable. And now he was stuck with Bill Foy indefinitely.

Hell, and damnation.

As he crossed the squad room, a constable looked up from his computer saying, "DI Foy would like to see you, sir."

"Well I wouldn't like to see him," he snapped, and strode into his office, slamming the door behind him.

"Blimey," said the constable to the man at the adjacent desk, "what did he have for lunch, I wonder?"

"Duck, I believe," said his neighbor.

* * *

What Stuart did not know was that Foy was sitting in his own office, amazed and a trifle bewildered by the phone conversation he had had with Professor Willard while Stuart was upstairs trying to stick a knife in his back.

"I've found the oracle bone, Inspector," Willard said, almost breathless with excitement.

"Excuse me?" said Foy. "You've what?"

"I've found the oracle bone. It was donated to the museum at the University of Caen eight months ago. I've just seen an article about it in a journal of sinology. I know the author very well, so I called to congratulate him and to find out how and where he saw the bone."

"This is amazing, Professor," said Foy. "What did you find out?"

"Apparently it was given to the university by a man named Henri Levesque who inherited it and a lot of other things from his uncle who died about a year ago. Levesque had no idea what it was, so took it to the university...he lives in Caen, by the way...and when he heard what it was, he simply gave it to them. A splendid gesture, don't you think?"

The gesture, splendid or otherwise, was of no interest to Foy. Hardly daring to hope, he asked, "Did you by any chance find out the name of the uncle?"

"Of course," said Willard, matter-of-factly. "I knew you'd need to know that. It was Alain Levesque."

"This is marvelous, sir," enthused Foy. "Thank you so much for letting me know. Now I must find out how Uncle Alain acquired the bone, if I can."

"Good," said Willard, "but I must say I'm a little disappointed."

"Why so?"

"Well," said Willard, sounding a little wistful, "I was rather hoping you'd find the bone here somewhere so I could have been the one to announce it to the world."

"Yes," said Foy, after a short pause. "I understand. But hopefully this means we'll be able to find Terry's murderer."

"Oh, I do hope so," said Willard. "That's the important thing."

Foy put down the receiver and turned to his computer. A short search revealed the late Alain Levesque — dead at the age of ninety-six — to have been a reclusive multibillionaire, reputedly connected at various times in his life with dubious financial transactions, arms dealing, and sundry other similar pastimes. He had, however, never been brought to book, and it was also noted that Levesque was known to have had a vast collection of art and antiquities. It had often been alleged he collaborated with the Germans under the Vichy government during the war, but those accusations were never proved.

Maybe that's how the good M. Levesque got his start, Foy reflected. Another Nazi connection. Interesting.

Foy picked up his phone again and talked to his contact in the French police. Charles Lebrun was an old friend and colleague, and he promised to follow up the lead.

"I will find out all I can about this guy for you, Bill," he said. "And from the sound of it, he's lucky to have lived as long as he did, no?"

After a few further pleasantries, Foy thanked Lebrun and ended the call. He felt both elated and impatient. Things were now moving a lot more quickly, and he felt like a hunter on the point of catching sight of his quarry before closing in for the kill.

Foy fumed with frustration for the next three days. What on earth was Lebrun doing? Why was it taking him so long? On the morning of the fourth day his patience, such as it was, finally ran out. He decided to give Lebrun until noon, but at ten-thirty-five, the Frenchman telephoned, apologized profusely for the delay, and then presented Foy with the results of his investigation.

Amongst the numerous documents ultimately transferred to Henri Levesque, the Trustees of Alain's Will had listed a diary. Lebrun arranged for the police in Caen to call on Henri, and they found he still had the book. With his permission, therefore, it was sent to Paris where Lebrun checked out all entries for mid to late February 2014.

"And there it was, my friend," he finished, a note of triumph in his voice.

"What did it say?" Foy asked, trying unsuccessfully to sound dispassionate.

"Aha, my friend," said Lebrun, with a laugh, "just you wait till you hear."

"I *am* waiting, Charles," said Foy, in some exasperation. "So, for God's sake tell me."

"All right, all right," said Lebrun, still laughing at Foy's impatience. "It said, *Received interesting Chinese artifact from Athena via my business agent.*"

"And the date of the entry was…?"

"The twenty-first of February."

"Perfect," said Foy. "Can we talk to the business agent, whoever he is?"

"It is a she, actually," said Lebrun, "and I have already interviewed her. She is totally innocent, I believe. She was simply told by Levesque she would receive a text message from a certain Paul Ellis, no doubt an alias, telling her where to collect a parcel for her employer. The text came from a disposable phone. She collected the parcel as instructed and never saw Ellis."

"It fits," said Foy. "I suspect Paul Ellis is Michael Barrow, and speaking of which, Charles, the couple who provided Barrow's alibi swore he'd never left Paris. Can you pull them in again and have another go at them?

375

They've been interviewed twice already but see what you can do."

"Okay Bill."

Following many grateful thanks, Foy arranged for Lebrun to email a written report to him and then sat ruminating on what he had heard. The word *Athena* had turned up and was clearly identified as the entity from which the oracle bone had been received. Athena was the supplier, and he was a sure as he could be that Barrow, alias Ellis, was the courier. Delivery had been made three days after Terry was killed, and two days after Barrow arrived in France. Plenty of time to catch a train to Caen.

"So," he said, under his breath, "how the hell do we connect Barrow with Ellis?"

Asking Barrow outright was pointless. He would undoubtedly say he'd never heard of Paul Ellis. He decided reluctantly he would have to wait and see if Lebrun could crack Barrow's alibi.

If I can collar Barrow, he thought, he might just be able to lead us to Athena, whoever, or whatever, that might be.

Chapter Twenty-Nine

"I passed," said Neeta Mahajan, with a radiant smile, two days later as she met Foy in the corridor by the lifts.

Foy looked blank for a moment, and she made a noise of mock exasperation with her tongue.

"My sergeant's exams, sir," she said, enunciating each word as though Foy were slightly deaf. "I told you, remember?"

To his chagrin, Foy realized he had forgotten it entirely. He began to fumble for words, but she let him off the hook.

"Never mind," she said, in bubbling excitement. "I passed. I got the letter this morning."

"Well done, Neeta," he said, recovering himself and pumping her hand. "I knew you'd do it. I'd give you a hug, only I'd probably get done for sexual harassment."

"Not by me, you won't," she answered, with another happy laugh, throwing her arms around his neck. She hugged him for what seemed a wonderfully long time, during which he found the feel of her young, strong body and the soft scent of her long hair utterly intoxicating.

Disengaging a trifle reluctantly, Foy grinned, congratulated her again, and then found himself struck by the realization of how many years it had been since he, himself, had opened that same letter and been similarly thrilled by its news. Resolutely, he pushed aside the gloomy thought.

"And I've something else to tell you, as well," Neeta was saying almost breathlessly. "I got word from Interpol."

"Yes?"

"I sent Weber's prints off to them, as instructed, and they got a hit straight away. He was in their database because the police in Colombia had found his dabs at the scene of a murder. Some bigshot gangster, apparently. Interpol wasn't brought into the investigation at the time, so they couldn't give me any details. I contacted the coppers in Bogota, the *Policia Nacional de Colombia.* There's my contribution to multiculturalism."

"Very impressive," said Foy, "but I'm more interested in what the Colombian coppers told you."

"I asked them to send me whatever they could, so they sent Weber's prints and I checked them out, just to be sure. All fine. But they also sent a second set of prints taken off a combine harvester delivered to the same place three months before the murder in question."

"A combine harvester?" asked Foy, his eyebrows raised. "What on earth...?"

"It was a big farm of some kind," said Neeta, "but that's not the point, sir. Guess who belongs to those other prints."

"This isn't a game, Neeta," he said, slight impatience in his voice. "Out with it."

"They belong to none other than Mr. Michael Barrow."

"*What?*" Foy burst out. "Seriously?"

"Very seriously," said Neeta, nodding. "And that's not all."

"Go on, then," he said. "This is all a bit hard to grasp."

"The bloke who was murdered liked to collect fine art, and he'd been suspected of building his collection through what the case files described as *other than legitimate means.*"

"What a surprise," said Foy. "How very prosaic of them."

"The Colombians did over the house where the murder occurred and found all sorts of stolen stuff, and amongst the dead guy's papers there was a reference to something called *the syndicate.*"

"What was the reference?" Foy asked. "What did it actually say?"

"It was a copy of a note to someone unnamed, but it instructed that person to postpone payment. His accountant, maybe."

By this time, they had reached Foy's office, and Neeta was seated in front of the desk, her long legs elegantly crossed, her familiar beauty heightened into sheer radiance by her excitement and happiness. Looking at her olive skin, her ebony hair, her fathomless dark eyes, and that wonderfully incongruous cockney accent, he sighed inwardly, then cleared his throat.

"Is there anything more in the files from Bogota?" he inquired, dragging himself back from nebulous realms to stark reality. Neeta shook her head.

"Nothing of any use. So, where do we go from here, Guv?"

"We go to pay a visit to Mr. Michael Barrow. We've enough to pull him in for questioning at the very least, but there's something you don't know. The French police were on the phone a couple of hours ago, and Barrow's Paris alibi has gone to hell. He left Paris, and I'm pretty sure he went to meet Paul Ellis in Caen, but what I'm not sure of is how the oracle bone fits into all this...if it does, that is."

"Are you going to tell Superintendent Stuart before we go, sir?" Neeta asked, and Foy gave her a grim smile.

Not bloody likely, he said to himself. He could readily imagine Stuart ordering him to stand off while he arrested Barrow himself, or, if nothing else, insisting he accompany Foy so the official report would show he commanded the operation as senior officer present.

Foy said, "No, I don't think I'll tell him."

Neeta nodded, but said nothing.

"Get Sergeant Fielding and organize the backup," he told Neeta, "and we'll go as soon as everything's in place."

She was gone in a trice, but Foy remained standing behind his desk for a few moments. He had no direct evidence against Barrow, he knew that. Everything was purely circumstantial. Carl Weber was now unable to testify concerning Barrow's stolen car. Even Barrow's defunct alibi and the bizarre connection between Barrow and a combine harvester in Colombia, of all places, still did not add up to proof of murder. He would just have to hope something would turn up at Barrow's flat, or that Barrow would incriminate himself somehow.

If I go arresting the wrong man now, he thought, Stuart will crucify me.

"But he's not the wrong man," he said aloud, as he left his office. "He just can't be."

Within an hour, just as darkness was enveloping London and the city was coming alive with streetlights and illuminated signs, the convoy drew up outside Barrow's building. He answered their knock wearing a satin smoking jacket and felt slippers, looking to Foy like something out of Charles Dickens.

"What's this all about?" he demanded, as Foy, Fielding, Neeta Mahajan, and two constables occupied his sitting room. "What's going on?"

"Fielding, Neeta, have a look round," said Foy, as the two constables took up station by the door.

"You can't do that without a warrant," said Barrow, angrily.

"Yes, we can," said Foy, "but forget that for now. Tell me, Mr. Barrow, have you ever been to Colombia?"

"Colombia?" said Barrow. "No, I haven't, not that it's any of your business."

"Well, then, are you in the agricultural machinery business?"

"Of course not."

"Then why were your fingerprints found on a combine harvester at a crime scene outside Bogota, the capital city of Colombia?"

"Obviously because someone made a stupid mistake," snapped Barrow, but a wary look had come into his eyes.

"I doubt it," said Foy, "but never mind. Tell me where you went when you left Paris for two days a year ago last February."

"I didn't leave Paris," Barrow said, hotly. "I was staying with friends. The ones you set the Paris police onto."

"Come off it, Barrow," Foy said, his voice harsher. "We know you left. Your alibi's blown. When your so-called friends heard there was a murder involved, they suddenly became a lot more cooperative."

Barrow's eyes narrowed momentarily at the mention of murder, but he maintained his façade of indignant aggression.

"All right," he said, "I probably did leave for a day or two. So what? That's not a crime, is it? I was very upset about Terry's death, and being the last person to see him alive, and so on. That sort of thing's a bit of a shock."

"Try again," said Foy. "We know you didn't hear about Terry's death until you came home. You said so yourself."

Barrow stared at Foy, his expression now less defiant. Foy intensified the pace.

"Ever heard of something called the Athena Syndicate?"

"No."

"Know a Carl Weber, do you?"

"No, I don't."

"Sylvia Becker, maybe?"

"No."

"Who's Paul Ellis?"

"I've never heard of him."

Barrow's answers came too quickly. He was wilting under the onslaught. Foy heard desperation in his voice.

At that moment Fielding came in from the bedroom carrying a clear plastic evidence bag containing what looked like a short metal cylinder.

"There's a silencer here, sir."

"And you said you didn't own a gun," said Foy. "Why keep a silencer, then?"

Barrow had no time to answer before Neeta Mahajan appeared with a bag of her own.

"It's all here, sir. Three passports. One's legit, but the other two are forgeries. Damn good ones, though. One's from the Netherlands in the name of Jan Vandermeer, and the other is from the UK in the name of Paul Ellis, complete with entry and exit stamps and a visa from Colombia."

Epilogue

No doubt thinking he had nothing to lose, and perhaps hoping for more lenient treatment in court, Michael Barrow confessed to the murder of Terry Preston, and then sang like an Italian tenor. Names and information poured forth from him in a flood. A few days later, after docking in Dubai, the captain, first officer, and several crewmembers of a certain Polish container ship were arrested at the request of Scotland Yard and the Polish police, thus causing considerable inconvenience to the vessel's owners. At one o'clock in the morning, a Chinese anti-corruption squad descended on an opulent home belonging to an official of the Shanghai Port Authority, flinging him into a van in his night attire, while at the same time arrests were being made in Beijing and Jinan. On the other side of the world, two Panamanian diplomats found themselves in prison, and later that week, in Jakarta's Jalan Surabaya market, the Indonesian police dragged the owner of stall number twenty-three out into the street and bundled him into a car, much to the consternation of tourists and locals alike.

Those arrests yielded information which led to yet more arrests as the net widened. Graham, arrested at Heathrow attempting to board a flight to Buenos Aires, at first confessed only to burglary, but under Foy's questioning he revealed the background to a murder in Romania Scotland Yard knew nothing at all about. After several high-level phone calls between Commissioner Drake and his Romania counterpart, therefore, a woman calling herself Anna was arrested in an upscale neighborhood of Bucharest, and shortly thereafter two motorcycle policemen turned hit men were apprehended as they arrived for work. Later, a terrified young museum guard was taken into custody as he attended his mother's funeral.

And finally, the net closed. In Berlin, Gabriella Becker, now near death and no longer able to speak, was arrested and conveyed to a prison hospital. At the same time, Sylvia Becker sat smoking in her sitting room in London with Lombardi at her feet.

"They'll never get to us, boy," she said to the dog. "Everyone has orders to stay silent, and they'll obey my orders. They always do, you see. There's nothing to worry about."

Leaning forward, she felt for Lombardi's glossy, golden head. As she stroked him, his ears pricked up at the sound of distant sirens, but Sylvia paid no attention. The braying wails grew louder, and louder still, until they abruptly ceased outside the building, but Sylvia sat where she was, unperturbed, smoking her black Turkish cigarette.

The End

AUTHOR'S NOTE

This story is set in both the present and the past. It unfolds against a backdrop of documented historical events, such as the fall of the kings of Xia in bronze-age China, the political chaos of China's so-called Warlord Period in the early twentieth century, and the Second World War in Europe, as well as in present-day Berlin, London, and elsewhere.

The historical record of ancient China is derived largely from contemporary inscriptions found on bronze ceremonial vessels and oracle bones, or from later texts, many of which were written years, or even centuries, after the fact. Because of this, the evidence can, on occasion, be inconsistent or even contradictory. However, King Jie of Xia and King Da Yi of Shang (sometimes called Tang, Cheng Tang, or Tian Yi) are known to have existed, and the general circumstances of their conflict — if not all the finer details — seem to be more or less accepted. The dispatching of Yi Yin as envoy from Shang to the court of Xia, and the flight of Zhong Gu from the court of Xia are documented, but I have fictionalized the circumstances.

The veneration of ancestors, often called *ancestor worship*, is referred to in the narrative and was a cornerstone of traditional Chinese religious observances. It persists into the present day, albeit with declining importance. The practice, best developed in China's southern provinces, has been known for centuries, and centers on the veneration of those from whom one is descended with the belief their spirits can influence the lives and affairs of those still living. Its origins most likely date from very early, and possibly even prehistoric, times.

Also mentioned is the concept of the *Mandate of Heaven*, a belief that a ruler rules only with the consent of the heavenly beings. The central point is that such consent may be withdrawn should the ruler prove himself an unrighteous man or otherwise unworthy of his position. It was believed that plagues, famines, and natural disasters portended the withdrawal of the mandate of heaven from the current ruler, and the concept was used many times throughout Chinese history as a justification for rebellion and the overthrow of emperors or whole dynasties. The notion of the mandate first appears in the historical annals of the Zhou Period (1045 to 256 BCE), which followed the Shang, but it is not impossible that its origins could be earlier. Thus, I have made use of it in Shang times in the story, and beg the reader's indulgence over this small piece of historical speculation.

More recently, the facts surrounding the large-scale and well-organized theft of artwork and antiquities by the Nazis are not in dispute, being supported by a wealth of documentary and physical evidence.

While I have taken care to preserve historical continuity as the story unfolds, I suspect I have taken something of a liberty in presenting the discovery and excavation of the tomb of the first king of Shang as being completed in one season. It is doubtful to say the least that so large and rich a site could be excavated and the artifacts collected and cataloged in so short a time, and apologies are offered to archeologists who may read this book. Although a more detailed description of the excavation over two or three seasons may well have been of interest to some readers, I have foreshortened it in the interests of time and word count.

Except for documented historical occurrences, the events described in this book are fictitious and the product of the author's imagination. Apart from known historical figures, the characters portrayed are likewise fictitious. If, through name, appearance, habits of speech, or behavior, any resemblance is found to any real person, alive or dead, such resemblance is coincidental and wholly unintentional.

The single exception to this rule occurs, not in relation to a person, but in the case of the guide dog, Lombardi, who appears from time to time in the narrative. There was, in fact, an actual guide dog named Lombardi — a golden retriever, as described. I use the name with the kind permission of Lombardi's former handler in memory of the faithful companion Lombardi was, and in tribute to service animals everywhere.

Charles Mossop
Parksville, BC
2020

Charles Mossop is now retired from a 42-year career as a post-secondary educator, administrator, and private consultant in international development. He lives on Vancouver Island on Canada's west coast. Partially sighted since the age of nineteen due to Stargardt's Macular Dystrophy, he enjoys gardening and playing piano and classical guitar when he's not writing or travelling.

He has completed a six-year term as a volunteer member of the National Board of Directors of the Canadian National Institute for the Blind (CNIB), and continues his service to the CNIB as a member of divisional and regional volunteer boards. In addition, he currently serves as an advisor to the board of the Canadian Council of the Blind (CCB) and as an officer of the World Blind Union (WBU), a consulting agency to the United Nations which advocates globally for the rights and independence of people who are blind or partially sighted.

www.ingramcontent.com/pod-product-compliance
Lightning Source LLC
Chambersburg PA
CBHW050026030726
47506CB00001B/133